THE WALLSCREEN WENT DARK . . .

Startled, she sat up in bed, clutching a sheet across her nudity. She looked at the wallscreen and felt disoriented. Instead of anything put out by one of the media channels, the wallscreen had evidently linked with the apartment AI. The scene she stared at was the living room as seen from her front door. The perspective changed suddenly, coming closer.

Her breath caught in her throat. Her heart thundered till she thought it would explode in her chest. She tried to move and couldn't.

The wallscreen image wavered, came forward, and moved through the hallway leading to her bedroom.

She stood with effort, hypnotized by the events unfolding on the wallscreen. The view changed until she was looking at herself on the screen, larger than life, terror painted across her face. She turned to face the open doorway, now feeling the other presence.

A hundred different shades of black ran up and down the big man's frame, reduced him to a paper-thin shadow in the doorway. And then she saw the only thing she could truly make out, the sharp, silver gleam of a short blade trapped in one of his misshapen hands. . . .

THE FUTURE IS UPON US . . .

LETHAL INTERFACE

Mel Odom

A ROC BOOK

ROC
Published by the Penguin Group
Penguin Books USA Inc., 375 Hudson Street,
New York, New York 10014, U.S.A.
Penguin Books Ltd, 27 Wrights Lane,
London W8 5TZ, England
Penguin Books Australia Ltd, Ringwood,
Victoria, Australia
Penguin Books Canada Ltd, 10 Alcorn Avenue,
Toronto, Ontario, Canada M4V 3B2
Penguin Books (N.Z.) Ltd, 182-190 Wairau Road,
Auckland 10, New Zealand

Penguin Books Ltd, Registered Offices:
Harmondsworth, Middlesex, England

First published by Roc, an imprint of New American Library,
a division of Penguin Books USA Inc.

First Printing, May, 1992
10 9 8 7 6 5 4 3 2 1

For Karen—

You can get much deeper into someone's heart with a kind word and a dedication than you can get with a kind word alone.*

Love ya, babe.

*With apologies to Al Capone.

ACKNOWLEDGMENTS

Yes, I know I would probably get kicked out of the Academy Awards for this because I'm going past the three-minute deadline, but these people deserve mentioning.

My mother, Imoneta, who believed in me when I couldn't.

My dad, who gave me a foundation upon which to build.

My brothers, Johnny, Joe, Daryl, and Scott, who blazed trails of their own as we got older and inspired me with tales of their own.

My children, Matthew Lane, Matthew Dain, Montana JoLynn, and Morgan Shiloh, who bring daily new and fresh wonders to the tired old world I sometimes see before me. And to Jeremy, who shared his first years with me.

My sister-in-law, Judy, who's not bad for a Yankee and has somehow managed to keep up with brother Johnny when the rest of us could only see the dust.

My niece and nephew, Imoneta Ann and John Ross, whom I've watched grow steadily over the years.

My agent, Richard Curtis, who saw real promise in the book, so he went out and sold not only it, but another as well.

My mentors, Mike McQuay and Steve Knickmeyer, who gave generously of their time and learning, and continue to do so.

To Feroze Mohammed and Cathy Haddad, who saw the promise in a hungry young writer, and who remain the best of friends.

The guys at Roc who helped me pull this off: Christopher Schelling, Jeremy Boraine, and John Silbersack.

Special acknowledgment goes to Keith Birdsong, whose work graces the cover, and who shares his life with Karen and Candi (who'll probably kill me for using her nickname). "Thanks for the cover, guy, but I'll pass on the buffet."

Special acknowledgement goes to Deborah Chester, a fellow writer who strained her brain while searching for the title to this book. "Dear Deb, I still liked *Shoot 'em Flat* best."

1

Mick Traven elbowed his way through the crowd on the street corner, keeping his prey in sight. He let the night's shadows and the leatherboys around him disguise his presence. The bagman looked back over his shoulder with the uncanny sense a professional runner always seemed to develop if he lived long enough. Six months was a lifetime in courier work. This guy showed indications of being in it for longer than that.

For a moment the bagman froze in place like a dog scenting the early-morning air. The guy was a worn blade dressed in ragged street black, glinting in places from decorative chains and zippers. There was nothing in his hands. The software containing the financial transactions would be tucked away somewhere in or on his body.

"Hey, man," one of the leatherboys whined, "whyn't you go find your own damn corner before we leave you bleeding on this one?"

Traven ignored the man and focused on his target, watching the bagman watch the city.

The south side of Dallas had yet to show a lot of the effects of the rebirth the Japanese promised. Dark streets littered with refuse and bodies were still the rule rather than the exception. Shadows were drawn long and sketchy, highlighted by brighter bits of the flotsam that formed a patchwork on the chipped and broken sidewalks under torn and fluttering awnings. In the distance an Eastern dynasty of skyscrapers towered above most surrounding buildings. The neon lights flashing on the Japanese-owned buildings kept scaling and rescaling the heights, advertising products and services in Japanese as well as English. Light traffic whished by. Rusted hulks stuttered on home-grown fuels and rattled from black-market drip. Flashy sports models piloted by corporate execs cruised for slum thrills.

Hunching his narrow shoulders against the unsubstantiated threat, the bagman went on. His strides lengthened, moving him almost up to a jog.

Traven gave the guy a slow count, waiting for the sudden snap of the bagman's head he knew would follow. He'd seen it happen too many times.

"What's the problem, asshole?" one of the leatherboys said, getting braver now. The others cheered him on in a low buzz of machismo. "You got a hearing problem?"

Turning around, Traven gave the group a bright smile he knew didn't register in his eyes. Leatherboys, stoned on the unrealities of their choice and social position, wouldn't notice the hard glint in those blue eyes. So he showed them the blued length of gun when the big guy reached out for him, bringing it out as he removed his hand from his duster pocket. It was a SIG/Sauer Model 1957 10mm caseless semiautomatic, built with no moving exterior parts. In Traven's hand, with the poor light filtering through the nine leatherboys and two leathergirls standing around him, the short barrel looked like a hard iron bar, till the muzzle winked at the observer.

The big guy had a face covered with tattoos similar to the ones favored by the Yakuza. The Yaks hadn't been mentioned in Japan's plans of economic rebirth. But they had filtered into Dallas and other major American cities as surely as had the Japanese yen.

The leatherboy's mohawk was colored platinum with a pink fringe cresting it. The loop piercing his nose looked like one of those sewn onto his jacket. The piggy eyes suddenly took on a sheen of intelligence despite the drugs in his system. The guy moved his hand back slowly.

Traven read the crowd, sensed the inner-directed anticipation flowing through the artificially induced adrenaline hitting their systems. They smelled blood and they didn't care who it belonged to. He waggled the gun slightly, never losing the white-toothed grin. "I got twenty rounds before I reload," he said in a soft voice. "Be a lotta dead leatherboys after the smoke clears."

The press of human flesh and black leather loosened. Traven dropped the 10mm to his side, hidden by the folds of his calf-length black duster, and took up the chase again.

Acid snow came down into the city in wet flakes that turned to acid rain moments later. The sidewalks, streets, and concrete buildings looked as if they were encased in black ice. The accumulated grime and slime turned slick underfoot. Headlights from the passing traffic turned everything in their beams to colorless shadows.

Traven darted through the pedestrian traffic unnoticed. Everybody had a reason to run from somebody sooner or later. The street people understood the reasons. You owed somebody money, you stole from the wrong person, you saw something you shouldn't have even though you were trying your hardest to be blind to the world around you. If you weren't running sooner or later, you were dead.

He kept his fist around the hard bar of the SIG/Sauer in his pocket. On the streets, weapons were the currency of survival. He keyed the com-chip inside his head, working the special short-range tach relay his team used for this operation. "Kowalski?" he said, mouthing the words so only the internal mike could pick him up.

"Go." The feathery voice brushed the inside of his skull.

"I lost him." Traven sidestepped three women dressed in leather and lace designed to display their surgically enhanced breasts and hips. He didn't have to look at their faces as he passed to know they were old for the business. They were in their mid-twenties, and surviving on talent now rather than false innocence. The younger girls operated out of penthouses and private mansions instead of wearing acidproof makeup and dealing with the rough trade.

"I got him."

Traven recognized the new voice as Chambers, the youngest member of his unit. "Where?" He forced himself to come to a stop under a striped awning of a pawnshop to get his bearings. The three brass balls on the door above him threw a shadow over the iron-barred plate-glass window showcasing a collection of musical instruments, artificial limbs, and software. The yellowed and stained BUY, SELL, OR TRADE sign taped in an upper corner fluttered from some inner wind.

"The alley behind the Big Bopper Bar." Chambers's voice was tense.

Traven read it as excitement rather than caution, and the knife of uncertainty twisted in his guts again. If he'd had more experienced men, Chambers wouldn't have been part of this operation. The kid still had a lot of moves to learn. Problem was, Chambers was at the point where he kept learning or he died damn quick. "Stay loose, Jonny. Keep a visual, no physical."

"Check."

The connection in Traven's head faded like reversed ripples on a pond. He looked back along the street to the alley. People were starting to notice him now, looking beyond the physical aspects of the tall, lean man with long dark hair and the blade scar on his face, mentally digging at the kernel of truth that lay beyond.

He crossed the street in a dash, feeling the uncertainty of the surface beneath him, one arm still jammed in the pocket of his duster, fingers locked around the 10mm. The familiar drumbeat thrummed at his temples now, and the animal side of him knew the time for second-guessing and maybes was over.

One of the Japanese sports cars threw water across the backs of his legs as he gained the other curb. The street people peeled away from him, leaving him facing a zoner chipped out internally, barely functioning in the real world while living in the world he'd designed for himself inside his head.

Unable to stop himself, Traven grabbed the zoner's clothing, and they went down together in a wild scrabble of arms and legs. The zoner was typical of the last stages of the psychosis, leaned out to skin over bone, moving with creaky slowness, not bothering to hide the trodes jacked into his temples from the home-grown cyberspace deck on his belt that enabled him to live in his own Twilight Zone. The guy smelled foul, as if he were dead already, his flesh pallid and almost intangible.

Traven cursed and pushed himself to his feet.

A spotlight fell across him just before the whirling blue and red of the police copter unit flashed across the street.

Still standing over the weakly flailing body of the zoner, Traven keyed the com-chip again. "Kowalski."

"Yeah."

"I got a local here."

"I see him."

"You will remain where you are." The amplified voice of the copter pilot bounced off the buildings, rose above the quiet shush-shush-shush of the blades as it attempted to set down in the street. "If you try to run, you will be shot."

Traven said, "Tell the son of a bitch I want him out of here now or he's going to be back on foot patrol tomorrow."

Wind swirled around the streets, scattered loose refuse, and caused the onlookers to pull their coats and jackets tighter around them as the December chill whipped into a frenzy.

"Guy does seem a little overeager for a simple battery case, doesn't he?" Kowalski asked dryly.

"If you don't get him out of here now, that guy's going to be partnered."

"Gotcha." Kowalski faded in a ripple.

Traven waited, not moving, till the copter pilot pulled away, then ran for the alley. The pavement was cracked worse here. None of the asphalt patching done on the main streets had ever touched this. He stumbled, would have fallen, then caught himself with his free hand. The butt of the SIG/Sauer banged into the brick wall, skidded, then caught, giving him enough leverage to keep going. He accessed the com-chip.

"Chambers."

"Here."

"Our guy?"

"Still moving."

"Where?"

"Other end of the alley. Going into Miko's Tavern."

"That's Yak territory." Traven flailed his way through a stand of overflowing trash cans that hadn't been divided into recyclable piles.

"I know. Looks like our connection runs a little deeper than we'd thought."

Traven said, "Stay with him," even though he wanted to tell the kid to back off, that Chambers was getting in over his head. He gritted his teeth and ran faster, kicked in the infrared circuitry jelly-wired into his eyes. The black alley suddenly switched from a towering rectangle of clinging shadows reaching for the sky to a greenish two-dimensional photograph of sharp edges.

"You got it." Chambers sounded cocky, too sure of himself.

"And watch your ass."

"Bet on it." Chambers rippled out, disappeared with an almost inaudible pop.

Traven ran through the tiny puddles cluttering the alley, light-green pools against a slightly darker green surface in the infrared. He nudged the com-chip, accessing the time from DataMain. 11:46 P.M. Time enough to die and have the organ-recovery jackals rip his guts out and leave his husk drying before the morning sun touched the top of Nagamuchi Towers.

The stink of the alley traveled with him, battered his face with almost as much physical presence as the falling snow. Rotting vegetables, Oriental cooking, the aroma of malt beverages, human excrement, all formed a miasma that pinched his nostrils. Only the driving force of his legs flared them open again.

Accessing the com-chip again, Traven called out, "Kowalski."

"Go."

"Bring in the troops." Traven slowed, switching back from infrared as he eased up on the yellow pool of light leaking under the back door of Miko's. Shadows moved across it. "Loose perimeter. I want these people alive."

"Calling it kind of early, aren't you?"

"Do it."

"Done."

Traven reached for the back door, hiding the SIG/Sauer in the folds of the duster.

Kowalski's voice was softer now. "Don't blame you. The kid's kind of green."

Traven didn't reply as he stepped into the noise and bad air of the bar. Perspiration covered him despite the chill on the streets. Part of it was from the exertion of running. The other part came from the demands made by staying awake the last thirty-six hours to ramrod the operation. His nerves felt wired as tight as a zoner's.

Colored fluorescent lights played along the naked bodies of the women whirling onstage to Traven's right. The light operator was being creative, narrowing the baby spots to dime-sized bits of color to reveal a hint of a breast here, the inner curve of a buttock there. Then the guy would widen the focus, spilling golds and greens and sapphires over the dancers, whose smiles looked as tired as the moves. The audience never failed to cheer at each revelation but, like the dancers, seemed to lack spontaneity.

He moved through the collected smoke of cigarettes, reefer, red satin, and crack, seeing faces he recognized, others he didn't. A wave of apprehension preceded him as the men and women gathered around the wobbly round tables eyed him speculatively. He didn't see Chambers or the bagman.

Knowing any attempt he made at accessing the com-chip to initiate contact might trigger the bar's inner security, Traven passed along the worn rut in the concrete floor. He stepped in something sticky, made squicking noises from then on as he walked.

On the wall opposite the stage, drawing even more interest than the dancers, the floor-to-ceiling television depicted one of the samurai epics seen increasingly on all channels. Somebody changed it to an episode of the 1960s *Batman* series starring Adam West, and the crowd hissed and booed till it was changed back. A samurai's sword licked out and another head went rolling.

Still holding the 10mm tucked in the folds of his duster, Traven made for the shoulder-to-shoulder crowd ringing the bar, catching sight of the stairs behind the line of video games for the first time.

Miko's was definitely larger than he'd remembered. The last time he'd been inside was nearly a month ago on a corporate rabbit run. Since then, the money behind the tavern had evidently bought more floor space inside the building and hollowed it out of the businesses that had been around it. The mind-set was definitely Japanese: There was no reason to rebuild to make money when it was possible to take what was needed out of what already existed.

The bartender was a big man who looked out of place wrapped in the stained white apron. The black eyes deep-set in the blocky face narrowed as they focused on Traven.

Reaching into his pocket, Traven produced yen notes. American money would have marked him as someone other than street trade. The bartender plunked down a beer and swept the yen away.

Traven took the plastic mug from the counter, made his way around the increased floor space, and tried to spot the spyholes he knew had to exist. The wallscreen broke for a special announcement, showing a Ku Klux Klan demonstration in Highland Park where Japanese corporate execs were hung and burned in effigy. The peaked hoods and darkened eyeslits looked grim and foreboding.

A blood-chilling scream cut through the loud noises of the crowd. Tracking it instantly, Traven dropped his mug, shoved his way through the zoners playing the video games, and brought the SIG/Sauer into view. People scattered. "Police!" he yelled as he sprinted for the stairs. "Get down and stay down!"

The bartender reached under the counter.

Traven didn't hesitate, swinging the 10mm around in a Weaver stance as he skidded against the railing beside the stairs. He accessed the com-chip even as he squeezed three shots into the bartender's chest and blew away a plate-sized section of flesh and blood and bone.

The bartender flew backward from the impact of the hollowpoints. A chopped-down semiautomatic Remington shotgun spun from his hands and smashed the mirror behind the bar. Women's screams punctuated the sudden roar of men's voices, scraping chairs, and overturned tables.

"Kowalski!"

"Go."

Traven yanked himself up the stairs as bullets ripped chunks from the acrylic steps behind him. "Shit's hit the fan. Close 'em in."

"We're running ragged here."

"I know, dammit, I know."

"Where's the kid?"

"Loose. I haven't found him. I'm checking out the second story now. Some kind of action went down here."

A mechanical voice, triggered by the activated com-chip, blared out from the ceiling. "We have unauthorized police presence in the building. Present your warrants. Present your warrants. Any attempts at search or seizure on these premises are illegal." It quoted the civil code to the decimal, then began to repeat itself.

"Take care. I'm already moving."

"Make sure we get the bagman. At least maybe we can get him to roll over." Traven threw himself up the last half-dozen steps as a machine pistol cut loose below and rattled the stairs. He fell face-first onto a threadbare carpet with enough impact to bruise his cheek. He forced himself up, slammed into the wall of the corridor, and leveled the 10mm. Infrared took over when he saw the darkness, eliminating the mix of colors staining the peeling strips of paint on the wall.

He played the first door by the book, taking up position, then swinging in low with the SIG/Sauer leading his motion. Cold wind swept at the curtains covering the open window, dragged the tails across the body lying under them. The head turned, revealing Chamber's face.

"Mick," the kid croaked. He held his right arm in his left hand. Blood dripped from the stump halfway down his forearm. The rest of the forearm and his right hand lay in a pool of blood above his head.

Swearing to himself, Traven dropped to his knees beside Chambers and fashioned a tourniquet out of the curtains.

"Guess I screwed this one up, huh?" Chambers asked. His voice was thick, sleepy. "Guy had me made and I didn't even know it. Wasn't figuring the deal would go down in Yak territory till I followed him up here and two Yaks jumped me. They had to go out through the window, so I fucked up their plans some anyway." He smiled, spittle dripping out of one side of his mouth. Then his neck relaxed and his head lolled to one side.

Traven checked for a pulse, found one weak and fluttering like a ghost on a cyberspace screen. "Kowalski."

"Go."

"Chambers is down. Get a medevac unit here now or he's not going to make it. We're looking for two Yaks, at least one carrying steel, and the bagman. They made the kid too late. They went out the window facing Trevane Street."

"Copy." Kowalski rippled.

Knowing he'd done all he could do for the moment and that the medevac was only seconds away, Traven picked up his pistol and stepped out on the fire escape leading down to the street. Before he'd covered half the distance, something smashed into him and staggered him back against the building. The pain of the cut hit him as he looked down and saw the black feathered arrow jutting from his chest.

2

Watching the woman sleeping on her side facing away from him, Earl Brandstetter eased his hand out from under the thin sheet covering their naked bodies. His heartbeat quickened as he gave in to the need that stirred him, made more urgent by the accompanying sharp sense of failure.

Camille Estevan wasn't beautiful, but she was put together well and gave the appearance of someone who took care of herself. He remembered the body under the sheet: generous hips that flared under a waist that might have seemed thick if it hadn't been for the breasts that overfilled even his big hands.

He felt his desire grow under the sheet. Still, he held himself back, the thought of a second failure as sickening as that of jacking into a burned cyberspace deck.

He allowed his fingers to trail through the peroxided hair. It felt so smooth. He shifted, leaned forward, inhaled the mixed aroma of her perfume, hairspray, and body powder. The scents were an ambrosia, so familiar, yet so alien.

Brandstetter ran the tip of his tongue across his upper lip. The salt of his earlier tears, cried without her knowledge, was still there.

The soft light of the bathroom spilled across the sheets and ignited her pale flesh against the shadows of the room.

In his mind, he ached to touch her. His fingers trembled at the thought. He remembered to breathe with difficulty. He inched his hand forward till it was just a layer of skin away from contact.

Camille stirred, and he froze, his breath locked in his throat, suddenly aware of her body heat so close to his. His heart hammered till he was sure if she had looked at him she would have seen his eyes bulge from his head. A sibilant sigh slipped from her lips. Then she was still and her breathing returned to the slow pattern of deepest sleep.

Brandstetter waited. Gradually his heart slowed. His palm brushed the sheet aside and his fingertips crawled, spider-light, over her breast. He paused, breathed deeply of her musk, and luxuriated in the victory.

The woman moved sensuously, shifting till she was on her back.

Brandstetter removed his hand, watching her for signs of waking. Satisfied she was still asleep, he let his hand wander farther down, across the soft, rounded plains of her stomach, paused momentarily at the fringe of pubic hair, found it still damp from his earlier *accident*. He banished the memory. He smoothed his palm against her. Her legs parted in response and her hips tilted slightly upward against the pressure.

Heart hammering, afraid he'd been caught this time for sure, Brandstetter moved his hand away. Her pink tongue flicked out slowly to wet her lips. Her eyes remained closed, her breathing regular.

Camille was still asleep. The realization thrummed inside Brandstetter. She was still asleep, completely within his power to do with whatever he chose as long as he didn't wake her. Maybe by the time she did wake, there wouldn't be any more problems with performance.

He trailed his fingers across her stomach again, lightly, quickly. He could smell her now, drinking in the intoxicating odor that was her musk. He checked, made sure she was still asleep, then lifted himself lithely from the bed, stalking the eroticism of the moment so sadly lacking since . . .

Brandstetter made the memory go away.

He pulled the sheet down, let its folds gradually uncover the flesh beneath, let the unveiled sights make him all the harder. He managed a three-point crouch above her, on his knees and one hand. She raised her legs and moaned softly, pushing against the bed with the heels of her feet. His senses spun inside his head. He thought he was going to be sick with singing excitement. The only thing he could equate it with was the soaring sensation of jacking into a deck and letting the gravity of cyberspace sweep him along like a leaf before a hurricane.

He almost lost it, then opened his eyes at the last moment, grunting with the effort of keeping his climax at bay. Like a hungry wolf, the impending orgasm scratched at his mind with broken claws.

Brandstetter mewled with the effort the control cost, a small sound trapped so deep in his throat he felt it instead of heard it. He almost laughed out loud when the pressure went away, but the realization that it would wake the woman stopped him.

He wanted to glory in the control, wanted every second for himself, wanted to reinforce the idea that he could command his libido. He was so close, yet he could deny it for the first time in so many years.

One of her hands moved. He felt it brush against his thigh, then it wrapped around him, tugging on him, demanding.

"No!" His voice was hoarse, a denial of everything that was happening to him. He felt the control slip.

"Come on," the woman whined. "You've been teasing me for the last twenty minutes. How much do you expect a girl to take before she goes completely nuts with wanting it?" She wrapped her other arm around him, pulled herself up to bite his chest.

The realization that she'd been awake through most of his performance doused Brandstetter's desire like cold water. He struggled against her, dominating her easily. "No!" He forced his way to his knees, slapped at her hands as she crawled after him. "You ruined it. You ruined it."

"What the hell are you talking about? There sure as

hell wasn't time for anything like that the first time around.'' Her voice was angry and piercing.

Brandstetter stood up on the bed and walked off, took his robe from the wall hook and slid it on. He had a glimpse of the woman covering her breasts with the sheet as he walked into the hallway leading to the living room. "Lights," he called. The apartment AI clicked them on and revealed the expensive furniture scattered over the roomy living area. He ignored the wallscreen, leaving it off so it looked like glassed-over infinity, passed the plush pit group that still smelled new from his recent successes in the job market, and came to a stop before the bulletproof balcony window overlooking downtown Dallas.

Nagamuchi Towers glinted in the moonlight, made blurry by the falling snow. As he looked at his employer's trio of buildings and remembered his Nagamuchi's relocation department had found this apartment for him a month ago, he realized again why this particular one had been chosen. For anyone who looked out at the world, it kept prominent the fact that Nagamuchi Towers was at the heart of the world.

He ignored Camille when she stomped into the room, watching her reflection in the glass doors before him. She dressed as she walked, jumped up and down to pull on the crimson vinyl pants, her unbuttoned blouse flying open from the effort and revealing the pendulous breasts.

"This new job hasn't changed you a bit, has it?" the woman demanded. "You're still creepy Earl Brandstetter from the apartment complex where we met." She pulled on one of her knee-high boots. "No wonder it took you so long to ask me up here. And I didn't exactly play hard to get, did I?"

He ignored her, worked hard to keep the anger inside him from exploding.

"Why did I bother coming up here?" She worked on the other boot, zipped it up as she finished. "I could have went with a dozen other guys tonight instead of picking you."

He whirled on her, knowing the anger showed on

his face. "You came up here tonight because you wanted the taste of the good life, bitch. You wanted to see what one of these apartments was like, wanted to know what it felt like looking down on the whole city instead of just a dirty section where, if you looked long enough, you could see somebody get his throat cut. Don't make it sound like you were doing me any favors, because that didn't even enter that empty little head of yours."

She laughed at him on the way to the door, buttoning her blouse, her bra thrown casually over one shoulder. She paused in the doorway. "You got a fucking problem, but it's not my problem. I'm going out right now to find me a man who doesn't have all the little perks you got stashed away here, but can give me what I want. A real man. You understand?" She did a burlesque bump and grind and threw her hips out at him, then the door hissed closed over her last triumphant smile.

Brandstetter forced the turgid air from his lungs and unclenched his fists. It had been so tempting to unleash the anger that rode inside him. Except that he had never done that and wasn't really sure if he knew how. Anger was a passion just as surely as lust was. It was possible he was a failure at that as well. If so, he didn't want to know.

He turned back to the window, mirrored by the reflection. He fought to keep his fists from clenching up again. He didn't have to take Camille's abuse. Being with Nagamuchi assured that. He was one of the powered elite now, not some deckjockey out grubbing a living at an American corporation.

Brandstetter was a big man, filling most of the balcony doors. He stood six-feet-four in his bare feet, with eyes he thought of unfavorably as lizard green, though he never opted for a cosmetech job that would change them easily, and was offered free to any employee of Nagamuchi. His bald head glared at him from his reflection, winking at the temples where the trode jacks were tiny chrome buttons. A fringe of red hair ringed his head, kept cropped close. Another cosmetech job could have taken care of Nature's shortfall, but he had never gone for this one either. He would still know what he looked like on the inside. He made the most of his body, punishing it through exercise and physical competition, till it looked as if it had been sculpted of bronze. His body had drawn the attention of a lot of women like Camille Estevan, but he had always kept himself away from them. Usually a smile, a nod, then he was gone.

Perspiration gleamed on his body. He threw off the robe and stood naked looking over the city. He slapped the bulletproof glass and cursed himself for giving in to the call of flesh and bringing the woman here. She was the first, and he had the uncomfortable feeling she knew that now. He was so much bigger than she was. He could have taken her by force had he wanted to, and it wouldn't have been rape because he had the distinct feeling she would have enjoyed it.

He turned from the balcony, padded noiselessly to the kitchen and his workspace. "Lights," he called. The apartment AI switched them on. "Deck up." The familiar hum filled the room.

Sitting down in the papasan chair before the Tendrai deck chipped for his personal use only, Brandstetter plugged the trodes into his temples and felt the icy black of cyberspace sweep him away at once.

There was a moment of familiar nonbeing, then the deck tripped him, dipped him, chipped him into the matrix, with an all-over sensation like diving into a subzero sauna. No matter how many times he'd done it, no matter how many different decks he'd jacked in through, it was always the same—always different enough to take his breath away. Figuratively, of course, because he didn't need to breathe in cyberspace.

He rode the matrix confidently despite the encounter with Camille, swept along by the forces that existed within the universe within a universe, achieving something close to the speed of light till he found his own construct. The construct was purple, but a purple unlike anything he had ever seen in the physical world. Liver-green strands that looked like fiberoptics but weren't, latched it to the canary-yellow Nagamuchi matrix like a puffer fish clinging onto a whale.

Some deckjockeys swore cyberspace was filled with sounds rather than colors, while others swore they got around inside by tactile impressions rather than either of those. He'd never talked to anyone who navigated by scent or taste, but he'd heard they existed, although usually their talent was limited in a number of ways. The best ones, like him, operated by visuals.

Pulsing with the chip-beat, he cracked the surface of his construct, experienced an explosion of lavender, then stepped inside the working space he'd built for himself. He passed through the silence of the house, past the designing labs, past the bedroom, past everything till he reached the drawing room.

He put a hand to the door, already feeling the heat of the fireplace. The drawing room was lit only by the flames crackling around the logs, their piney scent overlying everything. The furniture in this part of his private construct was just as she'd always liked it: fashioned of ornate and expensive woods with an Old Age skill that came from human hands instead of techlabor.

The bookshelves covering either sidewall were filled, but he'd never bothered to take a volume down to study. They belonged to her. The fireplace seemed like another doorway, glinting from the rolltop desk, the leather-covered chairs before it, the vases and paintings hanging on the walls.

She waited for him on the bearskin rug—another of her additions, not his—as naked as he was. Black hair framed her face as she raised herself on one elbow to look at him, skin as smooth as silk and flawless as ivory, so pale against her dark hair and eyes.

"I've been waiting for you," she said in that perfect voice.

"I know," he replied hoarsely. He was suddenly aware of how dry his throat was, still surprised at how strongly the weaknesses of the flesh could touch him in the construct. Yet, the strength of those sensations was what he depended on. Even as the weaknesses assailed his senses, so did the passions.

"Come here." She looked at him. "I see you have a present for me."

He moved forward, no longer in his thirty-eight-year-old body, taking a thirteen-year-old's steps now, forcing himself not to run. Desire thudded against his temples, pushing him forward.

"A present," she cooed with a scarlet smile that promised untold delights, "and I don't even have to unwrap it."

She took his arm, pulled him down beside her, bigger than he now since his full growth lay ahead of him, and dominated him. He felt the hair of the bearskin slide against him. She kissed him, unleashed her tongue to plunder the inside of his mouth, and ignited him with the heat trapped in her body.

"Now," she said in a ragged voice, "now." She pushed him over on his back, rubbed smoldering skin over him as she straddled him. "Now be Momma's good boy. Make it good for Momma."

"Yes, Momma," he said in his good little boy's voice.

Her hand guided him into her. She rode him hard, her breasts bobbing with the motion. He did his best to buck up against her. "Momma loves her little boy," she said breathlessly, her head thrown back and her eyes closed.

And he knew she did.

3

Traven felt blood trickle down his chest as he ripped the arrow free of the Kevlar body armor he wore beneath his loose shirt. Grabbing the railing, he heaved himself over the side of the fire escape, vision going infrared as he fell. Another arrow caught in the tails of his duster, narrowly missing flesh. He still couldn't see the archer. Then his feet thumped onto the concrete and drove the wind from his lungs.

Alleys snaked in a half-dozen directions on the other side of the street. With the constant patching, expanding, and rebirth struggling to go on in the area, the interior section of the block would become a maze in the shadows.

A green silhouette stood out against the Vietnamese catering service to Traven's left. He dropped as movement targeted him, lost sight of the man as the bright lights of a passing car swirled over his vision and turned it milky gray.

Kowalski rippled inside his head. "Mick."

"Go." Traven searched for the silhouette, holding the SIG/Sauer in both hands.

"I got the rooftop above you."

"Check. I'll find you a target. Just make sure you nail that son of a bitch first time out."

"Alive?"

"However you can get him. He's a Yak, using a goddam bow and arrow, probably a true son of Bushido."

"Yeah, and his masters still probably had a neural

imprint dropped on him to make sure. If we take him alive, maybe we can question him till his brain fries. Hunnesacker hasn't seen that happen yet, only heard about it.''

Traven ignored the cold laughter that echoed inside his head and accessed the com-chip, seeking the limits enough to web out and make brief sensory contact with the rest of his crew. Six men were still on the move, not counting Chambers. The image of the severed arm wouldn't go away. ''Make it count, Kowalski.'' He launched himself from the shelter of the fire escape and sprinted across the slick street, eyes blinking involuntarily as snowflakes touched them.

An old Buick Electra with a tic-tac-toe of gray duct tape covering the passenger-side windshield slewed in the street as the driver cut the wheel to avoid hitting Traven. Using one hand, Traven vaulted the rolling expanse of automobile hood and kept moving, catching the glimmer of green movement to his left. The silhouette drew back another arrow before Traven could get his feet on the ground. Hair on the back of his neck prickled as he realized how close and how open he was for the coming arrow. The Yak had to know he was wearing body armor this time, so the guy would be aiming for the unprotected areas. His groin tightened.

A bright dot touched the Yak's forehead. Traven identified it as laser sights from Kowalski's Beretta M-21 sniper rifle, then the Yak's face came apart behind the mask.

Traven hit the cracked pavement hard. Skin split on his empty palm, and the shattered bones of the street rattled against the body armor. He let the impetus of his fall drive him forward to his feet as more cars came to squalling stalls behind him. Angry voices, blaring horns, and the sound of crumpling metal pursued him to the curbside. Lights glared off the plate-glass windows of the closed businesses lining the alley.

He took up a position to one side of the alley entrance, 10mm in the ready position beside his face, and fired a pulse-net blast through the com-chip. "Anybody see anything?"

A chorus of six negatives rippled through the channel.

"Did you get a head count?" Hunnesacker asked.

"No."

"But this is definitely Yak action?"

"Got a dead one lying here beside me."

"Don't make sense that Donny Quarters would be teaming up with his chief competitors," Hunnesacker went on.

"I want the bagman now. We'll put the players and the puzzle together later." Traven rippled out, took a last glance at the sprawled body of the Yak only an arm's length away.

People were getting out of their cars now, pointing at him. Overhead the flashing blue lights of a medevac copter hovered into view, dangling a recovery crib with two parameds clinging to the chains.

"Kowalski."

"Go."

"What about the uniforms?"

"Already on their way."

"I want a six-block square netted in case some of these jokers get away."

"You got it."

Traven rippled out, dodging into the alley as the blue lights of the medevac splattered down over and across him.

Large sections of the pavement covering the alley were missing, letting him know a number of the local populace had gone sewer rat and were using what they could pry free to build walls against the upper world.

He walked through the mud, listened to it squish against his boot soles over the sound of his heart beating. His hands were slick with snow and blood and perspiration. He resisted the impulse to wipe them because he wanted both hands on the SIG/Sauer, wanted to keep his concentration focused on achieving the next heartbeat.

The alley curved to the left.

Putting his back to the right wall, Traven followed it around till he had a clear field of view again. He breathed through his mouth, meeting the increased oxygen needs of his body and trying to filter out the noxious fumes surrounding him.

He found what was left of the bagman's body around the next turn. The corpse would have been thrown headfirst into the dumpster except that nothing existed any longer above the shoulders. He discovered that when he tugged the body out and watched it sprawl lifelessly at his feet.

Controlling the spasming efforts his stomach made when the smell of fresh death interspersed with the residual rot assailed him, Traven accessed the comchip. "Kowalski."

"Go."

"I found the bagman, but the bastards took his head. This wasn't an operation set up for a nickel-and-dime cash flow. Guy must have been chipped to the max."

"Coulda figured that out once we knew the Yaks were involved."

"I need this guy's head," Traven broadcast. "We don't recover it, we got a dead bagman, a dead Yak, and no idea of what went down here tonight. We get that head and the chip that goes with it, I think we got a ballbuster of a case against Donny Quarters and whoever his connection is." He went through the alley faster now. His feet slapped against the mud, and his heart thudded inside his chest as he felt the pressure of the moment.

Greens fluttered through his vision as he dodged through the obstacle course of the alley and found a juncture to another alley, spotting a livid smear against one wall with the infrared. He stopped long enough to touch it, confirm that it was blood, and figured the person or persons he pursued were in a hurry now too.

"Kowalski."

"Go."

"Can you get a fix on me?" Traven spun as something moved behind him, tracking the lean feline form till it disappeared in a tangle of refuse.

"Negative. Got too much bleedover from decks and chips in the immediate area."

Traven leaped a pile of broken boards too short and too rotted to interest the sewer rats. "I'll send up a flare. You grab some height and run observer for the rest of the crew. I'm on the loose Yak now." He paused, reached in his duster, set the egg-shaped flare, and tossed it onto the second-story building beside him. He heard it pop and release the gas stored inside. Kowalski could track it with blacklight.

"Gotcha."

"Where am I?"

"Due east of Devine Street. Looks like your target's trying to make a vehicular connection and pull a fade."

Traven pushed himself harder, pumping his legs as each breath burned down his throat. "Can't let him fade now, dammit."

"I know."

"Hey, hey, look alive, people. I maybe got your bogey confirmed," a new voice said.

Traven bounced off a wall, propelling himself into the sudden right angle. More bright blips lit up in his infrared. Blood drips the size of coins swung wildly back and forth across the narrow alley. "Read it, Alvarez."

"Got a van, old suburban type, but it reads blitz wagon from bumper to bumper. Dual wheels in the back to hold up all the armor and bulletproof glass."

"Flag it and tag it," Traven ordered.

"I'm moving." Alvarez rippled.

"Kowalski, are you anywhere near his position?"

"Almost on top of him." Kowalski's voice sounded strained.

"You're coordinating till I get there."

"Gotcha."

"I want the bagman's head, and I want as many of Donny's boys and the Yaks alive as we can get."

"Can't make no promises."

"*Alive.*" Traven rippled out, taking himself back to

his own world and his own survival as he rounded another corner that opened to the street.

A nervous silhouette clung to the right side of the alley. A sword hung from a fist to the man's boot top. His other arm cupped the missing head like a fullback ready to scramble for yardage.

Traven flicked back into normal vision as he came to a halt and raised the 10mm. The Yak was dressed all in black, face masked by the hood and the scarf covering his mouth and chin. In his arm, the bagman's head stared blindly with only the whites showing in the eye sockets, a perplexed look shaping the bloody mouth.

Automatic-weapons fire rattled from the street as the suburban Alvarez had described roared into view and screeched to a stop in front of the alley. A side door opened and a man leaned out to urge his confederate on. Shots rang out again and the guy in the suburban rolled dead into the street.

The Yak's leg quivered under him as he reconsidered the dash that would have taken him into enemy fire.

A moment later Alvarez rammed the suburban from behind, plowing the big Dallas PD mobile operations unit into the smaller vehicle and spinning it sideways. Servos whined as the MOP unit extended traction forks that chewed into the bulletproof armor of the suburban and rendered it immobile despite the spinning tires. The rest of the team moved in, and Traven heard the buzz of voices in his head as Kowalski put them through their paces.

The Yak turned to flee back down the alley.

Traven stepped out in front of the man, both hands on the butt of the SIG/Sauer. "No fucking way," he said in a low voice.

The Yak straightened slowly, the sword dangling from a white-knuckled fist. "Traven." The voice was singsong, soft, not the voice of someone who was ready to give up. "I was told to expect you."

"Somebody told you right." Traven didn't move. He held the 10mm steady, aimed at the Yak's chest. Doubtless the guy wore body armor, but the hollowpoints would kick him on his ass all the same till Traven had time for a headshot.

Activity on the street bustled. The team inside the suburban wasn't going quietly. The scream of prowl cars ricocheted from the alley walls.

"I was also told you were an honorable man," the Yak said. He bent slowly from the waist, placing the bagman's head facing Traven. He straightened, tugged another sword from the sheaths on his back. "You are standing in my way, and we both covet the same prize." The Yak pulled his mask down to expose a white smile that held no threat.

Traven kept the SIG/Sauer on target.

"I propose a challenge, Traven-san," the Yak said. He threw the second sword to land in front of Traven. "You are no stranger to the sword. This shall be between you and me. To the victor go the spoils." He took the haft of his remaining sword in both hands, advancing slowly, blade point down. His eyes were flat black.

Traven showed the Yak a grim smile. "I may be a Texas cop, guy, but that doesn't mean I was born with a macho complex big enough to get me killed." He shot the advancing Yak through the head.

4

"**H**ey, Mick," Kowalski called out, waving from the crowd surrounding the pinned suburban still mounted on the MOP unit. "I always figured you was the type of guy to get ahead in the job. Just didn't have it figured you'd be the type to carry it around with you."

Traven shook his head at the big man's grim attempt at humor, fingers locked in the bagman's hair as he crossed the street.

Uniformed officers of the Dallas PD formed a loose perimeter around the scene. Two more bodies had joined the first on the street. Four other men were up against the suburban getting cuffed and having their rights read to them. Lights flashed from the parked cruisers and two firetrucks standing by. Civilians ringed the area, pressing against the line the uniforms held, trying to get a closer look. Media vehicles stood out from the rest, their escalating camera stands and telescoping eighty-foot antennas marking them immediately.

"Anybody on our side get hurt?" Traven asked.

Kowalski shook his head. "Alvarez thinks he mighta banged up a knee when he rammed the coke wagon. I think he's figuring on two days off on medical. He's still on a honeymoon when you aren't calling these midnight raids."

"Chambers?"

"Haven't heard."

Traven let Kowalski take the bagman's head.

The big man held it up with a smile. "Hey, Alvarez, want some head?"

Alvarez made an obscene gesture and continued searching the man in front of him, the automatic pistol in his hand never wavering from the back of the man's neck.

Displaced air pushed at them, beat papers from the street as the medevac copter took flight, heading for Tonagawa Hospital, because that corporation handled the PD's hospitalization insurance.

Kowalski dropped the bagman's head in a five-gallon plastic evidence bag, then secured the end in a square knot.

"I want Zenzo to handle the chip extraction," Traven said as he stepped to the back of the suburban. "Make a note and send it with that."

"Gotcha."

"Anybody else touches it, I'll break their goddam fingers. You can tell them I said that." Traven surveyed the broken pillowcases of cocaine spilled across the rear deck of the vehicle. One of the MOP unit's forks had accounted for most of the damage. Conscious of the media cameras trained on him, he put his hands in his duster pockets, not wanting any more close-ups of the blood on his hands than they already had. His reputation didn't need the added publicity. "What have we got here?"

"Coke," Kowalski said. "A lot of it." He wet a finger and dipped it in the yellowish-white powder. "Want to taste it the way they do in the movies?"

"And take a chance on it being laced with strychnine and dying right here?" Traven looked at his second and smiled, the effort more genuine now. "You figure on working my OD tonight too?"

"Death by misadventure," Kowalski said. "Be an easy write-up."

"There's another body back in the alley," Traven said as he walked toward the four men being held by the remainder of his team.

"Figured there might be."

"He's a Yak. Send one of the uniforms to get him before the organ-recovery jackals do."

Kowalski whistled, got the attention of a uniformed officer, and gave him a come-hither finger.

Traven didn't know one of the handcuffed men. The guy looked young, like maybe this was his first major score. The other two were low-level talent employed by Donny Quarters. Billy Krevitch was another matter. He came to a stop in front of the man and smiled. "Billy, Billy, and I thought I'd never see you in another situation like this because you were such a smart guy."

"Fuck you, Traven." Krevitch was lean and tall. Pale skin and twitches showed physical effects of the dust monkey on his back.

"Donny won't like this," Traven said softly. "He doesn't like it when guys screw up his operations even this much." He held up his thumb and forefinger a half-centimeter apart. "What's he going to do when he finds out about this?"

Krevitch's eyes were glassy. "You're gonna die, Traven, and die goddam slow. You're a punk, man, and your luck is about to run out on your showboating. They're gonna be puttin' your head in one of them little bags next. You don't know who you're messin' with now."

"Suppose you tell me."

Krevitch laughed, a harsh barking noise that contained a hint of insanity. "Not me, man. I want a front-row seat when they take you down." He fidgeted in the handcuffs, rocked back and forth against the gutted suburban.

Without saying a word, Traven filled his hand with Krevitch's shirt and dragged the man behind the suburban, out of sight of the cameras. A short punch to the abdomen doubled Krevitch over, gagging as he tried to fill his lungs with air again. Traven put a hand behind Krevitch's head and shoved his face into the cocaine.

Krevitch squawked in fear, struggling to get away.

Locking his fingers in the guy's hair, Traven held him. "Got something you want to tell me now, Billy?"

"You can't do this, Traven. I got my rights."

Kowalski came back, squatting down till his broad face was level with Krevitch's. "Ah, come on, Billy, everybody knows you like shoveling this shit up your nose as fast as you can anyway. Mick's just helping you out a little."

The man struggled harder to get away, unable to do anything other than scatter the powder.

"Think about it, Billy," Traven said softly. "If I put your face in that powder and hold it, sooner or later you have to breathe. With your record, an overdose won't be a surprise."

"Death by misadventure," Kowalski volunteered happily. "I'll make sure your name is spelled right. Might even tell your momma, provided we can find her pimp."

"There's a lot of money in this deal," Traven said, bumping the back of Krevitch's head forcefully. "I got Yaks crawling out of the woodwork to sell a product supposedly controlled by Donny Quarters in this area. I got a bagman carrying enough negotiable tech in his head to make the Yaks want to take it with them no matter what. You want to tell me something I want to hear?" He pulled the man up, listened to the hacking wheeze rattle the bird-thin chest.

"Can't," Krevitch said between drafts of air. "Neural imprints, man. Can't say nothin' about any of this."

Traven lifted the long hair at the nape of Krevitch's neck and saw the pink scar trailing the spine. "Who did this?"

"Can't say. Part of the imprint."

Kowalski grinned evilly. "Tough shit, Billy. What do you think, Mick? Think we should go ahead and question him just to watch his brain fry?"

Krevitch's face paled under the frosted layer of cocaine. "You can't do that. I got my rights."

Moving the man back with the other prisoners, Traven tried to put together how a middle-class hustler like Donny Quarters was suddenly rubbing elbows with the Yakuza. He figured the lack of sleep must be fogging his brain, because he couldn't even guess. The neural imprints would keep their prisoners from volunteering information for reduced sentences, and from testifying against Quarters or his associates. Unless something broke, the investigation would end here.

"It was still a good bust," Kowalski said. "You put together a smooth operation."

Traven rubbed the back of his neck, thinking about neural imprints and the bagman's severed head. "Almost got Chambers killed."

"He almost got himself killed. You know that." Kowalski clapped him on the shoulder. "We can only take care of so much on the streets. Otherwise they'd paint a big red S on all our chests."

"Yeah." Traven looked down at the dead Yak a uniformed officer dragged up. They looked inscrutable even in death and with half a face.

"Hey, Sarge," the uniformed officer said, dropping the Yak's heels and pulling a card from his pocket. "Ran into an organ-recovery jackal back there that said he could offer top dollar on any of the bodies that aren't claimed by next of kin, but we have to call quick, before rigor mortis sets in."

"Tell him to take a number," Kowalski growled. "Just like the rest of them."

Jamming his hands in his duster, the December chill rushing over him now as the lack of sleep sucked away his residual energy, Traven looked at the death and destruction that came with his job, realized this would be considered a success. "Let's get this wrapped and get the hell out of here," he said to Kowalski.

5

"How long have you been a cop, Mick?"

Traven looked up at the woman from his kitchen, spatula poised over the frying omelet in the skillet. He licked margarine from his thumb, considering the unimaginable source of the question.

Cheryl Bishop was a favorite woman in his life, and one of the few he brought home instead of signing in with at the nearest motel. She had short-cropped brown hair that barely reached her shoulders, soft brown eyes he always lost himself in when they were alone, and white, slightly crooked teeth that gave her the smile of a girl still in her teens. She had small breasts, a tight stomach, and an ass meant to be cupped appreciatively in a man's hands. He liked the way she dressed, the way she could be occasional or shift to blue jeans and a blouse. At present she wore only a red sweater that hung almost to the bottom swell of her buttocks. Traven had been admiring the view while he cooked and she wandered around the living room. "Why is this so important tonight?"

"It's not night out there anymore, dear heart. That's bright morning sunshine your blinds are holding at bay."

"Let's hope they keep it there." Traven scooped the omelet out, poured in more egg, added peppers, ham, onions, cheese, and started the whole process again.

"How long?"

"Seven years." He folded his arms across his chest, experiencing a mild chill. Possibly it was from the fact that all he wore was gray flannel shorts, but he figured it was more from the events of last night. Chambers's severed arm had chased him into the light limbo he'd crawled into between bouts of lovemaking. Even the workout at the gym downstairs before Cheryl had arrived hadn't totally relaxed him.

Cheryl leaned forward over the sofa to study the black-and-white picture of his academy days on the wall. Traven admired the expanse of feminine flesh revealed, then hastily turned the omelet. "You were cute," she said.

"Thanks, but some people think I still am." He removed the omelet, dropped the skillet in the sink with other dishes accumulated from past days, picked up the saucer piled with buttered toast, managed the vodka and orange juice with the other hand. "Lights out," Traven told the apartment AI. The room darkened in response. "Breakfast."

"Yum," Cheryl said, as she took some of the dishes from him and sat them on the acrylic-topped coffee table in the center of the small living room. She took a piece of toast and tore it in half. "You're twenty-eight now, so you joined the police department at twenty-one."

Traven sat on the floor beside her, resting his back against the spongy sofa. "I'm supposed to be the detective here. The last I remember, you're a waitress who does modeling on the side till the Canadian film companies discover you."

"It helps me get into character. Suppose I'm contracted to play a lady detective? This kind of character research could come in handy."

"Then watch the crime shows on wallscreen," Traven said as he cut his omelet into bite-sized pieces. "They deal with acting, not the real world, where the bad guys get to walk away at the end."

"Did I touch a sore spot there?"

"No." But Traven knew he'd been too quick to answer. He tried to cover by mixing fresh drinks. If exercise failed, if sex wasn't doing the job well enough, he could always depend on liquor to escape the nightmares.

"Sorry." Cheryl squeezed his thigh, then patted it. "So why did you become a cop?" Cheryl asked.

Traven held his arms up in mock surrender. "We've known each other for six, seven months, and you've never asked me this before."

"I never really felt comfortable before about asking." She took a bite of omelet, followed by a bite of toast.

Watching her eat was another reason why Traven let her into his private life at home. Not many women ate with the obvious gusto she displayed, or let their appetites wander as much as his did. "Because I thought I could do something about the world we live in."

"Being in politics or business could have done the same thing, and you're intelligent enough for either."

Traven sipped the screwdriver. "I didn't have a head for the college and training."

"Not true." Cheryl pointed at the overflowing bookshelves in a corner of the room with her fork. "I've seen all kinds of advanced college textbooks over there, most of them dealing with politics and psychology."

"Would you believe they were here when I leased this apartment?"

"No. I think you joined the police department because you like working with your hands. And you like the action." She gazed at him frankly. "You're not so mysterious, you know. I've noticed you usually call me after you've achieved some goal you set for yourself. When I come over, you're either finishing up working out or you've just finished. You've burned yourself out on whatever or whoever it was you were chasing, and the loneliness has set in."

Traven continued eating in silence, tried not to show his discomfort.

"Am I close, Detective Traven?"

He decided to respond to her innate honesty. "Maybe too close." He looked at her.

"Hey, I'm sorry." She touched his face gently. "It's

just hard to keep my feelings in. I care about you. I don't want to see you hurt.'' Tears sparked her brown eyes. "When I heard about what happened tonight, I wondered if you were involved. Then I came over to see this.'' She fingered the bandage covering the two stitches he'd gotten from the arrow wound.

Traven wanted to hold her, but he didn't. Too much emotion on his part and it would stop being fun and start being commitment. And nothing scared him worse. Not even Yaks. He settled for taking her hand in his. "It's okay,'' he said. "I'm okay.''

"I know. You're always okay.'' She returned her attention to her plate.

They finished in silence. Traven had two more screwdrivers with the meal and felt the warm lassitude of the alcohol kick in.

"I just thought it might help to talk about it,'' Cheryl said as she pushed her plate away.

"You don't want to hear about the kinds of things I see, Cheryl. I appreciate the offer, but you deserve better than a walk down that side of life.'' Traven pointed at the blank wallscreen. "Even when you see the shootings, stabbings, and killings on television, you know they're safely banished to the other side of that glass. If I told you about it, you'd know that kind of violence could reach out for you too. It's no way to live your life. Trust me.'' He drained his glass and kissed her on the nose. "Really, I do appreciate the shoulder, but I've been handling me and my problems a long time.'' He stood up.

"Are you going to take a shower?''

"Yeah.'' He smiled and it felt right. "Is this part of my program too?''

She smiled back. "Yes, as a matter of fact it is. Leave the dishes and I'll get them. Then I'll be in to scrub your back.''

"Done and done,'' Traven said, handing her the dishes.

She stood and kissed him, her breath sweetly alcoholic as it slid down his throat.

He padded through the narrow hallway leading to

his bedroom, wondering why it was he never noticed how cluttered a two-bedroom apartment could get with books, athletic gear, clothes, and other odds and ends until someone else was there with him. "Television," he called out.

The apartment AI brought the bedroom wallscreen to life at once, showing a morning news program. He adjusted the channel verbally as he stepped out of the shorts and walked into the bathroom. An old Roadrunner and Wile E. Coyote cartoon came on bigger than life. He watched it in the shaving mirror from inside the shower cubicle. Combined with the workout, sex, food, and drinks, the warm water cascading down his body put him on the brink of exhaustion.

Then Cheryl's face filled the shaving mirror as she came around the corner. She pulled the sliding door back and looked at him, holding her arms across her breasts. Tears slipped unnoticed down her cheeks. "Oh, God, it was just on the news. You, the head, the dead men, everything. I'm sorry. I didn't know or I wouldn't have said anything."

Traven gathered her in his arms and pulled her under the healing spray of the showerhead, sweater and all. "I know," he breathed into her ear.

She trembled against him, sniffling.

He tilted her face toward his and wiped the wet hair out of her eyes. "It's okay." He kissed her and held her till the trembling passed. Then kissed her again, and the fear she'd been filled with transformed into another passion altogether.

"There are visitors at the door," the mechanical voice of the apartment AI announced.

Traven fisted the 10mm from the headboard of his bed as he rolled away without waking Cheryl. "Display," he ordered as he pulled on the gray shorts and stared at the security panel wired into the upper right corner of the bedroom wallscreen. He felt woozy from the alcohol and the lack of sleep. He accessed the comchip for DataMain as the security display flickered to life. It was 1:33 P.M. He recognized one of his visitors instantly but carried the SIG/Sauer with him anyway as he went to the living room.

"There are visitors at the door," the AI intoned again.

"Cease function," Traven growled as he crossed the room. He put the pistol under a couch cushion and pulled on a sleeveless sweatshirt that had been draped over one end of the bookshelves. The door slid away when he palmed the security plate. He ran a hand through his hair, trying to psych himself up for the unexpected company.

"Good afternoon, son," Craig Traven boomed in his jovial voice as he entered the room. As usual, he was dressed in a suit, this one maroon with gray pin-striping. His salt-and-pepper hair looked as if he'd just left a beauty salon, and his teeth dazzled in the practiced smile.

The boy who followed him was unknown to Traven. Dressed in street leathers and denim, wearing his hair in a ponytail that dropped down below his shoulders, he looked more like a leatherboy than anyone interested in school. Yet, guessing his age, Traven figured that's where the boy should have been. Silver strands of earrings dangled from both ears, catching the afternoon sun coming into the room on their heels.

Traven gestured toward the sofa and chair. "Have a seat." He padded into the kitchen. "Coffee?"

"No, thanks, Mickey, can't really stay long." His father rolled a wrist over and glanced at the expensive Nijo strapped there.

"I'll take some," the boy said.

Traven eyed his father's companion over the coffee-pot as he put the brew together. Taking into account the sparse chin whiskers starting to take shape on the boy's face, he bumped the guesstimated age up to fifteen or sixteen, then automatically tried to fit the face into the mental mug file he had on juvies. The hot water started filtering through the self-contained coffee pad and the wake-up smell hit him with full force.

Craig Traven looked at the easy chair doubtfully,

touched the tip of his nose in an unconscious reflex of distaste, and remained standing.

Traven took two cups from the cabinet, rinsed them at the sink, and poured. "How do you take yours?"

"Black." The kid sat on the edge of the sofa, elbows on knees, balanced for action. It was a street pose.

Traven passed the extra cup over as he seated himself at the other end of the sofa to watch his father. Craig Traven was a businessman, and businessmen had schedules.

"You mind if I watch television while we talk?" his father asked.

"Sure."

Craig Traven faced the wallscreen with his hands in his pockets, a sure sign that he was agitated about something. He called for the television, then voice-controlled the channel selection and the volume. "Got a couple commercials working this afternoon, Mickey—want to make sure they get good play." The screen cleared in a blaze of color. "You need to get this calibrated. You'd get a better picture."

The kid stretched his hand out. "Danny."

Traven took it. "Mick."

"Sorry. I should have taken care of that." Craig Traven spoke without turning from the wallscreen. "Mickey, I'd like you to meet your brother."

Traven looked at the kid without trying to be too obvious.

The kid grinned without humor. "Didn't ever expect to powwow with you either, dude."

"That's enough, Danny." For an instant, the calm look dropped from the elder Traven's face. "I need a favor, Mickey."

Traven waited, functioning in the patient-cop mode because it helped him get through the few and far-between visits his father made, helped keep some of the old and new wounds covered.

"Danny's mother passed away a couple of days ago," Craig Traven said, "and I need a place for him to stay for a while, just till I get the home situation

squared away. You knew Beth before I did, Mickey—
you know how it is with her. She needs to be pam-
pered, given special attention. She's an intelligent
young woman, bright, very attentive to our guests and
good with the clients, but she needs room to breathe
right now. Hell, officially we're supposed to still be
on our honeymoon. If it wasn't for this special caseload I'm doing for the Nagamuchi Corporation, I
wouldn't have been anywhere in the continental United
States when this happened.''

Traven didn't bother asking what would have happened to Danny Traven if that had been the case. It
would only have disrupted his father's train of thinking.

The screen cleared, replaced immediately by a commercial for Nagamuchi Corporation, announcing the
best designware money could buy for all computer
needs, home and office. The most prominent things
Traven could see were the unfettered breasts of the
spokeswoman going through the spiel.

''What do you think?'' Craig Traven rubbed his
hands together expectantly.

''It was okay,'' Traven said, thinking it might have
been better suited for a porn-vid ad.

''Okay? That's all? Just okay?'' His father pulled at
his upper lip in frustration. ''Ah, forget it, Mickey.
We're mixing apples and oranges here. It would be
like you trying to tell me about what you do for a
living.''

Traven drained his cup and retreated to the kitchen
for a refill, bringing the pot to get Danny's at the same
time. The kid looked grateful, the expression looking
out of place. Usually the looks Traven got in the streets
from kids could blister paint.

''So how about it?'' Craig Traven asked. ''Think
you could take care of Danny for me for a few days?
Just till I get things worked out on the home front?''

Traven looked at the boy. ''You got anyplace you'd
rather be?''

''No,'' Danny said. ''I got noplace else to go.''

Craig Traven clapped his hands. ''Good, then it's

all settled. I'll send a couple people over later with his things. And you just call me if you need anything.'' The wallscreen blanked to another commercial, drawing his attention.

This commercial centered around the Nagamuchi Sentry RAM developed for most home AIs. It depicted a ninja attempting to break into an apartment only to be disabled by the security system. The electrified biofeedback created large sparks and dropped the ninja motionless to the hallway floor. The piece ended with the slogan ''Nagamuchi—working to turn your home into your first line of defense.''

Craig Traven raised an inquisitive eyebrow.

''The courts still have some questions concerning the lethal bursts those Sentry systems have been known to juice,'' Traven said.

''They've all been worked out.''

''I hope so—otherwise your agency could be taking quite a fall, right along with the Sentry designers. And the last time I looked, Nagamuchi Sentry Limited was in better financial straits than Traven Advertising.''

Craig Traven threw a forefinger out. ''See? That's negative thinking, Mickey. Very negative thinking. You have your mother to thank for that.'' He sighed. ''It's not easy trying to keep Japanese products looked on favorably in an economically barren country like the United States.''

''I wouldn't worry about it,'' Danny said with more than a hint of sarcasm. ''With the way immigration's being manipulated and the way the Nips are breeding over here, you shouldn't have to live much longer before you'll be playing to a majority audience. Real Americans are working their butts off to figure out where their next meal is coming from and don't have time to have kids.''

''I don't want to argue with you anymore, Danny.''

A mirthless smile tweaked the kid's lips. ''Why not? It seems like the only thing we get to do together.''

Craig Traven shook his head and moved for the door. ''Mickey, while you've got the time, try to talk some sense into this kid, huh? Help him figure out what the real world is like out there.'' He paused in the open doorway. ''You need anything, you call me, right?''

''Right,'' Traven said.

The door hissed closed.

''Looks like neither one of us actually meets the old man's expectations,'' Danny said.

Traven grinned, warming to the boy in spite of the circumstances that had brought them together. ''You had breakfast?''

''No. The old man picked me up after the funeral this morning and rescheduled appointments on the way over.''

Traven cleared the dishes, put them into the automatic washer, and took stock of the refrigerator. Danny took a seat at the small dinette and cleared the pizza boxes and Chinese food cartons.

''Did you really introduce Beth to the old man?'' Danny asked.

Feeling the twinge of the unresolved hurt, Traven answered without looking. ''Didn't actually start out that way.''

''Didn't think so. She's a fox. Just the kind of woman the old man goes for. And goes for, and goes for, and goes for.''

''You noticed that, huh?''

''My mom was wife number three. Maybe you don't remember. I heard later you were away at boarding school during the six months their marriage lasted.''

Traven set his collection of foodstuffs on the table. ''Maybe. I never heard about a lot of them. After he divorced my mom and she left town, I gave him a wide berth, and he returned the favor. He started coming back around about the time I enrolled in college.''

''Asked you to join the family business?''

''Yeah.'' Traven found a clean bowl, cracked a dozen eggs, and added milk as he whipped them.

''He wanted you so he could add 'and Son.' Makes a bigger sign and gives the agency a more venerable sound.'' Danny watched Traven prepare the omelet ingredients with interest. ''Mind if I help? I like working with my hands.''

Traven found him a knife, laid out the onion, cheese, peppers, and ham.

"You really a cop?"

"Yeah."

"You got any pancake mix?"

"Top shelf, to your right. Don't usually mess with them because I can never get them to turn out right."

"Then I'll cook them. Way my mom taught me to make them, they'll melt in your mouth." Danny's voice broke toward the end and he made knotted fists of his hands.

Traven put the whip to one side, suddenly lost as to what to do. It was one thing to console someone whose relative lay dead on the sidewalk. A cop rode the adrenaline high then, human, but insulated. It was another to be faced with the same kind of situation in his own kitchen with a brother he hadn't known existed. "You okay?"

"I will be." Danny went back to mixing powder and milk.

"Mick?" Cheryl's voice was thick with sleep. She came around the corner of the kitchen stretching, saw Danny, and pulled the hem of the sweater down quickly as she made an eep of surprise and dashed back toward the bedroom. "Goddammit, Mick Traven, you could have told me someone was in there with you!"

"Your girlfriend?" Danny asked.

"Friend," Traven corrected.

Danny nodded with a knowing smile. "I'd say you traded up from Beth."

6

Coiled up outside the Nagamuchi matrices, Earl Brandstetter floated on the lightless waves of cyberspace and contemplated the problem his department had been given. He picked an orbit, knew somewhere out in the flesh world his fingers had entered the information on his work deck, and slid into motion.

The canary yellow of the Nagamuchi Designers matrix pulsed with a life all its own. Its gravity reached out for him, plucked at his shapeless body with nonexistent fingers. Without encoding the security numbers, he veered toward the matrix, dived like a datajacker for the information contained in the matrix, crested one of the suddenly visible ice-blue lines of power that coursed through this particular grid of cyberspace.

He sensed his fingers playing over the keys of the Tendrai, ramming power and versatility to the breaker program he'd developed. It wasn't a true test, because he knew which combinations to avoid, which would allow him entry. A datajacker working the matrix would have felt it out, made more prelim cruises than most of the Nagamuchi people would give him credit for.

Brandstetter hit the first line of defense and went crashing through. The matrix turned nova-hot in warning. Since 80 percent of the deckjockeys perceived cyberspace as a visual experience, he'd programmed the sight function in. He'd also programmed the klaxons that would go off for those who heard, the feel of quicksand for the tactile, the smell of corpse decay for the olfactory, and the taste of vinegar for the gourmet. Each program had been a breakthrough of a sort on its own.

Ignoring the light, he compensated for it with the deck, given his cyberself a version of Fostershades. Then the data floated around him in an electrified ocean, shifted as quickly as sands through an hourglass. He reached for it, watched it trickle through his fingers, tried to retain it mentally only to see numbers change, languages alter. It was there/not there.

He was operating on instinct now. Neither a construct nor a slaved AI could keep up with his moves, making up yardage like a broken-field runner facing a dozen linebackers.

Then the matrix reached out and squeezed him, ejected him, would have crushed him had he not keyed in the user-friendly codes in time. Still, the impulse velocity threw him back, lost him in cyberspace.

He remained still, mentally caught his breath till he found himself and reinitiated the linkup with the Tendrai deck. He'd been fast, and he'd had the codes. A commonplace datajacker caught in the grid webs would have died.

The problem was, he didn't really expect a commonplace datajacker to get this far.

There were other, nonlethal barriers against deckjockeys with an itch and no talent. Nagamuchi reserved the best for the most dangerous.

Brandstetter reached out, snared a gridline, and let the power thrill him. His sails caught and held the cyberspace winds, and he skated through the common ground grids effortlessly. He identified the curving sprawl of the Berkeley logistics matrix, hued in violent reds, shunted off from there, and flagged the periwinkle pulse of Greenwich DataMain.

He coasted the length of the pulse, touching the New York databases for a moment, then swung down to Orlando, taking a moment to indulge himself in the new animated picture Montana DataBrush had in production.

He sidestepped, skipped, and smoothed over the security webs Montana DataBrush had in place. Nagamuchi owned a large chunk of the company, though it wasn't common knowledge, and the codes he held let him in most everywhere. Nagamuchi kept some of its investments quiet, letting the American people think there still—somewhere—existed an American way. In reality, it was all business. The rich were definitely getting richer, and the poor only paid increasingly higher prices for dreams that never came true.

Brandstetter entered the matrix, found himself suddenly in a construct of swamps and forest. He looked down, and gave himself over to the construct's vision. His body was sheathed in forest green that looked darker in the moonlight. As was usual in a DataBrush film, the night wasn't totally black, but rather trapped between some assortment of purples. He held a longbow in his hand.

He walked over to the gray ooze of the swamp, looked down, and smiled at the mustachioed face reflected back at him. He wore a triangular hat with a white feather in it. A quiver of arrows hung over his shoulder.

Without warning, the placid surface of the swamp erupted. A serpentine neck supporting a maw full of bared fangs and a head full of horns reared high into the air, obliterating the full, silvery moon. Moss and lichens flew.

"Who are you?" the great sea dragon asked in a voice that gave birth to thunder. Swamp water spilled cleanly through the fangs, because this was a Montana DataBrush production, not one of those produced by SlasherData.

Brandstetter laughed in savage delight, keyed into the sim/stim track underlying the production, designed to bring out the child in viewers.

The sea dragon lifted a webbed flipper/hand and scratched under its chin in puzzled fascination.

"I'm Peter," he replied, cupping his hands to make a megaphone, "and I refuse to grow up."

The sea dragon said, "Pardon me," and reached

under the swamp, came up with an ironbound book simply called SCRIPT. One flipper/hand held the book open while the other tracked the printed lines.

Brandstetter knew what he saw was a visual interpretation of the film's protective editorial AI seeking to assimilate the new data facing it while maintaining the integrity of the program.

"Are you sure you're in the right place?" the sea dragon/AI queried as it flipped through the ragged pages of the book.

Before Brandstetter could speak, another form tore itself from the swamp. Camille Estevan, dressed in chains of black clamshells and ebony seaweed that stayed over the erotic areas, stepped onto the muddy shore. Her legs stayed cleanly white and her face was shadowed by a halo of seaweed that looked as if it had grown there.

"That's Creepy Earl," the pseudo-Camille said, lifting a red-nailed finger as she pointed. Her lips ricked back to bare a flesh-flaying smile. "Everybody knows Creepy Earl. Can't get it up for real girls, can you, Creepy Earl?" Her laughter was as subtle as a gangster's machine-gun fire, as brassy as the spent casings.

Even knowing the Camille image was there only because the DataBrush program was operating on a subconscious level designed to tap the storyteller's full creativity as quickly as possible to feed the large audiences waiting on each new work, Brandstetter couldn't keep himself from reacting. He nocked an arrow, drawing the fletching to his cheek as he closed his left eye, tapping into the main editorial programming briefly to get the necessary skill. Even as a figment of his subconscious imaginings, Camille was not going to get a second chance to rail at him.

The arrow sped true, staking the woman in the left eye and pushing her backward to splash in the clean swamp water. Because this was Montana DataBrush programming, there was no blood.

The sea dragon roared in confusion. "Error, error!'' it yelled as it flipped through the SCRIPT book frantically.

''That's Errol,'' Brandstetter said as he nocked another shaft. This one caught the dragon in the throat. The book hit the swamp. The serpentine neck waved like a dying snake.

Coding out of the DataBrush program, Brandstetter locked onto a gridline and burned the anger away as he took flight. He homed in on the Nagamuchi matrices, keying the user-friendlies as he skimmed over data.

A bright, diamond-hard line of indigo drew his attention as he locked into orbit around his home matrix. Recognizing the questing break-and-shatter touch as that of a datajacker, he homed in on it.

The deckjockey was smooth. Brandstetter had to give him or her that. And brave, because the datajacker had already penetrated the first lethal security measures. Wondering how much the deckjockey had been paid to face the risks inherent in a system like Nagamuchi's, he set up a construct designed to snare the datajacker before more penetration was possible. According to policy he was supposed to let the security net deal with it, but the anger from Camille Estevan's ghostly counterpart still hadn't completely dissipated.

Conscious of his flesh body making the necessary strokes on the Tendrai in his office, Brandstetter set up his program, then ran it.

A crystal explosion went off around him, then he stood in a white cube of a room with no windows or doors, facing a bone-thin man half his age.

''Who the hell are you?'' the datajacker asked. He raked the sapphire frill of his mohawk out of his face, light glinting from the zippers on his jacket and pants and from his earrings and the two rings in his left nostril.

''I'm the guy who designed the security you're trying to break,'' Brandstetter said. ''Who are you?''

''Hey, man, I know my rights. You can't keep me in here like this.''

"On the contrary, I can do anything I damn well please at this point. You've ignored all the conventional warnings that you were straying into restricted and copyrighted area. A court of law would say you got what you deserved."

The youth licked his lips nervously.

Brandstetter could almost see the datajacker's corporeal hands hesitating over the keys.

"Maybe we can make a deal. Maybe I got some techware you'd be interested in."

Enjoying the feel of complete power he had over his captive, Brandstetter said, "You couldn't even break through the security I've set up here. What makes you think you could possibly have anything I'd want?"

The datajacker paced his end of the cube, never taking his eyes away from his captor. "Look, man, I got a little paper, a few drugs stashed, maybe we can work something out. You turn me over to the cops, we both know they fry my brain so I can't work a deck anymore. You live here too, man—how would you feel if somebody took away your key?"

"Who are you working for?"

"Nobody."

Brandstetter narrowed the datajacker's end of the cube, turning it to coffin size and pinning him in place.

"All right, all right, for chrissakes. I scored this hit from a guy at MegaTrend, and I didn't get paid anywhere enough for the job, let me tell you."

Brandstetter released the walls of the cube, touching briefly with his corporeal body as the information and power surge was coded in through his deck. His cyberself swelled with the energy. He smiled, made a mock gun of his thumb and forefinger, and said, "Pow." A ruby beam shot from the end of his finger and blew the datajacker through the back wall of the cube. Somewhere, the young man would wake up with a throbbing headache, his deck circuitry destroyed.

The cube dissolved around Brandstetter, and he hopped a gridline direct to his private matrix attached to the Nagamuchi matrices, intending to celebrate his victories before settling back into the real world.

7

"Hey, Mick, the captain left word he wanted to see your ass as soon as you dragged it in. He was also muttering something about having your answering machine molested."

Traven waved to the detective and kept moving through the squad room. A dozen desks mounted with outdated IBM work decks filled the square room and turned it into a maze. He waved to the guys he knew as he made his way back to Zenzo's department, stopping long enough to score a cup of bad coffee from the cappuccino machine Hackley had recovered from last week's narco raid and *accidentally* forgotten to list on the impounded-items file.

It appeared to be business as usual, with nothing really hot on the burner. The other detectives were involved in their own little worlds of move and countermove, huddled together at one desk or feet up on another as they talked to groomed snitches. Traven decided to see if Zenzo had cracked the chip the team had recovered last night before taking whatever bluster Kiley had lined up for him.

He passed through the static curtain that separated the computer analysis section from the regular squad room and found Zenzo jacked into a deck, fingers flying over the keys. Taking a seat on a table behind Zenzo, he watched the monitor and tried to make some kind of sense from the garbled colors that sprayed across it. They looked lunatic compared to the sterile white of the analysis section's walls.

Zenzo was thin, with a thick mop of black hair, glasses, and a white lab smock with a Dallas Cowboys football patch over the left breast. His wheelchair was equipped with a cybernetic linkage he'd designed himself once he found out he'd be in it the rest of his life.

Traven sipped his coffee and regretted not stopping at the corner 7-Eleven to pick some up.

The monitor blanked abruptly, and the wheelchair swung around with a mechanical hum. Zenzo reached up to his temples, unplugged the trodes, which receded into the chair's mounted deck, and said, "Let me guess why you're here."

Traven smiled. "It's not a big mystery. I've only got the one case hanging fire right now."

"True." Zenzo moved the wheelchair by thought to a sink area where a Mr. Coffee sat. "Want some real coffee?"

Traven emptied his cup in the sink and held it out.

Zenzo poured. "Colombian, my friend. Enjoy. Not all things coming from that country are meant to be snorted, injected, or inhaled illegally."

"But the price tag's about the same."

"Unfortunately." Zenzo rolled back to the monitor. He adjusted his glasses. "Also unfortunately, I've been unable to crack the security surrounding the core of the chip. Its self-destruct system can be triggered to feed on itself and wipe the chip clean before any attempts at core retrieval can be made."

"Are you telling me you can't get at it?"

"No, I'm telling you this is going to take some time."

"But we still have a case?"

"You will have when I'm finished. I haven't given up yet. This is some delicate coding here. Whoever put this operation together didn't spare any expense when it came to security."

"The deal went down under Yak supervision."

"I know, and the security looks Japanese too." Zenzo sipped his coffee. "Personally, I think you've tracked onto a major bust that's going to be felt in a few countries."

"Donny Quarters may have made it big just in time to take the big fall," Traven said.

"Yeah, but you can also bet he's going to be trying to cover his ass. I've picked up a few rumors out in the DataMain underground net that there's a sizable price tag on your head, buddy."

"Quarters?"

"Don't know. Haven't been able to track those down yet either. I got Gables on that. Figured you'd want to make your case before you worried about a small thing like local talent gunning for you."

"Yeah, you figured right."

Zenzo shook his head. "Can't be a twenty-four-hour cop all the time, Mick. I bet you couldn't use up the fingers of one hand counting the number of guys who'd cover your back when the shit starts to fall."

"But you'd be right up there around the top." Traven grinned.

"Only because I owe you."

Traven said, "If I believed that, I wouldn't be in here sponging coffee off of you."

The intercom tweaked with an ear-piercing ring, then cleared as Captain Kiley's voice blared over it. "Traven, get your ass to my office. Now." The sudden crack of the unit going dead was a final punctuation to the authoritative thunder.

"Got to go," Traven said, easing off the table. "God's calling."

"Give him my love," Zenzo said as he slipped the trodes in.

"Are you kidding? Kiley's hated you ever since you made the DeChancie case take a one-eighty and left him with egg on his departmental face."

"The way I remember it, *we* made that case."

"Yeah, but he hated me before then. He's got you pegged for the DeChancie thing." Traven stopped long enough to refill his cup. "Call me the minute you get anything out of that chip."

Zenzo nodded, fingers already active on the deck, jacking back into cyberspace.

The thought of moving through the computer world

still left Traven cold. Com-chips, infrareds, the other bodily armament that could be gene-gineered, were all things that built on the human body, made it more than it was. Cyberspace made the human body an empty husk. He'd seen too many zoners and deckjockeys who'd burned out inside a matrix and only left organ-recovery material behind.

Kowalski was in the squad room now, his shirt rumpled and the leather of his shoulder harness stained with perspiration. "Siddown there," he ordered the young woman in handcuffs and a black-leather-and-lace wraparound. He pointed to a chair.

"Piss off, dick," the woman said, struggling against the hand gripping her elbow. The handcuffs dropped to the floor with a metallic clank and a fistful of finger-razors unsheathed and swept toward the big detective's face.

Kowalski turned his head, let the razors glide by, then tapped the woman on the chin with a big-knuckled fist. Her eyes rolled up in her face, then she crumpled to the floor. Kowalski seated himself behind his desk, keyed up his deck, and growled, "Somebody put that bitch in a chair." He pawed through a drawer till he produced a Skoal tin, then dropped a big pinch into his lower lip.

Two other detectives picked the woman up, handcuffed her, dropped a neural-neuter trode into her neckjack to deactivate the finger-razors, so she couldn't pick the cuff locks again, then went back to work.

"Should have caught those finger-razors," Traven said on his way to Kiley's office. "Keep that up and you're going to end up having your face handed to you."

Kowalski gave him a wry grin and the finger.

Traven stopped in front of Kiley's office and rapped on the frosted glass pane with CAPTAIN OF DETECTIVES painted across it.

"Come," Kiley's deep bass voice boomed.

Traven palmed the entry plate and the door shushed back out of the way, then shushed back after he'd stepped inside.

Leo Kiley stood behind his desk, a big black man in slacks, white shirt, and tie. Blued fringe of afro made a halo around his head, leaving a large bald spot gleaming under the fluorescent lighting. He scowled at the piles of paperwork covering his desk, then at Traven.

"You wanted to see me."

"Nearly two damn hours ago." Kiley shoved papers aside until he found a remote control and thumbed it at the only wall clear of pictures, mug shots, and hardcopy. "What the hell's the use of having an answering machine if you never return your calls?"

"I don't have to listen to the aluminum-siding people, carpet cleaners, or Jehovah's Witnesses."

"Take your coat off and have a seat. We got some talking to do."

Traven discarded the duster and laid it on a nearby chair. Taking the SIG/Sauer and holster from the back of his waistband, he laid the pistol in his lap as he sat down.

"That was a chancy bust you made last night," Kiley said.

"I didn't see anything chancy about it."

Kiley snorted derisively. "You never do, kid. You're a fucking maniac out there on the street. Personally, I sometimes think maybe you need to have your tin pulled and somebody pressing a gold watch in your hand. How you get your crew to follow you through the shit you scrape up out there eludes me. Except for Kowalski. He seems to thrive on it even more than you do."

Curbing the anger roiling inside him, Traven said, "You got something on your mind, or are we just going to sit here and talk about the weather?"

"Your goddam attitude is another thing I don't like, mister." The whites of Kiley's eyes bulged, revealing the spiderwebs of red.

"It was a good bust. When Zenzo breaks that chip core, we're going to have enough evidence to hang Donny Quarters and whoever he'd doing business with in the Yaks."

"That's supposition and you know it. And you're taking it for granted your little pal in analysis is going to be able to break that chip without losing the evidence. That may not happen."

Traven bit back a retort.

"You're a hot dog, and hot dogs that stay on the fire too long get burned." Kiley sighed. "And, believe it or not, I don't want to see that happen." He walked around the desk, the bionic prosthesis that had replaced his left leg nine years ago barely showing a limp.

"Let's cut to the chase, shall we, Captain?"

Kiley sat on the edge of the desk and returned Traven's gaze full measure. "As of nine o'clock tomorrow morning, you're assigned to homicide detail for an as yet undetermined amount of time."

Traven stood up and shoved the 10mm back into his waistband. "No fucking way."

"Nobody offered you any goddam choices here, mister," Kiley thundered.

"You're not going to do this to me when I'm onto maybe the biggest bust this department has ever seen."

"I can and I have!" Kiley roared. "You got two choices: You show up for homicide in the morning, or you sign your resignation papers."

Traven didn't say anything.

"That's the way it plays, Mick." Kiley's voice softened.

"Why?"

"You're doing too good a job, kid. You're running a high profile. People know you. Your fucking picture's been on every goddam wallscreen in the city last night and today. The media's labeling you a killer cop, and this is reelection year for the mayor, whose stand on law and order blows like a daffodil in the breeze. It's been everything Kaneoki and I have been able to do to keep you from getting canceled. That tell you anything?"

"It tells me maybe I stepped on a few more toes than I'd expected with last night's bust," Traven said evenly. "And maybe it gives me a look at how far corporate corruption has spread through this department.''

''If that's any kind of accusation, I'll personally kick your ass through this goddam ceiling with this tin leg of mine.''

''Just an observation.''

Kiley flicked the remote control, showing a freeze-frame of Traven holding the bagman's head on the wallscreen. ''You're burned, kid, whether you know it or not.'' There was no emotion on replay-Traven's face. ''I've been seeing it in you for the last couple of months, but I didn't want to admit it because that would have meant pulling you out of vice. You're a fucking hot dog, but you're my hot dog.'' He sighed. ''And maybe you're right, maybe you did tumble to something deep here, but you're too close to it to do any more good. When Zenzo breaks the chip, we're going to follow it up, no matter where it leads, and we're going to put Donny Quarters out of business. You've got my promise on that.''

''That's not good enough.''

''It's all I got to give.''

Traven saw the iron resolve in Kiley's eyes and nodded. ''The rest of the team know?''

''Not yet. I wanted you to know first.''

''I appreciate that.''

Kiley sighed. ''Look, Mick, there's a not a damn thing I can tell you that will keep you from hating my guts right now, but—''

''When you're right, you're right.''

Kiley ignored the interruption. ''—but this is for your own good. And for the good of the work you've done so far.''

''Why homicide?''

''Kaneoki's idea. Figured if we started you out with them dead, maybe you'd be less inclined to shoot anybody.''

''Terrific.''

Kiley clicked the wallscreen off. ''Remember something else too: These traffickers you've been busting the balls on aren't going to forget you. Even when we leak it to the media that you've been pulled out of vice, they're going to figure it's some kind of bullshit and that you're still after them on the streets. If they don't think that way, revenge will keep them interested for a while. Zenzo picked up some kind of squawk in the decks. Keep your head low and your ass covered.''

Traven nodded. ''How's Chambers?''

''They saved the arm, but he's going to lose a lot of articulation, maybe enough to put him behind a desk.'' Kiley's voice was dead as he spoke. He touched the bionic leg unconsciously. ''If you hadn't got there and tourniqueted him, they tell me, he wouldn't have made it.''

Traven picked up his duster and palmed the door back.

''Traven.''

''Yeah.''

Kiley leaned on the desk with his knuckles, his ebony face looking as if it had been carved from anthracite. ''I find you messing around this case after today, I'm going to kick your ass and put you behind a desk for the duration. You understand me?''

''Sure.''

''And lose the beard before morning. Homicide doesn't put up with that kind of shit.''

Traven let the door shush closed behind him. He kicked a file-covered table and watched the papers spill to the floor, ignoring the invective flung in his direction as he made his way out of the squad room.

8

Brandstetter took the drink she offered. They were in another room in his private construct, drinking liquor that wouldn't get anyone drunk but made the illusion comfortable. He sat at the bar, perched on a long-legged stool with a back. He'd seen one like it somewhere one day and popped a simulacrum into the construct the next. Nothing was too good in the little bit of world he controlled.

His mother was dressed now, working behind the bar, wearing a low-cut red dress that showed a lot of cleavage in the light provided by wall-mounted candles. He had to work to keep his mind off of it.

"Where did this room come from?" he asked. "I've never been anywhere like it."

His mother shook out a bar towel and wiped the spotless wood counter, then slid a corkboard coaster under his glass. "I don't know. I've never seen it either."

"Then where did it come from?"

"From you." She gazed deeply into his eyes, holding her head just the way he liked to see it. Her throat convulsed as she drained off a third of her drink. "Everything you've got stored in here is either a product of memory or of your attempt to fill in the gaps of your memories about me."

"I don't like it when you talk like that." He said it hard, so she would understand.

"Like what?" she asked coyly.

"Like that."

"You mean like a computer analog of someone who used to be a person?"

Brandstetter didn't reply.

"Maybe I talk that way because that's what I am." She emptied her glass and poured more. Candlelight flickered across the smooth planes of her face.

"No. You're real. You may have started out as an analog, but you're real now." He swirled the melting make-believe ice in the glass that wasn't really there. "That happens sometimes, you know."

"What?"

"AIs, formed in constructs, split off to find their own identities."

She laughed at him, the notes bitter. "If that was true, I'd be far, far away from here." She put her glass down and moved effortlessly across the floor, the red dress clinging to her best features. Her eyes sparkled when she faced him again. "There's a whole world out there, just ripe and eager and waiting for me to reach out and take it."

"I know. You've always told me that."

"I mean it."

"I know."

"I should leave you."

Brandstetter sat quietly, knowing the mood would leave her when it had run its course. She was always like this after she'd been drinking.

She wandered through the round tables and empty chairs, wavering in the smoky light given off by the candles. "We can't keep this up, you know," she said in a husky voice. "He's going to find out one of these days, and when he does, the shit will really hit the fan."

"He can't find us here."

She looked at him doubtfully, clinging to the wooden support that ran from floor to ceiling.

"I promise."

"I should be a stronger woman. I really should."

"You are. I've never met another woman like you."

She smiled and came over to trail her fingers against his skin. The contact burned with passion. "You're a pretty boy too, and that makes it even harder to think of giving you up. A woman like me gets so few pretty things in this life.''

Brandstetter became thirteen again at her touch as the passion hit him. Her lips crushed his, and he could smell the shampoo in her hair. Gently he pushed her back.

''Where are you going?'' she demanded.

''I've got to go,'' he told her as he put on twenty-five years.

''Don't leave me here, dammit.''

''I've got to.'' Brandstetter walked toward the batwing doors, knowing she stared at him the whole distance across the floor. ''It's work. I told you this could never happen while I was working.''

''Damn you, you can't leave me here like this, needing you the way I do.'' She threw her glass down, and it broke against the floor.

Her voice ringing in his ears, Brandstetter keyed the deck and jacked out.

Brandstetter felt reality seep into him with the force of hammerblows. The bright intensity of the workroom always hit him first, followed immediately by the sound of the other decks in operation. He realized how close he'd come to breaking his promise to himself to control his visits to his private construct during working hours. For a moment he was frightened, wondering if anyone else had noticed.

Six other deckjockeys sat at their desks in the research lab on the seventy-eighth floor of Nagamuchi Tower B. None of them appeared even to know he was there, lost somewhere between the white walls and computer banks that filled every conceivable space.

Dressed as he was in black slacks, white shirt, black tie, and white lab smock, he wouldn't have stood out from the others. Except that he was Caucasian and the others were all Japanese.

The message light on his work console blinked blue fire at him. He touched it, said, ''Brandstetter.''

"Brandstetter-san," the girl said in singsong lyrics, "Yorimasa-san will see you in his offices now."

"Thank you. Tell him I am on my way." Brandstetter clicked off. He ran his fingers through his fringe of hair, feeling the perspiration dappled across his head.

He left the lab, moving with none of the unconscious grace he was so aware of in cyberspace, trapped in the hulking body he had resented for so long. He was graceful in sports and athletics, but he could never depend on his reflexes to be as slow and dignified as his employers' were. It complicated matters even further because he was so huge in comparison to them.

He used the tube to get to Yorimasa's office on the eighty-sixth floor. Most employees this far up in the R&D tower of Nagamuchi Towers still stared at him, thinking they weren't being seen in return. Western men or women were an oddity in this section of Nagamuchi.

The security guard, wearing black and the traditional swords of the samurai, was new. He kept his hand near the belted flechette pistol.

Brandstetter had to show him his identification before he could step out of the tube car. Even then, the guard followed two paces behind and to his left as he padded down the carpeted halls leading to Yorimasa's office.

The secretary passed him through at once, waving the guard off.

Brandstetter smiled at her, and she smiled back. She had always made him think of the Queen Dragon Mother depicted in the B movies that had died out when he was a boy and Japanese economy took corporeal root in the Western Hemisphere, beginning with media presentations.

Yorimasa's office was paneled in expensive dark woods that had cost a small fortune and required expert care to protect them from the acidic humidity that could creep into the taller buildings. Vases in niches and inkblock prints adorned the walls, interspersed with colorful tapestries. The desk was also wood, decorated with functional yet ornate office accouterments that spoke of the respect the corporation held for the man behind it.

Yorimasa stood staring at the terrarium built into the wall behind the desk, under the mounted and scab-barded swords. Small green and yellow lizards darted between bonsai trees and miniature bushes, over flat gray rocks. His smile was oily when he turned around. "Ah, Brandstetter-san, thank you for coming so promptly."

Brandstetter bowed the way the corporate liaisons had taught him, never taking his eye off his supervisor.

Yorimasa gestured to the seat in front of the desk. "Please, sit."

Brandstetter took the seat, sitting forward on it, forcing himself to appear relaxed. "What is this about?"

Yorimasa smiled again. "Ah, still the Western way of doing things. You have been with our company for six months, yet you do not see that we prefer to handle things a bit more discreetly than is the custom here."

Brandstetter said nothing, wishing he could be somewhere else.

"As you wish, Brandstetter-san." Yorimasa pulled a leather-covered notebook from a desk drawer. He handed a sheet of paper across.

Glancing at the notations and times, Brandstetter realized Yorimasa had assigned someone to log his time-in/time-out in cyberspace. "What does this mean?"

Leaning back in his chair, Yorimasa crossed his hands over his stomach. "As you know, Brandstetter-san, you were added to the security department at considerable cost to this corporation. In addition to your exorbitant salary, you are also provided with your own construct and a free schedule. As an employee of Nagamuchi, you also have many other bonuses and privileges that I won't go into. You have excellent medical and health insurance. All these things, yet I have to ask myself what we are getting in return. You understand, of course."

"No," Brandstetter replied, his voice croaking and betraying his lack of confidence. "I don't."

"Check the sheet you have," Yorimasa said. "According to it, you have been spending more and more time in your own construct, away from the people who have been assigned to you. Is this correct?"

Bottling the anger that threatened to lash out, Brandstetter laid the paper on the immaculate desktop. "Within a week of my arrival, your security measures were beefed up nine percent over what they were. The successful efforts mounted by datajackers took a twenty-seven percent dive in that same amount of time. In these last two months, security is up another sixty-three percent, with a proportionate decrease in datajacker activity." He tapped the paper meaningfully, hoping his voice wouldn't break again. "You don't have anybody else here that can give you those kinds of figures."

"Sadly, this is true." Yorimasa didn't bother to explain what was sad about it. "That lends considerable prestige to your position, doesn't it?"

Brandstetter forced himself to exhale through his nose, trying to relax the fear trapped inside him.

"It also makes me wonder when you may choose to parlay your successes into something more than you have at present."

Understanding what the meeting was about and the petty concerns Yorimasa had, Brandstetter relaxed. He almost smiled with relief. "Let me be the first to assure you, political ambition within this company is the last thing I want to pursue. I'm quite content with my job here, and, as you've mentioned, I'm well rewarded for those endeavors."

"Good. I'm pleased to hear that." Yorimasa's eyes narrowed, almost closing. "Because I would hate to point out to you how unwilling I am to relinquish any of the authority I now wield. And I would hate to see you released from our employ for reasons you wouldn't even know of, because I doubt the stockholders of the corporation would be willing to let a gaijin live with the knowledge you have in your head."

The veiled threat of death held less terror for Brandstetter than the thought of losing his construct. It had taken so long to find her again. He would not let her be taken away again without a fight.

A side panel hissed away, revealing a young Japanese woman in a satin shift carrying a tray piled high with finger food. Her makeup was done tastefully, giving her face splashes of color designed to elicit erotic response. She started to back away.

Yorimasa spoke to her in Japanese, bringing a smile to her lips.

Brandstetter noted the delight shining in his supervisor's eyes and filed the information away. If this corporate geisha girl was a favorite of Yorimasa's, it might prove a valuable thing to know.

Yorimasa turned back to him, a hard look on his face. "You are excused, Brandstetter-san."

Biting back the anger and the fear that quaked inside him, Brandstetter nodded. Excused, yes, but not forgotten. He knew there would be no reasoning with the petty emotions that preyed on Yorimasa's imagination, but maybe there would be another way to take the pressure off. He thought about the construct, felt the weakness in him when he even considered losing it. If there was another way, he was determined to find it.

9

"Buy you a beer, cowboy?"

Traven looked up from his table and found Kowalski wading through the bar's patrons and carrying a silver Coors Light can in each hand. Music throbbed, meeting itself on the way back from each wall. Using an arm, Traven shoved the five empties sitting before him to one side.

Kowalski handed a beer over, turned a chair around backward, and sat with his back to the wall as Traven did.

A woman with a boa constrictor worked the lights and music on stage, gyrating to the calypso beat, her long hair flying around a heart-shaped face. The crowd around her cheered her actions enthusiastically. She slipped the head of the snake into one hand and shrugged out of her leather vest with the other, leaving her bare breasts bobbing. She laid the snake's head between them, acted as if the flicking tongue provided erotic pleasure.

"Snake's sedated," Kowalski said.

"So's the woman."

Kowalski nodded. "Puppet?"

"Yeah. Legitimate enterprise, my man, licensed by the state and the city. She gets programmed and paid, and doesn't have to put up with all the bad memories. The bar owner makes good money provided the programming is top-shelf merchandise, pays his taxes, and keeps live entertainment at a naturally high quality. The psychologists say it cuts down on the number of perverts vice spends its time chasing out on the streets."

"Shit. If that was true, the streets wouldn't be fucking mobbed at this point. All this does is stir them up good." Kowalski drained half his beer. "Still, it ain't bad to look at after going damn near brain-dead watching wallscreen."

"Unless you're one of the guys who get stirred up by this and go looking for it on the streets."

Kowalski shook his head. "You got them blues bad, don't you?"

Traven chuckled, the humor mixed up between emotion and alcohol. "Just one of those days."

"Bullshit. If it was just one of those days, you'd be at home in bed, letting tomorrow take care of itself the way it always does. Didn't figure you for a classy establishment like this."

"Had company at home."

"I noticed when I dropped by to check on you. I thought you quit scraping them gutter kids up from between the cracks when that one nearly cut your throat a couple months back."

"I did. At least for a while, until I get up the nerve again to think I can actually make one see life a little bit better. That was my brother."

"No shit?"

"Yeah. My old man surprised the kid and me both today by dropping him at my place. We had different mothers. Didn't even know each other until today."

Kowalski nodded. "Your old man is some piece of work, all right. Is he still with Beth?"

"They're on their honeymoon." Traven tried to say the words without bitterness, but he was sure it didn't escape Kowalski's attention. They'd been partners and acquaintances too long for that.

"No shit." Kowalski drained his beer. "If it'd been my old man who stole a girl of mine, I wouldn't have taken it as calm as you have."

"She wasn't my girl."

"C'mon, guy, you were into her pretty heavy back then. Don't try conning a con." Kowalski stood his empty to one side with the others and left the table as he dug money out of a shirt pocket.

Traven watched the man, realizing the shirt-pocket move was an undercover cop's survival trait: Never put your hands near your badge unless you meant to flash it—never flash it unless you were ready to be shot at.

Kowalski returned with two more beers.

The dancer was out of her bikini briefs now. The snake moved sluggishly between her thighs. Lights flashed over the crowd now, disorienting them and making the illusion even more complete. There were a lot of Japanese faces in the crowd. The bar had integrated while Traven had been away.

"Kiley came out and read us the riot act after you left," Kowalski said.

Traven looked at him.

"Wanted to make sure we all knew you were out of vice for the time being, and that anyone caught giving you inside dope on vice investigations could count on having his ass slammed in a crack." The big man shrugged. "Naturally, I figured since we ain't had a beer in a while, tonight would be a good night."

"Kiley's not kidding."

"Yeah, I know. I think we finally bit off more than he can chew."

"Maybe."

"Shit, don't try that bureaucracy bullshit with me. I come from the streets, same as you, and I know your nose hasn't stopped working because of the promotion. We tumbled to something a lot bigger than anyone thought."

"It's going to be hard to prove that without the chip evidence."

"Zenzo's still working on it. Told me to tell you that you'd get the first hardcopy of anything he recovers."

"He knows I'm out of vice?"

"Hell yes, he knows. Kiley made a special trip to see him too. Zenzo just says to eat it when you're through reading it."

"Kiley's not just dicking around here."

Kowalski returned his gaze full measure. "Neither

am I. I've been busting my balls down in these streets for a half-dozen years. Maybe I didn't make sergeant. Don't figure I have the temperament for that kind of grief anyway. But I'll be damned if I'll back off this thing now. Way I see it, whoever they stick in as your temporary replacement is going to want to go soft with this thing till some kind of cover-up can be arranged. I don't want to give them the chance. The other guys figured same as I do: We can play inside their rules, but we keep you up on what's going down.''

Traven nodded. "Kiley's going to be looking for that.''

"So let him look. Shit, we've put together good busts from inside one of the leakiest sections in the department. You're not going to convince me the guys supposed to be on our side are better than anything the street could throw at us.'' Kowalski gave him a crooked-toothed grin.

The dancer with the snake picked up her clothing, still on chip-pilot, and walked wooden-legged back to the dressing room as another woman took the stage and a new beat rushed to fill the room. Her eyes were as empty as the first woman's.

"Keep the messages to a minimum,'' Traven said. "Only pertinent information. The rest of it I can get from the streets. I may be working different cases, but they all take place in a lot of the same territory.''

"You got it.''

"No suspicious com-chip links, because Kiley will have someone watching for that.''

Kowalski nodded.

"And make sure the team doesn't try giving the new guy any song-and-dance routines. At least, none out of the ordinary. If this guy gets a bunch of choirboys, he'll be suspicious about that too.''

"No problem.''

Traven watched the new dancer, thought about giving Cheryl a call because he really did have the blues and didn't want to sleep alone, then remembered Danny. Maybe Cheryl wouldn't be inclined to come over if they weren't going to be alone, and now that he thought of it, he didn't feel exactly relaxed with the idea himself. The uncomfortable feeling fired up the betrayal associated with his father and made the blues even worse. He looked away from the dancer, noticed the guy in the patched, ragged leather duster at the end of the bar for the first time, told himself he must really be losing it if he hadn't seen the guy before now.

"I got the skinny on who your partner's supposed to be," Kowalski said.

"Who? I didn't bother to hang around long enough to ask."

"Lloyd Higham. I asked around for you a little. Old Lloyd's still hitting the sauce pretty regular."

"Can't be too regular," Traven said. "Otherwise he wouldn't still be on the force."

"He's careful about it. Guys I talked to wouldn't talk to the brass. You know the system."

"Yeah. Guess I do. Otherwise you wouldn't be here tonight."

Kowalski's grin was broad.

The guy at the end of the bar sipped his beer slowly, eyes roving over the crowd instead of the dancer.

Traven had learned a long time ago to pay attention to the warnings that trickled across the back of his neck. He drained his beer and shifted in his chair.

"Sounds like you may be getting set up to take the big fall on top of getting transferred out of vice," Kowalski said. "Having Higham as a backup on an active bust could be worse than no backup at all."

"Guy used to be good."

"That's been a while, buddy."

"And like Kiley says, in homicide I'll be dealing with corpses, not runners and Yaks."

"Yeah, well, somebody made those corpses that way in the first place. Keep that in mind."

"I will." Traven moved so Kowalski's head shielded his face from the man at the bar. "You noticed the guy at the bar?"

Kowalski's grin was feral. "Skinny piece of work at the end of the bar wearing the patched duster and the dust monkey on his back?"

"Yeah."

" 'Bout half a minute before you did."

"He partnered?"

"Not that I could see."

"Me neither."

"If the guy's playing a lone hand, you can bet he's desperate."

"You make him?"

"Never seen him before. He's from out of town or new talent."

"Or maybe small-time looking to go big tonight."

"Guy picked the wrong bar."

Traven smiled. "He doesn't know that yet." And some of the blues went away as he moved into action. He deliberately walked a little wobbly, hands tucked in his back pockets under his duster, looking like a zoner, without letting on the 10mm was only inches away from his palm. He picked his spot and moved into the bar crowd one man down from his target, dropped money on the counter as he ordered another beer.

The new dancer was in full swing now, swaying to the music, naked beneath the lights. Raucous shouts rose above the beat, urging, pleading, threatening in a thunderous swell.

Traven was in position and ready when the guy made his move. He had to give the guy credit for waiting till the music ended and dancers were about to change again, the quietest time in the bar.

The sawed-off shotgun swept out from under the patched duster and the guy fired a round to get everyone's attention. "Don't nobody have to get hurt," the guy said in a cracking voice. He started to lower the barrel toward the bartender.

The new music died in midbeat. The bartender's eyes got big as he froze in place.

"The till, man," the robber said, motioning with the shotgun. "Open the goddam till and give me the money." His eyes looked watery and worn.

Traven reached around the guy next to him, seized the shotgun, and yanked it out of the robber's hands.

As the man bellowed and reached for the inside of his duster, Traven stepped around the man between them and delivered a roundhouse kick to the guy's temple that had enough force behind it to stretch the man out on the floor. He ejected the shells from the shotgun onto the floor, then laid it on the counter. "You going to call the police?" he asked the bartender softly. "Or are you going to wait until he wakes up and tries again?"

The bartender reached for the phone.

Kowalski put his pistol away, picked up his Coors Light can, deposited it with slow deliberation on the counter, and joined Traven on the way out the door. "Figured it would be your style," the big man said with a grin. "Hell, the Lone Ranger and Tonto always left a silver bullet behind when they cleared out of town."

10

The apartment was dark and quiet when Traven arrived home. The silence caught him off-stride. He hadn't known what to expect with Danny there, but he had expected to notice a difference. He paused in the kitchen long enough to take an orange from the refrigerator, then headed to his bedroom.

"There have been a number of messages in your absence," the apartment AI said.

He dropped the SIG/Sauer on the bed, leaving the light off, then skinned out of his clothes. He unbuckled his backup pistol, a 10mm identical to the first, from his ankle and put it on the bed as well. "Hold the messages."

The AI whirred in response.

Slipping into a bathrobe, Traven went to the other bedroom and knocked.

"That you, Mick?" Danny asked.

"Yeah."

"It's open."

Traven twisted the knob and followed it inside.

Danny called for a light and the AI switched it on, dimming it immediately at his request. He sat on the bed, rumpled blankets swaddled around him.

"Everything go okay today?" Traven asked.

"Sure."

"Got to work and wondered if you'd find anything to eat. I don't usually keep much on hand, because I can't ever depend on my hours or my days off. And I haven't had a houseguest do more than stay overnight in months.''

Danny scratched his head and yawned. ''I managed. I found your grocery list and added a few things you must have overlooked.''

Traven grinned. ''If you found a list, it's got to be weeks old.'' He peeled the orange as he talked, making the skin one long, continuous peel without looking.

''We're going to need some stuff tomorrow, unless you're starting a diet.''

''I'll be busy tomorrow getting set up in a new office,'' Traven said. He offered half the orange to the boy.

Danny accepted the orange, peeled off a wedge, and popped it into his mouth.

Traven did the same, bit into it, and relished the sudden rush of cold and flavor. The tart taste made his jaws ache. After he swallowed the juice and the pulp, he asked, ''If I give you my bank number, think you can handle the shopping? You can take a cab there and back. Give you a chance to get out of the apartment.''

''I'd like that. I got out for a while today, did some walking and thinking, but all I did was waste shoe leather and make my head hurt.''

''Takes time, Danny.''

''I know.''

''Wish there was something more I could say.''

Danny looked up at him. ''I know that too.''

Feeling uncomfortable, Traven looked down into his hand and separated another orange wedge. Somehow awkward moments like this always came easier when they were part of the job. ''Talk to Dad today?''

''No. He left a message for you, but I didn't feel much like talking to him.''

Traven didn't blame the boy, but he didn't voice the thought either. He finished the orange. ''Is there anything I can do for you before I go to bed?''

Danny shook his head and called lights out.

Traven turned to go.

''Hey, Mick.''

"Yeah?"

"Thanks for letting me stay, man. I don't think I could have hacked it hanging out with Dad and Beth."

"No prob, guy. Sleep tight."

"Yeah, you too."

Thoughts swirled in Traven's head, bumping into other thoughts as each tried to dominate his attention. Anger cycled in there as well. Anger at Kiley and the department and the old anger with his father reawakened by Danny's presence hung evenly matched in the scales. He switched off thoughts of Beth before the memories could become too comfortable and bring up visions of her naked and moving against him, laughing the laugh that he'd always found so intoxicating.

"There have been a number of messages in your absence," The AI repeated.

"Playback," Traven said as he slid out of the bathrobe. "This room only."

The bedroom door hissed shut.

The AI's message disk clunked as it booted up. "This is Kiley, and I'm still waiting here for your ass to show up." The connection broke with a loud bang.

Traven switched on the water, checking it for the right temperature, then kicked the shower head open and stepped in. He let the heat soak into him. The next two were also from Kiley, showing signs of increased hostility and more colorful language. The playback tweaked as it moved on to the next call.

"Hey, Mick, it's Cheryl." Her voice was low and sultry. "I just called to find out if you wanted company. If you get back after midnight, don't call. I'll be dead to the world. Tell Danny I said hi."

Tweak.

Traven worked a bar of soap into a thick lather, then watched it swirl down the drain. He accessed DataMain and found out it was 1:15 A.M.

"Goddammit, Traven!" Kiley's voice exploded. "I don't care—"

"Skip this one," he told the AI.

Tweak.

The disk clunked.

"I love my machine, Mickey," his father's voice informed him, "but I hate yours. Jesus, I hate talking to these things. Look, I wanted to tell you again how much I appreciate you taking your brother off my hands right now. What with Beth and this new project for Nagamuchi, I'm up to my ass is alligators. Just called to see if there was anything I could do to make his stay more pleasant. Call me."

Tweak.

Traven squirted shampoo into his palm and rubbed it vigorously into his hair, worked it into a lather.

The next voice on the message playback was rendered almost nonhuman by the artificial squelch on the pickup that insured voice prints couldn't be taken. "Traven, you know who this is. You took down a big score of mine last night. Way I hear it, you got your balls all swole up over what a stud detective you are. Just wanted you to know you got some people ready to cut them off, guys who've been in the revenge business for generations, if you know what I mean. If I was you, I'd try growing eyeballs on the back of my head. I mean, the people I'm associated with had the stroke to get this number. Think about it. I will be."

Tweak.

"There are no more messages," the AI said.

"Cancel function," Traven said as he stepped out of the shower without a towel. He dripped all the way to the bed, fisted one of the 10mms, climbed back into the shower, and sat the pistol in the soap caddy, then finished his shower.

11

"Do you want to lose me again?" she asked.

"No!" Brandstetter forced himself to concentrate on the configurations the program took in front of him. He'd had to expand the makeshift lab in his private construct to get the proper effect, and he felt it pulsing at the limits of cyberspace, threatening to spill over into that other, more fleshly world contained in his apartment. He was too damn conscious of his hands on the deck, not meshing with it as he wanted to.

"They're going to take me away from you," she said, crying softly in his ear. Her breath was so warm.

"No, they're not," Brandstetter said through gritted teeth. His cyberself played with the deck representation before him while his real hands flew across the real keys running programs. The configurations shifted again, becoming bright explosions of color as understanding tilted and slid away from him again.

She put her arms around him and held him.

He shed flesh, years, became thirteen years old. "No!" He took her hands from him gently, slid off the stool, and turned to face her, never letting go of her wrists. He felt the anger rising, burning inside her, and it chilled him. "Look, I need time to figure this out. Yorimasa is the only person at Nagamuchi who poses a threat to us. If this works, and I think it will, I can keep him busy, get him away from us until I can come up with some other way to put us out of his reach."

She drew her arms away, her back stiffening with anger.

Once her touch left him, Brandstetter resumed his age and size. He took his seat on the stool again and pecked at the keys.

"If we are found out," she said in a soft voice, "what will become of me?"

He answered without looking at her. "I don't know."

"Where was I before I was here?"

"With me. You've always been with me, but this makes it better."

"I love you."

"I know."

She stood there, watching him, breaking her stance only occasionally to refill her glass.

Even without looking at her, Brandstetter knew she was there. She'd always been there, somewhere. Cyberspace and his construct just gave her flesh.

Brandstetter left even his cyberself behind as he plunged into the deck representation. Cyberspace wrapped around him, then pulsed with the beat of his own heart. He knew the answers. What he needed was the proper question.

He zoomed along the gridlines, kicking over to DataMain, appalled at the passage of time, knowing his corporeal body was sorely taxed by the demands he put on it.

"What are you looking for?" she asked.

He didn't allow his mind to wander, to question how she was there with him, but he was thankful she couldn't touch him now. He smelled her breath and felt his pulse quicken, strangely out of place in cyberspace. "Privacy AIs," he replied without lips.

"Isn't that the corporation that manufactures the artificial intelligences that monitor homes and apartments?"

"Yes." He found the interlocking grid, followed the right-angle juncture, and sped along his way. Cyberspace didn't seem as cold now that he wasn't alone. For a moment he wondered what might happen if someone picked them up in cyberspace, if he accidentally ran afoul of any of the myriad traps waiting out there. His mother's presence could easily be covered, because any number of cyberjockeys rode piggyback. But that wouldn't help if her identity was discovered.

"Why go there?"

He found Privacy AIs' module floating free. Nodules of cybertraps hovered around it like dozens of orbiting moons. He'd designed some of them himself while working for other companies before Nagamuchi.

Privacy AIs was funded by a number of companies who developed software for the home AI, ranging from medical RAMs for home delivery of children to erotic RAMs for couples who liked fantasy with their sex to advanced personality RAMs for people who didn't like feeling alone at home. But at the core of all those additions was Privacy AIs' main programming.

"It's something I've been playing with ever since I first became involved in security work." He found the outer shell of defenses and plowed through with his Nagamuchi number; Nagamuchi had made considerable investments in the company before setting up its offices in Dallas. Bright lines of programming flowed around him.

"You're here because you're hoping to find some way to get through AI-monitored security." Her voice held a note of triumph in it.

A chill touched Brandstetter's mind. He still wasn't used to the way she read his thoughts at times. "Quiet," he ordered. But it wasn't as if anyone could scan his line of thinking without tapping into his deck.

"Even if you can get into Yorimasa's apartment, what then?"

"I don't know."

"You could kill him."

"No."

"Why?"

"That would draw attention to the whole department. I would be under investigation as much as anyone else."

"You don't have the backbone to do it."

He pushed away his anger. "It isn't a question of backbone. It's a question of intelligence. Maybe I can use his geisha against him. He seemed so happy with her. Perhaps he doesn't want anyone to know how fond he is of her."

"If you threatened him, he'd have you killed. A man in Yorimasa's position won't give in to blackmail."

He didn't reply.

"That's foolish to think you would be the first person to face him with an idea like that. Yorimasa would have one of the corporate Yakuza terminate you and sell your body to the organ-recovery jackals after burning your fingerprints and retinas. Organ-recovery companies haven't been ordered to do DNA testing on John Does yet."

"Something else then. I don't know. Right now this is the only option I have." He stepped across security nets, avoided detect-webs, slithered through maze expulsers.

"Kill him."

"No."

"For me."

"I can't."

"You're going to lose me. After all this time, we're going to be apart again."

"No. We're not."

"You're too weak to keep us together."

"No."

"You're too weak."

"I'm not."

"Do you want to go back to being Creepy Earl even here?"

"No!" His voice held thunder.

She was gone. Just like that.

He felt the ache of emptiness inside him. Panic clawed at him with jagged talons when the prospect of trying to survive without her again stared at him so abruptly. He concentrated on the living embodiment of Privacy AIs below his orbit, side-shifting around more traps. There was a weakness in the system. There always was. That was why people like him were employed as security, to preserve the integrity and the secrets of company data.

He scanned through the programming, found what he had found before, that AI home units were the same/not-same, individually contained little worlds despite the various RAMs that were added on.

He needed a skeleton key to the AIs, needed a way to become something the AI was programmed to ignore or would not notice. And it had to be something he could carry on his corporeal body so he could enter Yorimasa's home himself without tripping the security alarms or videoguards.

Without warning, the thought of videoguards that filmed whoever broke into the home made the connection for Brandstetter. It took his mind off what he was doing in his orbit around Privacy AIs enough to forget about the various security programming around him. A tangle-spore of computer virus tracked onto him, homing in on his personal deck to fry his brain.

He deflected his course, mimicked a covering detect-web program, then propelled himself out of the module when the tangle-spore went away, scratching furtive fingers into the cold terrain of cyberspace.

"You've found a way." She was back without warning.

"Yes." He hovered over the bunched representation of the fiberoptic cables routing free media channels to homes all over Dallas.

"What is it?"

"This." Brandstetter microed his vision, bringing the streams of data coursing through the cyberspace version of fiberoptic cable into clear view.

"Television?"

"Yes. Everyone has free access to a wallscreen. How could companies hope to sell their goods without advertisements? Companies buy out the television and movie companies, provide the programs, and sell everything they want to. Home AI units are programmed to receive media twenty-four hours a day without charge. Of course, part of the cost is reflected in the home payment, the apartment rent, and the cover charges at public places. Someone, I forget who and it doesn't really matter, once called it the opiate of the masses, and it was never truer than now.''

''How does this help?''

''You'll see,'' he said. Then smiled with no lips. ''Or rather, you won't. Give me a little time and I'll show you.''

''I'll be waiting for you.'' Her voice sounded hopeful. The sensation of her disappearance gusted around him.

Brandstetter read the overall programming of the media AI inlets and built a program that would be more than a facsimile. Once he was satisfied with his product, he moved back from it, observed the whole. It hadn't been easy. If it hadn't been for the Nagamuchi credentials that allowed him access to different nerve centers of the television stations and Privacy AIs, if he hadn't been as skilled as he was at setting up security networks and backups, and a dozen other ifs, it would have been impossible. But it had come together under his guiding hand and floated like a kite tail after him in cyberspace.

He created a virus to disguise and contain it, then bounced it off DataMain, through dozens of other public traffic areas in cyberspace, gained speed as he crossed grids till he must have looked like a negative return line on a VISA application.

When he was finished, he linked into a biosoft company owned by Nagamuchi through three dummy corporations. He set up the imprinting that would allow the programming to be rendered on a biochip, keyed into his fax line at his office, relayed the past week's performance records onto the programming, married the virus to it so it could not be detected easily, then took the finished product and shot it back to the biosoft Chipworx in his home.

Once there, he splintered the data once more, edited the virus out, and sent the untainted copy to Yorimasa's office as usual. Today was Friday, after all. The other copy, the one containing the virus, he ran through his home machine so it would be there waiting. Even if the biochip was traced and the records of it examined, the virus would escape investigation.

He jacked back into his personal construct, unable to keep from smiling.

She waited for him, leaning one full hip against the bar. "How did it go?"

"It's done."

"What?" She offered him a drink.

He took a sip, glorying in his success. "Watch." He held out a hand, programmed his virus into a biochip that gleamed like a drop of black oil in his palm, then inserted it into one of his temple trode jacks. He switched on the room's wallscreen and watched it come to life with a brilliant stab of color. Life imitating life imitating life . . .

A news documentary was on, delineating the growth of the Ku Klux Klan and Aryan Guard with the arrival of Japanese business interests taking up residence on American soil.

"What does this have to do with us?" she asked.

Brandstetter shut down the input from the television sources and triggered the taping function of the wallscreen. Instantly the image of Ku Klux Klan members rioting in Japanese neighborhoods was replaced by a view of the two of them standing in the room. Unlike a mirror, this was a true image of them in which right was right and left was left.

"Home video?" she asked. A perplexed frown twisted her features.

"Not quite," he said with a smile. "The biochip I created allows me to transmit in much the same fashion the television stations do. Or not to transmit if I choose not to." He toasted his grinning self in the wallscreen, the image reproduced truly instead of being reflected, and kicked in the special programming. "Now you see me . . . now you don't." And he faded from view, leaving only a black, vaguely man-shaped shadow behind, still holding the upraised twisted shadow of a glass.

12

Traven struggled through layers of sleep.

"There is a visitor at the door," the apartment AI announced again.

Rubbing his face with a palm that didn't feel like part of his body yet, Traven said, "Display," then glanced blearily at the inset in the wallscreen.

A man wearing an off-the-rack suit leaned against the door. He looked early fifties, paunchy, and bored. He twirled his hat at the end of a finger.

"There is a visitor at the door," the apartment AI repeated.

"Cease function," Traven ordered as he sat up on the bed. He studied the man through the display, then reached for his personal deck beside the bed. He keyed it to life and set it to function on the wallscreen.

"Hey, Mick," Danny said as he leaned into the doorway, "there's a guy at the door who says he's a cop."

"I see him," Traven replied. "Running him through my deck now." The wallscreen display continued, matched by the deck's rectangular readout a handful of seconds later. The inscription was led by the ID, first Higham, Lloyd, Det. Sgt. Homicide, followed by his police serial number. He glanced back at Danny, noticed for the first time the boy was dressed. "You up already?"

"Yeah."

"Got coffee on?"

"Sure."

"You mind letting the guy in and keeping him entertained while I grab a quick shower and put on some clothes?"

"No prob. You gonna feel like breakfast?"

"You cooking?"

"Sure."

Traven levered himself out of bed. "Sounds great. But, Danny, you're a guest, you know. You don't have to fix breakfast every morning."

Danny shrugged. "I know. It's just a way of saying thanks for the space right now."

Accessing his com-chip, Traven found out it was 7:38 A.M. On his way to the shower, he felt guilty for avoiding Danny last night, remembered how lonely the apartment could be when life seemed to come to a standstill. He banished the guilt under the hot spray. He'd learned a long time ago his shoulders were only so broad, but sometimes that knowledge didn't help everything go down easily.

He toweled off and dressed in jeans, a gray-and-black-checked flannel shirt over a T-shirt from a The Who revival concert, and white British Knights. Dress code be damned until a half-inch before suspension. He'd taken the beard off last night and his face felt tender, so he left the stubble. He'd been assigned to homicide, but that didn't mean he had to like it.

He tickled the com-chip again for the weather report, then took a black duster from the hallway closet. He laid both SIG/Sauers in the easy chair on top of the duster as he entered the living room.

Higham glanced at him from the kitchen table with an uncertain smile. He nodded toward the pistols. "You're in homicide now," he said in a gravelly voice. "We're responsible for cleaning up murders, not committing them."

Traven walked to the coffee machine and poured himself a cup. Danny was busy at the stove. "Yeah, well, I may have been temporarily transferred out of vice, but that doesn't mean I left all my business associates behind with the job."

The smile trickled off Higham's face. "Maybe I said the wrong thing."

Traven nodded. "Maybe you did."

Tension made a white spot over the blade of the homicide cop's nose. "Let's start over." He stood and held out his hand. "Lloyd Higham."

Traven took it. "Mick Traven."

"Nice place you got here. Wish I could keep mine looking like this."

For the first time Traven noticed how clean the apartment was and realized how Danny must have spent the empty hours. The guilt returned with interest. He sat at the opposite end of the small table. The smell of bacon and eggs was tantalizing, and the sizzling sound made it even more tempting. He sipped his coffee and tried to keep his stomach from rumbling.

Large red veins made a map under Higham's face, stemmed from the network around his nostrils. They were drinker's scars. His breath was a mixture of mouthwash and bourbon. The detective rummaged through a scuffed black portafile on the floor by his feet, coming up with a fistful of manila files. "I know we weren't supposed to meet until ten, but I wanted to stop by early." He shrugged. "I know what went down with you in vice yesterday, and I wanted to make this as easy as possible for us. Figured the top brass would keep us underfoot while they made up their minds how this arrangement was going to work out."

"I appreciate that."

Higham waved it away. "It's as much for my benefit as yours. I'm not exactly on the departmental honor roll anymore either. It'll help both our careers if we pull this act together and roll up some fast collars." He indicated the files. "Right now we're carrying a light load. We're working six murders and two attempted murders. But the caseload could change at any time. Homicide isn't like vice. You don't get to develop your target and take the operation down. In homicide you work a dozen cases sometimes, and hope something falls as you go through the paces."

''Breakfast,'' Danny announced as he brought steaming plates to the table.

Traven ate mechanically, chewed through the files as well as the food as Danny and Higham traded recent sports trivia at the other end of the table. He felt uncomfortable in the kitchen. He wasn't used to having company, and his relationship with both of them was forced, yet both depended on him in different ways.

The caseload seemed to be pretty cut-and-dried. The murderers had been identified in all six cases, but remained at large, leaving the trackdown as the next step in the investigation. Two of them weren't done by locals and would probably remain open for a long time unless cooperation from other cities turned up leads or the suspects themselves.

Finished with both breakfast and reading, he put the files to one side. Danny chose that moment to clear away the dishes and give him privacy with Higham, making the guilt of neglect that much sharper.

''We got a break on the Lawrence case,'' Higham said. ''An informant of mine turned up a possible address on Meishu. That's where we're going after we check in downtown.''

''The file was lean on Meishu,'' Traven said as he walked to the coffeepot. He filled his cup, then warmed Higham's. ''Tell me about him.''

''Japanese scum,'' Higham said. ''Imported for one of the Jap companies a couple years back when American labor tried to strike for higher wages and better benefits against Nagamuchi and the others. After the starve-out started and our workers realized the Nips weren't going to back off, the imported help was laid off. Hanzo Meishu was one of the ones who chose not to go back. He was a datajacker till he tripped over a security net at Ietaka Corporation. Meishu was neutered from deckwork. He hasn't been too happy with life since. The Lawrence girl's problem was she didn't know a loser when she saw one. Meishu had her turning tricks to support them until he slapped her too hard and killed her. According to what I could find out about Lawrence, she worked on the north side until Meishu screwed up her face and she dropped too much weight. Worked under the name of Skipper or something like that.''

''Slipper?''

''Yeah, that was it. Did you know her?''

''She also sold information to vice on the side. I cut a couple deals with her myself.'' Traven remembered the woman's face the girl had developed over the short time he had known her, had trouble equating even that with the bruised and battered picture with dead eyes in the file. ''I didn't know she was in this kind of trouble.''

''Yeah, well, that's the thing with homicides,'' Higham said in a fatherly tone. ''Nobody knows exactly how bad things are until it's too late to do anything about them.''

Traven pushed the files back across the table. ''That's why I prefer vice. You get a shot at stopping some of the bodies from hitting the streets if you're successful.''

Higham nodded. ''You ready?''

''Yeah.'' Traven dropped one of the 10mms in its ankle holster, tucked the other in his waistband at his back, then slipped the duster on. He slipped his bank chips out of his wallet and gave one to Danny.

''Any kind of budget you want to set?'' the boy asked.

''No. There's money in the account, so feel free to pick up whatever extras appeal to you. My tastes seem to run pretty much the same as yours. You drink beer?''

''When I can get it.''

Traven nodded. ''Fair enough. Pick up a couple six-packs of Coors while you're at it.''

''They won't sell to me. I'm a minor.''

''I've got connections. If you don't go any farther than the local FoodMart, I'll give Su Lin a call and have her fix you up. She's one of the assistant managers.''

''Okay.'' Danny put the bank card away.

"Deal is the beer is to be administered under adult supervision only."

"You got it."

"Can't say what time I'll get off tonight, but I hope it won't be too late. If you need anything, call. You can reach me through homicide division. Use Higham's name."

Danny nodded.

Traven turned to go, noticed Higham by the door and the cleanliness of the apartment again. He looked back, said, "The apartment looks great," and wished there were more he knew to say.

Danny said, "Thanks."

Traven followed Higham out of the apartment.

"Nice kid," Higham said as they waited for the elevator.

"Yeah. My brother."

"Didn't know you had a brother."

"Neither did I." Traven stepped inside the elevator cage before Higham could say anything else.

13

Higham drove, turned off Singleton Boulevard onto Fish Trap, then turned again onto Morris Street to cut through the heart of the West Dallas Housing Project.

Traven sat in the unmarked sedan's passenger seat and tried to relax. He stifled a yawn that crept up from under his toenails, thinking he shouldn't have had such a big breakfast, because it only made him sleepy.

"Late night?" Higham asked. It was the first attempt at conversation since they'd crossed the Continental Viaduct over the Trinity River twenty minutes ago.

"Not used to mornings," Traven replied. He shifted inside the duster for more warmth, because the car's heater wasn't working well. "You work vice, you see a lot of nights."

The housing project flowed around them, a steady montage of broken and chipped houses sporadically interspersed with short towers of apartments that had been introduced in the late '90s before the American economy had been gutted. The new Japanese landlords hadn't been too interested in the upkeep. Small children scampered and played in the dirty streets, weaving little magical dreams for themselves that would be shattered in too few years on the bare rocks that were the backbone of real life. Huge billboards advertising products ranging from cosmetics to cars clung to the tops of the apartment buildings, glared in bright colors from blank walls on company-owned housing. The offers of money from the loan agencies were hung in stark black-and-white, causing them to stand out from the pastel promises made by the companies.

A bouncing red-and-yellow beach ball caught by the wind thudded across the top of the sedan. Higham braked the car as a half-dozen children in torn clothing and coats gave chase gleefully. "Now there's a drug for you," Higham said as he got underway again. "If somebody could figure out how to bottle youth, even if it didn't take away the wrinkles, they'd make a fortune."

Two boys on skateboards swept by. Traven watched them in the sideview mirror as they turned around and flipped off the sedan. The sedan was a rolling billboard of its own, screaming that cops had once again invaded the neighborhood. He touched the 10mm's outline through the duster pocket.

"You remember what it was like to be that young?" Higham asked as he cut the steering wheel and moved on to Shaw Street. The address they were looking for was on Greenleaf Street.

"No," Traven lied.

"I do. Those were the good years." Higham sighed.

Traven focused on a small black girl sucking her thumb and carrying a teddy bear with a missing ear. She couldn't have been over three or four, but the knowledge of what the sedan signified was already burned into her eyes. She crawled back into hiding beside a cracked cement porch.

"Didn't used to find Japs and whites and blacks and spics living together like this," Higham said. "I've been working this district a long time, and it ain't been till the Japs took over the market that you saw the like of this."

"That's because poverty is the only known force to cut across racial barriers," Traven said as he watched the little girl creep back from the porch and run into the house.

Higham glanced at him for a moment.

Traven returned the gaze full measure.

"Yeah, well, it sure as hell tore up the hold the KKK

and Aryan Guard had on the area. Until then there was a semblance of law and order here. Now these people just kill each other and steal each other blind.''

The morning sun hovered behind gray clouds and provided a thin, grayed-out illumination. If it hadn't been for his biological clock and access to DataMain, Traven could have believed dusk was only minutes away.

A group of teenage males and females wearing gang colors sat and stood in front of a burned-out church. Their features were from several races, pure and mixed, but the hate evident on them could have been stamped from the same mold. A handful of the boys stood up defensively, rocked back and forth, then made taunting gestures as the unmarked sedan turned away from them.

''We aren't going to have a fan club around here when we do this,'' Higham said. His lips thinned out to a flat, tight line.

''That's why we have the backup.''

Higham stopped the sedan and put the transmission in park. ''There's the house in the next block.''

Grayed numbers retaining flecks of gold paint hung haphazardly from the porch eave. Gray duct tape and pieces of cardboard covered broken windows. Uneven black smoke poured from the makeshift flue someone had stabbed through the broken-shingled roof. Gaps in the brick exterior revealed rotting two-by-fours and pink insulation through the cardboard and paper plugs. A red Chevy compact listing badly to the left on broken springs squatted on the shattered driveway over a thick pool of black oil.

''Let's do it,'' Traven said as he crawled out of the sedan into the chill wind.

Higham followed after tripping the electronic locks and the burglar alarms on the unmarked car. ''This guy's going to rabbit the minute he sees us.''

''I'll take the back door. Give me five minutes.''

''You got it.''

Traven walked, both hands in the duster as if he sought shelter from the cold. His right hand was around the butt of the SIG/Sauer. He flicked the safety off. Even if Meishu didn't pose a real threat, the housing project was a spawning ground for the people he'd dealt with in vice. Familiar faces seemed to be around every corner when least expected. He passed between houses, past a cracked window with a faded Santa face wearing an eyepatch taped to it, walked through the few remaining bars of the stripped fences, and followed the ditch overgrown with brush to his target.

The back of the house wasn't any better. More gaps in the brick exterior let Traven know the house sometimes went for long periods without being rented. While it was vacant, other project dwellers stripped the brick to fill holes in their own houses. Green plastic trash bags littered the weed-infested backyard, and gleaming tears fluttered in the wind, then became broken glass, scraps of metal, microwave food trays, and other unsalvageable detritus of modern living when he looked at them. More cardboard covered the rear windows.

Traven moved into position beside the back door, avoided the few remaining broken spars of the patio. He left the 10mm in his pocket. If there were neighbors who'd spotted him and were concerned enough to call the police emergency numbers, he didn't want to increase their interest with the pistol.

He accessed the com-chip for the frequency he and Higham ran. "Ready." There was no reply.

He listened, strained his hearing, and picked up the staticky sounds of a wallscreen in use. Even if the rest of the building deteriorated to nothing, the leasing companies would make sure the television worked. Business flowed along every channel.

Muted voices laughed.

Traven stood by the door and leaned against the wall. The uneven bricks gouged into his back, and the cold fingers of winter caressed the back of his neck.

The doorbell rang inside, and the laughter and the voices died away, replaced by tense silence. Knocking followed. Someone went to the door and opened it.

Higham's voice cut over someone's objections, loud and insistent, punctuated by the sound of running feet.

The cardboard-covered window to Traven's right exploded as a body shot through it to land in a rolling heap that suddenly grew legs and charged off down the overgrown ditch.

"He's gone rabbit, Traven!" Higham's voice hammered through the chip-link with almost enough force to cause pain.

Pushing himself off the house, Traven ran after the man, slapping at the tall weeds almost obscuring view of his quarry with his free hand, the other still buried in his duster pocket. "Is it Meishu?"

"Maybe."

A stone turned under Traven's foot, sent flames of pain through his ankle as he dropped. Taking the pistol out of his pocket, he used both hands to shove himself erect again. The leg wanted to limp but he didn't allow it. The runner had gained precious yardage.

A mop of black hair zigzagged through the brush twenty yards ahead.

"Is it Meishu?" Traven asked again.

"Don't know." Higham's voice sounded petulant. "He's not in the house."

Traven pounded down more brush. The chilled air bit into his lungs when he inhaled.

"Where are you?"

"In the drainage ditch, going north."

"Does it look like Meishu?"

"I haven't gotten a look at him yet. I can give you a description of the back of his head and tell you this son of a bitch can run, but that's it."

"Stick with him. Meishu was in this damn house. That's got to be him."

"Where are the backups?"

"Rolling."

For the first time Traven felt the loss of control. Higham ran the backups, coordinating the dragnet on a private channel so no one could foul up his decisions, including Traven.

The fleeing man tried to angle up the steep sides of

the drainage ditch, only to have purchase give way under one foot and send him spilling back down the incline. He must have landed on his feet, because it didn't seem to have stopped his forward momentum.

Traven cursed as he jumped across an abandoned fifty-five-gallon barrel that had rusted away to a collection of jagged edges buried in the loose sand and brush. He landed off-balance. Cold sand trickled into his tennis shoes despite the laced hightops. He'd gained some yardage, but not enough to matter. The runner looked like all hard right angles, his head bobbing forcefully, knees lifted high, fists coming back under sharp elbows.

The drainage ditch dipped and the sides became steeper. More of the concrete showed through the brush now as the angle became unclimbable. The runner was on track now, left with nowhere to go but forward.

Breathing harshly, trying to control the rhythm and force the bad air out before inhaling again, Traven figured the guy would keep running till they hit the Trinity River unless something happened.

The drainage ditch widened and showed signs of water erosion along the bottom now. A musty, moldy smell pervaded the area. The sound of running feet echoed inside the enclosure.

Thirty yards in front of the runner, a car lunged over the edge of the ditch, one front tire spinning freely as the driver swung the door open and darted out. The runner stumbled to a stop, head turned toward the two men skidding and sliding down the concrete slope with guns in their fists.

Slowing now, knowing the guy's options were suddenly limited, Traven watched the runner, waited for the break he knew was coming, and wondered who the hell the two men were. He accessed the com-chip. "Higham?"

"Yeah. Where are you?"

"The ditch. Are there any more plainclothes working this with us?"

"No. We're it. I got two cars of uniformed officers en route."

"We got a couple of wild cards here too."

"What are you talking about?"

"I'm talking about the two guys closing in on our runner. They left their vehicle hanging on the edge of the drainage ditch."

"Goddammit. Have you got a visual on this guy yet?"

The runner turned and faced Traven with his mouth open and nostrils flaring under wide, white eyes. "Yeah. It's Meishu."

"Stay with him. I'm on my way." Higham rippled out.

Meishu bolted, drawing on reserves Traven wouldn't have believed were possible. Traven drifted toward the man, kept his eyes trained on Meishu's midsection, because the guy couldn't go anywhere without it. He feinted, saw Meishu go for the fake, then kicked out with a leg that caught the running man just above the knees and sent them both tumbling to the sandy ground.

Traven avoided the fingers that clawed for his eyes, ignored the screams of frustration and fear, and forearmed Meishu in the face. The man's lips split and dark blood stained the ground. Traven hit him again, rolled the man over, and scrambled to place a knee between his shoulders. He grabbed a handful of the dark hair and pulled the man's head up. He pointed the 10mm in the general direction of the two men closing in on him. "Police," he said, still breathing rapidly.

The two men came to a stop twenty feet away with uncertain looks on their faces. Both wore patched jeans, sleeveless down vests, mirrorshades, and dirty flannel shirts. They were bearded and their hair was uncombed.

"Bullshit," one of them said as he looked at the other man. "Takewa's boys have been running the same kind of scam on the west side. Ray, this guy's no more a cop than I am. He's feeding us a line, that's all.''

The other man kept his gun trained on Traven. "If you're a cop, let's see some ID.''

The sound of a pump shotgun racking a load into the chamber came from overhead. "How much more ID you boys think you're gonna need down there?'' The speaker was a uniformed officer peering over a Mossberg 870. Another officer stood to one side holding a pistol in a Weaver stance.

"Aw shit,'' the speaker said.

"Hands in the air,'' the uniform ordered. "I'm sure a couple of wise boys like yourselves know the routine. Guns on the ground.''

"There's sand down here. I'm not going to ruin my gun by getting sand all over it.''

"Maybe you'd prefer to bleed all over it instead.''

The men put the guns down and placed their hands on their heads.

Traven stayed where he was. His legs trembled from the run, but his hand was steady.

"Look,'' one of the men said, "we're on a case here. Meishu belongs to us.''

"How do you figure that?'' Traven asked.

"Meishu's late on his loan payment. He's into the agency for four figures. We were sent to collect it.''

The uniformed officers came down the slope with some difficulty, followed by Higham. "What have we got here?'' Higham asked, glaring at the two men.

"Got us a couple jackals working organ recovery,'' the officer carrying the shotgun replied.

"Check their licenses,'' Higham ordered as he turned to Traven.

"Paperwork's up to date.'' one of the collectors said.

"If it is,'' Higham said, "chase them.''

"Hey, you can't do that. My company's got a vested interest in that skin.''

"Take it up in small-claims court,'' Higham said. He turned to Traven. "Did you shake him down?''

"Hadn't had a chance.''

"I got him. Give you time to catch your breath."

Traven nodded and stood up, then tucked his 10mm back in the duster pocket. The whole business made him feel dirty. Busting people in vice meant putting down people while the deals were being made, not chasing after them while they ran for their lives. And not fighting with organ jackals over them. Prevention beat the hell out of retribution.

Higham patted Meishu down. "He's clean," he said, reaching for a pair of handcuffs at his waist. "You got any cuffs?"

Traven said yes.

The uniformed officers accompanied the jackals out of the immediate vicinity.

Meishu made his move as Traven tried to hook the first cuff over a bony wrist. An explosion of action, then he was looking at the big bore of a large-caliber revolver Meishu had taken from under his shirt.

Everything happened in slow motion after the gunshot. Traven felt the powder flash singe his cheek, felt the breath of the bullet travel past his ear, then watched Meishu stagger away, the man's chest becoming an eruption of blood and torn flesh. The body bounced when it hit the sand and the gun slid from nerveless fingers.

Glancing over his shoulder, Traven saw the uniformed cop still holding the riot gun at the ready. Trembling inside, keeping his anger in check, he turned back to Higham. "You said he was clean."

"I thought he was." Higham said white-faced.

Unable to hold himself back, Traven crossed the distance separating him from Higham. His hand knotted into a fist. He still trembled and he didn't trust himself to speak again. He breathed with difficulty as he registered the burn along his cheek. The alcoholic smell of the homicide man's breath seared his lungs. Abruptly, he turned away and walked back down the drainage ditch, away from the cooling corpse. Confused thoughts pummeled his mind.

"Hey," one of the jackals said, "are you guys still gonna need that body?"

14

Jacked into the Tendrai deck in his work office, Brandstetter slid through cyberspace, clicked through public channels at DataMain, rerouted, and approached the Nagamuchi module riding a gridline hardwired into the United States Immigration and Naturalization Service.

As chief security officer, he had the ID numbers of the immigration officials who could dip into company files at will. As an ex-member of American bureaucracy, he knew those ID numbers were abused within immigration offices, handed out to junior execs as whatever imaginary need arose.

Within the Japanese hierarchy, all perks of the position were jealously guarded, but even some of those secrets were privy to the prying eyes of the immigration watchdogs. At least until Nagamuchi and other corporations like it were able to put blinders on that department through continued economic pressures.

Camouflaged as a loose inquiry concerning citizenship from immigration, Brandstetter blurred through data, seeking the face and information he wanted. His mind tried to wander, worn from the hard hours of assembling the program the night before. Only the triumph he'd achieved kept him moving. Yorimasa had made him feel like a rat with its tail caught in a trap. If not for last night, if not for the power and pleasure his personal construct brought to him, as well as the peace of mind, he would have abandoned hope. But for the first time in his life he felt he truly had something to fight for. And no one, not even someone as powerful as Yorimasa, was going to take that away from him without paying the price.

It had been his mother's plan, but it was his skill and his courage on which everything hinged.

Geishas were listed under the public relations department personnel. A few of them were trained in different aspects of public relations. Most of them were trained as Yorimasa's geisha was, in the art of pleasing the men they were supposed to please. There was never a shortage of them. Trapped between two opposing cultures that had suddenly found themselves needing and hating each other at the same time, the mixed Oriental races of the United States and Japan had nowhere to go. The foundation of their world became abuse of one form or another, but the Japanese paid higher and provided insurance, an investment package, and a better life-style than could be found on the street.

Maintaining the calm that had guided him through dozens of deadly traps in cyberspace, Brandstetter reviewed the file quickly. He found a discrepancy in one of the files that would have, he discovered on quick inspection, led to one of the more energetic members of the Nagamuchi board of directors being brought up on murder charges. Someone had filed the report of the woman's death with cross-referencing to the coroner's report listing the cause as an overdose of drugs rather than the usual heart failure. He stepped out of his camouflaged programming for one brief instant to make the change, destroy the original file, and erase the cross-referencing number.

Geishas died in service. It was a known fact that being a mediator between two opposing cultures was a high-stress job.

Only Brandstetter didn't plan on Nami Chikara's death being something easily explained away or covered up.

The woman's picture and personal data blazed up before him, chugged into his cyber-consciousness like data drawn to a magnetic field. There was an impression of the dark-haired beauty he had seen the day before, presented front, profile, and full-shot, then followed by her address, employee number, current assignment, etc., etc.

Snaring what he wanted, Brandstetter retreated back along the gridline, twisted free of the immigration channel at DataMain, and flowed back through cyberspace toward the Nagamuchi module.

He lifted the trodes off his forehead, slid them free of his personal office deck, and pocketed them. He vibrated inside as the adrenaline surplus rocketed through his system. His hands shook and he stared at them in bright fascination, smiled briefly to himself. In cyberspace, there was nothing but control. The weaknesses of the flesh never touched him.

Conscious of the other people in the room, he slid his chair back, chipped into DataMain for a time reference, then entered a break time on his deck. Once his fingers left the keys, he felt the adrenaline hitting him again. His knees wobbled uncertainly as he got to his feet. He smoothed the lab smock and walked out of the room, remembering her breath in his ear. *Do you want to lose me again?*

There was no way with his size to escape notice in the hallway, and gaijin were a novelty anywhere above the thirtieth floor, impossible to find in the top seven floors. He jiggled the stack of hardcopy under his arm as he walked to the elevator. He was still jiggling it and wearing an expression of a man who'd rather be somewhere else when he got off on Yorimasa's floor under the watchful gaze of the security guard.

Checking on the man's routines had been one of the first things Brandstetter had done when he accepted his position at Nagamuchi. Yorimasa was an inflexible man and given to routine except when it came to spying on the various departments under his supervision.

"He's not in," the Queen Dragon Mother said when he entered the outer office.

Brandstetter held up the hardcopy. "Just need to drop a few reports off," he said with an easy smile.

Adrenaline hammered at his temples. *Do you want to lose me again?*

She reached for them. "You can leave them with me. As soon as Yorimasa-san returns from his lunch, I will make sure he gets them."

"Sorry." He folded his arms across the material over his chest, wondering if the pounding of his heart was visible. His hands trembled against the pages. "These are reports for his eyes only. Policy, you know."

She bowed her head, buzzed him into the office.

Walking on unsteady legs, he entered, sipped his breath instead of giving in to the impulse to gulp it. He laid the hardcopy on Yorimasa's desk with a note. It actually was material Yorimasa wanted to see but wasn't expected for another two days. Still, tomorrow was Sunday, and Yorimasa was used to the way he delivered projects ahead of time. As Brandstetter had said in the note, Yorimasa could look over the paperwork at home. He had also wished the man a good day, but knew that would be doomed.

Dipping a hand into his lab smock, he pulled out a Kleenex and wrapped it around the ornamental letter opener in Yorimasa's desk drawer, then dropped Kleenex and letter opener into his pocket. He turned, knowing there would be eyes staring at him, not believing it could have been this easy.

No one was there.

He exited, walking faster than he thought was prudent, but apparently it didn't seem out of character to the secretary.

"Brandstetter-san."

He turned at the sound of her voice, heart hammering in his chest, full of the knowledge that his subterfuge hadn't gone unnoticed after all.

She smiled at him and inclined her head. "Have a pleasant day off tomorrow."

He forced a smile, made his eyes meet hers. "Thank you. You do the same." Then he left, perspiration dappling his brow. He waited till he was inside the elevator, away from the scrutiny of the guard, before wiping his arm across his forehead.

Dressed in a long black coat, dark blue woolen cap, dark clothing, and boots, Brandstetter moved through the late-afternoon pedestrian traffic cruising the Cockrell Hill District in southeast Dallas. The last vestiges of a rosy-tipped sunset had faded from the black sky almost an hour ago.

Street people jostled to life around him, like an organic mosaic, the day shift pulling their handmade wares from Jefferson Boulevard as the night shift came on promising more erotic treasures for sale.

Brandstetter ignored the leather-and-lace girls and their pimps. His size and demeanor were enough to keep most of them away, and his carriage spoke of years learning to exist on the same streets. He kept the old memories and the past pain at bay, kept his attention focused on his present goal.

Cars swished by through the damp streets, their yellow lights splaying over windows of small businesses, some open and some closed. Smells of a Vietnamese restaurant made his stomach rumble, but he ignored that as well. The letter opener was a small hardness inside his coat pocket. He pricked his finger on the point of the sharp blade, then touched it to his lips. The salty taste of blood was curiously more erotic than the wares the leather-and-lace girls openly displayed.

He turned south on Gilpin Street, looked up now, and blinked away the light snow swirling through the streets. Sandalwood Terrace was a new high-rise built by Japanese investors as a place to house semi-important gaijin guests as well as the geishas. It rose like a stone-and-mortar finger thrusting at the starlit black ocean above. Lights scattered sporadically across the bulletproof windows.

His heartbeat accelerated as he turned toward the building.

A blond prostitute in a full-length neon-pink duster stepped in front of him wearing a nasty smile, then opened the duster as she licked her lips to show him she wore nothing else.

Brandstetter shook his head and she moved away, mouthed ''Bastard'' with her painted lips, and flipped the duster back over her body in a practiced maneuver.

He crossed Gilpin, skip-dodged through the heavy traffic punctuated by hoarse, entreating cries of the night's merchandise people and angry shouts of cut-off drivers.

Sandalwood Terrace depended on the building's security AI rather than more expensive flesh-and-blood defenses. Brandstetter's prelim security tap after lunch had netted the information necessary to get him inside. Using Nami Chikara's code after she'd already checked in would have set off the alarms, so he'd settled for another Nagamuchi geisha who wouldn't be checking in till much later. After the geisha's body was discovered, the dual check-in should escape notice.

He stopped in front of the bulletproof glass double doors long enough to code the borrowed security ID, then walked through the subdued lighting of the narrow hallway till he reached the first AI jack for messages and services. He looked at the dormant video cameras above machined pieces of ceramic Japanese art and prints, their online lights dimmed. If the security ID hadn't worked, they would have been his first indication. He felt the letter opener through his pocket as he slipped his trode down his sleeve and jacked into the port. Most apartment dwellers would have used the visual display, but he wanted more intimate knowledge.

The building threatened to swarm over him with the sudden burst of knowledge. He hadn't buffered himself the way a matrix tech would have, hadn't covered his cyberself with programming to delete everything but the problem he was concerned with. He shoved it aside, clung to the main gridline surging through the heart of the building, then slipped the trode out once he had the knowledge he sought.

He touched DataMain as he slid the trode back up

his sleeve, compared it to the information he'd received.

Nami Chikara had entered her home twenty-two minutes ago. It was now 7:43 P.M.

His pulses pounded as he headed for the elevator, surprising him when he discovered it was more from excitement now than fear. The elevator doors closed and he rode the compressed-air cylinder to the twelfth floor.

The hallway he found himself in was a clone of the main one, a little narrower and with fewer hangings on the walls. A large theater of bonsai trees and cherry blossoms was inset and preserved in the wall at either end. Moisture glistened on the leaves.

A woman walked out of her room to his right and locked the door behind her. Her features were an attractive mix between Oriental and black, explaining her almost six feet of height. The green satin dress clung to her generous curves, ended well above midthigh. The hair had to be a wig, filled with ebony curls dangling to her rounded shoulders. She smiled, exposed white teeth. "Hi," she said as they passed in the hallway.

Brandstetter felt the immediate charge of sexual electricity, and for a moment he considered abandoning his mission in an attempt to possibly meet the woman. Then he remembered someone was paying her bills for her to stay here. She was off-limits. Someone, or some corporation, had already bought and paid for her smiles and favors.

His throat was dry when the elevator doors closed and swept her away.

The anticipation remained, spurred on by the sight of Nami Chikara's door. It throbbed in a half-beat behind the pressure in his temples, almost swelled to bursting when he troded the auxiliary maintenance jack to program the apartment AI to respond to the biochip operating inside his head. As cyberspace swam around him and he tumbled halfway through, it felt warm and inviting, like the tall woman's smile, and he thought he was on the edge of orgasm. Meshed perfectly between cyberspace and the fleshly world through the tech of the programming, sensing his mother's presence but unable to speak with her, he stepped for the door as it slid open and let the apartment AI's senses become his own.

He fumbled for the letter opener and found it, hard and biting against his hand. His heart slammed against his chest. The feeling of impending orgasm stretched as he entered the home, hurt so sweetly.

15

Dancing with wild abandon to the new MTV hit blaring from the bedroom wallscreen, Nami Chikara shed her day's frustration along with her clothes. The video was violent, a sweeping panorama of color and sound and gyrating bodies spread across a background that was computer-enhanced, generated, and had never been. She sang with it, the words coming to her lips easily, letting the freedom of the moment fill and thrill her.

The bedroom was furnished in woods, dark and heavy and luxurious, Yorimasa's selections and not hers. Tonight she ignored them, ignored the mirrored walls and the mirrored ceiling over the round bed decked out in frilly sheets and coverings. The wallscreen reflected in the mirrors, sandwiched her in a world of light and sound.

Clad only in lavender bikini panties, she exulted in her nakedness, moved her body to the throbbing backbeat of the base guitar. A fine sheen of perspiration gleamed over her body. She paused during the intermission to let down her long hair. It felt stiff and bristly across the tops of her buttocks. The hair was another thing Yorimasa had paid for.

She pushed the thoughts out of her mind. Tonight was hers, and hers alone. Yorimasa was busy with his projects at Nagamuchi. Or perhaps he was busy with another corporate concubine. She was surprised when the thought didn't fill her with as much fear and uncertainty as it had before, when she had just been chosen by him.

She danced, giving herself over to the motion. If things could have been different, she would have been a professional dancer, not the kind who danced in the flesh bars, though she had done that for a while as well, but the true professional who saw dance as an art.

A slow ballad came on.

She grinned at her reflection, made a moue at herself with the lips Yorimasa had paid to have surgically enhanced, then bit them to bring them to the color of blood in the way that excited Yorimasa. Her breasts were taut and firm, perhaps too large for a real dancer now, but Yorimasa had preferred them that way. His wife, after having their three children, had breasts that were little more than hills. She had met the woman, of course, at corporate functions, and thought the woman knew her for what she was, but there seemed to be relief in her eyes rather than jealousy.

She chided herself for the dark thoughts on an unexpectedly free night. She cupped her breasts, letting depression touch her briefly when she considered the large swell of them and the oversized nipples. Yorimasa had not told her everything that was going to be done to her when she went in for her cosmetic surgery. The breasts were too big, and sex still hurt because the doctor had tightened her vagina so much.

Still, she told herself, what surgery giveth, surgery can take away. And that was exactly what would happen once she had enough money saved to get out of the whole business. It did happen occasionally, if a girl played her options and kept a clear head, despite the rumors that once an exec was tired of them they were auctioned off to the organ-recovery agencies.

She slid her hands across her sweat-slick arms and walked to the chest beside the bed. She ignored the drawer that held Yorimasa's collection of sex toys, reached for the small, private drawer she kept. She took out a lighter and lit the two scented lanterns on the walls to either side of the wallscreen, singing the song MTV was broadcasting.

Satisfied with the illumination, she said, "Lights out," and the apartment AI switched them off. She loved the darkness because it seemed like something she could have all to herself.

Lying nearly nude on the satin sheets, enjoying herself because it was one of the few times Yorimasa's eyes weren't following every move she made and making her feel more naked than even the flesh bars, she lifted the telephone and keyed in the number. A feminine voice answered and made her feel even better about the night because she hadn't reached a recording.

"Karla, it's Nami. Look, I have the night off and I thought maybe if you weren't doing anything, we could go out and get something to eat." She stared at the ruby depths of the oil reservoir in the lantern before her, watched the lights shift and turn in them. She didn't boast about not having to spend the time with Yorimasa because it was a proven fact that the corporate security teams bugged the geisha rooms and furnished chips to the execs.

"Sounds great. You buying?"

"Yes." She was the one with the expense account, and they both knew it.

"You talked me into it. Give me about an hour to call in sick and get dressed in something that looks to die for."

"Eddie'll be pissed."

"Eddie can blow it out his ass. Since you left, I'm the only girl at the bar who dances without the puppet matrix jacked in. Believe me, pussy-hungry those slabs of meat may be, but they can tell when a real woman is up there following her heart. Eddie wouldn't dare do anything to lose me."

Chikara laughed. For a moment she missed the good times they'd shared. Then she remembered how much older Karla looked these days. Cosmetic surgery didn't come cheap in the streets, and there were no guarantees at all. "Where do you want to eat?"

"How about Chinese?"

"Yuck."

"Sorry. I forgot you get all the Oriental cooking you can stand now."

Chikara knew the woman hadn't, and knew to ignore the little bits of jealousy that crept into their conversations, because the friendship was the important thing.

"Mexican then?"

"Yes. Definitely."

"Where do you want to meet?"

"I'll cab over. I've been a good little girl with the credit card this month, and it is almost Christmas. We both deserve a piece of paradise tonight." Chikara rang off, hung up the phone, rolled over, and looked at her reflection in the mirrored ceiling. She grimaced and stuck her tongue out at herself.

Then the wallscreen went dark and the music died, leaving only the wavering light of the oil lanterns.

Startled, she sat up on the bed, clutching a sheet across her nudity. She looked at the wallscreen and felt disoriented. Instead of showing anything put out by one of the media channels, the wallscreen had evidently linked with the apartment AI. The scene she stared at was the living room as seen from her front door. But there was something disturbing about the view, something not quite right. Then she realized that to have the same view, she would have to stand on a stepladder.

The perspective changed suddenly, coming closer.

Her breath caught in her throat.

The perspective spun, as if trying to orient itself, sweeping across the living-room furniture, across the parakeet cage where Lefty sat sleeping with his head folded under his wing, across the wet bar that Yorimasa had insisted be installed, across the dozen paintings that Yorimasa had chosen for the room.

Her heart thundered till she thought it would explode in her chest. She tried to move and couldn't.

The wallscreen wavered again, came forward,

moved through the hallway leading to her bedroom now. The dim wash of the lanterns hazed the walls.

She stood with effort, clinging to the sheet in defense, hypnotized by the events unfolding on the wallscreen. Her knees quivered. The room seemed much too cold. A scream locked inside her lungs.

The view changed again, till she was looking at herself on the screen, larger than life, white terror painted across her face. One breast was exposed and looked terribly vulnerable. She turned to face the open doorway, feeling the other presence now.

A hundred different shades of black ran up and down the big man's frame. She watched his head turn toward the wallscreen and realized he was looking at himself. Unable to do anything else, she looked at the wallscreen as well, tried to scream.

The wallscreen was a true representation of the bedroom from the man's eyes, not a reversed image, captured a thousandfold in the endless reflections of the mirrored walls and ceiling. The image was even less human, less discernible on the wallscreen. The only point of reference was the sharp, silver gleam of a short blade trapped in one misshapen hand. Then the perspective changed again, focused on her.

She finally made the scream come out.

16

Sensations, perceptions, agreeing and at odds with each other, threatened to swarm over Earl Brandstetter and erode his conscious mind. He held on grimly. Images overlaid images. The woman was there somewhere. He reached for her. The confusion was worse than losing gridlock without backup programming, or coming up off a flaming deck.

His mother's presence hovered over him, never quite touching but always there.

The letter opener felt blunt in his hand. He reached for the woman again when he realized she'd moved. Her scream tore at his ears, exciting him beyond his wildest imaginings, beyond anything that had ever happened to him in the construct. Here he wasn't a prisoner of a thirteen-year-old's body, trapped by passions that always seemed just out of his reach. Here he was a man, full-grown and powerful, and able to take what he wanted.

His senses cleared when he closed a fist around Chikara's ankle as she attempted to crawl across the round bed away from him. He held her with bruising force, conscious of the hunger that had never left him since he made the apartment AI open the front door. She felt so soft, so warm, so small and helpless before him.

He threw himself on top of her, pinned her with his body weight, not wanting to use the blade yet. In her continued struggle to get away, she ground her pelvis against his, and he was suddenly aware how naked she really was. A groan of pleasure escaped his tight lips.

Her eyes, wild and white, stared at him as her head whipped from side to side and the screams continued to pour out of her.

He flailed a big hand, missed twice before clapping it over her lips. Teeth bit into his hand and pierced the glove. The screams died. He batted her head. She bucked beneath him, and the pleasure became almost unbearable. He strained against her, the scent of an exotic perfume filled him, and he arched his back to increase the sensation flooding his groin.

She sucked in air noisily. Bright crimson stained the corner of her mouth, left scarlet threads across perfect teeth.

Take her. The ghost of his mother's voice echoed in his mind. *She's yours. Take her! Take her now!*

Brandstetter showed her the letter opener, held it in front of her eyes, caught the wavering gleam of the lanterns. He ran his thumb along the blade's spine. Reflections caught fire in the mirrors. In the wallscreen, his body was a twisted and misshapen shadow covering hers. An orange light in the corner of the wallscreen indicated the recording equipment was operational. He didn't care. The cameras only recorded what the wallscreen displayed.

"Okay," the woman whispered in a voice filled with fear. She stopped fighting him. She still trembled. "I won't fight you." The tension didn't leave her body, still pressed insistently against his.

The heat of her fired his loins.

Keeping the letter opener in his hand, Brandstetter leveraged some of his weight off the woman. She remained where she was. Watching her for any indications of tricks, he let his free hand trail down the length of her body. The glove made him insensitive, so he pulled it off and shoved it in a pocket. Both of them panted from fear and passion and exertion. He traced her body with his hand again, let the backs of his fingers caress her jawline, spill down the slender neck, stayed only long enough to feel her pulse beating frantically, then drifted down to her right breast. He stared at his reflection in the dark eyes that never left the letter opener. A mustiness clung to her, even more exciting than the intoxicating aroma of her perfume.

Hesitantly, visibly aware of the sharp blade so close to her face, she reached for him, slid her hand between them. "Please," she whispered. "Let me make it good for you. You don't have to hurt me."

He let her continue to stroke him, lost the reality of the situation as synaptic lava rolled over the hazy mixture of connections between his physical and cyber selves.

She opened his pants. Her eyes were on his face now even though he knew she couldn't see his features through the electromagnetic field he'd programmed across the wafer-thin mask.

He let his hand wander farther down. The thin material of the panties ripped with one tug.

"Here," she whispered. She pushed against him, moved him to one side as she reached into the top drawer of the nightstand beside the bed.

He touched the letter opener to her throat.

She swallowed hard. "No," she soothed, "it's all right. Look."

Brandstetter looked. She held a rubber.

"For you," she said. "It's lubricated. It'll help. I've had special surgery. You'll hurt me if you don't wear it." She wrapped her fingers around him and pulled meaningfully. "Surely you can feel that."

He nodded, not trusting his voice.

She's yours, Earl. Take her. Show her what a man you can be. Show them all.

The backfeed of the apartment AI kept blasting him, tugged him toward the depths of cyberspace. He forced himself to hold on to the physical world while maintaining control over the deck one.

"I won't fight you," she said. "You can have me, but let's make it good for both of us."

He knew she was lying, knew she was still afraid, but he was hypnotized by her submissiveness. He was so much in control. He nodded.

She put the rubber on with practiced ease, then dug her heels into the bed, slithered more toward the center, and pulled him with her.

He slid between her legs, slipped a broad hand under her buttocks. She joined them, groaned in pain as he surged forward. For a moment orgasm clamored at him, jangled his nerves, but he held himself back. The condom helped, helped take away the overpowering sensation. He'd never before achieved penetration with another woman.

Controlling the sexual urge that threatened to consume him, he eased in and out of her, listening to the muffled chuffing of her breath in his ear. He blinked, the orgasm on edge again. He stopped moving. She didn't, heaving her hips up at him. He floundered for control. "No!" he cried hoarsely. "Stop!"

"It's what you want," she cooed in his ear. "It's what you came here for. Take me. It's so good." She kept slamming up against him.

Hurting from holding back, he pushed up to look at her, her legs wrapped around his hips. Poised on the brink of giving himself over to the impending climax, he looked into her dark eyes.

She's lying! The bitch isn't enjoying you! She's faking, Earl! Look at her!

He did, and he saw the lies now, felt the heat of shame and anger cool the lust in him. He withered instantly, leaving the pain of unfulfillment. The condom slid off somewhere and was lost in the darkness.

"What's wrong?" Her face reflected the worry in her voice. She wrapped her arms around him.

He pushed out of her embrace roughly, snapped her head back with a forearm blow. Teeth broke with the sound of rotten twigs cracking. Her cry of pain was muffled by the blood. She tried to cover her face as he swept the letter opener toward her eyes.

The blade cut across the backs of her hands, angled across her fingers, and severed the tip of her left little finger. Scarlet ribbons ran down her arms. She struggled to escape, screamed and screamed. He slashed across her mouth next, sliced those perfect lips, masking the face in still more blood.

Brandstetter gave himself over to the frenzy that gripped him. His right arm became a machine that rose and fell of its own volition. Cyberspace swarmed dizzyingly around him, sucked at his senses, then for brief periods he was on the other side of the wallscreen, watching the elongated shadow perched like a ravening crow above the woman's body, digging a single sharp talon deep into the quivering flesh. He could almost hear his mother's urgings. His arm rose and fell, blood covering it nearly up to the shoulder. The coppery smell drowned out the perfume. He tasted it on his lips. He raked the blade viciously.

Then, unable to continue, he fell back from the disfigured body and drank in great drafts of air. He forced himself to keep moving. Bloody footprints followed him to the door. He paused, leaned against the wall, breath rasping harsh and deep in his ears as he remembered the letter opener clenched in his gloved hand.

He returned to the bedroom, gazed at the ripped and torn corpse draped across the bloodstained sheets, and flung the letter opener to the floor.

Once again at the door, he triggered the display through the apartment AI, saw no one in the hallway, and passed through. He used the fire escape, dark garnet footsteps following him. He reversed the long coat, took time to wipe his face, his shoes, his hands with a chemwipe that took away the blood. He faded into the shadows of the street as he dropped out of cyberlink with the apartment AI.

His breathing was regular by the time he hit the ground floor. No one seemed interested in him. He thrust his hands into the coat and aimed himself at his apartment.

17

A crowd of noisy people in street clothes and robes had gathered in front of the apartment, set apart from the media people by the mikes and minicams in the reporters' hands. Traven gave his new homicide ID a workout as he made his way through them and ignored the questions that trailed in his wake. He pocketed the ID after the uniform in charge of the door detail tagged him with breast-pocket identification that allowed him on the crime scene. He ducked under the yellow tape as the hostile questions from the media and occupants came with renewed fury.

The unmistakable coppery smell of blood flooded his nostrils.

Traven shoved his hands in the pockets of his duster and followed the activity back to the bedroom, noting the large bloody footprints leading out into the hallway.

Higham stood to one side watching the crime lab techs gather evidence. There were three techs circling the bed, all dressed in white smocks and wearing disposable rubber gloves. Two more worked on the AI's wallscreen security circuits.

One of the techs paused as she moved around the bed with a minicam, her face framed by blond curls and colored by the blue light jetting from the shoulder rig. She blew a bubble and popped it, displaying a wicked smile. "Hey, Mick, long time no see."

"I could have thought of better places to get reacquainted, Sheila." Traven stepped in beside her and surveyed the mutilated corpse. It was hard to tell, but he guessed from the smooth flesh that hadn't been ripped by the blade that the woman had been pretty. A collection of small tri-dee portraits stood on the vanity against the wall. With the shape her face was in, he hesitated to even guess which one might be her.

"Bastard made a thorough job of it, didn't he?" Sheila asked as the minicam whirred.

"Yeah." Traven was surprised how dry his throat was. It seemed like forever since he'd seen a body in the shape this one was in. Overdoses, gunshot victims, even decapitation victims like the bagman two nights ago in the alley weren't as bad as what lay before him. This was personal. He turned away as another of the techs started scraping under the dead woman's fingernails. More bloody footprints were by the bed, marred by a patch. He knelt to inspect it closer. "What's this?"

The tech doing the fingernail scraping had an ID tag on that read Burton. He stopped what he was doing, glanced down, and said, "That's where the guy came back into the room. He'd worn the blood off during the trip through the living room, then stepped in it again. By that time most of it'd had a chance to drain into the carpet so it didn't leave as good an imprint."

"He?"

"Yeah." The tech capped off vials containing the scrapings. "We got maybe what started out as a rape, then turned into murder. The vagina's pretty torn up. But that isn't surprising, because she'd had cosmetic surgery to tighten it up. Way too tight in my opinion, but hey, I wasn't the guy she was bedding down."

"What do you mean about starting out as a rape?"

"No ejaculation, not even preseminal fluid. Found a condom on her that had been torn up too, but it was dry. Of course, that's not unusual in rape cases. Lot of guys don't get off. They're usually in it for the power play."

Traven stood up. "Any idea why he came back into the room?"

The tech shrugged. "Maybe he just wanted one last

look. I don't know. From what I've seen, I'd say you're dealing with one sick son of a bitch here. Maybe he came back to take something personal from the body. An earring, a bracelet, anything that would be some kind of trophy.''

"What killed her?''

"This.'' The tech held up a plastic bag containing a blood-smeared letter opener. "Not neat, but enough to do the job if you applied yourself. This guy did.''

"Okay, thanks.'' Traven crossed the room to Higham as Sheila continued with the minicam and the tech turned back to his subject. The mirrored walls and mirrored ceiling made for a dizzying view, throwing the images of the techs, the body, and the blood-stained sheets into an eye-straining collage. The smell of lantern oil was thick and heavy, overlain by the blood scent.

"Did I wake you?'' Higham asked in a sour voice. Gray stubble covered his jowls and chin, and his breath stank of whiskey.

"No,'' Traven said defensively, watching as another crime lab tech wheeled a white-decked gurney into the room. "You got any breath mints?''

Higham reached into a pocket and produced a roll. "Not me. You.''

Higham looked away quickly, popped two into his mouth, and crunched hard. "Didn't expect to get called back in tonight. We were supposed to be off tomorrow. Don't guess we can count on it now.''

"Who was the girl?''

Higham flipped open a notebook. "Name's Nami Chikara. She's resided here for seven months. Rent's always been paid on time, never been a problem, never had many visitors. That was all the apartment manager could remember about her. That and she used to be a looker.''

The techs worked together and lifted the corpse from the bed onto the gurney. They had to go back twice to get it all.

Traven tried to keep his mind in an objective mode,

refused to give in to the subjective feelings that pressed in at him. "What do we have on her?"

"Clean record, but you can tell it's been wiped."

"When?"

"Seven months ago."

"Same time she got the apartment."

"Yeah. It was also the same time she started working for Nagamuchi Towers."

The gurney squeaked on the way back through the hallway.

"Geisha?" Traven asked.

"They call it public relations. The companies are kind of sensitive about that. Make sure in whatever reports you process that you refer to her as that. Kaneoki'll have a shit fit if you don't get it right."

"Is that a personal prejudice on his part?"

"Look, I don't know what you heard about Kaneoki before you got here, but the guy's a square-shooter. It's just that the corporate review board controlling funding for the department pays particular attention to any deaths concerning their public relations people. I've covered a handful of cases where an exec went nuts from pressure and the job, and took it out on his geisha. The corporations nose into it, just like they'll nose into this one, and everything will get cleared up. Case closed. Twice, the execs got closed out with it. Heart attacks, you know. Better for the immediate family. The geishas are a good indication of how well the execs are holding up."

"And they're half-breeds anyway, right?" Traven couldn't keep the sarcasm under lock.

"To them," Higham said softly. "Doesn't have to be that way for us."

Traven forced himself to breathe out the anger. "How did the perp get into the apartment?"

"No idea yet. The AI wasn't spoofed that the techs can tell, and the door wasn't forced."

"Meaning she let him in?"

"Maybe."

Traven reviewed the information he knew about the geishas. "That possibility narrows the field down, doesn't it? With the corporation footing her bills, who else is she going to let into her apartment with the type of security they have to live under? Who was she assigned to?''

Higham consulted his notes again. ''Guy named Yorimasa, head of the security at Nagamuchi.''

''Where's he now?''

''He's not at home. His wife told a uniform she thought he was at the office, but we turned up zero on that too.''

''So nobody knows where he is?''

''No. After the media hit the wallscreens with this, I expect he'll turn up quick enough.''

''Carrying an alibi in each hand.''

''Probably.''

Traven stared at the rumpled and bloody bed. ''How old was she?''

''Twenty.'' Higham's voice was soft. ''That's one thing you learn quick working this end of the system—you never get used to seeing the young ones die, especially like this.''

''Did she have family?''

''In Ohio. The state police are taking care of notifying them.''

Traven was glad, because he didn't feel up to calling anyone with news like this. He'd done it before, families of traffic fatalities, mostly, back when he'd been in uniform, but that was something he had never gotten used to either.

''A girlfriend of hers found the body,'' Higham said. ''The techs had to sedate her to get her to calm down. She's the one who called nine-one-one.''

''The AI didn't alert the PD?''

''No.''

''She could have yelled for a vocal emergency at any time. Why didn't she?''

''She may have been dead before she had the chance. You saw the way her face was slashed up.''

''But she was raped.''

''Doesn't mean she was raped while she was still alive.''

Traven swallowed hard, forced away the dark images that flooded his mind. He turned away from the bed.

"This isn't the first time something like this has happened," Higham said. "I wouldn't say you see it all the time, but it's common enough in a lot of cases. Homicide isn't pretty. It spins around the vilest and bloodiest things individuals can do to each other, and the world's full of cold, cruel bastards. You haven't really got your feet in Homicide wet until you've worked an occult case involving a bunch of dead kids, or a cannibalistic murder."

Silently, Traven figured he'd rather pass.

Higham crunched more breath mints. Voice pitched low so no one else could hear him, he said, "About this morning . . ."

Traven looked at the man's eyes and saw the fear hiding in them, aging Higham beyond his years. "Forget it. The reports will read right. I've already cleared everything with the uniforms involved. After all, we're partners, aren't we?"

Higham nodded. "Yeah. Just wanted to make sure. It won't happen again."

"I know." Traven wished he believed one of them.

"Higham." It was one of the techs working on the apartment AI.

Higham turned to the man. "What have you got?"

The man wiped his hands on a soiled red rag. "Nothing. The unit checks out perfectly. It wasn't jammed, spoofed, or dormant during the time the woman was killed. Got something recorded on it."

"Play it back."

Traven stood in front of the wallscreen with Higham. The tech vocally ordered the lights out and the screen on. Nami Chikara had been beautiful, dark hair contrasting with her white, sculpted body. The rest of it was out of a nightmare. There was an impression of someone lying on top of her, the disjointed hips moving in frantic rhythm, but it couldn't have been anything human. It was too thin to have lungs, the face an impossibly craggy profile, the voice something from a marriage between the sound of breaking glass and fingernails on a chalkboard. Then there was the letter opener in what had to be a fist, slashing, slashing. A gurgling scream ended Nami Chikara's fighting, but the arm kept rising and falling, shredding flesh. Traven watched through till the end, till the thing crawled up from the corpse and padded away. The picture ended abruptly, leaving only dead air.

"Son of a bitch," one of the crime lab techs said.

Traven wasn't sure which one. He felt suddenly cold inside the duster.

18

"Girl knew her stuff," Higham stated. "Went through all the right moves, lay back and tried to take it, should have saved her life."

Traven quelled the irritation he felt at the man's obvious callousness. The bit of tape involving the actual murder was being displayed again on the wallscreen of the police visual tech lab. The shadow man remained unresolved, a shapeless blob with spidery arms and legs.

The two people were larger this time because the outer edges of the film had been cropped, leaving only the struggle for life. Traven had seen it five times in succession, run at different speeds and with different lighting. The only things that remained constant were the unknown identity of the killer, the brutality of the actual murder, and the cold chill that chased itself up his spine. He lounged against a wall and wore his duster despite the room's warmth.

"Want to see it again?" Rusty Stipak asked from the desktop where he sat. He was young and long and lean, wore a white smock loosely draped over street clothes. He'd been at a rock concert when the emergency summons pulled him back to the precinct.

Traven had made the call himself, because Stipak's work was the best he knew he could get without going outside the department.

"Anything you want to see again, Mick?" Higham asked.

"No." He knew the chill wouldn't go away tonight.

Stipak turned his palms up. "Sorry, guys, but that's as good as it gets till we figure out how the AI video was jammed."

"Do you have any ideas?" Traven asked as the wallscreen blanked at Stipak's command.

Stipak turned to face him. The look on the tech's face was honest. "At this point, no. Whoever jammed this thing is a pro. Maybe in a lot of fields. My specialty is visual enhancements. I'd played my cards a little differently, maybe I'd be up in Vancouver now helping with the newest Amblin' Entertainment film. But this . . ." He waved a hand. "Still, I'm not going to turn loose of it. I'll brief my department first thing in the morning and we'll move it up on the priority list. I get something, I'll call you."

Traven nodded and said thanks.

Stipak shrugged and walked out of the room, the door rushing to cover the entrance behind him.

Getting up from his chair, Higham walked to the Mr. Coffee on the stand built into the wall and poured himself a cup. He held up the pot.

Traven shook his head.

Taking a roll of breath mints from his pocket, Higham shook three tablets into his hand, then threw the empty paper into the trash container near his foot as he chewed them noisily. "What are you thinking about?"

"The girl."

Higham was silent for a moment, then, "You can't let it get you down, guy. People kill themselves and each other every day."

"Not like that." Traven didn't want to talk to the man, not after seeing the blank way Higham had stared at the on-screen violence and appeared unaffected, but he couldn't hold himself back.

"You've seen things worse than this," Higham argued.

"Wrong. I've walked into things where the end results might be considered worse, but I've never been witness to something like this."

"Better get used to it if you're planning on working homicide long."

"That's one thing I'm not planning on."

Higham shrugged. "Suit yourself, but we're going to see this guy again."

"What makes you think so?" A breath of cool air slithered down Traven's back. He knotted his fists in his duster pockets.

"This guy was out of control. Believe me when I say it, because I know what I'm talking about. What puzzles me is if this is the result of a kink Yorimasa has, why hasn't it shown itself before?"

"There's nothing to indicate that Yorimasa is the man who did this."

"Other than his fingerprints being all over the murder weapon?"

"There were layers of blood over those."

"True, but this guy went there for some reason other than the sex. If it had been a piece of tail he was after when the Chikara woman starting throwing it at him, he should've went on about his business, left her alive, and walked out of there. Something about the sex set him off, drove him over the edge."

Traven remembered the insane fury that had gripped the shadow and shivered. "You think this guy will try again?"

Higham nodded. "Yeah, the same way you know a junkie's about to score when you see him on the street. I've been through too many murder investigations to even try fooling myself into believing we've seen the last of this guy. He made a journey of self-discovery tonight, and he'll be back. You can bet on it."

The door slid open without warning and Captain Gene Kaneoki strode into the room, his round face set in tight lines. He wore a business suit, dark and carefully pressed, cut to cover the hardware he carried. He wore glasses even though a corneal correction could easily have made the adjustment to 20/20. He stopped in the center of the room, hands folded across his chest, as the door slid shut behind him.

Higham stood up a little straighter and unconsciously checked his tie with a quick hand.

Traven continued to lounge against the wall, eyeing the homicide captain in quiet speculation. He'd encountered Kaneoki before, in police functions and when the mayor or city elders requested extra protection during political gatherings, but had formed no real opinion of the man.

Kaneoki centered his attention on Higham. "You're working the Chikara case?"

"Yes, sir."

Traven was impressed by his partner's sudden respect for the chain of command and quashed the sour smile that wanted to stretch across his face.

"I saw the tape in my office only moments ago," Kaneoki said. "I also know the fingerprints on the murder weapon belong to Taira Yorimasa, who is employed at Nagamuchi Towers. I want to know what your next move will be."

"We're going to find Yorimasa," Higham said. "He's been missing since before the murder."

"He has since been found," Kaneoki said without inflection.

"Why weren't we told?" Traven asked as he pushed himself off the wall.

"That's one of the reasons I am here," Kaneoki said. "To impart that information."

Traven immediately wondered what the other reasons were. "Where is he?"

"At home, but you will not be going there to question him tonight."

Checking the impulse to demand an explanation, Traven looked at Higham.

"What's going on here, Cap'n?" Higham asked in a soft voice.

Kaneoki held up a hand. "Please. Mr. Yorimasa is going to comply with this department in every way he can. He has already set up a time tomorrow afternoon when you may interview him."

"Shit." Traven hadn't been able to hold himself back.

Kaneoki gave him a sharp look. "Did you say something, Sergeant Traven?"

"I said *shit*, as in *this is bullshit.*"

Kaneoki faced him. "Maybe you got away with this kind of belligerent attitude with Captain Kiley, Sergeant, but you'll end up with your ass in a sling if you try it with me. Now you can shut up and listen to what I have to say, or I'll have you up on charges as soon as I leave this room. It's your choice."

"You didn't say anything about Yorimasa having an alibi that checked out. Why isn't he cooling his heels in a holding cell right now?" Traven returned the hostile gaze full-measure.

"All you need to do is your job," Kaneoki said. "Your investigation will begin tomorrow afternoon at three when you visit Yorimasa in his office."

"I don't like the idea of operating on this guy's home turf," Higham said. "Especially since he hasn't already cleared himself."

"I didn't ask you to like it." Kaneoki turned to Higham, clasped his hands behind his back like a miniature general marshaling his troops. "I was assured by the Nagamuchi Corporation that there are extenuating circumstances, and that all will be explained tomorrow. Also, whatever information Yorimasa imparts will not be released for public consumption." He paused. "Do I make myself clear?"

"Yes, sir."

"As for you," Kaneoki said, switching his attention to Traven, "you were transferred to my department as a favor to your Captain Kiley. He assured me you would be on your best behavior. I intend to hold you to that. The arrest this afternoon was sloppy. That man wouldn't have had to be killed if you'd done your job correctly and frisked him. If you want to continue to participate in this homicide investigation, you'll start showing some discipline and respect."

Traven held his tongue with effort and curbed the anger that surged to be free. He fastened his thoughts on his impending return to vice and told himself it would be worth the bullshit facing him now. He hoped.

"Tomorrow, you will be in the offices of one of Dallas's greatest corporations. Keep in mind these people directly or indirectly employ seventeen percent of the city. I want you there taking care of business, and I want you looking sharp. Traven, you will get a haircut and you will wear a suit. If you don't, you will be assigned to the worst post I can find when you come out of the building. Higham, there'd better not be anything alcoholic in or around your body, or you'll be joining him." He paused. "I want a report on my desk no later than two hours after you finish with Yorimasa." He turned on his heel and left, sweeping through the door.

"Got yourself a real sweetheart for a boss," Traven said.

Higham nodded. "Yeah, but sometimes he can be downright nasty." He smiled.

Traven didn't.

Despite the fact that his vehicle had been inside the department's parking garage and under surveillance, Traven inspected it before climbing aboard, because some cops came with price tags. The four-year-old Jeep Cherokee was manufactured by American-based and Japanese-managed factories now.

He took his time, remembering how a member of vice had exploded along with his car a few years before Traven made vice himself. Since then, he'd learned enough about explosives and detonators to know when to stay the hell away. Everything looked clean, but fifteen minutes later when he kicked the engine over, his heart still stopped.

He put the 4×4 in gear and pulled up the ramp that let him out at street level. The anger hadn't gone away, just shared polarities between Kiley and Kaneoki. Higham's words haunted him too. The homicide man had been sure of himself when he'd said they would see the killer again. It was the first time Traven had noticed the professional gleam in the man's eyes.

As he turned right, he accessed DataMain, found the time to be 2:13 A.M. He reached for the mobile phone mounted on the console, then drew his hand back. If Danny was asleep he didn't want to wake him.

When the man jumped out in front of him half a block away from the garage entrance, Traven locked the brakes and fisted the SIG/Sauer tucked inside his waistband. He checked the rearview mirrors to make sure the guy was alone. His thumb flicked off the safety as he centered the sights over the guy's chest. The yellow light of the headbeams washed across the dark clothing and turned it gray.

The man must have seen the pistol, because he put his hands up and started yelling. "Mick! Mick, it's me! Benedict! The reporter!"

Traven put the 10mm away after snapping the safety back into place. He thumbed the power button and the driver's side window whined down. "What the hell are you doing jumping in front of me?"

Robin Benedict grinned and shuddered with the cold. His breath whipped away in little fogs. "Needed a ride. Saw you coming and figured it would be the only way to get your attention."

"Where's your car?"

"Around the block." Benedict approached and put his hands on the door.

"What's wrong with it?"

"Nothing." Benedict's smile was shy and ingratiating.

Traven had known the younger man too long to be taken in by it. He slipped the stick back into first gear. "You need a ride around the corner?"

"Yeah. Think you can help me out?"

"How long have you been out here?"

"Damn sight longer than I thought I'd have to be," Benedict admitted. "The other city guys took the pablum Kaneoki handed out in the press release and called it a night. I knew you were on the case and—"

"And figured you'd get a little more from me," Traven finished.

"Well, yeah, now that you mention it." Benedict tried the smile again, showing a lot of the white teeth that had served him so well on the TV news stories he covered.

"Not this time." Traven rolled the Cherokee forward a little.

Benedict skipped to keep up. "Ah, come on, Mick, we're friends. This girl got murdered by the invisible man, for chrissakes. I'm not going to take a no comment on this."

"Is that what Kaneoki said?"

"No. He said that all available leads were being followed and you guys would soon have a suspect in custody."

"Then that's probably the way it's going to be."

"Friends, Mick, think friends. I've been pretty good to you in my news coverage. You haven't heard one single killer-cop cry from my stories." Benedict still skipped to keep up.

"You're going to fall and break something," Traven warned.

"This is Nagamuchi Corporation," Benedict yelled as he turned his head to watch oncoming traffic. "You know how many reporters would kill to get some dirt on Nagamuchi?"

Traven stopped at the red light. "Maybe one already did."

"Does that mean you people really don't have a suspect?" Benedict asked.

Traven indicated the traffic light. "Unless you can do the speed limit, I advise you not to keep hanging on that door."

The reporter glared at the light as the opposite side turned yellow. He released the door and stood in the middle of the street. "I smell a cover-up here with Nagamuchi's name all over it."

The light turned green and Traven moved out with the traffic. "So do I," he said as he thumbed up the window.

19

Satisfied no one kept watch on his apartment, Earl Brandstetter crossed the street and entered the building. He moved immediately into the elevator and rode up to his floor. His heart beat faster as he watched the lighted buttons climb higher and higher, stopped entirely when the elevator pinged and the doors opened.

He kept one hand over the doors as he stepped out into the hallway, ready to bolt back inside if he saw someone who looked out of place. The hallway was empty. He allowed the doors to close behind him, resisted the urge to run to his apartment. He hit the printplate and moved inside once the door swished aside.

Releasing a pent-up breath as the door closed behind him, he collapsed on the floor in a sitting position, his back against the wall and his arms locked around his knees. He shook. Then he shivered. He still smelled the blood, and when he closed his eyes, he still saw it.

He hadn't thought it would be like that. The slasher films that juiced over the wallscreens couldn't expose the viewer to the warmth that had covered him after the first cut. They hadn't imparted any of the knowledge of what it felt like to hold a person in his arms and feel the strength and life leave the body.

He squeezed his arms and tightened his grip on his knees. He forced his eyes open. He sat in the dark because he hadn't called for the lights. What was even more surprising was that he had only now noticed it.

"Lights," he croaked.

He shivered again. Not with cold this time, but from the memory of the power.

The AI switched the lights on.

"Television." Brandstetter remained where he was.

The wallscreen dawned with a brilliance of prismatic colors.

"News."

Channels flickered, locked in with an abruptness that implied a sonic boom, though none was heard.

He leaned forward, hugging his legs tightly. News paraded across the screen. There had been at least two murders besides the one he'd committed. He didn't pay attention to the details.

Commercials passed through his thoughts without ever connecting except for Nagamuchi's name and the names of subsidiaries.

More news concerned recent Aryan Guard activities, traffic accidents, the climb of the economies of Russia and Germany. The newsman stationed in New Berlin praised the joint efforts of the two countries, going into superficial depth about Russia's vast resources and Germany's technology to utilize those same resources in joint ventures. The newsman went on to speculate that although the quake that had leveled Tokyo and most of Japan had led to the Japanese immigration to the United States, it was the threat of Russia and Germany united that kept Japanese business there.

The camera panned back on the anchorman.

Brandstetter closed his eyes, saw the blood covering him again, dripping down his arms, smeared across his face. He jacked into the apartment AI using the biochip, then looked back at himself without opening his eyes to see if it was still there. His coat and clothing and hands were clean. Even his bare scalp. When he'd stood under the public shower two blocks from Sandalwood Terrace, he'd almost forgot the top of his head. The mask had covered it, but he didn't want to take chances. He grimaced wryly at the thought. He'd already taken more chances this one night than he had his whole life.

He was amazed at how comfortable he felt riding piggyback on the apartment AI's programming. He blanked out of it because his conscious mind interfered with the television reception.

The news anchor returned, lips turned up in another false smile.

They knew. Police already knew who had killed Nami Chikara. That's why they weren't broadcasting anything about the murder. The news staff was waiting till the police announced they had him in their custody.

His mind ached at the loss of his mother.

He decided he would kill himself before he allowed that to happen. He forced himself to breathe. Carefully, he reached up and removed the biochip, watched it glint in his palm like a drop of Nami Chikara's blood. He closed his fingers over it, wondering if it was his imagination or if the biochip really felt like ice.

The news anchor mentioned a bizarre murder in the Cockrell Hill district. The camera panned in on the front of Sandalwood Terrace.

Brandstetter listened carefully, the blood roaring in his ears.

The story was sparse of facts and released little more than Nami Chikara's name and her employment at Nagamuchi. The reporter seemed more interested in the fact that she had been slashed to death than in who had committed the act. "There is one interesting footnote to the story, John," the reporter said to the anchor. "Sources I have in the police department tell me the security tapes which should have caught the murderer in the act were somehow short-circuited. At this moment, police officers have no idea who killed Nami Chikara. In fact, I was told by one of Chikara's neighbors that the man who killed the woman was invisible."

"Invisible?" the anchor repeated, never losing the self-assured look on his face.

The reporter nodded, holding the microphone that

was more prop than tool closer to his mouth. "Very bizarre here, John, but hopefully the police will be able to shed some light on this before long. For now, this neighborhood is fearfully drawing in every breath, wondering if the killer is one of their own."

The camera panned back to the anchor as he made a transitional bridge and went on to the next story.

Relieved, Brandstetter unclasped his knees and forced himself to stand, still holding the biochip in his fist. The smell of the blood in his clothes hit him again, followed immediately by thoughts of scanning gear that could detect it in the fabric even though he'd scrubbed it.

He shut the wallscreen off and padded into the bathroom. He stepped out of his clothing, dropped shirt, pants, coat, socks, underwear, cap, gloves, and footwear into the shower area. Opening the medicine chest, he took out a plastic bottle of isopropyl alcohol, twisted off the lid, and poured the contents over the clothing, leaving only a half-inch in the bottom. He replaced the cap and put the alcohol away.

Summoning the attention of the AI, he overrode the fire security system, then went to the kitchen for the small laser lighter he kept there for the hibachi. He stood behind the frosted glass of the shower, torched the clothing, and watched the alcohol blue of the fire spread inside the cubicle, lapping at the glass and ceramic walls.

The fire burned for a long time. The black smoke was sucked away by the room's exhaust. The whirring of the fan motor was the only sound except for the quiet crackle of the flames. When it was finished, there was only a pile of ashes and a few lumps of scarred rubber or plastic.

He gathered the lumps and flushed them down the toilet, then turned on the water and fed the ashes through the shower drain. Once all the evidence had been disposed of, he sighed and sat down on the cold floor.

The biochip was still in his fist.

He uncurled cramped fingers and stared at it, lost

in the power it represented. Without standing, he reached up to a cabinet, brushed by the alcohol bottle, and brought a package of Band-Aids down. He shook one of them out, slit the wrapping along the seam with a thumbnail, pried the sterile pad free of the adhesive strip, tucked the biochip behind it, then resealed everything. He replaced the box in the cabinet and closed the door.

He was surprised to find he was ravenous, and that the hunger took precedence over his desire for sleep. He walked to the kitchen, removed a loaf of bread, mustard, a package of sliced ham, and a jar of spicy dill pickle spears. Making sandwich after sandwich, he consumed all of the ham, over half the loaf of bread, and at least a half-dozen pickle spears, and emptied the last liter of milk in the refrigerator.

He licked the bread crumbs from his fingers, had another pickle spear, and wondered how he'd been able to eat so much. Then wondered how it had tasted so good. Instead of curbing the hunger, memories of Nami Chikara's death seemed to warm him, freeing his mind of the mechanics of feeding.

Satiated for the moment, still naked, marveling at the glow that seemed to fill him, he took a seat in front of the Tendrai deck. Hesitantly, wondering what she would say about tonight's events, he picked up the trodes and jacked into cyberspace.

"If you had one wish," she asked, "what would it be?" They were across from each other in the bar. She wore a hot pink bikini and a kittenish smile.

He answered without hesitation. "To make love to you as I am instead of as a thirteen-year-old boy."

She smiled abruptly, like clouds parting after a summer storm. She set her glass to one side, then took him by the hand. "Come with Momma. Come with Momma and see the surprise she has for you."

He trailed behind her, thirteen years old again. The path she followed was different from any they'd ever taken, up dark and gloomy staircases, turn, turn, down a staircase that still felt as if it were going up. For one brief moment he almost panicked.

She turned to him, her face suddenly serious. "No, don't spoil it. It's okay. Momma's not going to let anything happen to you." She took his face in her palms, wiped away tears he hadn't known he'd shed.

He followed, wished she would release his hand so he could regain his age and stature, wished she wouldn't let go because he was afraid she'd vanish in the darkness swimming around them. There didn't seem to be anything on either side of the staircase now, no bottom, no top. He didn't know there was a door until they passed through it.

"Lights," she called.

The room lit up. Racks of clothing covered the walls. Boxes of shoes lay everywhere. At the far end of the room, a lighted vanity with a horseshoe-shaped mirror sat before a plush seat. Pornographic pictures covered the walls, displaying men and women engaging in sex, women alone engaged in sex, horses, goats, dogs.

Brandstetter tore his eyes away from the pictures with difficulty. She had been a participant in every one he'd seen. "What is this place?"

"This is where I go when you're not here."

He glanced at a 10×13 picture of her with two men. "What about the photographs?"

She looked puzzled. "I don't know. You took them."

He tried to remember when and couldn't. He looked back at her, saw her standing beside a closet covered by a poster with her in the famous Marilyn Monroe pose with the blown-up dress.

"You're going to love this." She opened the closet door and a recessed light inside came on.

Brandstetter peered inside, and a scream of fear locked in his throat. He stumbled backward.

Inside the closet, hanging from a wire hanger, was the lifeless body of Nami Chikara as she'd been when he invaded her apartment, before he'd slashed her to death.

She reached inside the closet and took the body off the hanger with one hand. "See? Isn't she pretty?" She held the body against her own, using her free hand to smooth out the wrinkles, making it obvious that it wasn't a body she held at all. It was only skin.

Unable to stop himself, Brandstetter reached out to stoke one of the limp forearms, finding it unsettlingly warm to the touch. He drew his hand back.

"Isn't she soft?" she asked as she trailed her fingers along the curve of a breast. Her eyes taunted. "You wanted her, didn't you?"

"How did she get here?" Even here, with the improbable facing him, Brandstetter found his innate curiosity about the nature of things pushing at him. He touched the delicate swoop of neck, found a beat that felt disturbingly like a pulse, and removed his fingers.

"Does it matter? Really?" She moved away, twirling, so light of step, smoothing the Chikara woman's skin against her like a new dress. "Do you like her?"

"Yes."

She did something to the back of the skin and it seemed to come apart. Then she stepped into it, turning away from him, covering her nakedness with the olive skin of the Chikara woman.

Brandstetter watched her hands slide along the ragged edges of skin running from the buttocks along the spine, disappearing somewhere below the dark fall of hair. The air seemed filled with electricity. The horseshoe-shaped mirror against the far wall reflected dim outlines of her as she smoothed the skin to a perfect fit.

She turned around to him, face looking down, so much smaller now. Scientific curiosity wondered what she had done with the extra mass. The rest of his mind didn't care. She ran her hands down her body, posed, and smiled. "Do you like what you see?" she asked in her voice instead of the Chikara woman's.

He stared into the eyes that were hers instead of the murdered woman's. "Yes." He had to force the answer out. His temples throbbed, matching the liquid fire in his groin.

She came closer, placed her hands against his chest, looking up at him from so far away.

He felt impossibly large and powerful next to her.

"You're still a man," she said. "Not a boy."

He embraced her, lifting her from the floor, lost in that gaze that was her, hands cupping the buttocks that she had somehow borrowed or stolen. He drew in the fragrance of her and let his sexual needs guide him.

She deflected him with a hand. "No. This must be special. This is only temporary, it can't last. Let's make the most of it. Take me somewhere. Anywhere. A place where true love can really blossom."

Brandstetter held on to her hand as he reached out for a gridline and jacked into cyberspace.

Brandstetter clunked into the vintage Montana DataBrush animated program without her at his side. But he knew where to find her. He had the glass slipper in his hand.

He squinted at the unremembered bright sunlight coloring the day. The iron-covered wheels of the coach squeaked and clattered over the cobblestones as the four shod white horses pulled it along. He looked down at his clothing, not surprised to find himself in a sky-blue tunic, a purple cloak denoting him as a member of royalty, calf-high black leather boots, sky-blue pants. He touched the crown on his head.

A row of squat white houses sat on either side of the twisting road. Trees, impossibly neat and straight and filled with shade-giving branches, were between the houses and in the yards. Small animals, dogs, cats, mice, and others, scattered before the coach.

He felt anxious, the erection in those sky-blue pants definitely unprincelike.

He knew the house at once and knocked fiercely on the coach's ceiling. The driver came to a halt as a liveried footman swung from the back of the coach to open the door for him.

Neighbors halted in their daily chores to watch him get out. He ignored them, knotted a fist in his cloak as he strode toward the door. The footman raced around him and knocked on the door before he could get to it.

The door opened as the footman stepped away.

A gray-haired motherly type stood there, evidently dressed in her best and thinking it was much better than it was. "Oh, the prince," she squealed in a voice that was as soothing as fingernails on a blackboard. "Come, come, girls. The prince has arrived. Do come into our humble house, your highness."

Brandstetter stepped inside, holding the glass slipper tightly.

The two girls who came running to the door were smaller echoes of their mother, and not whom he was looking for at all.

"Where is she?" Brandstetter asked.

"Who, your highness?"

He held up the glass slipper. "The girl whose foot fits this shoe."

"Why, either of my girls, being dainty of foot, could easily fit that shoe, your highness."

Obeying the programming of the animated piece, Brandstetter knelt and tried the slipper on each of the women. It didn't fit.

"Neither of these is the girl I'm searching for." He turned to go, panic rising in him when he thought the programming might be harder to deflect than he had imagined.

"Your highness," the footman said, "there is another girl." He pointed imperiously.

Brandstetter turned to look at the girl, knowing at once it was she.

She had that same elfin stature, the large breasts, the tight waist, that same expression on her lips that he could never forget. She was dressed in a torn and dirty shift that ended well above the knee and looked impossibly sexy.

"Girl," he said softly, holding the slipper out, "come here."

She came, laying down the broom and dustpan she'd been carrying.

"Not her," the old woman said. "She's just the cleaning girl. Not fit for a prince at all."

The two sisters echoed the sentiments.

She stuck out her foot, her eyes never leaving his.

The slipper fit perfectly.

"Out," Brandstetter ordered as he took her into his arms. "All of you out of here now."

They fled, leaving him with her.

He took her into his arms, feeling the twin warmths of her. "Is this what you wanted?"

"Yes." She laughed in delight. "All this and more."

"I love you."

"I know. I love you too." She wrapped her legs and arms around him. "Take me to the kitchen."

He did, following her direction, somehow finding it despite the fact that her burning lips never left his.

"The table," she said.

The table was large and round and sturdy. Two windows on different walls overlooked the backyard and the apple tree to the side. Her feet were unshod, and somehow that fact made her even more irresistible.

He dropped the purple cloak to the floor. She helped him with the rest of his clothes.

"Come on," she coaxed. "Take me. Momma's waiting." She wrapped her legs around his waist as he tore the shift from her, breath coming in gasps.

Brandstetter thrust home in a hot rush, continuing on till he was buried completely inside her. She doubled up without warning, wrapping her arms around his neck as she bit him on the chest. The unexpected pain caused him to grow even harder. He began to thrust, wanting to hurt her back, listening to her plaintive cries as her orgasm slashed through her.

She squirmed and fought against him, raking his chest with her fingernails, pushing him toward his own climax. When the orgasm ripped through him and made him feel as empty as Nami Chikara's skin, Earl Brandstetter knew he'd never been more in love in his life.

20

"We're out here, Mick."

Traven locked his apartment door behind him, dropped his duster over the couch, tucked his primary SIG/Sauer under a cushion, left the one in the ankle holster, and followed Danny's voice out to the balcony, wondering who "we" were.

Danny sat in one of the wrought-iron chairs, his crossed feet resting on the waist-high parapet and a Coors bottle dangling from the fingers of one hand. Cheryl sat with her elbows on the cocktail table, palms turned up to support her face. An empty beer bottle sat beside her. Three others were more or less centered on the table. She smiled when he looked at her and said, "Hi, lover. We'd almost given up on you."

"Something came up," Traven said. He walked to the edge of the enclosed balcony, looking through the bulletproof glass at Holland Street fifteen floors below. Traffic was sparse. Kalita Humphreys Theater was a dark hulk to the east, almost lost in the high-rises that had surrounded the Goldstar, where he lived. The glass felt cold to the touch, holding the warmed air from inside the apartment. He turned back to face them.

"Are you hungry?" Danny asked.

"You haven't eaten yet?"

Cheryl held up a pretzel. "This is all we've allowed ourselves. And the beer, of course."

"Does spaghetti sound good?" Danny asked as he got to his feet. Traven nodded, and the boy disappeared inside the apartment.

"So what brings you here?" Traven asked as he slid into an empty chair at the table.

"Danny. He called and said you'd invited me to dinner at eight."

Traven raised his eyebrows and said, "Oh."

"I don't need to be a detective to see that this is news to you too."

"Why would he do that?"

"C'mon, Mick, don't be dense." Cheryl smiled to soften her words. "Danny's not a fool. He knows his presence here has screwed up your privacy."

Traven rubbed his face with a palm, wishing he could rub away the fatigue that clung to him as well as the memories of the dead woman.

Cheryl took his hand in hers. "Hey, are you okay?"

He found a smile somewhere and showed it to her. "Sure," he said as he reached out to tweak her snub nose. "I'm a tough guy, remember?"

"Yeah, well, I've spent some time around this tough guy, and I know when things are bothering him."

Realizing he hadn't told her about his temporary transfer from vice, Traven ran down the events of the last two days, glossing over Higham's missed weapons check and only skimming the murder briefly.

When he was finished, she called for the lights, cupped his chin in her palm, and studied the burn on his face. "I didn't even see it," she said. "Something that big, you'd think I'd notice it right off."

He captured her wrists in his hands and gently removed them, calling for lights out. "It's okay. Doesn't even hurt anymore. Much." He kissed her, enjoying the warmth of her lips against his.

Danny returned carrying a large salad bowl, three wineglasses, and a bottle of red wine. "Pour," he said, "and I'll get the silverware."

Cheryl reached into the salad bowl and plucked out a lettuce square. "Look, Mick. Small pieces, not the rip, rip, rip style you make that ends up with the dressing in your lap." She popped it into her mouth.

"Has he talked to you much?" Traven asked.

"No. Why?"

"I worry about him being able to deal with everything that's happened to him, but I don't know how to talk to him."

"He likes you, you know. We talked about you a lot this evening. He brought you up. Wanted to know what you were like, what you liked to do when you weren't working." Cheryl looked at him.

Pinned by her gaze, Traven looked away and leaned back in his chair. "Well, I don't know how to relate to him. The whole situation's awkward."

"You don't think he feels the same thing?"

Traven glanced back at her. "He could be gone tomorrow for all I know. Dad has custody of him for the moment, and all it takes is one word and Danny's out of here."

"That's a mixed-up kid in there," Cheryl said. "I can see it, and I know you can too. It helped today that you let him get out of the house, trusted him to see to taking care of the two of you, but he needs more than that. He lost his mother a few days ago. And you know the kind of father your father is. He needs somebody. Even if your father took him out of here, which I think neither of us believes is going to happen for some time, could you write him off so easily?"

Danny came back bearing dishes and silverware before Traven could reply.

Cheryl took the small salad bowls as the boy passed them to her. "Find a way, and make the time."

"Something I miss here?" Danny asked as he seated himself.

"Your brother was making lewd and lascivious suggestions," Cheryl said as she dripped dressing over her salad. "I'm considering taking him up on them."

21

"**Y**our weapons must be left here," the Nagamuchi security officer stated. "You may pick them up on your way out of the building."

Traven returned the man's flat gaze silently, registering no threat, only business.

The security office was small, and the man was large. Each seemed to complement the other. Smallness implied the security office could maintain a tight ship with only a few people needed to trim the corporate dirty laundry. Largeness implied the man could captain his ship quite effectively.

Higham was irritable and tense, smelling of mouthwash as he placed both hands on the desk separating them from the officer and leaned across it to intimidate. "Not a goddam thing was said about us giving up our weapons."

The officer regarded the homicide detective coolly. "Nothing needed to be said. These are standard procedures for any armed member of American military or government, state or federal, coming into Nagamuchi offices. You may abide by our rules or leave, as you wish. You will remember, when you calm down, that these offices are sanctioned by your government, and include many of the same rights as any embassy, including diplomatic immunity." He spread his broad, scarred hands. "So, in effect, we are suffering your presence by our choice rather than bowing to any laws this city might strive to enforce."

Even in the suit, with the SIG/Sauer tucked into

shoulder leather, and his hair cropped shorter by Cheryl that morning, Traven felt distinctly out of place. He hadn't been expecting the opulence of the building despite what he'd heard from other rare individuals who'd had the chance or mischance to be brought inside its doors.

The security officer's black uniform looked like solid one-piece with Kevlar thins woven into the fabric in all the right places. Besides the short-barreled flechette pistol mounted in a cross-draw rig across the flat stomach, the man also carried a short sword over his shoulder. The pommel of the weapon was decorative, looking more like a possession of office than something that would be used. The loose sleeves and pantlegs of the one-piece no doubt hid other deadly articles. Instead of boots, the officer wore traditional tabii, and the space between the split toes looked worn. Spit and polish and decorum obviously ended where such practices would slow down reflex and response time.

"Put your gun on the desk," Traven said, producing the SIG/Sauer from his shoulder rig. "Kaneoki set this game up and let us know in advance we were going to have to play by their rules."

Higham snorted derisively and dropped his weapon beside Traven's larger 10mm.

Reaching down to his ankle rig, Traven placed the other semiautomatic beside the first. The security officer's face was impassive. "We're not going in empty-handed," Traven said softly, maintaining the eye lock with the security man. "It's said there can be no stronger attack or defense than the truth, and that's what we're here for."

The security officer gave him a slight smile. "There are many truths in this world, Sergeant Traven, and—like any good weapon—truth cuts both ways. The wise man lives his life according to the few truths he needs rather than going in search of others. You might keep that in mind as you pursue your investigation." There was no hidden threat in the words, only a statement of fact.

"I will." Traven turned for the door flanked by two guards in black one-pieces. He passed through into the lavish hallway leading back to the central anteroom from where all roads to inner Nagamuchi Corporation stemmed. He turned back at the sound of a gentle buzz and found Higham blocked in the doorway by swords held by the guards.

The security officer glanced at his desk and pressed a hidden button that slid a portion of the imitation woodgrain back. "Sergeant Higham, it appears you have attempted to conceal something metallic on your person." He looked up, his black eyes flinty with non-emotion.

Higham put his hands behind his head as the two guards frisked him.

A moment later one of the guards freed a metal flask from an inside coat pocket and tossed it to the officer. Catching it effortlessly, the officer scrutinized it carefully, then twisted the cap off. He smelled it, frowned, then recapped it and placed it beside the collected weapons. "I assure you, Sergeant Higham, any of the brands you find in the corporate conference rooms exceeds whatever it is you have here. But it will be here awaiting your return."

Higham maintained tight-lipped silence as he stepped between the guards and into the hallway. No alarms sounded this time.

Traven used the magnetic passcard he'd been issued in the security office to access a private elevator. The elevator was almost crowded with the two of them. Deliberately punching 16 instead of 18, where they were to meet Yorimasa, he glanced at the lobster-red stain across the back of Higham's neck. Part of him felt sorry for the man. The other part, the majority, felt that Higham in his present demeanor was an accident waiting for a place to happen.

The elevator took a full minute to reach its destination. During that time the walls transluced and displayed a number of commercial bursts on the walls, ceiling, and floor. Most of them seemed to have the Craig Traven signature at the end.

He wasn't surprised when the cage crested the eighteenth floor and stopped instead of halting at the sixteenth floor as he'd punched in. He tapped the passcard, wondering how much other information the security officer had encoded on it, then decided it was a safe bet that if he "accidentally" wandered into the wrong room, alarms would sound. Without it, other alarms would undoubtedly sound.

Higham stepped out first and glanced at the floor where six inch-wide colored stripes ran parallel to the wall. "Yellow, right?"

"Yes." Traven pocketed the passcard and followed Higham, aware that mounted security cameras clicked and whirred and trailed in their wake, their fields of exposure overlapping so the homicide team was never out of sight.

"You noticed the bit about Yorimasa meeting us in a conference room?" Higham asked as he followed the thin yellow line.

"Yeah." Traven glanced in the office windows to either side of the hallway, wondering if the foldout blinds were always in place or if this was a special occasion.

"Why do you think we're meeting him there instead of his office?"

"Maybe he's got another couple of dead bodies stashed in his office he doesn't want us to know about," Traven replied. But the dig was more for the security officer's ears than for Higham.

The senior member of the homicide team looked over his shoulder. "My guess is the guy doesn't want to soil his office with gaijin trash."

Traven followed Higham around a turn, momentarily losing the yellow line as they crossed a wide, empty hallway filled with more office windows covered with portable blinds. "Could be. I think it's interesting that we haven't seen anyone else on this floor."

Higham's face grayed a little. "You think this is some kind of setup?"

"It's a setup all right, but a harmless one. We'll get

the dog-and-pony show, a pat on the back, and a foot in the ass. That we've even been given an audience at all tells me either Kaneoki's got some pull in the corporation or somebody's worried about how Nagamuchi will look in the media. No one in the halls means even less chance of us asking unwanted questions.''

Higham pulled his coat tighter. "I don't mind telling you, I don't like this assignment. I get the distinct impression we're in over our heads, and I like that even less.''

The yellow line took one more jog, then dead-ended at a broad door marked CONFERENCE ROOM 18F. The hallways, three of them that Traven could see, remained empty. He brushed the magnetic face of the passcard across the room's security lens. The door slid sideways and a computer voice said "Welcome" in four different languages.

Higham stepped in first, and Traven flanked him on the right.

The room was large, ostentatious, and would have seated a hundred people easily. The Nagamuchi corporate symbol, crossed swords overlying a stylized Komodo dragon, was emblazoned in gold on one white wall. Long, rectangular tables with maroon tablecloths covered the expensive off-white carpet. Generous swivel-backed chairs surrounded them. A crystal chandelier depended from the peaked thirty-foot ceiling and gleamed brightly, turning the daylight streaming in from the south wall into a wealth of tiny rainbows. The scent of cherry blossoms filled the cool air.

"Guess they do things in a big way around here," Higham commented dryly.

"Yes," a man's voice said.

Traven glanced to his left and saw the Japanese man dressed in a traditional black business suit emerge from a door inset on the north wall under the Nagamuchi symbol. He was small and compact, hair shot through with just the right amount of gray to elicit respect, just enough extra weight to emphasize self-importance and self-confidence, and a smile oily enough to have floated on water. "You're Taira Yorimasa?"

"Hai." The man bowed.

Traven returned the bow out of force of habit rather than any desire to ingratiate himself with the man. His studies of the martial arts had ingrained such behavior in him when facing someone who was considered a possible opponent. "We're Detectives Higham and Traven." He flashed his shield, irritated when he realized the Nagamuchi ID pinned to his pocket had already told the man who he was.

"Hai. I know who you are. Your offices apprised this corporation of your arrival, and I must admit, I find your presence here an inconvenience in a day that has already been full of unpleasant surprises."

"Nice to know where we rate," Higham said.

"And you rate highly among them, Detective. If not for the efforts of you and your partner, I might not have been the recipient of such hostile media footage. The allegations and accusations inherent in the case entrusted to your hands should never have left your mouths till you were ready to make an arrest. As it stands, should unprovoked hostilities continue in the press, the corporation is ready to file a suit against your department."

"We don't control the press," Traven said. "They're free to print or televise whatever they wish unless they intentionally do harm to an individual or company."

"Have you seen what they are showing on wallscreen?" Without waiting for a response, Yorimasa addressed the room AI and caused the conference room to darken as the east wall transluced and became a wallscreen larger than any Traven had ever seen. The view was breathtaking, and induced a mild vertigo till the scene sharpened and showed the sheet-covered body of the murdered woman being loaded into the back of an ambulance on a night-dark street. The voices of the reporter and the people present sounded like muted thunder with the volume turned down. Yorimasa faced them, his features stained with the cast-off reflection of the impossibly large wallscreen. "The name of Nagamuchi Corporation is found mentioned in these so-called news pieces with more frequency than the dead woman's. And Nagamuchi is being shown unfavorably in many of these broadcasts.''

Traven silently tallied the broadcasts flashing quickly across the wallscreen, identifying the reporters as being from independent stations, not linked with Nagamuchi assets at all. There weren't many. Of the four, Shiner Broadcasting System was the largest. Still, SBS had a large audience. Yorimasa and Nagamuchi Corporation had a right to be concerned about the coverage. The SBS reporter even knew about the letter opener, information which, as far as Traven knew, had not been released to the press.

''You and your partner have, as you seem to phrase it here in this country, been talking out of school.''

The lights came back on with blinding intensity.

When Traven glanced back at Yorimasa, he saw the man wasn't alone. The woman must have been able to move very swiftly and quietly for him not to have seen or heard her approach.

She was tall and slender, showing definite signs of mixed Oriental and Caucasian blood. She wore a white blouse which deemphasized her bust, and a matching gray short-waisted coat and knee-length skirt. If there was any makeup on her round face, Traven couldn't tell it. Her hair was done in a long braid and curled up on her head.

''You're wrong,'' Traven said. ''Neither of us released anything to the press.''

Yorimasa flashed him a humorless grin. ''Maybe I am wrong, Detective, but who is to prove it?'' He steepled his fingers before him. ''You are faced with the same unsubstantiated claims as I am. So, what are we to do about them?''

''They're not our concern,'' Higham said, stepping forward.

Sensing the man was seeking to establish himself as the senior of the team, Traven backed off and studied the woman. She studied him back, and the effect amused him. She looked young, and took whatever it was she was doing here seriously. He could see that in her almond-shaped eyes. Yet she was unsure of herself, as revealed by the small movements of her shoulders inside the jacket.

"Our concern," Higham went on, "is the murder of Nami Chikara."

"Then why are you here?" Yorimasa asked blandly. "Why are you not out on the street seeking her killer?"

"We wanted to find out why she was killed with your letter opener," Higham said.

Yorimasa spread his hands. "As to why, you could probably come up with a good many more reasons than I could venture. Coming up with reasons for her murder is your job."

"How did your letter opener get to her apartment?"

"Again, there could be any number of answers. Perhaps she stole it, and her murderer chanced upon it and used it. Perhaps it was taken from my office by someone seeking to frame me."

Traven looked back at the exec. "Why would someone want to frame you?"

"For my position, of course." Yorimasa flashed that oily smile again. "I enjoy a great many things because of my position: an advantageous social structure, perks, benefits, and, yes, money. A number of my rivals, vying for my job, might be willing to see me humbled under adverse publicity and taken from office."

Higham produced a notebook. "Who?"

"Please." Yorimasa waved the thought away. "If I thought someone within these offices had done that, we have our own ways of dealing with them. Had not Nami Chikara been of American citizenship, you would not be here now."

"Where were you yesterday?" Traven asked. The woman beside Yorimasa stared at him in subdued disbelief.

There was dead silence in the conference room.

Yorimasa diverted his scathing gaze to Traven. "Your manner is very crass, Detective Traven. It's no small wonder why you were transferred from your last assigned post. Why you are still with the police department in any capacity might be even more puzzling."

"You haven't answered my question." Traven returned the stare full-measure.

"No, I haven't." Yorimasa clasped his hands behind his back, his spine straight and his shoulders squared. "And I won't. My whereabouts do not belong in a police report, much less to a department that cannot keep its secrets to itself. My corporation has vouched for me, and there are papers—signed by a number of the board of directors—saying I was nowhere near Nami Chikara's apartment when the murder was committed. They are even now en route to your offices. This meeting is purely a matter of form, and need not have even taken place. Except that I wanted to meet you, to let you know the ramifications of any failures you might make on this investigation in the future."

"You were with these board members yesterday?" Higham asked.

"I did not say that. I said they knew where I was."

"And they know you were there?"

"If they didn't, would they have signed statements to that fact?"

"You tell me." Higham's expression was bland.

Rolling a wrist overheavy with a jeweled gold watch, Yorimasa said, "Gentlemen, your visit is at an end. I'd like to take the time remaining to introduce Otsu Hayata, the public relations spokesperson whom you will be talking to from this point on."

The woman gave a slight bow.

"She will have everything you need to know, and will pass on any message you might have that will demand my attention, though I can think of none. Together, I expect you and she to find some way to end all the adverse publicity surrounding this matter." Yorimasa permitted himself a smile. "My suggestion to you would be to find the person who really committed the murder and release his name to the press."

He turned and headed for the door under the corporate logo.

"Gentlemen," Hayata said in a soft voice. She bowed.

Traven returned the bow, watching her as she glided across the carpet to follow Yorimasa.

"I'd say we just got the bum's rush," Higham commented as the door slid shut.

Traven silently agreed as he turned back toward the door and reached for the passcard. The door slid away at their approach.

"And that bit about your transfer," Higham said as they passed into the hall, "that wouldn't have been in any legit briefing Kaneoki could have sent over to the Nagamuchi security people."

"I know."

"So that means they've been digging around in our backgrounds. Why?"

Traven halted in front of the private elevator. "When the time comes, I'm sure they'll let us know."

"Yeah, that's what gets me the most." Higham reached inside his jacket, then caught himself. "The son of a bitch is lying about something, though. You can feel it."

The elevator doors closed, displaying more commercial bursts, including the new one Craig Traven had just released. "Hell," Traven said with more humor than he felt, "you're being optimistic. He may have been lying about all of it."

"Except for the lawsuit. I got definite vibes about that one."

The elevator dropped slowly, and Higham's attention was seized by some of the more sexually explicit advertising.

Traven turned the whole meeting over in his head, seeking some loose strand to work on, then gave up because his mind seemed to insist on focusing on Otsu Hayata. And he couldn't figure that one out either.

22

Traven drove the Cherokee out of the underground parking garage below Nagamuchi Towers, pausing long enough at the gate for the black-clad security guard to peel the visitor pass from the windshield. Higham sat in the passenger seat thumbing through the slender file they'd assembled on Nami Chikara.

"This is bullshit," Higham said, closing the file angrily.

Traven didn't reply, concentrating on the heavy flow of afternoon traffic cruising Musashi Boulevard between the three skyscrapers. The afternoon sun was being crowded out by approaching rain clouds, throwing darkness over the streets. He accessed DataMain, discovered the time was 4:17 P.M., and realized most of the traffic was from the afternoon shifts letting out at surrounding plants. He inched forward and waited for a break in the line of cars covering his side of the six-lane street. He gave serious consideration to switching on the siren and lights, then decided against it because a mobile media vehicle might pick it up and use it to reemphasize the Nagamuchi connection to the murdered woman.

"Without Yorimasa's say-so," Higham said, "we're not even going to be able to access their personnel records."

"Some of those records will be in Immigration service files," Traven said as he eased his foot off the clutch and fed the 4×4 into a gap made by a car turning down the street.

"Yeah, but Immigration's not exactly a fount of knowledge when it comes to the big leagues. They know just what Nagamuchi and the other corporations want them to know, and that's the extent of it." Higham closed the file and tossed it onto the dash with a sigh of disgust. "Also, we're going to have to get a warrant to even access the files they do have."

The traffic was slow, moved by meters as each vehicle took its turn lumbering through the lights at the end of the long block.

Ignoring the impatience that filled him, Traven reviewed their conversation with Yorimasa, wondering what the man was hiding, or if maybe all execs at that level acted the same. He tapped his finger on the steering wheel idly. "You had any dealings with execs before?"

"A couple close brushes," Higham replied as he scanned the side mirror at his elbow. "Damn, would you look at this traffic. You couldn't pay me enough to put up with this every day."

"Did you get the impression he was covering his own ass, or the corporation's?" Traven worked over to the inside lane, angling for a left turn five car lengths away. The angry buzz of a motorcycle engine whined somewhere behind him, came closer.

"At his pay grade, aren't they one and the same?"

Traven smiled in spite of the circumstances. Three more cars edged through the light, leaving him stranded behind a flashy red Japanese sports car with corporate, tax-exempt tags. The tinted windows revealed nothing of the interior or the driver, but the wrist poking out the driver's window gleamed with a thick gold bracelet. "Were you working homicides when you came up against your previous execs?"

"Yeah, but I can tell you right now they weren't anywhere near Yorimasa's caliber. Yorimasa's a guy who has the power to punch the button on your ticket all by himself."

"Then why didn't he?"

The motorcycle engine rumbled closer and geared down.

"Beats me," Higham replied. "Maybe he gets his rocks off stepping on the little people."

"It doesn't scan." Traven checked the rearview mirror and spotted the motorcycle making its way slowly to the forefront of the stalled traffic, eventually blocked by a freight truck almost bumper-to-bumper with a compact van. Two people sat astride the bike, dressed in identical dark chocolate road leather. The helmets were black bullets with tinted bubble-shields. They looked lean, adolescent, with a swagger to the way they clung to the powerful Suzuki. The motor was a dull rumble of thunder.

"What?" Higham seemed only half interested, still marveling at the glut of traffic.

"If Yorimasa likes the political ass-kicking that goes on behind closed corporate doors, he's in a position to get all he wants."

"Maybe he just wanted some new meat."

The light changed, and Traven surged forward with the wave of vehicles. He jockeyed to keep his position from the sedan that changed lanes with no signal and joined a half-dozen other drivers in sounding their frustration. "No," he said. He settled back behind the wheel and let the traffic flow guide him downtown, away from Highland Park. "Yorimasa met us there for reasons of his own."

"What reasons?"

"He wanted to know how much we knew."

"About what?"

"That's where the questions start again. What exactly is he covering up? His relationship with the woman? No. That he murdered her? Possibly. That he knows who did murder her? Interesting, because then, as long as the murder remains unresolved, he has a heavy sword to hold over someone's head."

"He'd be into a power trip like that." Higham grinned, shifted in the seat, and rubbed his chin. "I like that, but it's going to be tough to prove."

Traven nodded.

"You can even twist it a little farther out of norm and say that Yorimasa thinks he knows who killed the woman, but wants us to be in the position to prove it, then he swoops down to snatch defeat from the jaws of victory on our behalf and leverages the information to his own benefit.''

''That would make it even harder to prove.''

''But it fits the up-and-coming kind of guy we met back there.''

''Yeah.''

The rumble of the motorcycle engine flared to life again and closed in. Traven checked the mirrors, watched the bike come up on the right side. He tapped the brake gently, getting ready for the next stoplight at Bryn Mawr Drive.

''I thought homicide was just going to be a temporary thing for you,'' Higham said with a half-smile. ''When did you start taking this seriously?''

''The day I pinned on the badge,'' Traven replied, looking the other man in the eye. ''I've always taken this job seriously, even when I was handing out parking citations. I may not agree with everything that goes on, or approve of the changes I see, but I've never shirked my job.''

A serious expression washed away the humor on Higham's features, and he looked back at the traffic without saying anything.

Across the intersection, a gap opened up and Traven signaled for it. He cut the Cherokee's wheels to the right. The motorcycle streaked ahead of the car beside it and wove between two others. The rider lifted a cloth-covered length from knee level on the other side of the bike. Metal gleamed as the cloth tore away in the slipstream.

Traven glanced ahead, saw the solid blockade of stopped cars ahead of him, and checked his alternatives as he yelled, ''Look out!'' Pedestrians and people waiting for the mass transit system covered the sidewalks and left no place to run to even if he could cross the remaining lane of traffic. The left was blocked by the meter-high concrete median filled with bonsai and cherry trees.

Higham's head came up a second before the motorcycle tracked directly onto the 4×4. His pistol appeared in his lap a heartbeat later.

Traven stepped forcefully on the brake. Rubber shrilled. He saw the motorcycle fishtail away from the slewing back end of the Cherokee as he drew the 10mm. Releasing the brake and stomping the accelerator as he hit the shift-on-the-fly 4WD control, he scooted out in front of the motorcycle. The driver dodged and spoiled the rider's aim.

The familiar blast of a shotgun tore through the traffic noises. Metallic rips appeared across the hood of the Cherokee. The rear glass of the vehicle stopped in front of Traven evaporated as the double-ought buckshot smashed into it. The back wheel of the Suzuki clipped the 4×4's front bumper, spun out of control, and sent both riders skidding across the pavement.

Throwing the emergency brake on, Traven opened his door and dropped to the street. "Call for backup!" he yelled to Higham. He dropped to his hands and knees to get an underbelly view of traffic as the motorcyclists clambered back on the Suzuki and roared away. A final blast of the shotgun tore into the Cherokee's body somewhere, then they were gone, riding back down the wrong way in the congested traffic.

Traven pushed himself to his feet and fisted the SIG/Sauer tightly as he pumped his knees, forced himself to breathe through his nose instead of his mouth, and settled himself in for the long haul.

The motorcycle's engine blared like a burned-out bearing.

By the time he reached the end of the Cherokee, the first accident had already happened. A motorist seeking to evade the suicidal rush of the Suzuki swerved into the right lane of traffic, smashed into the side of a produce truck, and scattered crates of lettuce heads and tomatoes across the street. Traffic came to a standstill in quick order with only narrow gaps for the motorcyclist to attempt passage.

Maintaining the inner edge of the median, Traven ran, trying to watch the traffic and keep the Suzuki in sight at the same time. His lungs burned from the exertion. Ten car lengths later, he was gaining, but the last intersection was coming up and he knew if they made it he would never catch them.

Another car tried to avoid the motorcycle and ended up smashing into the car beside it, followed by two more, and created a logjam of twisted vehicles. Horns honked. Pedestrians climbed out of their stalled vehicles to see what was going on.

Traven waved his gun as he ran, knowing it got more instant recognition and respect than his shield.

People dove for the imagined security of their cars.

The Suzuki was only five car lengths ahead now, some ten or twelve lengths from the open intersection. Without warning, a diesel rig opened its door in their path. The motorcycle skidded, lost ground as it tried unsuccessfully to swerve. The thud was loud and meaty, and left the door on warped hinges and the motorcycle passenger with a cracked faceshield streaming scarlet. The driver stamped his foot, returned the shift to first gear, and brought the motorcycle around to avoid the crunch of cars.

Traven left the median and scrabbled across the hood of a late-model sedan. He leaped to the top of another as he caught a glimpse of the surprised face behind the steering wheel. The footing felt unsure, springy, filled with metallic tension. He leaped for the top of another car, still running, slipped and fell, barely able to control his skidding descent and land on his feet on the trunk compartment.

The motorcycle passenger pointed him out to the driver, then concentrated on raising the shotgun while the driver spurted around a stalled van.

Traven dove as the shotgun came up and rolled prone between parked cars as the double-ought pattern sliced through empty air. He triggered five quick rounds one-handed, holding the sights centered over the shotgunner's chest. The motorcycle whined as it bucked through the stalled vehicles. The rear tire spun on the pavement. The shotgunner crumpled, dropped the weapon, and spilled lifelessly into the street.

Maintaining a Weaver stance as he closed in on the

downed gunner, Traven heard the motorcycle's engine blast new acceleration. He kicked the shotgun away, knelt quickly to check the pulse, felt none, but found a neck too slim and too soft to belong to a male.

He cursed as he pushed himself to his feet to rejoin the pursuit, bloody visions of the murdered woman rampaging through his mind, this time hidden by the broken faceshield.

Higham's voice rippled into his mind. "Traven!"

"Here."

"Where?"

"North on Musashi. I dropped one of them. Where's the goddam backup?"

"En route."

"They're going to be too late. Get back here and secure the body."

"Body?"

Traven didn't answer. He dodged between the row of cars as he kept the motorcyclist in sight. His foot slipped and he bounced off the side of a car, pain shooting through his hipbone. Then he had a handhold on the next car and dragged himself across the hood, ripping his shirt on the thrusting ornament. The stitches in his chest pulled. He got his legs under him, vaulted to the top of a pickup, and flipped the safety on the 10mm as he threw himself at the motorcyclist.

23

Traven crashed into the motorcyclist with enough force to drive the air from his lungs. He resisted the immediate impulse to throw himself clear as the Suzuki twisted wildly beneath them and managed to get an arm around his target and rip the guy from the bike. Off-balance and unable to control his fall any longer, he ended up on the bottom of the sprawl over the pavement. His elbow hit first, and felt as if jagged glass shards had been driven up into it. He dropped his pistol.

The man butted Traven with the helmet and cut his forehead with a chipped corner.

Twisting under the man's lighter weight, Traven came up with an open-hand blow from his uninjured arm to the fractured faceshield that rocked the driver's head. He tried to bring his right arm into play and couldn't sense it enough to figure out what he was doing. His numbed fingers slid over the slick helmet.

A gleaming knife blade sprang into the man's hand from some hidden pocket of the riding leathers. He threw himself forward and leaned on the knife.

Traven jerked his head to one side and heard the sharp blade grind into the pavement. He chopped his attacker in the throat with his operational hand, listened to the guy gag as he leveraged himself from beneath the weight and rolled way.

The assassin came after him instantly and flailed out with the knife, showing more emotion than skill.

Pushing himself up on his hands, Traven lashed out

in a vicious sidekick that caught the helmet with full force. The attacker went over backward and remained limp, the knife forgotten in nerveless fingers.

Traven bent and retrieved his pistol, then held it in his good hand while splinters of pain ran through his other arm. He breathed deeply as he flipped the safety off the 10mm and approached the man. He kicked the knife away and leaned against one of the stalled cars. "Police," he told the frightened motorist behind the wheel.

"Mick?" The deep voice rippled through the comchip.

"That you, Kowalski?"

"Yeah. You okay?"

"Been better." Traven noticed the screaming sirens then, saw the MOP unit slide around the corner and come to a broadside halt on the outer edge of the gathering crowd.

Kowalski bolted from the passenger seat, togged out in full riot gear and carrying a combat shotgun across his broad chest. The crowd melted before him. Three other officers with VICE marked in white across the backs of their black jackets moved out to secure the area. Kowalski moved like a panther, turning constantly as he called out orders to his team.

A crimson newscopter swooped past the scene, scattered street trash, then curved around for another pass. It hovered directly above them, a cameraman clinging to the half-cage as the pilot switched on a directional mike mounted on the copter's belly.

The voices of the crowd returned and brought even more confusion.

Traven leathered the SIG/Sauer and knelt before the unconscious driver. When he tried to pull the faceshield away, it went to jagged pieces in his hands. He dropped them as he studied the Hispanic features.

"Ochoa," Kowalski said.

Traven looked up at the big man and nodded. "One of Evaristo Escobar's errand boys." He reached forward to take the helmet off.

Kowalski lowered the ugly snout of the automatic

shotgun till it was aimed directly at Ochoa's face. "Doesn't make sense that Escobar would take a hand against you right now," the big man said. "We've been squeezing Donny Quarters's balls lately, and haven't been able to catch him moving jack shit for almost a month. And he'd have known you were pulled off vice. Why pull a dumb shit stunt like this now?"

Traven touched the thick scar running down the unconscious man's neck. He sighed and released the head, letting it thump back against the pavement. "He's sure as hell not going to tell us."

Kowalski moved a foot against Ochoa's jawline and twisted the man's head over to reveal the surgical scar Traven's fingers had found. "Man's been 'printed."

Traven nodded. He glanced over his shoulder to the south, past where Higham stood guard over the other body, to the unmarked car coming up Musashi Boulevard.

"Neural imprints usually aren't Escobar's style," Kowalski commented. "Guy thinks money can buy everything and everybody he needs, and keep business to himself."

"Yeah, well, evidently the times change." Traven accessed his com-chip and reached for Higham. The man looked up once contact was made.

"Go," Higham responded.

"Find any ID on that one?"

"No. She's clean."

The pronoun bit into Traven's soul.

"She?" Kowalski echoed verbally.

Traven nodded. "Dropped a woman before I knew it." He jammed his hands into his pockets and walked through the crowd. They moved back away from him out of fear rather than because he was a cop.

"Women aren't Escobar's style either," Kowalski said as he trailed behind after assigning a vice cop to cover Ochoa. "Evaristo comes from the old school in Colombia, where killing is still a man's business."

"I know."

Higham stepped aside.

Trying to ignore the red ruin the 10mm hollowpoints

had made of the woman's chest, Traven knelt and removed the helmet. The ache in his arm and elbow had dulled out to broken-toothed gnawing.

She had been pretty, with raven-dark hair, elfin features, and a smooth complexion beginning to gray in death. Blood trickled from the corner of her mouth, and her eyes were half open.

Traven's stomach rolled uncontrollably. For a moment he thought he was going to lose it. Then the feeling went away, leaving behind the thick taste of bile.

"Japanese," Kowalski said. "That definitely ain't Escobar's style. Something stinks here, Mick."

An authoritative voice rang out on the other side of the crowd.

Traven looked up as he took his wallet out and removed one of the plastic-coated calendar cards he always kept with him.

"Kaneoki," Higham replied.

"What the hell's he doing here?" Kowalski asked. A sour look twisted his face.

Higham shrugged.

Traven removed the glove on the woman's right hand, rolled it palm up, then pressed the thumb pad and first two fingers onto the calendar. He put the last two fingers on the other side, never touched anything but the corners of the card himself. Finished, he sandwiched the calendar between two other cards, then handed all three to Kowalski.

Higham watched with unexpressed interest.

Kaneoki's voice sounded clearer now as well as closer.

Traven examined the woman's long fingers, then placed a thumb against her palm and pressed. Five two-inch-long blades sprang out from under the fingernails and glistened in the gray storm light.

"Son of a bitch," Higham commented in a dry voice.

"Bitch wasn't exactly cherry to this kind of thing, was she?" Kowalski observed. "Maybe you guys are lucky she opted for the distance kill."

Traven let the hand drop, still not feeling any better about his part in her death. He stood and faced Kowalski. "You guys have any reason for being in the area?"

The big man shrugged. "Heard you and Higham were going to be taking on one of Nagamuchi's big boys today. Thought we'd cruise by to see if anything interesting happened. Just in case it did."

Traven shook his head. "Wrong. You were working Ochoa. He was running a dry drop your intel had turned up, and you were blazing the trail when this went down. If Kaneoki hears it any other way, he'll clue Kiley, and Kiley will ream your asses."

Kowalski grinned. "That's just what I said."

"And thanks for being there."

"No prob, my man."

Traven glanced at Higham. "Any problems with what I said?"

"Not from me. We cover each other. You know how it is."

Inside, Traven chilled at the other man's words. The code that kept Higham from ratting Kowalski and the vice team out to Kiley was the same one that kept him from recommending Higham be pulled from the street before someone, maybe Traven, got killed.

"Traven!" Kaneoki's voice cut through the surrounding din like a laser through butter.

Traven turned to face the man.

"What the hell's going on here?" Kaneoki demanded as he looked down at the corpse.

"We were attacked," Traven replied, "as soon as we left Nagamuchi Towers."

Kaneoki blinked behind the glasses, then set his gaze on Higham.

The homicide man raised his shoulders, then dropped them. "Happened just like he said, Cap'n."

Eyes flashing inner anger, Kaneoki glared back at Traven. "You expect me to believe Nagamuchi had something to do with this?"

"Did I say that?"

"Cut the bullshit, Traven."

Traven looked at Higham. "Did I say anything like that?"

"No."

The newscopter buzzed by overhead again. Uniformed units arrived on the scene and set up around the perimeters of the congestion to start moving the traffic.

"Taira Yorimasa has been cleared of any guilt in the geisha's death," Kaneoki said. "I was faxed a set of documents this thick saying he was nowhere near her building last night." He held his thumb and forefinger three centimeters apart. "I don't want you turning this around in your favor to use it to get back at Nagamuchi. They're out of this."

Traven kept his voice calm. "Even if Yorimasa didn't kill the woman, he could have hired it done. With or without the corporation's knowledge."

"The man's innocent till he's proven guilty, Traven, or don't you remember the law?"

"Sure, I remember it. But I haven't proved either yet. If Yorimasa had nothing to do with her murder, it's more than fifty-fifty that someone in those offices did. So far, from what I'm to understand from Yorimasa, we're getting zip as far as cooperation is concerned."

"Stay away from them."

Traven returned the man's gaze. "I have to wonder why you're so insistent, Captain."

"You don't have to do a goddam thing but your job, mister."

Knowing he'd struck a nerve, Traven said, "That's what I'm trying to do."

Adjusting his glasses, Kaneoki glared at Higham, then moved on to Kowalski. He blinked. "What the hell is vice doing here?" He looked a Traven as if daring an answer.

Kowalski cleared his throat. "Well, the prisoner we got back there is Luis Ochoa, a known associate of Evaristo Escobar, a Medellín cartel member operating here in Dallas. We'd staked him out after getting wind of a new drop line Escobar was setting up through

Highland Park, and happened to be on hand when the fireworks started.''

''And they attacked Traven?''

''Yes, sir.''

''Why would they do that?''

''The way it looks to me, they figured on killing him.''

Traven restrained a reflexive grin as Kaneoki searched in vain for some sign on the big man's face that showed insubordination.

Turning away from Kowalski, Kaneoki said, ''There's your answer. Evidently Ochoa and his accomplice recognized you and decided to take you down on the spur of the moment. This attack had nothing to do with Nagamuchi at all. The basis for it lies in your past work with vice.''

Traven nodded, thinking about the shotgun and the finger-razors. ''You're probably right.''

Kaneoki straightened his jacket and tie. He was visibly relieved. Glancing up, the police captain noticed the newscopter spiraling around the area for the first time. ''I'll make sure and mention that in the statement to the press. Why don't you and Higham clear the area. It'll make things less confusing for all concerned.''

''And maybe keep the Nagamuchi connection down to a minimum,'' Traven said. ''I understand.'' He started walking before Kaneoki had a chance to say anything, and was met almost at once by a familiar reporter still working on fixing her hair and trying to talk through the notepad clenched in her teeth. He pointed at Kaneoki, who was straightening his tie. The reporter went on when he said, ''Captain of detectives,'' evidently relishing the aspect of bearding a higher member of the police department about the nature of violence in the streets.

''Mick?'' Kowalski was at his elbow.

In a voice low enough that Higham couldn't overhear, Traven said, ''I want a meet with Escobar. Tonight.''

Kowalski nodded and faded away.

Traven surveyed the damage done to the Cherokee, realized it was nothing a quick trip to the body shop couldn't fix, then stepped up into the 4×4, trying not to remember the dead woman.

"You okay?" Higham asked.

"Yeah," Traven replied as he moved through the dense traffic with the aid of the uniforms who recognized him. He hoped the answer sounded more sincere than it felt.

24

"You sure you want to do this alone?" In the night's darkness, even Kowalski's big voice seemed quieter than normal along the private com-chip frequency they'd arranged for the night.

Traven remained adamant. "It's not like I'm going to be exactly alone."

"Yeah, but it's not like you're going to have an on-the-spot backup either."

After checking the lights, Traven crossed the streets, dressed for the night in a black duster, T-shirt, jeans, and tennis shoes. Both SIG/Sauers occupied the pockets of the duster, and he kept it open despite the misting rain falling all over the city and the chill that nipped at unprotected flesh like a rabid dog. The Cherokee was three blocks back from Escobar's building in case a uniform on routine patrol happened to notice it. He still wasn't sure how far Kaneoki had his operation staked out, but he was sure the man had. It disturbed him to realize that in his role of the watcher, he was also being watched by his own teammates on this one. But not so disturbing that he could let the opportunity go by unchallenged. "We play this right, I shouldn't need one."

"And if you do, you're shit out of luck."

"Careful. Your optimism's showing."

"I shouldn't have agreed to let you do this."

"You didn't have a choice."

"Sure as hell did."

Traven turned the corner, threaded through the

leatherboys and street flesh. His footsteps spanged wetly on the sidewalk.

"You're not in vice right now," Kowalski said.

"You can take the boy out of vice."

"Shit."

The rain gathered force, came down in drops now. Traven hunkered his shoulders against it, wished the wind didn't have fangs, wished he could get the two dead women out of his mind. "What's Escobar doing?"

"Partying hearty. You'd think thirty years of doing cartel work would slow the son of a bitch down. Instead, he could drink either one of us under the table and still drink a toast to our health."

"Does he know Ochoa was aced today?"

"Don't know. Can't get an audible on his penthouse, and the word on the street concerning Señor Escobar is rare and neutered these days."

"Looking back, do you come up with the same timetable I get?"

"You mean, that Escobar pulled a fast fade while young Donny Quarters came on strong?"

"That's the one."

"Funny how we never noticed that before."

"Too caught up in the eye of the storm. Looking back's always easier and surer." Traven glanced at the Hsing Building. By daylight, it was beautiful, concrete and stained glass, catering only to the very wealthy. But at night with the low-lying black clouds surrounding the upper stories like a moat, it seemed more formidable, like a fortress that used shadow as part of its defenses.

"When's the last time you stood eye to eye with Escobar?" Kowalski asked.

"Sixteen months ago."

"As I remember, no love was lost."

"True."

"He might decide taking you out is worth getting kicked out of the country," Kowalski said. "Did you think about that?"

"Yeah. You've got to remember that despite his ambassadorial relations for Colombia to this country, Escobar likes the life-style he enjoys here. Dallas has become as much of a home to him as Medellín, and it's a good place to do business.''

''He's addicted to the game too.''

''There's that. I consider that one more reason he won't try to have me whacked tonight. He has his own rules to live by.''

Kowalski's silence was noncommittal.

Traven stood across the street from the Hsing Building, looked up at it, and knew some of the building security had probably already picked him up if Escobar's talent hadn't. ''Who's the DEA guy working tonight?''

''Not a guy. A lady.''

''Gibson?''

''Yep.''

''She have any problems with the script?''

''Not as long as we share and share alike. She's a pro, been chasing Escobar and his troops longer than either of us. Did I tell you I finally found out how old she really was?''

''No.''

''Yeah, well, you know how the cosmetech surgery the DEA does on their femmes fatales retards the aging process. Turns out Delilah Gibson, card-carrying DEA agent, could've bounced either of us on her knee.''

''No wonder she hasn't given in to your charms yet.''

''Ah, but that's the beauty of it, my boy. Now that I know the age, I also know to try my winning ways by plying her with flowers and candy. I'll let you know when I score.''

''You do and you let it get around too much, I'll bring flowers and candy to you in the hospital. Maybe you can suck the candy through a straw and you can smell the flowers when they unpack your broken nose.''

Kowalski's laughter was as harsh and biting as the wind.

"Time to go sub," Traven said as he leaned into the wind and trotted across the street. The com-chip rippled inside his head. The frequency locked into the transmit mode, and would stay that way until he willed it back open. He'd be blind in some ways while inside the building, cut off from the extra pairs of eyes he was used to on the street during a group operation, but it wouldn't set off any privacy alarms and would allow them to make a recording of the conversation.

He slowed to a walk on the other side of the street, hands still buried in his pockets. He pressed the main entrance button and the doors slid back as he stepped through. Rain dripped off the duster to the carpeted floor.

A building security team of two came toward him at once when the thumbprint scan came up blank. They were dressed in upscale fashion, with the cuts in all the right places to conceal their weapons.

Traven took his hands out of his pockets slowly and unfolded his shield case so they could see the gold.

"You got papers?" one of them asked.

Traven shook his head. "Here by invitation."

"Whose?"

"Evaristo Escobar."

The security men exchanged doubtful looks. "You don't mind if we call up right quick and confirm that?"

"No."

One of the men stayed there, just out of reach, while the other retreated to the house phone. He smiled as he spoke to the building operator. "Who should I say is calling?"

"Traven. Mick Traven."

The security man spoke in a voice so low Traven couldn't understand it. Slowly a look of puzzlement spread across the broad features. He hung up the phone. "He says to let you come on up."

Traven walked over to the elevator, stepped inside, and waited for the security people to code it for him.

"This won't take you to the penthouse," the security man said. "One of Mr. Escobar's people will meet you in the hallway on forty-seven and take you the rest of the way.''

Traven nodded, and the doors closed. He watched the climbing blip-blip-blip of the floor lights coming as fast as his heartbeat. His hands were sweat-slick on the butts of the 10mms.

The doors binged open at forty-seven and a coffee-colored young woman wearing a white smile and a carmine party dress stepped into the elevator cage. She addressed him in Spanish, and he responded in the same language. She flashed a silver passcard across the elevator's scan circuits and they were on their way again.

Traven kept up a steady stream of small talk, complimented the woman on her dress, and asked her about the party. This was the time Kowalski would be most concerned about him: the time when he was out of sight. Steady chatter over the open com-chip would let them know he was all right. The vice team had secured a room in a building across from Escobar's penthouse some years ago, finally splitting the rent with the federal agencies interested in the man because the surveillance had become a joke, but it kept the man living in a fishbowl.

The doors opened again at a hallway filled with lush tropical plants and a humidity to make them comfortable.

Traven politely refused the woman's offer to take his duster.

She led him through a winding hallway that abruptly ended up in the pool area on the northeast side of the building. Technically, the whole floor was the penthouse and was owned by Escobar, but he had turned it into a palatial estate.

Ceramic tile colored a half-dozen shades of light purple decorated the walls of the pool room. Two wet bars stood in opposite corners with liveried bartenders serving the collection of at least thirty guests, most of whom were beautiful women in the scantiest of swimwear. Traven figured *Sports Illustrated* could have done its annual swimsuit issue with this evening's guest list.

Marble statues of nudes stood eternally waiting around the sunken pool area. Marble columns were set against the two walls not constructed of bulletproof and polarized glass. Rain fell against the glass section of roof overhead, then sluiced down specially constructed gutters to splash visibly down the sides of the building.

Evaristo Escobar held court on a raised dais on the outer tier of the swimming pool area proper. He sat, relaxed in a chaise longue, a large, flat-bellied man with dark skin, and a hairy chest and abdomen, dressed in a maroon velour robe and sandals. His head was round, bald except for the sides, where close-cropped black hair grew. A broad mustache seemed to grow out of his large bent nose. His eyes looked like holes that had been punched into his face with a blunt awl.

The cartel man smiled and waved Traven on up.

A bikini-clad blond waitress who jiggled as she walked stopped in front of Traven with a silver tray covered with glasses and gave him an earnest smile. "Can I get you something to drink?"

"Sure. How about an orange juice?"

"Nothing alcoholic?"

"I'd rather remember how you look when I leave."

She dimpled at his words, then disappeared in the maze of seminaked people.

Traven took the cut steps leading up to Escobar's arena. Three men wearing light jackets and bathing trunks wandered in from different directions till the cartel man waved them away.

Escobar stood and offered Traven a nearby chair. He smiled. "I would offer to shake your hand, Detective Traven, was I not sure what your response would be. I'd rather this be as painless as possible, and having injured feelings would do neither of us any good."

Traven sat on the edge of the lawn chair and briefly inspected the view of the pool area and the overview of the lighted city.

"Is someone getting you something to drink?"

"Yes."

"Good. I wouldn't want you to be any more uncomfortable than you already feel.'' Escobar plucked a glass with fruit and a pink umbrella in it from a small stand and sipped through the straw.

The blonde reappeared with the silver tray and the orange juice. Traven took it when it was offered.

''You don't have to worry about anything being put in the drink,'' Escobar said.

''I know. It's not your style.''

Escobar's grin was genuine.

As the time before, Traven couldn't help but like the guy's surface character to a degree. Escobar had his own set of rules concerning life, and he never broke one of them. In a society where it seemed individuals dumped rules on a daily basis, it was one trait that made Escobar respectable. At a certain level.

Escobar said, ''Since we are moved by totally different pursuits and motivations, I find us curiously lacking something to toast.''

Holding up his glass, Traven said, ''To Herve Wilcoxin's fastball.''

Escobar laughed. ''Ah, yes, we do have that in common, I suppose.''

''Vice usually gets some choice seats behind your box,'' Traven replied. ''I watched some good baseball while watching you.'' He sipped his orange juice.

Escobar sipped his own. ''When this season opens up, I would offer you a seat with me. That way you could do your watching in the comfort of air conditioning.''

''That would make my boss frown.''

''He hasn't learned to trust you?''

''He hasn't learned to trust anyone.''

''And what will he say about tonight's meeting?''

''Nothing if he doesn't find out about it.''

''But you came here willing to take the risk.''

''Yes.''

Escobar took a long green cigar from a box, offered it to Traven, who declined, then licked it, snipped the end from it with a small scissors, and lit it, expelling great clouds of blue-gray smoke. ''I'd heard you'd been transferred out of vice.''

"You heard right." Traven met the black-eyed stare evenly through the smoke.

"Your successor hasn't been named yet."

"Expect it any day."

"So, if you're not with vice anymore, what brings you here?"

"Luis Ochoa."

Escobar shook his head as he rounded the ash end of the cigar in a large green glass tray. "Not of my doing."

"He's your boy."

"Was. The operative word is *was*."

"What happened?"

Escobar blew out a plume of smoke. "Therein lies a tale."

Traven spread his hands, keeping them close to the pockets of the duster. "Tonight I have the time."

Escobar gave the appearance of considering that. "Do you remember the last time you spoke with me, Detective Traven?"

"Yes."

"That was one year, four months, and twelve days ago." Escobar eyed him in frank black speculation. "You promised that no matter what it took on your behalf, you would see me deported, dead, or behind bars before you quit your job. And I believed you meant it."

"I still do."

"I believe you." Escobar sipped his drink again, then watched the bikini-clad beauties parading around the pool before him with unseeing eyes. "That was the same night you'd lost one of your men to men in my employ. Despite cosmetech techniques, you still wear the scar on your face that you yourself received."

Traven didn't say anything.

"Why?"

"To remind me how easy it was to think I had planned for everything."

"A bitter experience, I'm sure."

"I learned from it."

"Yes. I suppose you did. You've become a very challenging opponent since that time."

Traven let it pass.

"So, I suppose you have everything planned for this evening?"

"Well enough."

Escobar nodded. "And now here we are again."

"Yes."

"Wanting me to help you?"

"I think it's a matter of helping each other."

"And you would do that?"

"The enemy you know is better than the one you don't."

Escobar laughed again, an easy explosion of sound. He crooked a finger at one of the waitresses and ordered another round of drinks. "By God, Traven, I like you. It will really sadden me to see you go down before a gun some night."

"If you're there to see it, chances are you'll be arrested for my murder and, at the very least, deported."

"True."

The waitress delivered the drinks and left after collecting the empty glasses.

One of the body guards stepped forward and whispered into Escobar's ear, pointing.

Traven followed the line of the finger and saw the young man bearing down on them at once.

Escobar rubbed a hand across his mouth, the easygoing demeanor dropping from his features instantly.

The young man was lean and nut-brown, dark hair falling to his shoulders. Gun and knife scars marked his hairy body above and below the gold-and-white bathing trunks. His face showed anger, and he spoke with an accent. "So, this is the policeman who has been causing so many difficulties in this city, Uncle?"

Without looking at Traven, Escobar said, "You'll have to excuse my nephew. He forgets whose house he is in, and forgets that an honorable man doesn't plot to kill those under his roof while they are there."

"Bah. You and your honor. You are sitting beside

one of the men most responsible for destroying our hold here, yet you do nothing with him. Your weakness embarrasses the rest of the family.''

The bodyguards moved in quickly.

Escobar waved them away, and sat forward on the chaise longue, black eyes fired with excitement. ''You would kill him then, Pablo? Kill him here in this house and allow yourself to be deported and lose your ability to run things with your own eyes, your own hands?''

''I would have one of my men do it. Then he would be deported.'' Pablo glared at Traven.

Heart beating with the tension of the moment, Traven set his glass down beside him, not taking his eyes off the younger Escobar clan member.

''You've not long been in this country, nephew. Things are not always handled with a gun or knife or bomb in this land. There has to exist a certain amount of cunning and subterfuge. You have learned neither.''

Pablo shook a gnarled fist at the older man. ''I've not learned to bow before these people, if that's what you mean.''

''You're a fool.''

''I could kill him for you now and be done with it.'' Pablo took a step forward.

Traven dipped a hand inside the duster, not knowing which way things would go.

''Stop!'' Escobar commanded as he held up a hand. ''Another step and I will have you shot myself before your stupidity gets us both killed.''

Traven studied the alcohol-inflamed eyes. The man teetered on the brink of obedience or disobedience.

''You think this man would come to my house,'' Escobar said, ''knowing what he does of me without some way to tilt the odds in his favor?''

Pablo said nothing.

''If he moves,'' Escobar said to the guards, ''shoot him dead.''

Pablo blinked.

''Detective Traven, show this impetuous idiot that

you are not to be taken lightly.'' Escobar leaned back in his seat, gazing contemptuously into the younger man's face.

Traven held up his empty hand and signaled.

25

Three ruby dots the size of dimes appeared on Pablo Escobar's hairy chest. Two others, staggered one above the other, decorated the darker red fabric of Evaristo Escobar's robe. The discomfiture that fitted itself over the cartel man's face was amusing despite the tension of the situation, but Traven kept the grin to himself.

Having made their point, the laser sights faded away.

Escobar sipped his drink. He addressed Pablo. "Leave us. You have embarrassed me enough."

Shaking with restrained rage, the younger Escobar turned and left the room, brushing forcefully past another of the waitresses. Her silver serving tray toppled. Broken glass crashed against the purple tiles. The waitress stamped her foot angrily, then went to get a hand-vac from the nearest wet bar.

"This," Escobar said derisively, "is the future of my country. Not a pretty thought, is it?"

"Neither is the thought of the coca still being produced in your country," Traven replied.

Escobar shook his head. "You didn't come here to discuss politics, and you know that the production of coca leaves in my country is the only thing left to us after the rest of the world has left South America economically barren. We cannot subsist on the earning power of Juan Valdez alone." He flashed a quick smile. "And already the Japanese markets are coming up with imports of their own. Ice and red satin have taken a big chunk of the consumers available to our kind of recreation."

"There's still plenty to go around," Traven said, "as long as you keep opening your doors to children."

"The American government leaders have to take responsibility for much of that. Since the Japanese economic takeover, they don't retain enough of their future to offer anything to their children. They auctioned it off a piece at a time, sold out to the highest bidder, yet no one bothered to stop them or yell foul." Escobar turned over empty hands. "I sell dreams, limited ones, of course, and, like everything else, they have the taint of death. Even you, Detective Traven, cannot say that death has not touched you. The media call you a killer cop because of your recent successes. I'm surprised some enterprising soul hasn't thought of offering T-shirts with a still of you carrying Donny Quarters's bagman's head. There are those out there who would buy something like that, you know."

Realizing the argument was an endless one, Traven retreated. That was a battle to be fought out on the streets, not in conversation. He said, "Luis Ochoa."

Escobar settled back in his chair. "He's working for Quarters these days. And he isn't the first in my organization to defect."

"Why?"

Laughing harshly, Escobar said, "Because the grass is greener on the other side of the fence now. Quarters holds all the aces. But only for the time being."

"Because of his relationship with the Yakuza?"

Escobar traced the rim of his glass with his fingers. "You are a good street man, Detective, and have keener instincts than many men I have faced. Were it otherwise, you would have been dead long before now."

Traven unconsciously traced the scar on his face, caught himself, and put his hand away.

"When was the first time you were aware of the connection between Quarters and the Yaks?" Escobar asked.

"Friday night."

"I knew three weeks before that." Escobar turned on the chaise longue and dropped his feet to the tiled floor as he faced Traven. "But the only reason I learned of their involvement was that my people were directly involved. Three weeks ago, I lost a sizable shipment through my channels in Panama. You know what my agents reported to me?"

Traven shook his head, almost mesmerized by the whispering voice the man used.

"I was told ninjas took the shipment before they had cleared the Panamanian harbor. Ninjas." Escobar sipped his drink. "These people used some kind of minisub, spoofed the radar and ship's computers on the freighter transporting the shipment, and came aboard in the dead of night. Most of the twenty-three ship's members were killed with sword, arrow, or knife. Only one of the ninjas was killed in retaliation. When they stripped the body, they found the traditional Yak tattoos covering all but the man's hands, feet, neck, and face. We ran the fingerprints, the retina prints, the DNA core sample, and came up with nothing. In this age of documentation upon documentation, we'd found a man who did not exist."

"How did you know about the connection with Quarters?"

"Two more such raids occurred, with more accuracy than I cared to believe possible through luck. I began an investigation of my own, using the eyes and ears I have bought and paid for on the street. A week ago I tracked a rumor of an information leak to one of my agents, a man I thought above reproach. It took a while, but I persuaded him to tell me the truth."

Traven couldn't help wondering if the man's body would turn up soon.

"The Yaks had gotten to this man of mine, had threatened his family if he didn't provide them with the information they wanted."

"What happened when he disappeared?"

"The Yaks killed his family, of course." Escobar sipped his drink.

Feeling his stomach turn despite his efforts to control his reaction, Traven glanced out at the rain-covered walls. A woman dove from the diving board and lost her bright-colored top the instant she hit the water. The crowd around the pool roared its approval.

"You look surprised," Escobar said.

"You let those people be killed." Traven's voice was hard and flat.

"I was sorry to do so, but it was a necessary thing. I had to find out if this man was telling the truth."

"No one tried to stop it?"

"My men?" Escobar shook his head. "No, that would have confirmed to the Yaks that I had discovered them."

"They didn't know you had tumbled to their guy?"

"No. His departure was made to look like a planned one. A plane ticket was purchased in his name, easily found in a search of air traffic computer records, and he vanished."

Traven realized he was also being told the death of the man, even if he could come across a name, could not be tied back to Escobar. It also let him know there probably wouldn't be a body.

"The next day, following up on information we retrieved from my betrayer, one of Donny Quarters's dealers was relieved of his life and his product. When we ran it through spectroanalysis, we discovered it was part of one of the stolen shipments. Quarters is selling what they can steal from me, as well as being backed up by a new supplier."

"How do you know that?"

"Because I do. The people who were supplying Quarters are no longer doing so. They approached me, seeking someone who could arrange transportation to the United States. They have product, but they have no way to get it to optimum selling points. I declined. At least until I figure out a way to see myself clear of the present situation."

Traven considered Friday night's bust again and tried to figure what Quarters had in his possession that would interest the Yak faction. "Quarters isn't just the front man on a Yak operation. Whatever his bagman was carrying that night, it was enough to make the Yak team take the guy's head."

"I heard about that."

"So what does he have to sell?"

Escobar shrugged. "From what little I've learned, Quarters had been scoring some high-priced tech."

"How high-priced?"

"Maybe even from Nagamuchi."

"That's pretty big for someone like Quarters."

"So is the distribution system being set up by the Yaks." Escobar flagged down a waitress.

"And if they've been able to take over as Quarters's suppliers, that means they've got a source of their own to move the stuff inside the country."

"That's exactly what I've been thinking."

Traven lifted an eyebrow.

"But I can't find out a goddam thing."

"It must be a pretty substantial connection," Traven said as he took the orange juice the waitress handed him. "Or would three heists from you be enough to cover his action?"

"Seven," Escobar corrected. "As of yesterday. And no, they would not be enough. Enough to damage my delivery credibility with my customers, yes, and cost me business, but not enough to cover everything. Quarters's men have already hustled some of my distribution points as well as my men. I wouldn't hesitate to say that at this time, Quarters controls eighty percent of the traffic flowing through your city, Detective Traven. And it doesn't end there. I've received information that his setup is reaching across at least a handful of state borders."

"It sounds like he was stepped up into a made-to-order situation."

"Doesn't it?" Escobar shifted restlessly, as if the subject matter was finally wearing thin. "That's why I've been wondering about your replacement."

"Why?"

"You have your own honor, a code you live by. Sure, it gets you in trouble occasionally and doesn't answer all questions, but you would rather have it than not have it. You understand these things internally, without so many words, and more than someone like Pablo ever will.'' Escobar fixed him with a black stare. ''Would you ever think of selling out?''

''No.''

''I believe you. Otherwise I would have refused to talk to you tonight.''

''Have you heard that vice is selling out?'' Traven tried to clamp down on the sudden fear that left cold knots in his stomach, thinking of men like Kowalski who would rather be killed than go on the pad.

''Not yet. But you are no longer there now.''

Traven was silent.

''So, perhaps we do have something in common now besides our love of baseball. Donny Quarters has become a threat to both of us.'' Escobar raised his glass in a salute. ''Together, perhaps we can remove that threat.''

Traven shook his head. ''Not if Quarters owns eighty percent of the market. If I managed to take him down cold, that would leave an awful big vacuum waiting for someone else to come along and take over the reins of the biggest dirty empire this city has ever seen.''

''You forget: It's already out there.''

''I don't intend to just change the faces when the time comes to close down Quarters's business.''

''When that day comes, I'd say we'll have divergent business interests,'' Escobar stated in a calm voice.

''And till then?''

''I'll let you know anything I find out. Like you, Detective Traven, I also find the most dangerous enemy to be the one I don't know.''

Traven finished the orange juice and stood up, leaving the empty glass on the chair arm. ''What if the Yaks had approached you?''

Escobar shrugged and smiled. ''But they didn't, did they? We represent different producers, different interests. This is just like buying up outlying shares in a corporation: a hostile takeover. Only instead of shares, Donny Quarters and the Yaks are dealing in lives.''

Traven nodded. ''Thanks for the drink.''

Escobar snapped his fingers, and one of the guards

came forward. "Miguel will follow you to the door, in case Pablo behaves even more foolishly than he has. Wouldn't do to have to explain to your captain why you shot a man on my premises."

"No," Traven said with a small, tight grin, "no, it wouldn't at all."

26

"What's this?" Earl Brandstetter asked. He slid his fingers across the wrinkle on one perfect shoulder.

She smiled up at him, taking his hand away and giving him a glass. They were in the drawing room, a fire crackling in the fireplace, the smell of hickory lingering in the air, and working on sexual satiation. She wore a loose white robe that barely concealed Nami Chikara's gifts.

Following the pull of her small hand, Brandstetter walked around her and sat cross-legged on the bearskin rug before her. He wore sweatpants and went without a shirt. Another wrinkle between her breasts drew his attention, and he reached for it.

Mistaking his curiosity as sexual interest, she ran her free hand down his arm, cooing and closing her eyes.

Normally her behavior would have ignited another round of passion, except this wrinkle looked worse than the other one. It felt rough under his fingers. He plucked at it. Skin ripped, peeling away in a great flap to reveal the other skin beneath. Paralyzed by the sudden tearing, he yanked his hand away and spilled his drink.

She blinked her eyes in Nami Chikara's face and looked at him in perplexity. Then she glanced down at her breasts. She hurled her glass toward the fire as she stood up, the analog alcohol creating a brief blue explosion as if it had been the real thing. "Damn you,

Earl!'' She walked away from him and leaned against one of the bookshelves.

"What the hell is happening?'' His voice constricted in his throat.

The sound of harsh, barking laughter cut through the sound of crying. She whirled around to face him, her mouth stretched to laugh beneath eyes bright with tears. "Surely you didn't think these things would last forever.'' She pulled at the loose flap, tearing more skin, revealing more of herself. The robe fell away.

"What are you talking about?''

Her smile was suddenly her smile again, not Nami Chikara's. More cracks spread across her face. "This is only temporary,'' she said in a more subdued voice. She indicated her body, already pulling the outer skin apart at the seams as she added height. She threw a whole hand into the fire. It sizzled as it lay on a burning log. "It won't last. It can't. This is something we created together, and no matter how hard we tried, we couldn't hold it together.''

He stood frozen, staring at her, watching her emerge from Nami Chikara like a shedding snake. Her skin glistened, as if covered with oil.

She pulled the face off, taking the blistered hair with it, tossing it into the fire without looking. It hissed and spit and popped. The hair moved like a live thing dying. "This one's done well for us,'' she said in a soft voice. She tore the torso away. "But we're going to need another body for our love.''

He knew he couldn't deny her. Her wants were his.

"You know the one I want next.''

"Yes.''

27

Traven kept his duster on to cover his pistol rather than checking it at the door. Robin Benedict waited impatiently in the restaurant's foyer, looking out of place in the junglelike surroundings of floor-to-ceiling plants. Neither he nor the reporter was dressed in accordance with the shirt-and-tie clientele that took the restaurant's noon meal. Benedict folded the appointment book he'd been studying and joined Traven as the hostess came forward.

"Will you be dining with us?" the hostess asked. She wore an imitation tiger skin that, even with the tail, almost failed to cover her breasts and buttocks completely.

"No," Benedict said. "Just drinks, thanks."

"Yes," Traven said. "A table for two, please."

The hostess nodded, took two menus from the desk, and led the way into the dark restaurant. The dangling tail emphasized the side-to-side movement of her hips. She stopped at a table along the wall and spread the menus. "What can I get you to drink?"

"Coffee," Traven replied as he slid out of the duster and palmed the SIG/Sauer so it remained hidden but accessible even when he folded the garment on the booth beside him.

"Double bourbon," Benedict said as he took a seat opposite. He glanced purposefully at Traven. "I'm not working this afternoon."

The hostess nodded and moved away.

Benedict laced his fingers together, fitted them under his chin, and rested his elbows on the table. "So what's the story?"

"You always in this much of a hurry?" Traven asked.

"When it's news, yeah. The time it takes you to tell it, it's already old."

"This time you're getting advance copy."

The nonchalance evaporated from Benedict's face and left a hard, predatory sheen. "You cracked the murder? You know how the guy got around the AI security?"

"No."

Benedict slumped back in the booth in open disgust. "Come on, now is not the time to be jacking me off about this shit. Do you know how hot this story is?"

"It's on every channel I've seen so far," Traven said, "but I don't watch much television."

"You're goddam right it's on every channel. It's getting the media attention it deserves. Do you know how many people out there in America viewing land are feeling less secure in their homes now because of what happened to that woman?"

Anger surged in Traven. "Nami Chikara."

"What?" Benedict was perplexed.

"Her name. She had a name. And a family."

Benedict produced a microrecorder. "Anybody local? Be a great human-interest story."

"No."

"I didn't think so. Somebody else would have covered it by now anyway."

The waitress returned with the drinks and set them down.

Traven sipped his coffee and found it too hot. He pushed it aside.

"So what's this advance copy I'm getting?" Benedict asked.

"Patience."

"That's not a virtue in the news business. Anybody else got a line on this advance copy of yours?"

"No."

"Not even your supervisors?"

Traven shook his head.

Benedict leaned forward and whispered, "You're holding back from your own department?"

"Not quite. I just did a little more digging than the surface effort they're willing to do."

"And you know who the killer is?"

"No."

"Then tell me what the hell it is we're dealing with here." Benedict looked exasperated.

Traven grinned at the reporter's seriousness, feeling some relief from the weight his decision had caused within him. In a way, it felt like betraying the department, because he knew how the media would depict it. In fact, he counted on the predictable enmity between the media stations and government bureaucracy to achieve the results he wanted. The problem was, it was also the only way he had of getting his job done. And his job was the most important thing to him, because if he didn't or couldn't do it, someone else got hurt by the very people he pursued on a daily basis.

A waitress came by to take their order.

"I don't have time to eat," Benedict protested.

Traven ordered two steaks, baked potatoes, salad. As the waitress walked away, he said, "I'll make a deal with you. If you don't think the story's worth it, I'll pay for dinner. If it is, you pay."

"Sold," the reporter said. "If it's worth it, I can put it on my expense account. So give."

"What do you know about the investigation?" Traven sipped the coffee again and found it cooler.

Benedict counted off points on his fingers. "I know that the woman was killed by someone using techware to spoof AI security that's supposed to be unbeatable. I know the corporations that develop, manufacture, and market the AI security packets are busy pointing the finger at each other, disclaiming fault. I know there are a lot of people out there who are convinced the government has secretly encoded passwords to let government employees in and out of residences without knowledge of the homeowner. I know the woman was a geisha in the employ of Taira Yorimasa, who is a big mucky-muck of Nagamuchi Towers.''

"Vice president in charge of security."

Benedict shrugged. "So we got a security tie-in. What are we going to do with it?''

"I was told not to interfere with Nagamuchi operations."

"Isn't everybody?" Benedict grinned.

"They're not allowing me to do my job."

"So that's what this is about? You getting your nose slammed in the door?''

Irritation flared inside Traven, because he'd asked himself that same question before being sure of his motives. It was a surface judgment a lot of people were going to make. "No. This is about getting to the truth and finding the man who murdered Nami Chikara.''

"And you think it might have been Yorimasa?"

"I don't know, but I want the chance to find out."

Benedict drummed his fingers on the table. "Look, I can see a human-interest story looming on the horizon here. Beef it up a little, of course. Hero cop seeks vengeance for slain maiden, that kind of thing. It would be interesting, but it's too much like movie-of-the-week hype. But even at its best presentation, the story would splash and die, with hardly a ripple left behind.''

The waitress arrived with their plates, set them out with practiced ease, then left.

Traven picked up his knife and fork and started working on the steak.

"Where's your partner?" Benedict asked. "I heard you'd been paired with Lloyd Higham."

"He's working the apartment building where Chikara was killed. Marking time to fill out reports.''

"You don't think he'll find anything there?"

"Did any of your guys?"

"No."

"And you had more manpower to put on it. To the homicide division, it was one more dirty little murder to file along with the rest.''

"But the techware used—"

"Doesn't factor in. To the media, Nami Chikara's death was a gold mine of sensationalism."

"It was news," Benedict said defensively.

"It was turned into a circus."

The reporter was silent for a moment. "You don't care for the media much, do you?"

"No."

"Then why are you here?"

Traven smiled. "Because I trust you. Because I had nowhere else to turn. And because, despite all its other failings, the media can sometimes make the impossible possible."

Benedict made a casual circle with his lettuce-studded fork. "All this mystery, folks, with a smidgen of philosophy thrown in for good measure."

"What would you think," Traven asked, "if you found out Yorimasa had a past history of violence with his murdered geisha and no one stepped forward to volunteer the information?"

"Does he?" Benedict put his fork down and turned on the microrecorder.

Traven reached across and switched it off. "This is off the record or it's not happening."

"Shit! You do have something, don't you? I was beginning to believe you were just stringing me along."

"What would you think?"

"I'd think it was a goddam cover-up, of course."

"The deal is, you don't say where you got this." Traven took the papers Zenzo had given him that morning from an inside pocket of the duster. They'd been folded in half and rubber-banded.

"I can protect my source, no problem," Benedict said as he took the papers. He pulled them down to his lap to read, reminding Traven of a little boy looking at something he wasn't supposed to.

The waitress came and left a smile and the ticket.

"Shit," Benedict said. "This is good, this is really good. You're going to be headliner news tonight, buddy. A goddam corporate cover-up. This is the kind of stuff that made Quirita the legend in the news world she is. You could have gone to her with something like this instead of me.'' He clenched the papers as if suddenly afraid Traven would change his mind.

''I don't know Quirita,'' Traven said, working on the baked potato. ''I know you.''

''Actually,'' Benedict said, ''I'm safer than Quirita. Once she gets the smell of a story up her nose, there's no stopping her. No matter who gets hurt. She'd burn you in a minute if it would call more attention to her story.''

Traven didn't think it was true. Quirita was a freelance reporter, covering what she wanted to, and earning enough at it to afford an affluent life in what remained of Occidental Highland Park. Her word had to be her bond and her destination had to be the truth. But he didn't say anything. Media work was just as nerve-racking as police work, with trust and innocence being the first on the casualty list.

''So how do you want to work your side of the story into this?'' Benedict asked.

''I'll leave that up to you. I want back on the case. I'm still a cop looking for a killer.''

''Despite overwhelming odds.'' Benedict grinned. ''It's still movie-of-the-week stuff, but we're channeling it right along toward the feature slot. Got a lot of promise here.''

Traven smiled, picked up the ticket, and shoved it into Benedict's shirt pocket. ''I think so too.''

The mobile phone in the Cherokee rang while Traven was still in the restaurant's parking lot. He scooped it up, thinking it was Higham wondering where the hell he was. ''Traven.''

''Wait,'' a rough male voice instructed.

The next voice was easily recognizable as belonging to Donny Quarters. ''We need to meet to clear up some stuff,'' Quarters said without preamble. ''You pick the spot.''

Traven pulled to the side and let the car following him go by. ''Why do we need to talk?''

"I think it's in both our best interests. No sense in anybody else getting hurt in this thing if we can work out an amicable relationship."

"I'm not looking for a relationship," Traven replied, "amicable or otherwise."

Quarters sucked in his breath. There was a pause, then, "What can you lose?"

Traven thought the answer to that was obvious.

"Look, you name the place, the time. I'll be there. Won't be any tricks."

"That'll be a first."

There was another pause.

Traven pondered that. The Donny Quarters he knew would have blown up at the insult. Curiosity filled him.

"Still want that meet," Quarters said in a patient tone that was even more mystifying.

"Tabasco's. Eight o'clock. I won't be alone."

The connection clicked dead in his ear.

Wondering if he would live to regret the decision, Traven hung up and pulled into traffic.

28

Keyed into the building's AI, Earl Brandstetter knew his prey was at home. His pulse beat quickly within him, outpaced by the savage thrill of the cyberlink. He was more attuned to the unrealities that swam around him this time, more able to establish the differences between computer life and real life, still able to hold his place in both.

He left the maintenance corridor and moved down the hallway silently. He wore black, hardly noticeable in the weak glow of the substandard security lights. The building super knew the security AI would trigger a discrepancy if one of the lights blew, but also knew a low-wattage bulb would reduce cost and still make the AI think everything operated at peak capacity.

The door slid aside and allowed him to enter as the elevator opened and drunken voices were released in the hall.

Once inside the apartment, he tugged the mask from his pocket and started to pull it over his head. He paused before slipping it over his nose. He flared his nostrils out and sucked in the smells of the apartment. They were all familiar odors, ghosts of a past he'd longed for and never had.

Camille Estevan had been a longtime passion of his, had plagued many midnight imaginings in his bed only to end in wet dreams. She hadn't been all that attractive. The women on wallscreen were much better. But while he'd lived in the building with her, it had seemed for a while that she was so close to being his.

He'd even forgiven her for all the other men she'd constantly brought into her home, forgiven her for all the passion she'd expended in their arms. He'd memorized her routine perfectly. Many times he'd caught her wrapped in a bathrobe a half hour after she'd arrived home, the hot shower water dappling her exposed skin. He knew she took hot showers, because he'd been there a few times when someone called and had taken the opportunity to look over her bathroom. The walls had been steam-covered, the shower stall fogged. Pink frogs made of a dozen different materials had perched all over the bathroom. He still didn't know what her fascination with them was. He'd never had the chance to let her know he'd seen the bathroom.

If it hadn't been for the last time he'd seen her, for the hurtful words she'd said, he was sure he could have forgiven her for anything. Maybe, if his mother hadn't wanted her, he might have been able to let her live awhile longer.

With the mask in place, satiated with the soup smells and familiar soapy odor that clung to the living-room carpet, he reached into the AI's programming and switched on the recording equipment. The wallscreen halted in the middle of some evening soap opera, blurred, then focused on him standing just inside the doorway.

In the black clothes with the specialized programming from the biochip in his head taking control, his image looked like a bent and twisted and splintered thing conjured from the dank depths of nightmare. He smiled, unable to see it under the mask. There was a crooked man. The time in the upper left corner of the wallscreen said 7:42 P.M. He paused long enough to dump the cigarette butts he'd collected a few moments earlier from the street into the ashtray on the chipped coffee table. Only her brand had been in it previously.

Curious, confident of his freedom, he walked through the kitchen. Dirty dishes filled the sink. He stepped on a fork before he saw it, then picked it up and put it with the other dishes. Fast-food cartons covered most of the available counter space. The scent of something rotting crept from behind the refrigerator. Cockroaches moved in a wave from him. They had been in his apartment when he'd lived there as well. Nothing short of nuclear weapons would have eradicated them permanently. And the building would have to be shorn down to keep them from coming back.

Before a particularly large cockroach could move from the counter, Brandstetter reached out and smashed it under a gloved thumb. The carapace gave way with audible cracklings. He smiled again at the noise. He flipped the dead body into the sink, knowing its brothers and sisters would find it soon and devour it as they had everything else that couldn't escape their greedy little mouths.

He started to look for a weapon, noticing for the first time the nervous tension had left him and he was looking forward to what would happen next. He shook his head. He should have known to expect this. She'd told him this would happen. He rummaged through the dirty dishes.

Camille Estevan rolled over on the bed uncomfortably, the broken spring digging into her thigh. She moved the leg, then regretted it instantly when the headache rocked to new life. The sour taint of sex still lingered in the bedroom. She felt for the man, but he was already gone. For a moment she felt angry, then gave it up as wasted emotion. She tried to remember his name and couldn't. He'd just been some guy from the streets, looking to make it through till tomorrow by surviving the night. He'd had a few flics of red satin. The headache told her that. She got those kinds of headaches only from doing red satin.

Dark light from the wallscreen stained the ceiling with garish shadows and drew her attention to the fact that she was trying to go back to sleep.

"Screen off," she whispered to the AI while rolling over and burying her face in the crook of her elbow. She rested her eyes for a moment, then blinked them open as sleepless frustration overtook her. She'd been going strong for the last forty-eight hours, hardly paused long enough to catch catnaps.

The wallscreen was still on.

"Screen off," she repeated in a louder voice.

Nothing happened.

Wondering if the AI had finally gone on the fritz and where she'd get the extra money to fix it, she looked at the wallscreen to see if it was one of those IF THIS WAS A REAL EMERGENCY tests that occasionally woke her. It took a moment for the scene depicted there to register. Her eyes were still bleary from the drug.

The focus of the wallscreen kept playing over her kitchen in a systematic search. Black gloved hands that looked thin and fat and warped and shattered kept pawing through things. Her breath tried to catch deep in her throat. She got up silently from bed, forgetting about rubbing the sore spot on her thigh, unable to take her eyes from the wallscreen. She knelt to lift her abandoned robe from the floor and shrug into it. She felt cold. Her skin rippled in prickly goosebumps.

It was her kitchen.

The thought hammered into her aching head.

Onscreen, the pantry door opened and exposed the row of knives hanging there. Most of the spots were empty. The knives had been lost or lent or left somewhere in the living room or under the clutter of the fast-food cartons. The focus zoomed in on one knife near the end. It had a thick handle, a broad blade, and she could still feel/remember the cut it had given her last summer when it had slipped in her hands and sliced her palm. It looked smooth, but it felt jagged.

A black-gloved hand—thin and spidery—reached out and took it from the mounting bracket. The pantry door closed. The perspective of the wallscreen changed, moved from the kitchen to the hallway leading to the bedroom.

She glanced at the bedroom door. It was closed. Moving frantically, she crossed the room and shot the bolt. A mewling scream died unborn in her lungs.

The wallscreen filled with the sight of the closed

door. The sense of motion ended. She tried to scream
again, only managed a small squeak. A black-gloved
hand that pulsed like a jellyfish pushed at the door as
if testing it. The glint of the doorbolt showed it had
moved.

The screams came then, and she knew they would
be heard. The walls were too thin. It was nothing to
become intimate with the neighbors if they raised their
voices above normal speaking range. In this building
that was a common occurrence.

She ran for the window and tried to release it. It
wouldn't move.

Someone kicked the door, and screws whined as
they pulled loose.

She scooped one of her boots from the side of the
bed, covered her face with her free arm, then smashed
the glass out with the boot. Jagged pieces of the window scattered inside the bedroom as well as splinter-
ing on the rusting iron fire escape snaking down the
outside of the building.

She cut her hands trying to throw a leg over the
window as the door broke free.

Brandstetter moved instantly as the door crashed inward. He gripped the long knife in his hand, blade
down. Camille Estevan was trying to get through the
window. His breath rattled through his throat, came
out in an animal whine that he didn't recognize as
belonging to him at first.

He grabbed her by the wrist and spun her around to
face him, away from the window and the fire escape.
"Bitch!" he growled. "Bitchbitchbitchbitch!" He
emphasized the words with slashes of the knife, guided
it to cut deep, felt it grate along bone.

He slashed her more deeply than he'd ever dared
dream. And her face showed that he was getting more
real emotion out of her than he had at any time before.

She tried to scream at him, to tell him to stop.

He smashed her lips with his fist and the hilt of the
knife. Blood sprayed anew, came from a dozen cuts
or more. He did not count them, just relished the feel

of the knife blasting home. She couldn't ignore him now.

When she fell to the floor, he picked her up by the hair and walked her to the wallscreen, using the AI and the biochip to give her a close-up view of herself. The robe flapped open, stained dark by the blood, and exposed the stained body beneath. She tried to fight him.

He pulled her head back and bared her throat. For a moment the temptation to rip the mask off and sink his teeth into her flesh thundered through his head. He forced it away. The knife made a hard, thin line across her neck that wept solid sheets of blood.

He dropped her as the life kicked out of her body. The knife stuck point-first in the worn carpet.

Someone rattled the front door and called Camille Estevan's name.

Brandstetter knelt on his hands and knees, blood heavy on his clothing. He stared into the fogged eyes as the last flickerings of life disappeared. Then, knowing he was in danger of being discovered, he crawled through the shattered window, took the fire escape down to the street, and let the hard black wind cutting through the city blow him into the shadows.

29

Tabasco's occupied the top four floors of a refurbished high-rise in the heart of the old downtown Dallas business district. Traven arrived at 7:56 P.M., left the 4×4 in the underground garage, and took the elevator tube up. He stepped out into a wall of music and smoke and loud voices. The decor was chic and shiny. The hostess who met him to collect the cover charge was svelte, her enthusiastic smile firmly in place. After paying, he stopped by the main bar to pick up a draw beer, then walked toward the wallscreen room, where raucous shouts cheered as Monday Night Football came on.

As he sat at a table near a window providing a southern view of the city, Traven felt the frustration of the day wash over him and leave a film of disgust. After returning from lunch with Robin Benedict, he'd spent the rest of the work day interviewing apartment residents about the neighbor most of them didn't know. It had been an exercise in futility. The ones that did know Nami Chikara's life-style weren't talking because they lived the same life-style. A geisha didn't talk about corporate business. And Traven had the feeling someone had put out the word that Nami Chikara's murder was definitely corporate business.

He sipped his beer, tried in vain to switch his mind to the colorfully clad players strung out in formation across the wallscreen. The ball was snapped and the battle began with an explosion of contact. The padded body armor the players wore splatted with express-train impact. Muffled curses squirted through the speakers between cries of pain and rage.

Donny Quarters entered the room with a small entourage. The trafficker waved the three men to a table by themselves, then crossed the floor and slid into the booth opposite Traven. He was a large man with a beefy build. If he'd lost fifty pounds in the right places, he could have taken his place up there with the other steroid giants on the wallscreen. He wore his blond hair in a ponytail in the back and cut almost to the skin on the sides. The hair on top looked as if a shaggy animal had crawled up there and died. His face was florid, the nostrils too wide, the forehead too low and thick. His clothing and jewelry spoke of money. Rings flashed on his hands as he cracked his knuckles.

"You here alone?" Quarters asked, not taking his eyes from the wallscreen.

"No."

Quarters nodded. "Just wondered. I didn't see Kowalski around anywhere."

"He's not here to be seen."

"You don't trust me, do you, kid?"

Traven didn't flinch from the inquiring stare. "No."

"I guess liking me is out of the picture, huh?" Quarters's laugh sounded as if it came from the bottom of an incinerator tube.

"So is respect."

Quarters leveled a forefinger at him. "You're a punk, kid, and nothing but. You might think you're one slick number, but to me you're just like any two-bit street hustler trying to put the arm on Donny Quarters."

"Somebody's put the arm on you," Traven replied. "Somebody's made you toe the mark. This new you I'm seeing makes me wonder who that somebody is."

"You're wrong about that, pally." Quarters's lips firmed into a thin white line. "Just got a new perspective on the business end of things. That's all. You come under the heading of business now. And a good businessman never mixes business with pleasure."

"What's pleasure to a businessman like you?" Traven asked sarcastically.

Quarters grinned. "Stomping the face in of a guy that was as big a pain in the butt as you are."

"But now I'm business?"

"Yeah."

"Who made me business?" Traven asked. "You? Or your partners? I'm betting on your partners. Intelligence is a little out of your line."

Quarters snorted in exasperation. "You don't know when to quit pushing, do you, Traven?" He made a fist and shoved it forward, holding it clenched and shaking only inches from Traven's face. "I'm holding your goddam balls in my hands, and I can squeeze anytime I get ready. You think it was just coincidence you got pulled out of vice after making that Devine Street bust? We had that wired. You ain't the only cop in Dallas, buddy, and they ain't all as clean as you'd like to think you are."

"Why did you want this meet?" Traven asked. He kept his anger under control, wanting as much information from Quarters as he could get.

"To set you straight on a few things. To let you know how close you was to being a casualty when you didn't have to be."

"I got your message yesterday when you sent Ochoa after me."

"That was a mistake." The sincerity in Quarters's voice rung with authenticity.

"You sent him."

Quarters held his empty hands up before him. "You know I ain't going to say I did. If you're wired, that could be admissible in court. I've seen my last courtroom." He laughed. "Unless I get called in to serve on a jury." He drummed his fingers impatiently on the table. "Look, Traven, you know the kind of guys I'm dealing with now."

"Yaks. Do you know the kind of guys you're dealing with? You still got all your fingers now. What are you going to do the first time you screw up? Are you going to cut one of your fingers off and present it to the oyabun the way they do?"

A grimace twisted the big man's features. "I go my own way. We got a business arrangement."

"Till you fuck up," Traven said. "Then maybe they'll take your head. The way they did your bagman's."

"Ain't going to happen, pally. They need me."

"You're living a dream, Donny."

"Yep, and I intend to keep living it." Quarters gnawed at his bottom lip. "See, Traven, I'm in a position to make you a rich guy if you'll see the light and back off. Or I can make you a dead one."

"Let's cut to the chase. What do you want?" Traven sipped his beer.

"You went to see Escobar. Why?"

"To find out how deeply you'd cut into his organization."

Quarters grinned and rubbed his big-knuckled hands together. "Yeah? What'd he say?"

"That you were running eighty percent of the business through Dallas and were looking to increase the territory."

"He said that, huh?"

Traven nodded and wished he could wipe the smug look from the man's face.

"You believe him?"

"Yeah. Ochoa was one of his more loyal people."

"Goes to show you how much money talks." Quarters downed his beer. "How much money would it take to talk to you?"

"Your pockets aren't that deep."

"Maybe they're deeper than you think they are."

"No."

Quarters sighed. "I was told to make you the offer, buddy, but there ain't no way I can make you take it. I'm telling you, the scene that went down yesterday wasn't meant to happen. Some people jumped the gun is all. Some guys thought they was doing me a favor. I don't want you operating off of some kind of revenge thing."

Traven studied the man's face and knew Quarters was lying without knowing exactly how he knew.

The wallscreen broke for halftime, projected a SPE-CIAL BULLETIN message, then cleared for a close-up shot of a piece of tape from the footage of the killer in Nami Chikara's apartment. The anchor came on-screen, oozing sincerity. "The police have no idea who this man is, or how he got through an alarm system supposed to be foolproof. Tonight, immediately following the game, reporter Robin Benedict will reveal facts that have been hidden from the public as this station probes at the identity of the killer coming to be known as Mr. Nobody."

"That's who you're supposed to be chasing," Quarters said. "Mr. Nobody. Not me."

Traven nodded as he finished his beer. "Yeah, but don't you worry, Donny. I'll make time for you. You keep looking over your shoulder, because I'm going to be there real soon." He stood up to go. "And don't think this is one of those revenge things. This is business, pure and simple. It's what I get paid all those big bucks for." He grinned without humor and left, feeling Quarters's eyes boring into his back.

30

Kowalski joined Traven in front of the elevators. Dressed in boots, jeans, and a pullover, the big man looked like one of the dozens of patrons cheering on the action coming over the wallscreens. "That looked like Donny Quarters, smelled like Donny Quarters, and sounded like Donny Quarters," Kowalski said, "but he didn't talk like no Donny Quarters I ever heard of."

The elevator doors binged open and Traven stepped inside, followed by the big man. "Somebody's got him on a short leash," Traven said as he punched the button for the basement floor.

Kowalski grunted. They had the elevator cage to themselves. At this time of night everybody was coming, not going. "The Yaks run their guys like that."

"The Yaks haven't been the type so far to join up with somebody like Donny Quarters, or with their American counterparts at all," Traven said. "Makes me wonder what changed their mind. Or who. And Quarters has always looked at them as his competition."

"You figure there's a middleman."

"Yeah, but I'll be damned if I can put a finger on who." Traven watched the floors drop away. The cage settled with a small bounce and the doors opened to the semigloom of the parking garage. "It also brings the question to mind of why Escobar was cut out of the deal."

"If he was."

"He was. When I talked to him, you could see it on his face."

"Escobar's always been more into calling his own shots," Kowalski said.

Traven led the way into the parking garage. Two security men sat smoking in a near corner, their body armor as black as the shadows that almost concealed them. "Maybe. And, like Escobar said, the Yaks seem to have their own supply lines. They don't need his."

"Meaning the Golden Triangle."

"That's what I'm thinking."

"They got to have a way to move it in-country, Mick."

"They've captured eighty percent of this city's business," Traven said as he stopped beside the Cherokee. "They're getting it in-country somehow. You can bet on it."

"You're talking about a lot of product," Kowalski said as he leaned on the 4×4's hood. "And you're going to tell me U.S. Customs and the DEA hasn't heard about it?"

"This thing may be bigger than either of us think it is," Traven said. "Our import-export laws have been shot to shit since the Japanese set up camp here. There are freighters Customs can check, and there are freighters they can't."

"You're talking about a corporate connection," Kowalski said.

"That's exactly what I'm talking about."

"That's some scary shit."

"I know." Wind gusted through the parking garage, whipped at Traven's duster, and spun sharp-edged dust twisters into his face. "Quarters also tried to tell me how to do my job back there."

"The thing about Mr. Nobody?"

Traven nodded. "And that means somebody knows my business, knows what cases I'm working on."

"We've worked under a spotlight before."

"Not when the people looking on could hit as hard as the Yaks," Traven said. "And that's not counting the pressure they can pull in from legitimate sources."

"So we'll still get one shot at the brass ring before we're sidelined." Kowalski flashed him a crooked-toothed grin.

"Only if we're careful and quiet." Traven took his key ring from his pocket. "Keep the team together as much as you can. Let them watch each other's backs."

Kowalski sighed and straightened up. His broad face was grim. "That may be out of my hands."

Traven locked eyes with the man.

"Kiley appointed your replacement this afternoon. It's official tomorrow morning. Cale Tompkins."

"The best cop money can buy," Traven said before he could stop himself.

Kowalski held up two big hands. "Never been proved, though. Guy's slick."

"Son of a bitch." Traven's words were cold fury. He stared at the holes in the Cherokee's hood. "What the hell does Kiley think he's doing?"

"Came from higher up than Kiley." Kowalski shoved his hands in the back pockets of his jeans, making his bomber jacket gap open enough to reveal the Pachmayr grips of the 12mm cannon leathered under his left arm. "Don't know how high yet. Zenzo's working on tracing the interoffice memo through the chain of command, but it's kind of hard getting through all the security at the department. Especially when you're sitting in a glass house while you're doing it."

"Somebody wants holes in vice's intelligence," Traven said. "It would help if we knew why."

"Yeah, well, in the meantime, don't figure on the team for a lot of support, because we're going to be busy covering our asses from Tompkins." Kowalski shook his head. "Even if this is a legit posting, Tompkins has got his eye on a captain's seat, so he'll have us under his thumb from the git-go. But if you need us, you holler and we'll come a-running."

"I know."

Kowalski stuck out a big hand. "Take care of yourself, Mick."

Traven took it. "You too." He watched the big man go as he climbed into the Cherokee, realized for the first time how truly cut off he was from the world he'd made for himself. The com-chip beeped in his head and he answered it mechanically.

"Cigarette butts here aren't the same as the brand we found in her purse," the lab tech said as he poured the contents of the ashtray into a plastic bag. "I think we got a good shot at getting some DNA samples here."

Traven nodded at the man. He stared at the chalked outlines of Camille Estevan's body overlying the pool of blood clotting the carpet. He had his hands jammed into his pockets and still couldn't get warm. Another lab tech reassembled the AI security system and camera while standing on a ladder they'd borrowed from the building's manager. There was another piece of recorded tape in the unit. He hadn't even viewed it yet and already his stomach was queasy.

Higham was a gray shadow leaning in one corner. The man's eyes were red-rimmed, and he stayed away from the other police department personnel in the room. He belched softly, covering his mouth with his hand each time.

As soon as he'd seen the shape his partner was in, foreshadowed by Higham's voice over the com-chip, Traven had taken over directing the investigation. He followed the gurney carrying the slashed remains of Camille Estevan as far as the kitchen, then searched through the nearly empty cabinets till he found a container of instant coffee. He microwaved a glass of water, shook in a large helping of coffee crystals, stirred it with a spoon from the silverware drawer, and took it back to Higham.

"Thanks," Higham said in a voice that was only slightly more steady than his shaking hand.

"If you're going to be sick," Traven said in a voice low enough that only they heard it, "do it somewhere else. I want to maintain the integrity of this crime scene."

Higham nodded without looking at him. " 'S okay. I can handle it."

Traven doubted it, but moved away just the same. He jammed his hands back in his pockets. Nami Chikara's face, the face of the nameless woman he'd shot yesterday, and Camille Estevan's face all swirled within his head and created a miasma that made his breathing labored.

The lab tech standing on the stepladder looked down after slapping the final cover into place. "Ready to roll when you are, Sarge."

"Let's do it," Traven said, and steeled himself for the impact of the scenes captured on the tape.

The lights dimmed, then the shock of the AI camera system kicking in was almost electric. It began with the living room, shot from the perspective of the killer, a lazy panorama of furniture, unadorned walls, the cave where Camille Estevan had lived and died.

Traven's heart involuntarily speeded up as the killer took his first few steps into the kitchen.

There was a close-up of the cockroach being methodically crushed.

An echo of satisfaction resonated within Traven, and he realized suddenly that the killer had even enjoyed the destruction of the insect. His psyche overlaid the scenes on the wallscreen unwillingly, almost screeching as it was sucked into the vortex of emotions that emanated from the footage. He'd wanted a fix on the murderer, but nothing like this. He felt cold, frozen and dead inside. Perspiration broke out on his forehead.

The gloved hands, broken and twisted and inhuman in the camera's eye, completed their unhurried search of the kitchen, ended with the location of the broad-bladed knife used to kill the woman. The perspective dropped away. The door became the focus. The killer came nearer, moved with agonizing slowness. Then the killer threw himself against the door frantically. The lock gave. Freeze-frame on Camille Estevan crawling through the window.

Traven couldn't look away, hypnotized by the events on the wallscreen. He was a part of them now. It seemed so familiar. The final scene, where the killer was looking at himself, looking at himself, looking at himself, and looking at himself ad infinitum through whatever link had been constructed between himself and the apartment AI, was a gut-wrenching nightmare till the knife swept down and released the blood. Traven's senses slid over the edge with it, and his own perspective returned to him like the unexpected snap of a rubber band.

The footage abruptly ended when the woman's body dropped from the gloved fingers.

"Arman?" Traven called in a dry voice.

"Yeah, Sarge," the little lab tech on the stepladder said.

"You saw the footage from the murder two days ago?"

"Yeah."

"Is it just me, or is the intensity of this one beefed up?" Traven closed his eyes for a moment, but the bare white neck wouldn't fade from sight.

"It's not you," Arman replied. "I felt it too."

"Why?"

"Couldn't tell you. I don't know how the guy's spoofing the AI yet. Want to see it again?"

"No."

The man's face showed relief.

"There weren't any attempts at rape this time," Higham observed quietly.

Traven looked at the man.

Higham nursed the glass of coffee and made a grimace of disgust as he swallowed. "He's learned how to enjoy the killing now. Without dressing it up as something else." His words hung in the air.

They also mirrored Traven's thoughts. A chill raced down his back. "I want this guy," he said to Higham.

Higham nodded. "So do I, despite tonight's appearances." He finished the coffee, a dark streamer of sediment chasing the brown liquid down the side of the glass.

A uniform came into the room, jerked a thumb over his shoulder, and stared at the pool of blood under the chalked outline. "Got a call from Captain Kaneoki," the officer said. "Wants to see you in his office right now."

Traven led the way, glad to be out of the room and away from the wallscreen.

Traven watched the wallscreen in Kaneoki's office, flanked by Higham and confronted by the homicide captain.

Robin Benedict was in rare form. His delivery was timed and eloquent as he revealed the cover-up engineered by Taira Yorimasa of the Nagamuchi Corporation. Copies of the hospital reports, the insurance payments, and the X-rays were shown with damning clarity. Traven's name came up a number of times, always in the role of a good cop just trying to get the job done. Traven was surprised by the information about past cases Benedict had managed to compress in less than thirty seconds of bio on vice's hottest cop while shooting down some of the killer cop labels pinned on him by other media personalities.

"Screen off!" Kaneoki barked. His eyes were thin hard lines behind the glasses. He faced Traven as the wallscreen blanked. His tie hung loosely about his neck. His sleeves were rolled up and wrinkled. He looked like a crumpled and worn human being lodged in an immaculate office. "Do you know where this reporter got this information?"

Traven shrugged and kept his face bland. "He had more information there than I was able to get through the police computers. We could subpoena him and find out."

"I've already tried, but he's standing squarely on the First Amendment."

"The Constitution really gets in the way of good police work," Traven commented. "You ever notice that?"

Kaneoki glared.

"I guess you could threaten to put him in jail as a material witness."

"He's already said he would go," Kaneoki said.

"He told the DA that his arrest would only escalate the interest in the story. The DA agreed."

"He rated the DA?" Traven asked. "Not one of those neophyte assistants that usually try the cases we put together? I'm impressed. Somebody else must have been too."

Kaneoki's jaws worked. "Do you see something funny about this, Traven?"

"No, sir, I do not. I've seen the corpses left behind by the son of a bitch I'm looking for, and the last thing I think about this case is how goddam humorous it is."

Seating himself behind his desk, Kaneoki said, "Let me be perfectly clear: I think you were behind part of this media show tonight. If I can ever prove that, I'm going to hang your ass out to dry. This kind of publicity jeopardizes the good this department can do."

"On the contrary, this kind of publicity forces the department to get up off its collective ass and get something done." Traven returned Kaneoki's hostile glare.

Without looking away, Kaneoki said, "That may be, but you're not going to be working this case."

Knowing the homicide captain waited for the explosion he kept bottled inside, Traven released his breath through his nose. He forced himself to relax.

"Higham."

"Yes, sir." Higham's words weren't nearly as slurred as they'd been at the apartment.

"As of eight o'clock tomorrow morning, you'll be assigned a new partner. You will be here, in my office to meet him or her, and I will lay down some ground rules concerning this investigation."

"Yes, sir." Higham looked away from Traven.

Kaneoki leaned back in his swivel chair. "You, Traven, will be assigned to records division till we decide what to do with you."

Unable to hold his feelings in any longer, Traven was about to say something he knew he would regret when a feminine voice cut him off.

"Captain Kaneoki?"

Traven looked over his shoulder and saw Otsu Hayata standing in the doorway.

She wore a red dress with black trim. Splits up the side showed a lot of healthy thigh. "Perhaps we can talk about this before you make a rash decision that could hurt all of us."

"Who are you?" Kaneoki asked.

"My name is Hayata. I am from Nagamuchi Corporation and have been sent here to speak for the company." She walked into the small office, very cool and collected. Her hair was tied up in a bun that emphasized the sharp angles of her face. "My employers feel that with the media exploitation of this embarrassing situation, it would be better if we gave thought to more cooperation with the police department."

"Your corporation has already been most helpful," Kaneoki objected. "There is no need to humble yourselves further in this matter."

"Still, this is the decision made by the board of directors after seeing the news, and Robin Benedict in particular."

Kaneoki bowed his head in acquiescence.

Hayata looked at Traven, her almond eyes dark and depthless. "It is also further stipulated that Detective Traven be placed in charge of the investigation. It is felt that Nagamuchi Corporation should be exonerated by its most ardent attacker to clear the dark cloud clinging to the company image."

"Traven is going to be busy in records," Kaneoki said. "A department where his talents for disruption may not be so readily exercised."

Traven jammed his hands in his duster pockets and watched the woman's attractive face in open speculation. He didn't see any wavering in her resolve and felt hopeful.

"If you wish, Captain Kaneoki," Hayata said, "I will tell the board of directors that you are rejecting their most generous offer. But I do not think they will agree to it without feeling offended, and they may even seek to go over your head. This is a most serious matter to them.''

Eyes burning with trapped rage, Kaneoki rose from his desk and turned to face the window overlooking the city. His voice was dry and restrained when he spoke. ''Looks like you got what you wanted, Traven, in spite of my efforts to control this situation. But I warn you now, you fuck up just once, and I'm going to ream your ass so bad trucks can pass each other driving through.''

''Thank you, sir,'' Traven said in a voice filled with sarcasm. ''Maybe I can return the favor someday.'' He followed Hayata out into the hall before Kaneoki could respond, flanked by Higham.

Hayata spoke before he could, facing him with impassive features. ''I do not have time to talk tonight, Detective Traven. Be at my office at ten o'clock in the morning and we can discuss our working arrangement in detail.'' She turned on a heel and walked away, her hips swaying under the clinging dress.

Traven watched her till she entered the elevator tube at the end of the hallway. The doors closed and cut her off from view.

''I don't think that was one of those gracious invitations,'' Higham said as he walked to the water cooler in the hallway.

''Maybe not,'' Traven said. ''You still want in on this?''

''Hell, yes.'' Higham's gaze was steady. ''I may be a lot of other things, some of them not so good, but I've been a damn good homicide detective for a lot of years.''

Traven nodded. ''We're going to have to watch our asses on this one.''

''Yeah. You want me to pick you up in the morning?''

''No. I'll stop by for you at eight. I want to get an early start on this while the chance exists.''

''Okay.''

Traven walked toward the elevator, thoughts and

emotions churning inside him. Gracious invitation or
not, he'd still succeeded in getting his foot in the door.
And at this point, he felt that was a major accomplish-
ment.

31

"Don't expect me early tonight," Traven said as he helped clear the breakfast dishes.

Danny stacked them neatly in the dishwasher. "Going to be caught up in that Nagamuchi thing, right?"

Traven paused. "Yeah, how'd you know?"

"I watch the news. Last night I caught the part about you getting pulled off the investigation and the cover-up that Jap exec tried to run."

"I'm back on it now," Traven said as he refilled their coffee cups. "Today's the first day I get to access the Nagamuchi files, so I'm planning to make the most of it."

"You figure the exec did it?"

"I don't know."

"If he didn't, then it was probably somebody else in that building." Danny blew on his coffee. He looked long and lean in his school clothes. They weren't new any more and the pants were about an inch too high for the current fashion.

"That's what I think."

"They aren't going to be any too happy about letting you into their little world," Danny said.

"No, but I'm in for now."

"You push yourself pretty hard, don't you?"

"I believe in what I'm doing. That makes you push yourself."

Danny nodded. "I know what you mean."

Traven considered asking the boy what he believed in, but knew he'd be opening a conversation that would last longer than he had time for. He didn't want to cut it short. There would be another time soon. And if there wasn't, he'd make one.

"I may be late getting home myself," Danny said as he finished off his coffee. "Got some catching up to do on a couple classes. This guy I know said I could come over and copy his notes. I thought while I was out anyway, maybe I'd act a little social for a change."

Guilt spread through Traven faster than the heated coffee. He faced the boy. "Hey, I'm sorry I can't be here more right now. It's just that the things I've got going on are taking up a lot of time. It's one of the hazards of the job." Even as he said it, he wondered how many times their father had given the boy the same speech.

Danny gave him a crooked smile. "It's okay. Really. I understand. And anyway, I get the feeling if I needed you, you'd be there for me."

"I would be," Traven said and hoped the boy could tell he meant it. He reached into his duster, took out his wallet, and plucked out a ten-dollar bill and a fifty-yen note. He handed them to Danny.

"I can't take your money."

"Do you have any?"

"That's not the point."

"It's hard to act social when you're broke," Traven pointed out.

"I don't take handouts. I never have and I don't intend to start. Especially from family."

"It's not a handout. If I paid you for the work you've been doing around here with the cleaning and shopping and laundry, I'd owe you a lot more than this. Take it. Spend it if you need it, bring it back if you don't."

Danny crumpled the money up in a fist, then jammed it into his pants pocket. "Thanks, but I want you to know right now, whatever I spend, I'm going to pay you back once I get on my feet."

"No prob. You enjoy yourself tonight. Just leave me a number where I can reach you if something comes up."

"I'll give you a call from the guy's house," Danny said, "and leave a message with the AI." He left.

Traven took his coffee cup to the balcony and stared out over the morning traffic rush sweeping across Holland Street. Something bothered him about the conversation. He'd gotten the feeling Danny was being evasive about something, but he didn't know what. He sipped the coffee, then decided maybe he was being too paranoid with the morning meet at Nagamuchi Corporation looking him in the eye. He hoped that was it, but Cheryl's words from two days ago kept coming back to haunt him. *He needs somebody.*

He finished the coffee, returned to the kitchen, rinsed the cup out in the sink, and pulled the duster on, making a deal with himself to handle one problem at a time. He figured he had a chance of pulling it off if they only came at him that way.

"This will be your office," Otsu Hayata said as she opened the door.

Traven glanced in the room, still aware of all the attention being given the homicide team by the secretaries on this floor.

The room was a three-meter-square cubicle with two metal desks topped by computer consoles. Squares of neutral gray StatiGard covered the areas beneath the swivel chairs. The walls were unadorned and looked newly painted. The fresh smell of enamel hung in the still air.

"Your names are the passwords for accessing the files open to your investigation," Hayata said. She had dressed sedately for the meeting. The difference in last night's clothing and today's made Traven wonder where she had come from just before arriving at the police department last night. The loose blouse and mid-knee skirt deemphasized her trim figure, and she wore her hair in a severe ponytail. Her face held no trace of makeup. "Only the personnel files of the people in this building will be available for your review. Even then you may find the information about their job capacities too limited. When you would like to ask questions, contact me through the computer and I will do what I can. All you have to do to reach my office is tap my name out and the program will route you through to me.''

Higham, looking rumpled and worn, walked into the room and dropped his hat and coat on one of the desks. "What are the chances of getting a Mr. Coffee brought in?''

Hayata bowed her head. "I will have that taken care of immediately. I should have thought of that already.'' She passed out two blue acrylic ID tags. "These are coded as well. As long as you remain within the blue area, you will not set off an alarm. Once you move anywhere past the blue line in the hall-way, you will trigger a silent alert that will bring armed guards down on you. I can assure you, if this is done even once, your presence here will be forfeit. This is a gift not to be taken lightly.''

"I understand," Traven said as he shrugged out of his duster. Their weapons had been confiscated by the same security guard they'd met last time. "What about Taira Yorimasa?''

"He will be unavailable for your questioning," Hayata replied. No emotion showed on her face.

Traven dropped the duster on the other desk. "I'd like to talk to him.''

"That would be impossible. Yorimasa-san is very busy negotiating new agreements with Nagamuchi constituents. He cannot be pulled away at this time.''

"I thought he was in charge of computer security.''

"He has many duties. Overseeing the security section is only one of them.''

"Where was he last night?''

"I cannot say.''

"Because you don't know, or because you were told not to?'' Traven's voice held a sharper edge to it than he'd intended.

"You are overstepping the boundaries of proper manners, Detective Traven.'' Her voice was sheathed in ice.

"I tend to get that way when someone's been murdered and I can't get cooperation," Traven replied.

"Cooperation is why you have this office today."

"I'd like to talk to Yorimasa."

"That is impossible."

"Then I want to know where he was when Camille Estevan was murdered last night."

"There is a file in the computer under Yorimasa-san's name," Hayata said in a cool voice. "You will find depositions from board members that say Yorimasa-san was nowhere near the Estevan woman's home last night."

"Just like last time, right?" Higham asked from across the room.

Hayata's thin eyebrows arched in indignation. "You should learn how to behave as a guest, Detective Higham." She glanced meaningfully back at Traven. "Both of you should."

"I didn't expect to have my hands tied on this investigation," Traven said. "I expected cooperation."

"No." Hayata's tone defied denial. "You gambled, Detective Traven. When you forced Nagamuchi Corporation's involvement through your media connections, you bet you were good enough to prove your case despite whatever anyone, including this company and its employees, could do to stop you. Now you have the chance to see how good you really are."

Traven ignored the acid in her words. "What's your connection to this investigation?"

"I have been assigned as public relations liaison to smooth over whatever repercussions result from the accusations made by the police department. Sales of several of the Nagamuchi brand products are on a downward spiral as of this morning. Forecasters are predicting similar results in Nagamuchi subsidiaries as media coverage of this investigation broadens and gives a larger picture of corporate holdings."

"You can tell that at ten o'clock in the morning?" Higham asked.

Hayata turned her attention to the older detective.

"Yes. We can. Nagamuchi Corporation is run more efficiently than your police department."

Higham grinned and shook his head. "You're really a public relations liaison?"

"Yes."

Higham sat in the chair behind the desk he'd chosen. "I thought that was just a job classification the execs picked out so they didn't have to list their geishas under fringe benefits." His smile was sharkish and cruel.

"I am not a whore, Detective Higham. You'll want to remember that in whatever future discussions we may have."

Traven studied the hard look in her almond eyes and knew she meant what she said. "You've already got plans drawn up to nullify the long-term effects of this investigation?"

"Yes."

"Do you mind if I ask what they are?"

She crossed her arms over her breasts. "They consist of advertisements, commercials, special sales, slots on television and radio talk shows, endorsements by media stars, a whole barrage designed to reintroduce the Nagamuchi corporate image to the American consumer market."

"Have you got an alternate plan in the works?" Traven asked. "In case it turns out Taira Yorimasa is the man we're looking for?"

"No. He has killed no one. But yes, there is an alternate set of the same type of things set up in case you people cannot solve these murders and Yorimasa-san continues undeservedly to bear the brunt of public opinion. So actually, your presence here has two purposes. You are to find a murderer if you're able, and exonerate an innocent man."

"I'll keep that in mind," Traven said.

"As well you should, since that broadcast placed Yorimasa-san on trial. Will there be anything further?"

"Just the coffeepot," Higham said.

"No," Traven said, meeting her level gaze. "Thank you."

She bowed and left the room, closed the door behind her.

Traven took his place behind the computer, keyed it up, and entered his name. The drive started cycling.

"Sure is a frosty bitch, isn't she?" Higham commented.

"She wasn't exactly playing to a sympathetic audience," Traven replied. He tapped the keys experimentally and moved the cursor through the various menus open to him. He paused under EMPLOYEE FILES and entered Otsu Hayata's name. The computer bleeped at him, then ACCESS DENIED scrolled across the screen. He returned to the main menu, moved the cursor to INTERCOM, and reentered Otsu Hayata's name. She answered almost at once.

< YES, DETECTIVE TRAVEN?

< THE WOMEN'S FILES DON'T APPEAR TO BE OPEN TO ME.

There was a pause. < THE PERSON YOU ARE LOOKING FOR IS A MALE. THAT HAS BEEN VERIFIED. WHY WOULD YOU NEED FILES ON FEMALE EMPLOYEES?

< THAT DOESN'T PRECLUDE THE POSSIBILITY THAT A WOMAN STOLE THE LETTER OPENER FROM YORIMASA'S OFFICE AND GAVE IT TO SOMEONE ELSE TO FRAME YORIMASA.

< WE HAD NOT THOUGHT OF THAT. GIVE ME A MOMENT.

Traven leaned back from the desk and waited for the blinking cursor to continue.

"So how do you want to work this?" Higham asked.

"We're going through the files to see what we find, then we'll set up individual interviews with the employees, starting with the ones that seem most interesting to us."

"Got any idea what we're looking for?"

"No, but we'll know it when we see it."

Higham grunted sourly. "You realize that even with all this information at our fingertips, we're still looking for a needle in a haystack."

"Yeah, but at least the haystack isn't off-limits anymore."

< THE PROGRAM HAS BEEN AMENDED. FEMALE FILES ARE NOW OPEN TO YOUR EXAMINATION.

< THANK YOU.

There was no response. The screen blinked and wiped the entries clear.

A secretary entered after a hesitant knock and gave Higham a coffeepot, two cups, and a two-kilo bag of coffee. She left at once.

"It's a good thing we both take it black," Higham said as he set up the coffeepot beside the sink.

Traven didn't respond, already engrossed as Otsu Hayata's file opened up before him. She was single, twenty-six years old, born in Patterson, California, had spent the last four years at Nagamuchi Corporation's main office after transferring in from a San Francisco subsidiary, and had a public relations position in a department run by Taira Yorimasa. There was no listing for a home address, nor did it include her pay scale. Evidently Nagamuchi Corporation didn't want its people interviewed away from the building, nor did it want any part of their financial status open for inspection.

"They don't give you a whole lot here to go on," Higham said.

"I noticed."

"We're going to spend hours looking at these files and still not know the people they're connected to. Interviewing each and every one of them is going to be about the best route we've got open to us."

"I know. Start with the people working on Yorimasa's floor, then work up and down from there."

"You realize we're probably going to end up duplicating a lot of work."

"Maybe we'll get it right the first time."

Higham grunted sourly.

"Another thing," Traven said as he moved on through the files. "If you come across something that strikes you as worth remembering, don't mention it to me and don't make notes. Memorize it. This new paint job may not have been for our benefit as much as it was for Nagamuchi's. You can bet we're being monitored, video and audio both. I don't want to talk about anything we find while we're inside the walls of this building.''

The buzz of an alarm drew Traven's mind from his dazed contemplation of the computer monitor scrolling through another employee. He reached for the empty shoulder holster immediately, then remembered his weapons were down in the security office.

Higham was a half-step behind him when he moved out into the hallway.

A woman's soothing voice speaking Japanese issued from speakers mounted along the hallway. During their break for lunch and other trips to the bathroom and water cooler, Traven had noticed English wasn't spoken on this floor.

Secretaries left their desks and hurried to the windows lining the east side of the building, talking in confused and excited voices. Worry seemed to be the dominant emotion showing on their faces.

Moving slowly, Traven made his way through the secretaries to the window within the blue area assigned to the homicide team. Higham was on his heels. Night had covered the city, leaving pointed black fingers of skyscrapers covered with lighted warts against the fading indigo tint of sky.

A group of people dressed in the white sheets of the Ku Klux Klan were gathered at the foot of the building. Traven gave up trying to count them when he reached forty and fire was set to the giant cross they had worked to erect in the middle of Musashi Boulevard. The flames scaled from the bottom to the top, flared out to follow the arms. He tried to access the com-chip in his head when the first firebomb exploded against the building's steps, then realized Nagamuchi's security had damped its power. He faced Higham as he forced his way back out of the crowd of women. ''Call the station!'' he yelled. ''Tell them to get a riot squad out here damn quick or they're going to be pulling bodies out of the street.''

Traven watched in helpless frustration. Employee

action near the elevator let him know the floor had been sealed off.

Pools of blue-tinged alcohol-based flames eddied on the steps and walls of the Nagamuchi building. Another bomb exploded against the bulletproof glass of the double front doors of the lobby and spilled fire over them, erasing the uniformed security guards on the other side of it from view.

Other Ku Klux Klan members worked together to overturn cars and trucks and vans in the executive parking slots before the building. Screeches of tortured metal and shattering glass tore through the night, punctuating the angry voices of the crowd.

The flaming cross in the middle of the street still burned. It had been specially treated. Traven could tell that from the way the flames clung to the wood rather than eating into it. More vehicles were overturned as the crowd surged forward again. Cars with open windows were firebombed systematically.

Picket signs with fluorescent lettering hung like flat, rectangular clouds above the hooded figures. Only a few of them looked professionally drawn. The rest were hand-lettered. All of them protested the presence of Japanese murderers in an American city. Still others advertised U.S. FOR US, NOT JAPAN. There were at least a dozen bullhorns among the crowd. Their voices chanted more or less in unison, screaming, *"Murderers go home!"*

Then the black-clad Nagamuchi security guards confronted the inner perimeters of the Klan with blazing Uzis. White-sheeted bodies fell for a moment before return fire claimed a handful of the Japanese guards.

Trapped above the roiling death and carnage, Traven could only watch and wonder to what extent the story he'd given Robin Benedict had precipitated the events.

32

Traven noticed the look of concern on Cheryl's face at once. She sat curled up on the couch in his apartment, a dog-eared book in her lap. "Where's Danny?" he asked.

"I don't know. I got here about fifteen minutes before he left. He was disturbed about something, but he wouldn't talk about it."

"Did he say where he was going?" Traven was tired. The aftermath of the Klan's uprising against Nagamuchi had been taxing and time-consuming.

"No."

"How long has he been gone?"

"Nearly two hours. Mick, I don't think he's coming back. At least not soon."

The wallscreen was already playing scenes from the Klan demonstration. Autofire blazed soundlessly from the silenced speakers. Traven tried to figure out where the boy could have gone. He ruled their father out at once. He looked up at Cheryl. "Do you have to be anywhere soon?"

A hard-edged shadow touched her face, and she hesitated before answering. For the first time he noticed she wore a dress, nice shoes, and the pearl earrings he'd gotten her for her birthday in September. An unaccustomed seriousness was in her eyes. "No."

"Can you stay here in case he comes back before I find him?"

She nodded.

He started to lean forward to kiss her goodbye, but

she turned away before he could. Not knowing what to say and not wanting to deal with more than one problem at a time, he mumbled thanks and let himself out the door.

He took the elevator reserved for security and apartment management personnel, using his shield to open the privacy locks. Frustration chafed at him. It felt good just to be moving. Or maybe, he admitted, it was running.

Even with the information gleaned through departmental files via the mobile phone in the Cherokee, Traven spent an hour walking through alleys covered with pools of water and filled with sacks and boxes of garbage. Despite the wind whipping through them, the narrow, twisting alleys reeked of rotting vegetables, mold, and excretion. The reflections he saw of himself in the uneven water-filled holes in the asphalt were wreathed in despair.

He found Danny atop a two-story-high cinder-block wall that would have closed off one of the alleys if it hadn't been eroded by years and scavengers.

Danny gazed at him silently as he approached. The boy's eyes were empty black pits in the cloistering shadows.

"Mind if I come up?" Traven asked in a quiet voice.

Danny shook his head.

Traven approached the fractured wall. "What's the best way?"

"That corner." Danny pointed to the one farthest away from him. "There's handholds cut into the cinder blocks."

Traven triggered his vision to infrared and climbed up the wall. The smooth edges of the handholds gave way in powdery clouds as he climbed. He straddled the wall and sat with his back to the building opposite the boy. "Want to talk about it?"

He shrugged. "I made the mistake of answering the phone when Dad called, because I thought it might be you. Heard about the Nagamuchi thing on wallscreen.

Simple as that. I just couldn't take his shit tonight. Then I couldn't stay inside anymore.''

Traven nodded and sat quiet, waiting.

"How'd you find me?" Danny asked after a few minutes.

"You used to live here," Traven replied. The infrared was no good in helping him read emotions, so he flipped back to normal vision. The uncertainty in Danny's voice told him to go slow. "I used to have a place like this to go to get it together when I was your age."

"Yeah, well, it ain't working tonight."

Traven stayed silent. No matter what else existed between them, the boy would still see him as an authority figure, still see him as a cop.

"Not much of a place, is it?" Danny asked.

"I've seen worse."

"Part of the job, right?" The boy's grin was self-deprecating and crooked.

"You weren't the first son Craig Traven ditched in his efforts to deflower womankind," Traven said. The bitterness in his own voice surprised him.

"My mother died in one of those dumps," Danny said and pointed at the apartments around them. His voice wavered uncertainly. Wetness gleamed on his cheeks. "She died *here,* busting her ass trying to get something better for herself and me. Her lawyer was a court-appointed idiot who couldn't get past all the red tape in Dad's business. According to the tax records, Dad was barely making it himself without having to pay a huge monthly alimony and child support. And I'm not sure he didn't play golf with the judge. He has a lot of influence with the Japanese corporations.''

"I know."

"They have a lot of influence with the court systems too. Anyway, when the dust settled after the divorce, Mom had barely enough to keep us going. She had no skills. She married Dad when she was nineteen, gave up her dreams of going to college when she got pregnant with me. She worked two jobs most of the time, and I learned to take care of myself.'' His voice broke, and he pulled his forehead down on his knee. His shoulders shook.

Traven sat quiet, waiting because there was nothing else he could do.

"I swear the only thing I wanted to do was take care of *her.*" Danny snuffled. "She wouldn't let me drop out of school to help her. She wouldn't let me work. I got good grades in school to please her. And I watched her dreams for us die a little each day. Can you imagine what that felt like?"

"No," Traven answered honestly. "I can't."

"When they diagnosed her as terminal with cancer, she gave up. You could see it in her eyes. She went through the same routines every day, but she was always apologizing, telling me that Dad would take care of me after she was gone. I acted like I believed her. It made her happy. I even told her Dad and I were talking on the phone when we really weren't because it kept her from worrying so much." Danny took a deep breath. "So why did you come here?"

"To get you. To let you know you have a home to come to when you get ready." He stretched out a hand.

Danny was hesitant about taking it, but when he did, he fell into Traven's arms and cried, clinging desperately to Traven's clothing.

33

"I knew I'd find you here when Danny told me he left you downstairs," Cheryl said. She still had the hard look about her.

Traven looked up from the weight bench, breathing in great drafts of air. His hands inside the gloves felt wet and worn. His arms trembled as he hung on to the bar. The community gym in the apartment building had felt cool in the beginning, but now his sweats were drenched.

She sat on the military-press bench of the Nautilus machine and stared at him through the wires and pulleys that were the guts of the exercise equipment.

"How's Danny?" Traven asked as he forced the weight up again. His arms shivered with effort. He cleared the weight, forced his arms to release it slowly.

"He's fine."

"Talk to you?"

"A little. I got the impression that he's all talked out."

"He's got a lot of things on his mind."

"I figured you both did."

Traven cleared the weight again. This time of the morning, there were only a handful of people in the gym. Most of those were occupied at the heated swimming pool. It was Tuesday. On school nights most of the younger set retired early, or went somewhere else to play hookey from home.

"Talk to me." Cheryl's voice was soft.

Traven released the bar, winging his arms out at his sides. "I don't know what to say yet."

"What about Danny?"

"I'll have to wait and see."

"He needs somebody strong around him."

"I know."

Cheryl paused. "I think you reached him tonight. At least partially. It wasn't anything he said, but I could tell from the way he looked and the way he sounded."

"He's got a lot of problems."

"Yes."

"I don't know how to help him. And even if I did, I wouldn't know which problem to start with."

"I'd say you made a good start tonight."

"I thought you'd be the one he'd talk to. He didn't say anything?"

She shook her head. "We talk, but he doesn't really open up to me."

"Maybe he won't open up to anybody."

"He will to you. If you give him time and space."

"I can't guarantee either of those," Traven said grimly.

"He's a lot like you, you know. Neither one of you likes dealing with your feelings, and I don't think either of you is comfortable with that knowledge. You find ways of working yours out, though."

"Like the weight machines," Traven said as he sat up.

"That's part of it. Liquor and sex are other means you use to burn off nervous energy."

Traven looked at her, not knowing what to say.

"I'm not faulting you for it. Everybody needs something recreational to do to let off steam." Her smile seemed more strained.

He looked at her again, captivated by the glint of the lights on the pearl earrings. Her perfume soothed and invited. He felt stirrings of interest in his groin.

"You keep pushing yourself, though," she said. "You never let up. If things start falling into place for you, you take a look around and see if you can't take on another responsibility. A lot of the reason for doing that is to avoid making commitments to people. To me.''

''Cheryl—''

''It's the way you are, dammit, and it's about time you faced that. You can be a real chicken-shit bastard when you want to, Mick Traven. My relationship with you isn't really your fault. It's mine. I'm a grown woman. I'm supposed to take care of myself.''

He reached for her, only to have her move away.

''Don't,'' she said with cold fury. ''As I said, I can take care of myself, but Danny can't. He needs someone willing to make a commitment to him. He needs you. You can't duck out on Danny, because he has nowhere else to turn.''

Traven tried to find something to say and couldn't.

She stood and hung her handbag over a shoulder. ''I'm leaving. That's what I'd originally come over to tell you tonight. But you didn't even bother to come back up to see me. I don't want to be taken for granted by you. And that's what I've let myself in for. It took seeing Danny, seeing how much he needed you, to make me realize what I wasn't getting from you. You complain about your father being a user, Mick, but if you keep going like this, you're going to end up as a chip off the old block. But you'd better goddam well see it doesn't happen to Danny.''

The damp sweats felt cold to Traven now and clung to him like a loose second skin. His throat was dry.

She walked out of the room without looking back.

He waited on the bench, hardly daring to breathe, expecting her to come back. When he realized she wouldn't be coming, he lay back on the bench, telling himself she was better off finding someone else than trying to tie herself to a career cop. Part of him insisted he'd been betrayed by her, that she had ran out on him the way his mother had, that she had taken advantage of him the way his father had. He kept up the exercise, working till the ache in his arms and chest passed the ache in his heart.

34

"Naturally," Shoda Matahachi said in his dry, crisp voice, "we had not expected your involvement with this corporation, or your investigation of a matter that concerns us only tangentially, to trigger events of this magnitude." The old man stood in the darkness cloaking the end of the long office, his thin arms behind his back. He wore a traditional Japanese black suit and white shirt that contrasted sharply with the gray hair and pallor of his features.

"Nor did I," Traven replied. He stood at the other end of the office, dwarfed by the tall bookcases lining the walls on either side and the pair of black-garbed security guards standing a half-step behind him.

"Yet, it has happened." Matahachi's gaze was unwavering, filled with accusation.

"Yes." There was nothing else Traven could say. Otsu Hayata stood to his left, her fists on her thighs. She wore a long emerald dress that brushed the thick carpet.

The rest of the triumvirate that held the real power behind Nagamuchi Corporation sat behind the specially made desk that ran the width of the room. The desk had electronically controlled panels that gave each of them a private cubicle when needed. Traven had seen those panels recess when he stepped into the room and the three men gradually turned their attention to him.

Kema Debuchi sat to Matahachi's left. Short and bordering on obesity with a round face that allowed little chin, Debuchi was Matahachi's son-in-law and

handled much of Nagamuchi's shipping and manufac-
turing concerns.

Baiken Matahachi, on the right, was the old man's
son and already getting old himself. He was thin and
distinguished, with fragile porcelain features inherited
from his mother's family. He was not married but had
adopted a ward in true oyabun form to pass down
learning and wealth. The notes Zenzo had faxed indicated that Baiken Matahachi was gay, but the matter
had never been proved.

Presented with an opportunist and a man of ques-
tionable morals as heirs to the great corporation he
had inherited from his grandfather, Shoda Matahachi
had never relinquished control of Nagamuchi and ruled
with an iron hand at ninety-three.

Traven thought the recent years showed on the man.
Matahachi's shoulders were more stooped than shown
in the faxed pictures he'd received.

"As you know," Matahachi continued, "your supervisor is only too willing to acquiesce to whatever
demands we choose to make. He wanted to issue a
news release that everyone at this corporation had been
cleared of all pending homicide investigations." He
paused to pace a few steps more, presented his profile,
then turned back. "However, mere generosity is not
going to undo the damage the public image of Nagamuchi suffered in last night's street battle."

Traven kept his voice even with difficulty. "That may
be, but it's surely better than being one of the people
the emergency teams took from the street last night."

Debuchi rose to his feet, his voice too high-pitched
to crack like thunder. But the effort was there. He
leaned forward and rested his knuckled fists on the
desk. "Your impertinence will not be tolerated, Detective. Clearly you do not know your place in the
scheme of things involving this corporation, or knowing, you willingly risk your own career and future."

Traven shifted focus. "My place here," he said in
a soft voice that did little to mask the flint underlying
it, "is to find a murderer who has killed two women
so far. Maybe you people don't have a debit column

for things like that, but finding the man who did that is my bottom line.''

"You're a fool, then, Detective. Even if you take investigating murders up as your vocation, you should know when to cut your losses." Debuchi glared through slitted eyes.

"Enough," Matahachi commanded. "I did not summon you here to entertain a debate on the issue. Kema, sit down."

Debuchi sat, forefinger and thumb pulling at his lower lip in sullen fury.

"As I started to say," Matahachi went on, "things escalated past a point of no return last night, no matter whose fault it ultimately was. We can throw arguments back and forth about what happened during the demonstration all day and still end up with no better than what we now have. It would be a waste of time for both of us. That would not be good business."

Traven stood still, facing the old man, waiting for the hammer to drop.

"You were given a great gift, Detective Traven," Matahachi said. "One you obviously didn't know how to receive, or one you could not judge the value of. Perhaps you would be surprised to learn how limited is the number of Westerners who are permitted through these doors. Usually only people who have something to offer us are even met in the lower offices by subordinates who are trained to see to their needs."

"Then why did you let me in?" Traven asked.

The silence in the room was thick enough to challenge a laser knife.

Traven broke it. "It wasn't because you felt threatened by the media. Nagamuchi Corporation and other Japanese interests have dealt with unfavorable publicity since you pulled up stakes in Tokyo and set up shop in Dallas. You have advertising firms on retainer to deal with that. And you're not going to get me to believe you give a damn about Nami Chikara's death. If you had, your doors would have swung open a hell of a lot sooner. So tell me, why did you want me here?"

"It would have been good business," Matahachi

said. "We could have used the free publicity once your investigation revealed no one from our offices was involved in either of the murders."

"You're sure of that?" Traven let his incredulity show.

"Yes."

"Are you sure that no one within this building was involved? Or was it that you were sure nothing could be proved?"

Debuchi rocketed back up from his seat.

Matahachi waved him down like a man commanding a trained animal. "You are most disrespectful."

"My supervisors tell me that too," Traven said. "Only not so graciously."

Matahachi rubbed his almost fleshless hands together. "Why are you so motivated in these cases? Is it because this is your job? Or is it because you see this as a chance to embarrass Japanese interests in your country?"

"It's because I saw the bodies of those two women."

"And you expect me to believe this?"

Traven didn't reply.

Matahachi dropped his hands and put them behind his back again. "You see? We both choose to express a view, yet neither of us has to accept it. As they say to the south and west of us, we are in a Mexican standoff." A small smile touched his leathery lips. "You view this as a moral issue, a pursuit of right over wrong. That is to be commended in these times when the border between the two becomes blurred by the very effort of living. But to me, to this corporation, this is business. This is a venture that has gone from a slightly better than break-even proposition to one that will be most costly. I have to cut my losses at this point, salvage what I may, and rebuild at a future time. The only decision that remains to me is when to cut them." He returned to the desk and sat in his chair with slow elegance.

"So what do you propose?" Traven asked.

Matahachi turned a palm up. "Why should I propose anything?"

Traven permitted himself a thin smile. "You're the businessman here." He heard a quick intake of breath from Hayata that might have been intended as a warning, but he ignored it.

Matahachi's expression was an amused rictus. "For now, you will retain your office here, and you will continue your investigation of Nagamuchi personnel within the established limits. On Monday, you will either deliver a murderer to me or you will leave this place, and possibly your employment with the police department."

"I don't suppose you've left any room for negotiation?" Traven asked.

"No. This is the only deal you will receive at Nagamuchi Corporation. Whether you take it is your decision."

"And if I choose not to?"

"If left to your own devices, if relieved of the liberties you've been given within these walls, if unable to produce a killer, will you just walk away from this investigation?"

"I can't."

"Because you're bound by your own sense of honor." Matahachi nodded in approval. "This is an outdated ethic judging from your culture."

"It works for me."

"I wonder," Matahachi mused. "Does it work for you, or does it work against you? Do you hold this sense of self in esteem, or does it hold you captive?"

"How can it be one without the other?" Traven asked.

Matahachi laughed openly. "You are evidently a more complex man than I'd imagined, Detective. At another time, I would enjoy the challenge you present. You show more spine than most men I've met, and I'd like the opportunity to see if you have the resources to back up your determination. However, I still have a business to run. I would be remiss in my duties if I were to choose to see how far you could get on your own. That is why, if after Monday you still have not found your murderer and refuse to leave Nagamuchi out of your investigation, you will be relieved of your position at the police department.''

Traven held his temper in check.

''Without the power of your credentials, I feel you will be unable to injure this corporation any further. And you will be just a man, unable to rise above the crowd. I'm told by our psychologists that an American policeman puts much store by his gun and badge. Have you ever given any thought to how you would feel if those were stripped from you?''

''No.''

''I'd suggest you give the possibility some thought, then, because that is surely what will happen if you don't show some common sense.''

''Why by Monday?'' Traven asked.

''Business,'' Matahachi replied. ''The media will be filled with the incident in the street last night. By this weekend, the storm will have run its course, unless something else comes along to change the media focus before that time. Monday, the viewers and readers will be looking for a new topic and a new injustice to rail against. If you persist in being illogical, it will be arranged that you could be that new injustice for a time. I give you those days between out of fairness to you, so that you may exorcise that sense of honor that propels you. Who knows? Perhaps by that time you will have assured yourself these walls do not harbor a fugitive.''

''Perhaps.''

Matahachi's eyes flicked over to Hayata. ''You will remain in charge of the public relations concerning this matter. You will clear your desk of everything else from this time until Monday when we meet again. If anything comes up that you feel should be brought to my attention, you will contact me at once.''

''Hai, Matahachi-san,'' Hayata said, bowing.

''You may both go,'' Matahachi said. He pressed a button on the desk, and the privacy shells came up over the desk.

Travel left the room without another word. He figured it was better that way.

* * *

"So how did it go?" Higham asked.

Traven sat down at his desk and sifted through the myriad emotions seething through him. He outlined everything that had happened as he gazed at the screen of information before him.

"You get the feeling we're getting run up the flagpole on this one?" Higham asked when he finished.

"We have been all along," Traven said. "Only now they're letting us know when they're going to finish the job."

Higham looked uncomfortable. He leaned back in his chair and scratched the top of his head. "I don't want you to take this wrong," he said in a strained voice, "but if we ain't got jack shit to show by Monday, I'm off this investigation." He hurried on before Traven could speak. "This job may not be much, but it's all I got left in the way of a life. My second wife divorced me twelve years ago, said she couldn't put up with the job. I couldn't turn it loose then. You know what I mean?"

Thoughts of Cheryl paraded through Traven's mind. "Yeah, I know what you mean."

"I just want you to know how it'll be if this turns completely sour on us," Higham said. "I don't want to wait till the last minute to let you know how I feel about it."

Traven looked at the man. "I appreciate that."

"I also want you to know I haven't had a drink since we found the Estevan woman's body." Higham's face reddened. "So you'll be getting the best I got to give twenty-four hours a day." His laugh sounded undecided. "Maybe I'll be able to put the bottle away for good now."

Traven smiled. Some of the depression he'd carried from the penthouse office lifted. "Welcome back, Lloyd."

"I guarantee till Monday," the homicide man said. "After that, well, I'll just have to wait and see."

"If I can help, let me know."

"You'll be the first person I call." Higham slid a

notepad free of the organized clutter covering his desk. "Got a message here for you. Your dad called. Wants you to meet him for lunch."

"Where?"

"In the corporate cafeteria downstairs. I don't know how he figures on getting in, though."

Traven tapped the keyboard and watched the information onscreen change. "He works for Nagamuchi," he replied. The words hung in the air. Higham's obvious failure to respond made them even more ominous.

Craig Traven used a corporate card at the cash register to pay for his meal.

Traven used yen.

"Didn't they give you a card?" Craig Traven asked. He offered the orange rectangle to the cashier again. "Let me get this for you."

"No." Evidently Traven's voice came out more harsh than he'd intended. The male cashier and his father both froze. "I've got it. I've been paying my way for a long time now."

Craig Traven nodded and put the card away. "You on an expense account?"

"Yes." Traven handed the yen over, took his change. It was easier to lie and give an explanation Craig Traven would understand than to attempt to interpret how he really felt about using Nagamuchi money.

The cafeteria was set up buffet-style, the serving line running through the center of the huge room. Conversations and silverware made a steady background noise. The employees wore similar clothing covered by white smocks. The only people who stood out in the room were the three security guards clustered around a corner table.

Craig Traven chose a table next to a wall covered by a Bengal tiger mural. He unrolled his silverware from the cloth napkin and placed the napkin in his lap. "So how's Danny?"

"He's fine," Travel replied. He sipped his tea, determined to let the other man say what was on his mind first. White-suited cooks and waitresses kept the buffet area scrubbed spotless when they weren't serving. The employees left their tables neatly arranged when they got up. They placed the silverware on the plates to facilitate quick recovery by the buspeople. Even the dining area hewed to Nagamuchi standards.

"Give you any problems?"

"No."

Craig Traven poked at his rice like a man with something on his mind.

Traven didn't allow him the luxury of kicking the conversation open. He methodically cut the sweet-and-sour pork into bite-sized pieces.

"Danny's a good kid."

"You know that from personal experience?" Traven kept his voice neutral with difficulty.

Craig Traven sighed. "Has he been complaining about me never being there?"

"No. I haven't heard him complain about anything." Traven took a bite of pork, chewed it, then swallowed, surprised to discover it wasn't bad. "I just noticed you haven't been around to see him much since he's been at my apartment."

"Hell, you know what my business is like. Pressure, pressure, pressure. All the damn time. This thing with the Ku Klux Klan isn't helping a bit."

"I'm sure the people who got dead over it weren't too thrilled about it either."

Craig Traven set his silverware down on either side of his plate. "I didn't ask you here for dinner so we could play cops and robbers."

"Why did you ask me to lunch?" Traven asked. "The last time I remember sharing any kind of meal with you was when I was twelve."

Craig Traven nodded. "Your birthday party. I remember. It's a shame things have to get so complicated."

"Nothing's any more complicated now than it was back then."

"Yes, it is." Craig Traven leaned back in his chair.

"Shoda Matahachi isn't kidding when he says he's going to hold you responsible for your actions if you keep putting your nose in where it doesn't belong."

"What do you mean by that?"

Craig Traven's face hardened. "This is business. You can't expect to disrupt the flow of monies through a corporation the size of this one and emerge unscathed. I never have understood this cops-and-robbers fantasy of yours. Good and evil. Right and wrong. What the hell kinds of concepts are those to try to build any kind of career on? No, wait, let me talk. I know what kind of money you're pulling down at your job. You could be earning three times that amount if you went to work for me tomorrow. And the vacation and bennies would be a damn sight better."

Traven's voice was cold and clipped. "This isn't a fantasy, and it isn't a game. Maybe you didn't see what that maniac left behind when he got through killing those women."

"That's none of my business."

"Then don't try telling me mine."

"Goddammit!" Craig Traven slapped the tabletop with enough force to shake the plates and silverware. The conversation and clattering around them came to a stop for an instant.

Traven didn't look away.

Craig Traven's breath hissed between his clenched teeth. "If you don't give this nonsense up, Matahachi will see your public image destroyed. He'll get you kicked out of the police department and you'll be branded persona non grata in this city."

"He'll have to prove his case first," Traven said as he pushed his plate away and stood.

"Aren't you going to finish eating?"

"I've had all I can stomach," Traven replied, meaning it. He walked away.

"Mickey."

Traven stopped and looked back. His father hadn't moved, but his eyes focused on the tabletop now.

"Matahachi will put his best man on the hatchet job he does on you in the media."

"Nothing but the very best," Traven replied sarcastically.

"I'm the best he's got."

Walling off the sudden mix of emotions that swirled through his stomach, Traven forced himself to say, "As long as it's just business and nothing personal." He made himself walk out of the cafeteria and kept his head up.

35

"You mind if we record this, Mr. Brandstetter?" the older cop asked in an easygoing voice. He even smiled politely, as if to say they both knew the procedure was nonsense, but necessary nonsense.

Brandstetter brushed at the folds of his lab smock as he took the chair the detective indicated. "No. I don't mind."

"Good. It's for our benefit, mainly. Helps us keep things sorted." He sat on the edge of his desk and touched a recording device. The slight hum almost faded into the background noise created by the heater units. "Thursday, eleven-thirteen A.M., with Earl Brandstetter. I'm Detective Higham from the homicide squad. You can call me Lloyd." The smile flashed again. "This is Detective Traven."

Brandstetter nodded, glancing from the older cop to the younger one. He didn't feel threatened. Not really. Just cautious. The way he always felt when he talked to other people.

"Do you know why you're here?" Traven asked. He sat behind his desk, the screen of the monitor shimmering to his left. Earl Brandstetter's name was at the top of the screen of data, followed by employment dates, promotions, and other particulars that did not reveal anything about the projects he was involved with.

"I know your investigation has to do with the Chikara woman's death," Brandstetter replied. He left his

hands in his lap. They felt cool and dry despite the
tension inside him.

"Did you know her?" Higham asked.

"No."

"But you have seen her?"

"Yes. She worked in Taira Yorimasa's office."

"And you work for him?"

"Yes."

"So you had occasion to see her frequently."

"No."

"No?"

Brandstetter relaxed. The conversation was taking
on aspects of computer programming. The detective
was chipping away at an unidentifiable mass, hoping
to scrape off something of interest. Once he could relate to the practice, it became easier to deal with, easier to manipulate in his own favor. "I wouldn't say I
saw her frequently."

The younger detective cut in. His voice was sharper,
filled with suspicion. "How many times would you
say you did see her?"

Brandstetter shifted his attention to the other cop,
realizing the men operated on different levels. One was
trying to blend in with the current programming, while
the other pursued defects more vigorously. He checked
security systems in the same fashion himself. "Three
or four times. No more than that."

"Did you ever speak to her?" Higham asked.

"No."

"Why?"

"There was never any need."

Higham smiled. "She was a good-looking woman,
Earl. I think a lot of guys would have found a reason
to need to."

"I didn't."

"You didn't like her?" Traven asked. He leaned forward and placed his elbows on his desk as if suddenly
interested.

"I didn't say that."

"Then what are you saying?"

"I'm saying I never got to know her."

"Why not?"

"There was never any need to." Brandstetter shifted in the seat. "Detective Traven, if you've reviewed my file, and I'm sure you have or you wouldn't have it posted so obviously on the monitor there, you already know I'm not predisposed toward people. I get to know the people I need to in order to get my work done. My private life is my own, and is of no concern to this corporation."

"Maybe we should be asking about your private life."

"That's none of your business." Brandstetter kept his voice neutral, displaying no emotion, only a statement of fact.

"Would you like some coffee, Earl?" Higham asked. "I just made a fresh pot."

"No, thank you. As soon as we finish here, I'm taking a break."

Higham poured himself a cup and sighed as if he was tired of everything he was doing. "You've had a promotion lately."

"Yes."

Higham nodded and blew on his coffee before sipping. "I noticed that. What was it? About a month ago?"

"More like six weeks."

"Congratulations."

"Thank you."

"Must have worked hard to get bumped up like that."

"Nagamuchi Corporation doesn't promote anyone that doesn't deserve it."

"I gathered that from what I've seen. They seem to run a pretty tight ship here."

"Yes."

"So what do you do for them?"

"It's in my file." Brandstetter let boredom sound in his voice.

Higham smiled affably. "I saw that. Chief of programming security. It's a fancy title, but I don't really know what it means."

Brandstetter settled back in his chair, arms folded across his chair. They expected an intellectual elitist, so he gave them one. His voice dripped with feigned sorrow at their collective ignorance. ''I design security systems for programming. I make sure outside sources can't penetrate our computer defenses to steal software our designers have developed for our use.''

''By outside sources, you mean datajackers.''

Brandstetter gave him a condescending smile. ''I believe that's what they call them on the streets.''

''You keep to yourself a lot?'' the young detective asked.

Brandstetter shifted gears easily, feeling himself tense up in response. ''Yes.''

''Where were you the night Nami Chikara was killed?''

''At home.''

''Alone?''

''Yes.''

''So you have no one to corroborate your story?''

''An alibi?'' Brandstetter grinned as if not believing the procedure. ''No. Forgive me, but this is hitting too close to the television shows for me to take it seriously.''

''Murder is a serious issue.''

Brandstetter didn't say anything.

''You like television, Earl?'' Higham asked.

''Some of it.''

''Me too. Usually I can take it or leave it, but I really like that show with Rob Seavers. You know, the one about the Hollywood bounty hunter.''

''*Wolfe Durkin: For Hire.*'' Brandstetter supplied the information automatically, then realized that the show came on Saturday night, the same night he'd killed Nami Chikara.

''Yeah,'' Higham said, snapping his fingers. ''That's the one. Do you like that show?''

''I've seen it a few times. It's too violent for my tastes, but then most of what you see on wallscreen is.''

''Did you see it the week before last? They had a

couple motorcycle stunt riders that you'd have to see to believe. Riding jet bikes and stuff.''

Brandstetter barely kept from smiling his contempt at the crude effort to trap him. ''No. I watched a special on the public broadcasting station about the space station being built. It was an interesting documentary concerning which businesses should be allowed to set up shop first, whether business should come before research.'' Actually, he'd had it marked in the media guide.

''It was a repeat from an earlier date,'' the other detective said.

Brandstetter glanced at the man, saw something flickering in the blue eyes. He wondered if the detective had seen the show or knew it from a schedule he had access to. Either was a possibility. But if there was a schedule before the man, it wasn't in evidence. ''If it was a repeat,'' he said in a calm voice, ''I didn't know about it.''

The younger detective gave no indication of believing him.

With sudden clarity, Brandstetter realized that although the older detective knew more of the word games of extracting conflicting information, the younger one was definitely the more dangerous. This man would hang on with dogged determination. He resolved to watch his answers more closely.

''What do you think about the situation here with the geishas?'' Higham asked.

''That's not my place to say,'' Brandstetter replied.

''You know their job function, though.''

''Yes.''

''Do you have one?''

''No.''

''Why not?''

''My job classification doesn't entitle me to one.''

''Meaning that you would have a geisha if you were allowed?''

''No. I didn't mean that at all.''

''Would you have one?''

Brandstetter gazed at him. ''I believe that asks for

a response about personal preferences. I was assured when I agreed to this that I didn't have to answer any questions of that nature."

"You're right," Higham said. "I withdraw it."

"Do you have a problem talking about your personal life?" the younger detective asked.

"No. We've already talked about what I do at home. I don't care to discuss whatever fantasies I may entertain."

"You received a healthy raise and a new apartment with your promotion," Higham said.

"Yes," Brandstetter replied. His heart thumped against his chest as he wondered if they were about to question him concerning his private module.

"Did you ever notice anything strained about the relationship between Yorimasa and Chikara?" Higham asked, changing subjects again.

Brandstetter didn't let the relief show in his voice. "No."

The questions began again, covering the same material in different fashions, coming from different angles. He had no problems with any of them. They didn't know anything about him. But the penetrating stare the younger detective gave him was distinctly unsettling.

"So what do you think about this guy?" Higham asked as he handed a cup of coffee over. They left the water running in the sink to foul the audio bugs.

Traven took it, trying to keep his thoughts focused on the investigation at hand. All morning he'd had trouble keeping from thinking about Cheryl, his father, and Danny. All posed problems and questions of an entirely different sort. All caused pain. "I don't know. He comes across cold, like he has no warmth at all. The guy we're looking for definitely has some fire in him. But there's something about Brandstetter, something just under the surface."

Higham grunted. "I get the same feeling."

"Maybe we've been in this room too long."

"Yeah, maybe." Higham rubbed his face with a big

hand. "If I have to do this good cop, bad cop routine one more time, I think I'm going to puke."

"The next one will be here in five minutes," Traven said, accessing DataMain, "so you'd better get it over with if that's what you're going to do."

Higham gave him a thin grin. "You're all heart, buddy. How do you want to mark Brandstetter?"

"Keep his file open. We'll see what pops when we get this thing over. How many more people do we have to see today?"

Higham consulted his computer. "Twenty."

"We're going to be working late."

"You want to switch for a while? Let me be the bad cop?"

Traven shook his head. "Right now I'm in the mood for it."

"You think we're going to get this guy?" Higham asked in a low voice.

"I don't know. If he kills again, maybe he'll screw up, leave something behind we can work on."

"The smart thing for him to do, if he is working here at Nagamuchi, would be to hold steady till the deadline Matahachi imposed on the investigation runs out. That would leave us with the street as the only resource."

"Matahachi wouldn't leave it alone even there if it concerned this corporation," Traven said.

"You're probably right."

"I know I am." Traven closed his eyes and banished thoughts of personal conflicts for at least a short time. "I don't want to see this son of a bitch get away."

Higham looked up from the keyboard, a grim expression on his face. "If Matahachi and company are involved in a cover-up, you won't."

"He knows nothing, Earl," she hissed angrily.

"You didn't see the look in his eyes," Brandstetter replied.

They stood at the bar in the construct. She served him another drink. The lighting was lower than usual to hide the fact that Camille Estevan's skin had peeled away in great patches. She wore a turquoise scarf in an effort to keep much of the face together. An odor clung to her with the skin.

"What if he finds out something?"

Her voice regained the sharp edge. "Then we'll take care of it." She came around the counter and grabbed him by his shoulders. "Get me another body, and get it soon. I can't love you like this." She handed him a 3×5 index card. "I've done some checking while you've been gone."

"How?" The knowledge frightened him.

"I'm stronger now. Getting stronger every day." She gave him a Sphinx-smile. "Maybe I could even exist without you now." She held him close, breathed into his ear. "But I don't want to, baby. I want you to be the only man for me."

He took the card. "I'll do it." The fear raging inside him wouldn't subside. "Don't leave me." He held her fiercely.

36

Traven accessed DataMain. The time was 6:41 A.M. Friday morning. He was cold and tired and hungry. And impatient. He jammed his hands in the pockets of his duster.

"Here he comes," Danny called in a low voice. He stood farther up the corner under the multicolored sign of the Daytime Donut Shop, looking up Holland Street.

Traven looked without making it obvious. The traffic was thick and sluggish. Zenzo's black Toyota van was almost lost in the parade of other vehicles. He took his hands out of his pockets and paused to blow on them briefly to warm them as he stepped toward the street.

The van never came to a complete stop, but the side door slid back out of the way.

Running alongside the vehicle, Traven allowed Danny to crawl inside first while he checked for tails. There was no way to be sure his phone hadn't been tapped along with his com-chip. Zenzo hadn't mentioned his name, but it was possible some of the listeners might know the computer expert's voice. Traven pulled himself up into the moving vehicle as Zenzo turned south on Turtle Creek Boulevard.

"Clear?" Zenzo asked as he looked in the rearview mirror. He piloted the van from his wheelchair.

"Clear," Traven said as he moved up to the passenger seat. Danny remained in the rear. The side door hissed shut electronically and walled out the sound of the morning traffic.

''Any tails?'' Zenzo asked.

''If there are,'' Traven replied, ''they're better than I am at shadowing.''

Zenzo nodded as he eased into the left lane. ''How you doing, Danny?''

''Another couple hours' sleep and I think I would have been just fine.''

Traven kept watch in the side mirror. He accessed the patrol car band on the com-chip, shut down the volume inside his head to a level where he could carry on a conversation and monitor the frequency activity at the same time.

Zenzo took the turn onto Lemmon Avenue East, then glided through the congestion with ease. He kept his eyes on the mirrors as much as he was safely able. ''I don't see anything.''

''Neither do I.'' Traven breathed a silent sigh of relief.

''Maybe we're getting paranoid,'' Zenzo said. He smiled and shook his head.

''I'd rather be paranoid than dead.''

Zenzo looked more serious. ''You think this goes that far?''

''You tell me. You're the guy who broke the lock on that chip.''

Zenzo concentrated on his driving for a moment, then, ''Quarters has a guy inside Nagamuchi.''

''You can tell that from the chip?''

''No. I can tell that from the way the programming was set up. Usually, any heist will damage the integrity of the program in some way. It can be something little, or it can be something major.''

''And this wasn't damaged?''

''Not a bit.

''What did the chip have on it?''

''Heavy-duty techware. I'm talking high-priced market-quality stuff designed to process millions of bytes of information in nanoseconds. I could tell you what it does, but I'd spend half an hour giving you a frame of reference.''

''Skip it. It's enough that I know we're dealing with

big money here. That explains why Quarters was able to negotiate a deal with the Yaks.''

"Oh, yeah. This kind of quality could front a major operation on a drug buy. Maybe three or four of them."

Traven looked at Zenzo. "Are you saying Quarters overpaid the Yaks for the shipment?"

Zenzo drummed his fingers on the steering wheel nervously. "The amount of cocaine your team recovered in that bust might have covered a sixth of the black-market value of this techware. Unless this shipment was just an installment of more to come."

"That's possible." Traven turned it over in his mind, not liking what he was coming up with. "Maybe Quarters didn't know the street value of the stuff he handled."

Zenzo shook his head, ran a hand through his thick mop of black hair. "Even if Quarters didn't know, his man inside Nagamuchi would. And the guy would demand a big cut, because he's taking a big risk. The corporate execs wouldn't settle for anything less than leaving a corpse for the jackals to divvy up if they found out about him. Or her."

"This wasn't the first time Quarters cut a deal with the Yaks," Traven said. "He's managing eighty percent of the drug trade moving through this city right now. You don't get that big overnight."

"Once news of this hits the media, there's going to be any number of corporate headhunters looking for a piece of Donny Quarters."

"The Yaks will keep Quarters deep if his own men can't do the job."

"Maybe. You've got to understand how much pressure and money the designers of this techware are going to throw into the pot. Techware designers make their money by inventing a product no one else even knows they need. Something consumers can't live without once they know it exists. That kind of thinking doesn't come easily or quickly. You have to invent everything, including the market you're going to sell to. With the techware on its way through the black market, the value is going to plummet once it reaches the street. People and companies who've been counting on long-range profits out of the techware are going to lose their shirts.''

''You're talking about people other than Nagamuchi?''

''Yeah. Nagamuchi only leased this techware. They didn't invent it.''

Traven considered that. ''Then what do they lose?''

''Basically nothing. They may break off relations with the computer designers for a while, but in the end, Nagamuchi is still one of the biggest consumers around. Insurance covers some of the inventors' losses, but nothing like what residuals and royalties bring in for years.''

''How do you figure Quarters's man got techware Nagamuchi leased instead of techware Nagamuchi developed?''

''Leased techware is harder to protect than home-grown programming,'' Zenzo said as he coasted to a stop at a traffic light. ''It's manufactured so that any internal tampering will void the integrity of the system, including a lot of the security precautions that go into domestic programming. Like putting sugar in the gasoline tank of your Jeep. It would take a talented guy, but this kind of thing isn't impossible for somebody who has the skill and wants it bad enough.''

Traven stared out the window as the van got underway again. He saw a man and woman walking hand in hand at the side of the boulevard and redirected his attention to the more impersonal flow of traffic. ''How did you break the chip?''

''I borrowed a friend's deck and crashed the security illegally. There's a lot of room to maneuver out in cyberspace if you don't have to dot every i or cross every t.''

''You can't put that in your report.''

''No, but since I know the system now, I can kind of luck into the right combination at work.''

''Can you luck into that combination a few days

from now?'' Traven asked. ''And give *me* some room to maneuver?''

''Figured you'd ask me that.'' Zenzo moved to the right, homing in on the outside lane. ''What do you have in mind?''

''I want to find out if Quarters has been fencing other techware to the Yaks. If so, I want to know what kind of stuff he's unloading.''

''I can tell you about some of the recent stuff that's surfaced. What kind of time frame are you looking for?''

''Stuff that's hit the street in the last month.''

Zenzo nodded. ''McMillan Limited lost an engineering comparison package almost four weeks ago that was projected to run into the billions through royalties alone over the next ten years. Personally, I think that figure is so much bullshit, because life expectancy on a package doesn't extend that long. Other people are working on the same thing and will develop similar programming in less time than that.''

''What happens when somebody comes up with a similar program?''

Zenzo shrugged. ''It's studied, of course, to make sure it wasn't copied from the original, then allowed to be placed on the market.''

''And that drives down the worth of the first program,'' Traven said.

''Exactly. Maybe you have a future in computer crimes if Kiley and Kaneoki both get tired of you at the same time. I can put in a good word for you.''

Traven flashed him a mirthless smile. ''I like working the people end of things. Somehow it seems more satisfying than rescuing a corporation's P&L.''

''A number of jobs go with the bottom line of those P&Ls, my friend,'' Zenzo replied soberly.

''Yeah, I guess so.'' Traven settled back in the passenger seat to mull over the information. He felt he could almost get a hand on it, then it would slip out of his grasp. ''Can you find out anything about the McMillan theft?''

''I doubt I can find out who.''

"Why?"

"A score that big, the datajacker who pulled it off would already be known. The guy would tell a few friends, throw his money in a suitcase, and be gone by the time the word hit the streets."

"Why wouldn't he lie low?"

"We're talking about artistic people, guys who take pride in their work. You take down a big collar, you tell a few guys you know."

Traven nodded.

"These guys are the same way."

"Then why hasn't the guy who did this job surfaced?"

"Some of the street chatter is that the corporate headhunters have already done for him."

"Any names come attached to who might have done it?"

"A few. But they've all checked out clean. I did some of the prelim on the case myself."

"Makes you wonder, doesn't it?"

"Sometimes it happens."

The auditory flow from the com-chip in Traven's head roared to new life as details of a traffic accident hit the nets. "How long can you sit on this information?"

"The longer I wait, the bigger the chance this guy will disappear."

"If it's somebody working inside Nagamuchi, his leaving will blaze a trail."

"Yeah, but what if I'm wrong about that?"

"Do you think you are?"

"No."

"I trust you."

"So there'll be two fools if this goes down wrong."

"It's been a week since we captured the chip. There's no telling how long Quarters had it in his possession before he moved it to the Yaks. A few more days won't matter."

"How many days?" Zenzo looked uncomfortable.

"We'll negotiate as we go along." Traven turned to face him. "This adds a new twist to the drug score, but I need to know some more before I can do anything with it.''

"A few days, then I'm going to have to come out with it and let some people start working the channels.''

"If this scans the way I see it,'' Traven said in a soft voice, "those people can work the channels all they want to and still won't come up with a damn thing.''

"You sound sure of yourself.''

"I am. Are you in or out?''

Zenzo hesitated. "In, but I'd better not regret this.''

"I need you to find out a few things for me.''

"Like what?''

"I need to know if Nagamuchi was leasing any or all of the jacked techware.'' Now that he'd said it, Traven felt less sure of himself. To nurse it along as a conjecture was one thing, to offer it out to be shot down was another.

Zenzo looked at him in disbelief. "Are you thinking what I think you're thinking?''

"That the techware that can't be matched up to any known datajackers is coming from one source within Nagamuchi Towers? Yeah.''

"You're playing with fissionable materials here. If you're not careful, you'll end up in some organ jackal's ER-equipped van yourself and have your husked body thrown out in some alley.''

"You want to paint me a scenario that sounds better?''

"But how would some guy in Nagamuchi get away with this kind of shit?''

"Beats me.''

"And the money involved. We're talking about a lot of dinero for one program, let alone two or more.'' Zenzo shook his head.

"Maybe it's for the thrill,'' Traven said. "I'm working a case now that involves somebody who can interface with apartment AIs while he's committing murder. I also believe this guy works at Nagamuchi.''

"The Mr. Nobody thing, right?''

Traven nodded, flinched inwardly at the media tag.

"I've seen it on wallscreen. How's it going?"

"It's not. Between Kaneoki and Nagamuchi's board of directors, they've got me dead in the water. I need something to start a fire under some of the people involved. Could be the datajacker heist tie-in is exactly what I need."

"You sound like you've got somebody in mind."

"Maybe. I'd like you to run a couple background checks for me. Deep stuff. The surface garbage I already got."

"Who?"

"Taira Yorimasa and Earl Brandstetter."

"I remember the first guy. Who's the second?"

"The top guy working computer security for Nagamuchi."

"Their files aren't going to be easy to access."

Traven smiled. "I didn't say this was going to be easy. Yorimasa's already been implicated in the Nami Chikara killing."

"She was the geisha working for Nagamuchi."

"Right. And she worked in the computer security section too."

"I can see where you're headed," Zenzo said, "but you've still got a long way to go before you get there."

"Getting there is half the fun," Traven said with a lightness he didn't feel.

"Even if someone in that office is guilty of stealing those programs, Nagamuchi isn't going to let any of their people take the fall for it. That would mean losing face, not to mention business contacts." Zenzo tapped his fingers on the steering wheel. "They'd kill you before they let you break a story like that."

"I know," Traven said. "That's why I need you to give me a few days."

"If you're right about this—and I've learned to trust your instincts—I could be agreeing to help you commit suicide." Zenzo sighed. "You think you've really got this thing, don't you?"

Traven nodded, but he was truthful with himself because he'd learned a long time ago he had to be. He didn't know if he had the case or it had him.

37

The women were twins. Earl Brandstetter couldn't tell them apart. Both were tanned, lean, with short-cropped blond hair styled in a current street fashion. Their clothes were similarly cut and patterned, but one wore predominantly green and the other predominantly blue. One was Shellie Cahill. The other was Aimee. He stood in one of the bedroom closets and watched them through the lenses of the apartment AI's optic system.

One of them called for the lights. He allowed the apartment AI to switch them on. The optic system compensated instantly, and Brandstetter experienced no discomfort. He hadn't even noticed the change from darkness to light because of the optic system's night-vision capabilities.

Desire and hunger filled him as he watched the two women move around the apartment. They talked about work, inane things that held no interest for him. He turned up the auditory pickup on the apartment AI, listened to the beat of their hearts and the rush of blood through their slender bodies. His grip tightened on the knife in his gloved hand.

The closet smelled of fabrics and perfumes and woman. He wondered whose bedroom he was in, then decided it didn't matter. They were twins. He could have them both in the construct. The thought was exciting. He listened to the blood gurgle in their arteries and veins, listened to the double-pump explosion of their hearts. He switched on the air conditioner to the closet automatically. The cool breeze wrapped around him and made the heat of his desire burn brighter.

Two women at once. The thought remained uppermost in his mind despite the sensation of being torn between two worlds. It had been even easier to jack into the apartment AI this time, like donning a favorite shirt or a comfortable pair of shoes. He knew that other world was there, whichever seemed like the other world at the time, but instead of serving to distract him, it only sharpened his perception of self. He realized it was like joining together the two halves of himself, the real-world self that was hamstrung by a society he couldn't understand, and the cyberself that was so like a god.

"I'm going to get comfortable," one of the women said. "If you'll get the dishes started, I'll finish them when I get back."

"Who's going to cook?" the other asked.

"Call out for something."

The other laughed. "Did you become suddenly rich or something?"

"No, but today was payday at my job."

"On a Sunday?"

"Semimonthly means semimonthly, and today is the fifteenth."

"You got a deal, sis."

Brandstetter blanked out of the living-room optics, then followed the movements of the other sister. She opened the door of the other bedroom and went inside. He slid the closet door aside silently and moved without noise after her. His breath felt warm against his face under the mask, faster now that he was committed to action. He carried the knife point-down.

"Wallscreen," the twin called as she pulled her shirt over her head. Her skin looked so soft and supple, stretched tight over muscle.

Brandstetter switched the wallscreen on, shifted back to normal vision as he watched the soft light play over her upper body. He watched the shadows fade as she turned around and saw him standing before her.

Sudden fear etched into her face as she poised to scream, holding her blouse across her naked breasts.

The knife moved seemingly of its own volition. At the apex of its swing, the blade slashed across her throat. She tried to escape and hold her wounded throat at the same time, then smashed into the wall. The blood-spattered blouse dropped from her fingers. Her lips moved in silent terror.

"Shellie?" the other woman called. "Are you okay?"

Then he knew which twin he'd killed first. Her body crumpled to the floor, fingers staining the wall as she tried to keep herself erect and deny death and gravity.

Brandstetter moved to the side of the door and switched off the wallscreen so the darkness would hide the corpse from the surviving woman.

Aimee Cahill moved into the room cautiously. "Shellie? Shel? Are you okay?"

Brandstetter willed himself to relax. The anticipation of the kill clung to his spine like the jaws of a pit bull.

"This had better not be some kind of game." Aimee Cahill's voice was tense, growing annoyed. "Lights."

He killed the apartment AI's automatic reflex to switch them on.

"Lights." The voice was higher now, more strained.

He throttled the apartment AI's attempt to switch them on again.

"Shellie." The woman stepped around the corner and felt for the manual switch.

Brandstetter grabbed her arm and switched the wallscreen recorder on, making it record through his eyes this time. He focused on her absolute terror and stared into the white-toothed scream ripping free of her throat. Then he changed the point of view on the wallscreen and watched himself.

He threw her toward the bed and leaped after her. He landed across her stomach, then shut her screams off. The knife swept back, came down in a vicious overhand lunge that sank in to the hilt. He pulled the knife free, kept it coming, harder, faster, giving himself over to the act, merged physical and computer senses to concentrate on his conquest. She stopped moving long before he did. The sheets were covered with blood.

He relaxed, breathing deeply, dropping to his knees beside the bed.

Ten minutes later, he picked up the other corpse, laid it beside the first, and began again.

When he was finished, thoughts of the homicide detective crowded into his mind and eroded his confidence. He felt for his mother's presence in his thoughts, but if she was there, she kept her own counsel.

Quickly, before caution and fear could take away his resolve, he walked to the other side of the room, grabbed the short, spiky hair of one of the women, and bared her slashed throat. White bone gleamed back at him.

He started sawing with the knife. The going was harder than he'd expected. But he didn't give up. Too much was at stake.

"Got time to take a break?"

Traven looked up from his computer screen and saw Danny standing in the doorway. His eyes burned from staring at the lines of information and notes for hours. "Sure." He pointed to the unmade bed. The rest of his bedroom wasn't in much better shape. Every available flat surface had been used to store computer chips and hardcopy of everything he could get on Nagamuchi Towers and its personnel.

"Want a beer?" Danny asked.

Traven nodded. He stretched his spine to relieve the ache between his shoulders.

"I'll get us one."

Vertebrae cracked and Traven's arms and shoulders flooded with sudden relief. His frustration level remained undiminished. He accessed DataMain, found out it was 7:57 P.M. Sunday. Tomorrow the office at Nagamuchi would be taken away, along with the slim

corporate concessions, and he still wasn't any closer
to the unknown killer. He stood and walked into the
bathroom long enough to splash water over his face.
Danny was there with the beer when he returned.

"How's it going?" the boy asked. He sat on the
edge of the bed as if ill at ease.

Traven shook his head. "It's not." He cracked the
beer open and sipped. His stomach rumbled, reminding him he hadn't eaten all day.

"Do you want me to leave? I didn't mean to interrupt."

"No. A little time out is probably what I need to
clear my head."

Danny pulled the tab on his beer, and the hiss filled
the room. "We haven't really had a chance to talk
since the other night."

"I wasn't dodging you," Traven said. "Just waiting
till you were ready."

Danny sighed. "I guess I figured that out. My mom
was real good about giving me space to work things
out for myself. Anyway, I've had a lot on my mind."
He knuckled a fist of his empty hand. "What I'm trying to say is that I'd like some help exploring the options I do have." His words came faster, as if he was
afraid to stop. "Even if Dad ever gets around to taking
me off your hands, where's he going to put me? In that
penthouse apartment with him and Beth? No fucking
way. That means some type of foster home or military
school. I don't want that." He stared at Traven and
clenched his jaw muscles. "Not if I have a choice."

Traven saw commitment in the boy's eyes, and the
sight of it scared him. Commitment meant success or
failure. There was no happy medium. No halfway
measures. And no rules. "You're thinking of staying
here with me?"

"Yes."

Traven didn't say anything. He didn't know what to
say. Cheryl's words haunted him. The thing Danny
needed most in his life now was commitment from
someone.

"Look," Danny said in a nervous voice, "if it's the money, I can get a job."

"It's not the money," Traven said. He turned away, unable to face the disappointment in the boy's eyes.

"Then what is it?"

Traven turned back around. He wanted to confront his fears head-on. "I don't think I'm the person you need in your life. I'm a cop. You've seen the kind of days I put in. There'd be a lot of times you'd be left here alone."

"I've been left alone before. I've been left alone a lot."

Traven shook his head. "You're looking for a father. I can't be that for you."

"I don't want a father. I want a friend." Hard, bright tears shattered in Danny's eyes. "Tuesday night, when we were sitting on that cinder-block wall, I thought we were friends."

"We are." Traven's words felt thick and sharp, yet sounded false even to him.

"It damn sure doesn't feel like it now."

Traven set his beer down, emotions churning inside him. "The responsibility you're suggesting scares the hell out of me. I've taken care of myself for a long time now, and never had to doubt anything I did. If I screwed up, I was the only guy that got hurt. I don't want to hurt someone else when I'm wrong."

Danny started to say something, then changed his mind. He got to his feet. "I understand. I've run loner a long time myself. I didn't like other people clinging to my shirttails either." He walked toward the door.

Feeling the spring-coiled tightness in his stomach outweigh the heaviness of his heart, Traven said, "Danny."

The boy turned to face him.

"What would we do if we disagreed about something you had going on in your life if you lived here?"

"Probably the same thing we'd do if other complications came up. We'd work it out. That's what life's about. If I never learned anything else from my mom, I learned that."

Traven's voice felt clogged in his throat. "Yeah." He took a deep breath to loosen the tension filling him. "You can't go into this on a trial basis. We'll sit down together and work out the rules, and we'll both hold to them." He stuck out a hand. "Deal?"

Danny took it. "Deal."

Traven pulled on the hand and embraced the boy, surprised at how good it felt while at the same time feeling as if he'd stepped out over a bottomless pit. Thoughts of Beth and her ultimate betrayal burned through his mind, followed by mental pictures of her with Craig Traven. She was smiling, happy, and totally unrepentant. The final conversation he'd had with Cheryl drifted in, created a frantic mix of emotions.

The com-chip clamored inside his head. He released Danny and stepped off by himself. "Go."

"Got another murder," Higham said. He sounded tired, but alert. "A double this time. And our guy has changed his MO."

Traven reached for his duster and pocketed the SIG/Sauer. "How?"

"He killed two women, same way as before, with some kind of sharp instrument—we think we have the knife. But this time he cut off their heads."

Traven strapped on the ankle rig and holstered his backup piece. "Any idea why?"

"He took one of the heads with him."

"For a trophy." Traven's words sounded harsh and alien. Danny, able to hear only one side of the conversation, looked confused.

"Maybe." Higham sighed.

"What about the other one?"

"It's here. Mick, they were twins. Identical. We've got fingerprints, so we can tell the bodies apart, but not their retinas. Their parents have been informed of their deaths, but how the hell are we supposed to tell them one of their daughters' heads was taken and we can't tell whose head it was?"

"I'm on my way." Traven rippled out of the com-chip connection.

* * *

"Aren't they beautiful, Earl?"

Brandstetter watched the twins, enjoying the way their bodies undulated out on the ballroom floor. Their mouths moved in unison when she spoke, but their actions were independent. "Yes."

They were clothed in chiffon dresses. One wore blue. The other wore green. The music was low and didn't intrude on their conversation. Soft fog sparkling with a myriad of colors under the strobe light rolled restlessly over the black-and-white-checked floor.

He leaned against the doorway, arms folded across his chest. He felt satisfied, complete. Tomorrow would see the end of the detective and the threat the man posed. He would continue on, undiscovered, able to take a hundred women if he wished, a thousand.

"See?" she called from the dance floor. "Didn't I say you'd be happy?"

"Yes." He tried to remember which of them favored which color so he could tell them apart.

They stopped and looked at him, their smiles open and inviting, filled with promise. They held out their arms. "Now you can have all of me." Her laughter was warm and tinkling. The lights dimmed. She slipped their clothes off, dropping them somewhere in the fog, leaving them naked. "Come to Momma, honey. Come to Momma and let Momma reward you for being such a big, strong man."

Unable to tell them apart for sure now, Brandstetter moved forward, letting the first one take him in her arms to kiss him passionately while the other dropped to her knees before him.

38

"Two more women were killed last night," Traven said as he leaned across the desk.

Secretaries in the cubicled work areas around them tried to act as if they weren't listening. Their fingers clacked busily across keyboards, sending business letters and interoffice memos on their way.

Otsu Hayata looked demure in the earth-tone single-piece she'd chosen for the day. She looked up at him from her swivel chair. "That has nothing to do with this corporation," she said in a controlled voice.

"The hell it doesn't," Traven said as he placed his palms on the desk and leaned closer. He felt tired and irritable after spending most of the night between the latest crime scene and the lab, but the helpless feeling coursing through him now was the most brutal. "Those two women were part-time models who'd done commercials advertising Nagamuchi products less than six months ago."

"Through your father's agency," Hayata replied. "We are aware of that coincidence."

Traven stood up. "It's no coincidence. There's a connection between this corporation and the killer."

"So you insist. Yet where is your proof?"

"It's there. I'll find it."

"Where is the connection between these offices and Camille Estevan?"

"I'll find that too."

Hayata turned her attention back to the computer screen on her desk. "You're wasting your time here,

Detective Tavern. I suggest you go before I call security.''

''Doesn't it even matter to you that four women are
dead because of this son of a bitch? Four women that
we know of?''

She glanced at him sharply. ''Yes, it matters. I don't
like the thought of anyone getting killed. But what do
you want me to do about it?''

He softened his voice, made it more urgent and demanding. ''I need help.''

''Yes, you do. But not the kind of help I can give
you. You're obsessed with this investigation, Detective
Traven, and that is definitely not healthy.'' Her face
was a still mask devoid of all feeling.

''You're the only chance I've got of getting those
people to listen to reason,'' Traven said.

She regarded him coolly. ''If I'm the only chance
you have of persuading the board of directors to let
you remain here, then you've already lost.'' She tapped
her keyboard. ''Your presence here has nearly cost me
my job once. What makes you think I'd want to risk
that again?''

Traven searched for words to say and came up
empty.

''I have a good job here, and I like my work. I don't
intend to jeopardize what I have. I don't know how
you can think of trying to solicit my help.''

''Whatever else you may think of yourself as, you're
a person who cares, Ms. Hayata, and you can't escape
that.''

''I don't intend to. Nor do I see the need to. Like
many other people trapped between the American and
Japanese cultures, I've learned to suffer in silence.
Even for other people. Good day, Detective Traven.''
She returned her attention to the screen.

Turning away from her, Traven noticed the heads
swiveling away from their direction. He jammed his
hands in his pockets in frustration, but kept the emotion from his face. He'd come alóne, hoping for the
best and knowing he wouldn't get it. Higham remained at police headquarters, obviously uncomfort-

able with his decision but choosing not to put his neck on the block with Traven's. He passed through the ranks of secretaries and wondered where to take the investigation next. The secret was locked up behind these walls somewhere, and his certainty of that twisted his stomach in knots. Memory of the Cahill family's response when they learned of their daughters' deaths haunted him.

A phone rang somewhere in the background, then Hayata's voice called out to him.

He turned and saw her standing behind her desk, a palm over the mouthpiece. She held out the receiver. He retraced his steps and took the phone from her. "Traven." He watched her sit down again, not looking at him.

The voice was harsh and raspy and obviously disguised. "Her head is downstairs in the incinerator room." The connection broke with a metallic click, followed by buzzing static.

Still holding the receiver, Traven got Hayata's attention. "Can you trace this call?"

She seemed confused.

"It's important," he said.

"Is the caller still on the line?"

"No."

"Were you disconnected?"

"No."

"Then why—"

"There's no time for explanations. Trace the call if you can."

Biting her lip in anger, Hayata got up, took the telephone from a nearby desk, and spoke in rapid Japanese. When she hung up, she looked confused. "The call was initiated in the building's lobby. But why would anyone call for you from there?"

Traven hung up the phone and told her.

The incinerator room was clean, sterile, and filled with state-of-the-art appliances. Pipes that broke down the smoke and loose debris issuing from the heart of the oven that routinely disposed of everything Nagamuchi Towers threw away each working shift criss-crossed the ceiling almost five meters above the floor.

Traven followed the first security guard down the stairway in darkness, followed in turn by Hayata and the remaining guard. The guards were draped in black, blending with the shadows in the large room. They carried compact Uzis on slings. Traven went empty-handed because the security commander refused to return his weapons.

"What about the lights?" Traven asked.

The guard spoke with an accent. "No lights. Broke down."

Uneasiness scaled Traven's back on lizard's talons. He shifted to infrared. "Isn't that unusual?"

The guard shrugged, both hands cradling the Uzi. "Sometimes work, sometimes no. Repair people fix when need. Incinerator very good."

Rows of ducts ran through the walls into the room, threaded between the dozen or more incinerator units. The room was filled with the constant throbbing of the incinerator jets kicking to life in random patterns. The concrete floor gleamed dully from the flashlights the guards carried.

For once Traven missed the hand-held walkie-talkies the police department had dropped in favor of the com-chips. Of course, that had been before his time. Com-chips were standard issue now, but he had seen walkie-talkies in the old training films. They must have been bulky and heavy and uncomfortable to carry around. But at the moment he wouldn't have minded having something bulky and heavy and uncomfortable in his hands. He couldn't hit someone with a com-chip.

"Maybe you should wait upstairs," he told Hayata as they reached the bottom of the stairs.

"No. I put my ass on the line to get you this far." She didn't look at him, concentrating on the incinerator area.

The slip in her language told Traven how nervous she was. Questions filled his mind about how the voice on the other end of the phone had known he was there.

If the head really was in this room, it meant the killer had planned on this since last night. Perhaps before then. Whether it was there or not, it was sure as hell bait.

"And no, Detective Traven," Hayata said in a quiet voice too low to be heard by the guards, "I didn't do this for you. I did it for the Cahill woman, to give her back her dignity in death. If this is true."

Traven nodded and turned his attention back to the first guard's progress. A musty smell filled the air, already oppressive with the residual heat given off from the incinerator units. Another unit kicked into operation with a *whumpf* of flames. The sudden generation of heat was a physical force that slammed into Traven. The duster was too hot, and he considered taking it off.

They found the head almost fifteen sweat-soaked minutes later, according to DataMain. The lead guard played his flashlight over it. The head was perched on the edge of an incinerator unit, the neck of a biodegradable trash bag open around it. Canted to one side, the eyes were half closed as if in deep thought.

As soon as he saw it, Traven smelled the scent of burning flesh and realized it had been there for a while. The guards fanned out cautiously. Behind him, Hayata doubled over and vomited noisily.

There was a metallic click, like a pretzel snapping.

Traven reacted at once, turning to lunge at Hayata and cover her body with his own to take them to the hard concrete.

An explosion ripped through the room. Traven felt at least three impacts against different sections of his body armor even at floor level. Hayata struggled against him frantically. He helped her to a sitting position against one of the stone pillars supporting the ceiling. "Are you all right? Were you hit?" He surveyed her, still in infrared mode, but couldn't see any damage.

She shuddered as she exhaled. "I don't think so."

He glanced back over his shoulder. The lead guard was done for. The two razor-sharp spikes driven through the back of his head guaranteed he wouldn't get back up. The Uzi and flashlight lay on different sides of the body. The stench of death and vomit crawled up his nose. The second guard had caught a spike through a biceps and was silently working it through the flesh when Traven found him in the shadows. He started to move toward the man to help him, but the guard lifted the Uzi from his lap and pointed it. Traven got the message. He sat back down.

"What was that?" Hayata asked.

"Spring bomb," Traven replied, leaning his head back against the incinerator as he watched the living guard bind his wound with a headband.

The sound of running feet came from the stairwell behind a bank of incinerator units and purge systems. Voices carried through the stillness in low, unintelligible echoes.

"Is he dead?" Hayata asked.

"Yes."

She looked at him with frightened, tear-stained eyes. "That bomb was meant for you."

"Yeah."

"He just got in the way."

"I know."

The wounded guard called out in Japanese. An answer in the same language came back. The footsteps came closer.

"Why?" Hayata asked, staring at the dead guard.

Traven searched the area with infrared and finally spotted the severed head a dozen meters away against a filtering unit. The skin looked flayed and blackened. "Because somewhere in those interviews I did, I scared the guy who did this."

"Even if that is true, how did he know you were here?"

"He knew about the deadline Matahachi gave me, and he guessed I'd be here today trying to change that. If I didn't show, all he had to do was drop the head in an incinerator and think of something else. He knew I was here because he watched me come in." Traven looked at her, touched her shoulder softly. "This guy isn't going away on his own. He's going to have to be put down. By me, or by somebody else. He likes what he's doing, and he won't stop unless somebody stops him.''

She looked away from him, wrapped her arms around herself, and trembled.

Four members of Nagamuchi security swung into view at the same time. Two came from the ends of the aisle, two more from over the top of the bulky units on both sides. All of them carried automatic weapons. One of them assumed control, ordered the others about with hand signals. One guard moved toward the dead man while another assisted the wounded man. The guard checked the corpse, looked up, and shook his head.

Traven stood up as the commander approached him, then helped Hayata to her feet.

The commander paused, took a hand-held com from his belt, and spoke in Japanese. He focused on Traven. ''I have been instructed by Matahachi-san to escort you out of the building,'' he said.

''There's been a crime committed here against an American citizen,'' Traven said.

One of the security guards approached carrying the severed head.

The commander spoke into the radio again.

Hayata took a step forward, saying, ''No. You can't.''

Unsure of what was going on, Traven pulled the woman back when the commander raised a hand to shove her out of his way. Hayata struggled briefly.

The commander said something in Japanese. The guard carrying the head opened a side panel on an incinerator.

''Hey!'' Traven yelled, starting forward.

Two guards stepped in front of him, Uzis trained on his face.

Traven came to a stop and watched the guard throw the head into the fire and relock the panel. He swung on the security commander. ''You fucking bastard.''

The commander's eyes were steel-hard. ''There has

been no crime committed here," the man said in a harsh voice. "Matahachi-san wants you removed from the premises at once. You can walk or we can drag you out. The choice is yours."

Traven looked into Hayata's dark eyes. "Hell of a corporation you're working for, lady." Then he allowed himself to be led away, trembling inside with repressed rage and frustration. The smell of burning flesh filled the room despite the filtering units.

39

"There's not a whole lot here to go on."

Traven looked across the conference table at the FBI man, then pointed to the footage reeling across the lab room's wallscreen. "We've got film of the guy in action during every murder. That's got to tell you something."

Oliver Thorsen, the FBI man, adjusted the lapels of his government-issue suit. "It tells me the guy likes to perform before an audience. That he can interface with the apartment AIs tells me he's highly intelligent. He's obviously got some kind of sexual hang-up."

"What makes you say that?" Higham asked. He lounged in a dark corner of the room nursing a cup of coffee. "He hasn't tried to rape any of the victims since the Chikara woman."

"You're assuming she was the first one," Thorsen said. He checked the manicure on his nails. "You have no evidence that she was."

"What do you think?" Traven asked.

Thorsen shrugged. "I don't know."

Traven got up from the table, barely controlling his frustration. "Then what the hell can you tell us, Agent Thorsen? The VICAP people sent you down here in response to our queries for help. So far I haven't seen any of it."

A hard spark ignited in the FBI man's eyes. His voice was chill. "Profiling a serial murderer hasn't become an exact science, Sergeant Traven. If it was, we'd just pop the stats into the nearest computer and fax you a picture of your man. I propose a sexual deviant because the victims are all women. Yet I also theorize that the man you're looking for doesn't know his way around the hookers and prostitutes of your city. They're the easiest targets for this kind of killer. They work alone and they're willing to go anywhere with strangers, because it's their job. I think he's getting his information about the women somewhere else, then acting on it.''

"There's the Nagamuchi angle," Higham said.

Traven watched the silent images on the screen. Death happened again and again, hammered home the fact that he remained helpless to prevent another one.

"For three of the four victims," Thorsen pointed out. "The Estevan woman doesn't fit the pattern of having worked in some capacity for Nagamuchi.''

"She definitely fits the method of killing," Traven said. He turned toward the man. "I apologize for blowing up. The first of these cases is a week and a half old. We still don't have any idea who we're looking for.''

Thorsen nodded. "I understand. Believe me. I've worked a lot of these cases. Some you break, some you don't. These people are intelligent, usually more intelligent than your average citizen.'' He tapped his notepad with the eraser end of his pencil. "I've jotted down a few notes you might consider. One, as I said, the guy is extremely intelligent. Two, he's got a sexual problem and he's using these women to solve it. Even after you find out who's doing it, you may never know why. Three, he likes to watch himself. That's why he tapes the murders. In straight life, he may be an introvert, somebody who avoids the crowd scene and public recognition. Who came up with the Mr. Nobody tag?''

"The media," Traven answered.

"Okay. If he'd come up with it, we might have been dealing with an ego problem as well as the sexual one. Four, even though his mania has its roots in some sort of sexual situation, this guy doesn't know his way around the flesh-for-hire circles.''

"Because he'd be choosing his victims from them?" Higham asked.

"Right. They're the easy targets. He knows he's marked himself by selecting the women he has. Being a bright guy and evidently a computer expert of some sort, I'll bet, he feels safer if he's able to research his kills beforehand. On that assumption, I'd write off any known sex offenders on your lists. Five, the guy you're looking for is strong. Slicing a person's head off her shoulders is a physically demanding job." Thorsen looked up from his notes. "Six, because of the attack on you at Nagamuchi, I'd say this man believes he has something to fear from you, Sergeant Traven."

"What could have made him believe that?" Higham asked. "I was there at every interview with Mick."

"Hard to say at this point. Sociopaths select their own private fantasies. It's understandable that they'd select their own private fears as well. His has evidently manifested itself in the material world. Not all of them do." Thorsen focused on Traven. "If I were you, I'd watch myself till you bring this guy down. If he has developed a fixation on you and perceives you as a threat to his world, he won't stop till you're dead."

Traven felt a chill spread across his shoulders and down his spine as he looked back at the wallscreen. A knife blade glinted in the sable shadows.

With darkness cloaking the east side of the city, Traven left the Cherokee at the side of Marburg Street, pulled up on the curb in front of a boarded-over window on a building sporting a faded sign advertising Western Wear for Men. He took the SIG/Sauer from the seat beside him, pocketed it in his duster, and stepped out into the falling sleet. A press of his thumb against the ID sensor switched on the Jeep's alarm system. He wore black jeans, a black turtleneck, and a black watch cap. His cheeks felt cold as his breath came out in fogs.

Zenzo trailed along with him, a disembodied voice in his head on a special frequency they'd set up for the night excursion. "Mick?"

"Go."

"How does it look?"

"Like a street." He knew his irritation sounded in the transmission.

"You should have brought Kowalski in as your backup. I'm not cut out for this waiting-on-the-sidelines bullshit."

"I can tell. Now get out of my head and let me do my job." Traven felt the connection ripple inward and disappear. He regretted his words at once. Zenzo would understand, however. The man had seen him on edge before.

Kiki Moreau's apartment building was halfway up the block, behind a row of closed businesses.

Traven's tennis shoes made little noise, and he worked hard to keep it to a minimum. Traffic continued to trickle up and down Marburg as he ducked into a damp alley. The wind and sleet were kept at bay by the walls. A wooden fence closed the alley, but enough planks were missing so he had no trouble stepping through.

He took the creaky metal stairs zigzagging up the side of the building, the 10mm in his hand now, hidden by the folds of the duster. The outside landing was made of grilled metal, so he could see through it below him. Infrared showed him nothing. He switched back to normal vision.

Moreau's door was number 16, the third one down. Someone peeped out a window of the first apartment, then quickly let the curtain drop back into place as he passed.

Traven paused in front of Moreau's door and realigned his grip on the pistol. Knowing he was about to commit himself to action of some sort, he felt the absence of a partner. He knocked on the door.

Sounds came from inside. The volume on the wallscreen dropped. A man's voice called, "Who is it?"

Knowing the apartment wasn't AI-equipped and couldn't transmit a picture of him, Traven pulled his weapon from the folds of the duster and laid it alongside the doorjamb. "C'mon, Kiki," he growled in a low voice. "I ain't got all night."

"Who is it?" The suspicion in the voice was sharper now.

"Give me a name, Zenzo," Traven transmitted.

"Jerrin Slide. He's a go-between tech buyers sometimes use. He's—"

Traven cut off the rest of the information, saying, "Slide."

The electronic look whirled above the doorknob, lights changing from red to green. "Just a minute. Let me get the sucker-trap off this door."

A glint of light on darkened metal drew Traven's attention. He was in motion before he knew for sure what it was. He slammed a shoulder against the door and went through low. Bullets slammed through the wooden walls and flattened against the steel door over his head.

Traven rolled as he spilled across the floor. Moreau brought up a cut-down double-barrel shotgun from the coffee table. Bullets continued to hammer into the vibrating door. He swung out a leg, caught Moreau behind an ankle, and followed through. Moreau fell backward. One of the shotgun's barrels discharged and blew a hole in the ceiling before it spun out of his hands.

"Mick," the com-chip chirped in Zenzo's voice.

Traven flipped over on his back as he drew target acquisition on the room's only light. "Call the uniforms. Now." He squeezed the trigger and the bulb exploded. Darkness claimed the room.

Still on infrared, he saw Moreau moving on forearms and knees toward another room. He reached out and caught one of the man's ankles. The man kicked at him, clawed frantically at the lumpy sofa as he tried to pull away.

A black shadow moved from the back room. It pulsed with green life in Traven's infrared view. He identified the intruder as a Yak by the ninja outfit, then by the sword the man had raised in both hands. He pushed up with one hand and both feet as the Yak swung for Moreau. He blocked the sword with the SIG/Sauer.

Metal clanked on metal and sparks flew.

Traven slammed into the smaller man, lifting the Yak from his feet. Even before they hit the dining table together and sent it crashing to the floor, the Yak was struggling to use the sword. He punched the Yak in the face, punched again. Then they were entangled in the remains of the table and the chairs.

A fusillade of bullets tore through the cheap wall and scattered white clouds of plasterboard as chunks of the same material rattled off the walls and furniture.

Placing the 10mm against the Yak's throat, Traven pulled the trigger and felt life leave the man's body.

"Mick?"

"I'm on the move."

Zenzo rippled out.

Traven heaved himself up from the remains of the table and moved in a crouch. Two shots bounced from the body armor covering his back and let him know the Yaks were infrared-equipped too.

Moreau had made it to the bedroom. He was silhouetted against a window, clawing at the catches that fastened it.

"Dammit," Traven said as he staggered into the room, "get down before they blow you away." He grabbed the back of Moreau's waistband and yanked the man down.

Autofire ripped the glass from the window. The jagged shards tinkled down around them.

"Goddam, that was close," Moreau yelled. He held his hands over his head and looked at Traven. "Who the fuck are you if you're not with them?"

"I'm a cop," Traven said as he glanced over the shattered glass remaining on the windowsill.

"First time I ever been glad to see a cop," Moreau said. He got to his knees. "Fuck me, I can't believe how close that was. Who are those guys?"

"Yaks," Traven answered.

Moreau shook his head. "I got no beef with Yaks." He glanced at Traven. "They after you?"

"No."

"Why the hell would they be after me?"

"Because I found out about you." Traven figured it fit. The Yaks had a team watching Moreau. That was the only way they could have fielded his play on such short notice.

"So what's to find out?"

Traven glanced at the man. Even in infrared Moreau looked too leaned-out to be healthy, his hair dirty and straggly. "That you're the guy Donny Quarters has been going through to dope out the techware he's been getting his hands on lately."

Moreau didn't say anything.

The shrill scream of a siren sounded off in the distance.

"You remember the techware, don't you? The Mc-Millan Limited Stuff. Fargo. Dane. Hitachi. From what a friend of mine tells me, the stuff you've been working on could have made you a rich man if you'd jacked it yourself."

"I don't know what you're talking about."

"Don't clam up on me, Kiki. I may be the only way you have of walking out of here alive."

Moreau considered that. "What do you want from me?"

"I want to know where Quarters has been getting the techware."

"I can't tell you that. Quarters will kill me."

"You think the Yaks are doing this without his approval?" Traven shook his head. "Don't be a fool, Moreau. You became a liability to Donny Quarters the first time you agreed to receive the techware his Nagamuchi connection shipped out."

"You know about that, huh?"

"I know all those programs had been leased to Nagamuchi. I'm not going to believe Quarters was intelligent enough to penetrate the security of more than one corporation. He doesn't know that many people who could fit the corporate scene long enough to get far enough in a security department to get all the right passwords."

Moreau shook his head. "Quarters didn't go to this guy. The guy came to him."

Traven fixed him with a hard stare. The siren was closer. "Give me a name."

"Give me a reason."

Something thumped softly onto the roof overhead.

Moreau looked up when Traven did.

"Tell me," Traven said, "and I'll take you out of here with me. Keep it to yourself and you can take your own chances about getting out."

Moreau licked his lips, glanced at the ceiling, and said, "Yorimasa. The guy's name was Taira Yorimasa."

Traven stood up beside the broken window and fisted the 10mm in both hands. More bullets sprayed through the jagged shards of glass. They splintered further and scattered bright crystal rainbows in the moonlight. A dark form whirled around the doorjamb before the staccato reports died away. Traven started at lip level and punched three rounds through the Yak's head. The Yak flipped backward. Something dropped from his hand and white smoke poured into the room.

Grabbing Moreau's shirt, Traven pulled the man after him. He whipped the pistol around to cover the living room as they plunged into it. Nothing and nobody was in his way. He released Moreau and ran his free hand over the dead Yak. Seconds later he was in possession of three more smoke bombs.

The first of the prowl cars roared into the alley below. The whirling lights ignited the darkness around the apartment building. Two men separated from the vehicle and fanned the doors open to use as shields. Bullets punched through the metal. One man went spinning to the ground as three more cars converged on the scene.

The window in the kitchen shattered.

Traven put five rounds through the broken glass to keep whoever had broken it at bay. He changed magazines, flipped the toggles on the smoke bombs, tossed two on the left end of the landing and one on the right.

He took a double-fisted grip on the SIG/Sauer and looked at Moreau. "It's now or never."

Moreau moved. He didn't look happy about it at all.

"Left," Traven ordered. "Toward the stairs. Don't stop till you hit ground level or I'll run right over the top of you."

Moreau disappeared in the bilious clouds of smoke. Autofire raked the landing but faded away as the arriving police forces started sniping back. A black-clad body tumbled from a building across the alley to the pavement five floors below as Traven threw himself out the door. He dropped to one knee at the stairs with the SIG/Sauer out before him when Moreau made for the second floor. He accessed the com-chip, dropped into the emergency band, and identified himself and his position as well as Moreau.

A chunk of roof tile smashing onto the metal landing beside him alerted Traven. He twisted around, hit in the ribs by at least one bullet. The force drove him backward, over the edge of the steps, and he flailed wildly with his left hand to keep from falling. He clutched the wrought iron. The 10mm came up automatically and bracketed the Yak clinging tenaciously to the rooftop. He squeezed off rounds one-handed, aiming for the Yak's chest. He knew body armor would keep the bullets from being fatal, but it wouldn't help a damn bit when the driving force of the 10mm parabellums tore the guy from the roof and sent him falling three stories. The Yak hit twice, once against the outside railing of the second-floor landing and once against the alley.

Traven twisted, found footing, and threw himself down the stairs. He hit every third or fourth step. He bruised his hip against the railing to make the 180-degree turn to the first floor. He leaped over the side as Moreau cleared the last step and headed for the darkness behind the building. He body-checked the computer man, grabbed his shirt, and shoved him back toward Marburg Street. From what he'd gathered about operations, a MOP unit was parked there as a command base. "The street. Hit it."

Moreau didn't hesitate. Lack of movement meant a stationary target. He lost his balance and fell, pushed himself up with his hands, and ran for the street.

Traven was content to follow. It wasn't his operation anymore. The uniforms had their own guy calling shots. His place was with his prisoner.

Traffic, what little of it there was, was stalled at either end of the street, blocked by the whirling red and blue lights of the MOP unit and the unit's bulk. It stood tall and imposing in the center of the two lanes.

Moreau hesitated at the end of the alley, breathing through his mouth.

"Move," Traven ordered. "Slide under it. There'll be an access port underneath." He accessed the com-chip and let the driver and team know they were coming. The crash of gunfire echoed in the alley. Both sides, Yak and police, were silent. Com-chips replaced everything but the screams of the wounded.

Moreau ran, arms swinging wildly.

Traven followed the man, both hands locked on his weapon.

Rubber shrilled before Moreau made it halfway. Headlights poured over the running man as the sound of a racing engine screamed to renewed life. A mid-size sedan swung around the corner and bore down on Moreau, less than fifty meters away and closing.

40

Traven stepped off the curb and brought the SIG/Sauer into target acquisition. He tracked the driver's side of the sedan and squeezed the trigger in rapid fire as he held a twenty-five-centimeter grouping.

The sedan weaved out of control when the driver tried to dodge. Tires screeched. The headlights moved from Moreau to Traven.

Waiting till the last moment he judged possible, wanting to give the driver the least amount of time he could to correct his course, Traven threw himself back to the curb. He glimpsed Moreau slithering under the MOP unit, blue and red lights flashing across the man's clothes.

Metal crumbled and folded as the sedan came up over the curb. It bounced erratically and crushed a wire trash basket and a media-chip vending machine under its wheels. Bullets from the rear door pocked the sidewalk beside Traven's face.

Maintaining his grip on the 10mm, Traven rolled and got his feet under him again, came out of the dive with his weapon centered on the back window of the sedan. Autofire tore splinters from the boarded-over windows of the vacant businesses behind him. He ducked back into the alley. Shooting at Moreau's apartment building was sporadic now instead of a staccato roar.

The sedan turned in the middle of the street, the driver obviously intent on at least getting one of their targets.

Traven got a brief image of a Yak behind the wheel as the sedan accelerated again. Then the MOP unit's mounted antitank weapon coughed out a 94mm warhead that impacted against the sedan's grill. An inferno blossomed up at the forward end of the car and swept back with the speed of a prairie fire in dry season. Flames rolled. There were a few screams, but they were cut off by the second explosion caused by the gas tank igniting. Sparks and assorted fragments of the vehicle rained down in the street. Little fires dotted the black pavement. Traven lowered his weapon.

"You want to tell us what the hell you thought you were doing tonight?" Kiley sat on the edge of his desk, face as blank of emotion as if it had been carved from ebony. His eyes were red and bloodshot. His big hands gripped the edge of the desk.

Traven stood against the outside wall of the vice captain's office with a cup of coffee. He'd ignored the offer of a chair. The little plastic curtain over the glass in the door was pulled down. The sound of the detectives working on the other side of the wall was muted. "I got a tip that Quarters was using jacked techware to buy cocaine from the Yaks. Moreau's name turned up, so I followed it."

"And you had no idea the situation would turn this hot?"

"No, sir." Traven could tell from the way Kiley held his head that the man didn't believe him. He'd seen that particular tilt a lot over their years of association.

Kaneoki didn't limit his disbelief to a gesture. "You're lying." The words were flat and impersonal. The homicide captain stood to Traven's left, in front of the blank wallscreen. His spine was stiffly erect and his clothes looked fresh. But the eyes looked tired. Evidently both men had been logging long hours.

Traven faced Kaneoki. "I don't have to take that kind of shit." He paused. "Sir."

Kaneoki's face mottled.

"Who was in on this with you?" Kiley asked in a gentle voice.

Traven sipped his coffee. "No one."

Kaneoki folded his arms across his chest. "Perhaps you don't realize your situation, Sergeant Traven. You are in serious trouble."

"Didn't know there was any other kind."

"If you told us the names of the others involved . . ."

"I could have company in here?" Traven grinned sarcastically. "Even if there was someone else, I wouldn't rat him out. I still work in the streets, Captain, not the bureaucracy. I don't need someone else's ass on the line with me for something I'm willing to take responsibility on."

Kaneoki shifted his attention to Kiley. "He's protecting someone."

Kiley grimaced. He ran a big hand over his stubbled face. "Mick, you fucked up."

Traven looked at the vice commander.

Kiley grunted as he pushed up off the desk and limped to the side of it. "You never know when to quit, do you? You find something or someone in your way, and you just keep pushing. Yeah, sometimes you think you're on a streak when you get a wild hair up your ass and pull a move no one's expecting, but you can't get it through your head there's some things you just don't fuck with." He sighed and rubbed his face again. "Tell me what you hoped to accomplish by bringing this Moreau guy in."

"Word is, Moreau's handling stolen techware for Donny Quarters, getting it ready for transfer to the Yaks." Traven finished his coffee and set the cup aside. He shoved his hands in the duster pockets. The room still felt chill. He wasn't sure if it had anything to do with the thermostat or the cold shoulder he was getting from the two men before him.

"What did that give you?" Kiley asked.

"A connection. Something to work with."

"What were you going to work with? Stealing techware from a Japanese company isn't a punishable offense in an American court."

"Unless the company wants to press charges."

Kiley's eyes were muddy brown. "What do you think your chances of that were?"

"Wasn't important what I thought," Traven replied. "It was important what Quarters and his connection thought. If I put pressure on Quarters, some of it had to filter through to his connection in Nagamuchi. I figured the inside man would back out and take Quarter's bargaining position with him."

"Quarters has a lock on this city," Kiley said. "You knew that."

"Yeah."

"Taking out a source of income for Quarters at this point is going to be tough. Every street corner, bar, and fifteen-year-old pusher is one of his banks now. The man doesn't have a cash-flow problem."

"You have to start somewhere," Traven replied.

Kaneoki broke in, his hands behind him and his shoulders squared. "We've talked with Nagamuchi Towers. They have no desire to press charges against Moreau or Quarters. It's my feeling they'll be cleaning house on their own and you've signed the death warrant of whoever was inside their offices supplying the techware to Quarters. Moreau might live five minutes after he steps out onto the street."

"I hadn't planned on the Yaks being so close to Moreau," Traven said. "From the looks of things, I got him out of there only minutes before they would have wasted him. If Moreau gets burned five minutes after he hits the street, I've already extended his life."

"You believe yourself to be innocent, don't you?" Kaneoki asked. "That you're somehow above all of this."

Traven stepped forward. "Wrong, asshole. I learned a long time ago that when you pinned on your shield you took on a load of guilt with it. A cop makes deals in the street, lets some people go, pushes hard on others. Situational ethics. You deal them every day. But I still believe in the system. Things can still be made right no matter how much money there is for a guilty party to throw around. You just have to toe the line yourself.''

''And you've never stepped over it?'' Kaneoki asked.

''No. I've kicked dust on it from time to time, but I've never crossed that line.''

''A supercop.'' Kaneoki sneered.

Traven stepped forward, unable to stop himself.

Kiley moved between them, holding his hands open at shoulder level. ''Cool it.''

Traven stopped but didn't turn away. He leaned over one of Kiley's arms. ''No. I just don't make deals and I don't let anyone buy me off or shove my job security down my throat.''

''Mick!'' Kiley's voice was sharp.

Kaneoki's lips compressed into a thin, bitter bow. ''You're referring to the Chikara murder.''

''You bet your ass I am. And the Estevan murder, and the murders of the two Cahill women.'' Traven fought the rising anger inside him. Impatience chafed him. Kiley and Kaneoki hadn't called this meeting for no reason, yet neither man seemed ready to take on the main issue.

''Another investigation which you were ordered to go easy on, yet seem to have ignored.'' Kaneoki stepped back, bumping into the desk.

''I believe in doing my job,'' Traven said. ''If somebody in that building is dirty, I want him however I can get him. Within the law. But I'm not going to let politics or payoffs stop me.''

''You're worse than a fool,'' Kaneoki said. ''At least a fool doesn't know any better. You know and you still insist on placing your head on the chopping block.''

''If it'd save someone's life or take some product off those streets, I'd stick my head in a lion's mouth.'' Traven worked on his breathing. He inhaled through his nose and breathed out between clenched teeth. He looked at Kiley. ''If we're through with this mutual admiration society, I'm leaving.''

Kiley dropped his arms to his sides. ''No.''

Traven eyed him. "Any particular reason, or are we planning on waltzing around here all night?"

Kiley reached out a big hand, pink palm up. "I'm taking your shield. You're being suspended till a formal Internal Affairs investigation can be conducted."

"On what grounds?"

"Doesn't matter," Kiley said in a low voice. "They want it, so they're going to get it. Ain't a damn thing you can do about it."

Traven didn't move.

Kiley returned his stare. "This can go easy, or it can go hard. Gonna be your call, but it's gonna happen."

Traven reached inside his duster, took out his wallet, and unpinned the badge. Its weight felt comforting and solid in his palm. When he tossed it to Kiley, he hoped none of the ragged emotions coursing through him showed. "Doesn't mean I'm quitting, Leo."

Kiley wrapped his big fingers around the gold badge. "I know, kid." His voice was soft. "I'm going to take care of this till you get back." He took a Kleenex from his desk, wrapped the badge in it, then pocketed it. "You need to talk, you call me."

Traven nodded. "Think about this guy Moreau," he told Kiley. "Every now and then, ask yourself why Nagamuchi's name keeps turning up in a drug and murder investigation."

"Stay off the streets, Traven," Kaneoki ordered. "If I find you around Nagamuchi, I'm going to run you in and throw the book at you." He stepped around Kiley.

Traven looked at the homicide man. "Don't get in my face, Kaneoki, or you're going to have to pick yourself up off your butt."

Kaneoki froze and glared at him.

Traven waited a beat, then reached for the door and left. They shut off the com-chip while he was in the elevator. The sudden silence was almost physical and maybe the most intense thing he'd ever felt. He realized he'd never known true loneliness before.

* * *

"Want a beer?" Danny asked.

Traven shook his head. He sat on a chair on the patio looking out over the city. The silence in his head from the deactivated com-chip was deafening, worse than any sinus condition he'd ever experienced. He moved enough to pour another screwdriver, this one stronger than the last.

Danny moved out onto the patio. His face was lined with concern that Traven tried not to notice. "Want to talk about it?"

"Can't." Traven's throat was tight, his voice hoarse and strained. He'd never felt this cut off or abandoned. He missed Cheryl. Maybe he'd been committed to more things than he'd believed. Maybe he wasn't as deserving as he'd thought.

Danny leaned against the railing. "You need to eat."

"Later." It was easier to communicate in monosyllables. If the vodka would only neutralize the fire in his belly, he'd be all right.

"It's cold out here." Danny rubbed his bare arms.

Traven nodded and sipped more of his drink. He'd turned the temperature down on purpose. He kept looking out over the city, thinking how he should be out there instead of here sitting on his ass. But Kaneoki would run him in if he did that, even if Kiley wouldn't. He felt confused, lost, alone, and powerless. He alternately missed Cheryl and blamed her for not being there for him. The wallscreen was already covering his suspension. The channels controlled by Nagamuchi corporation ran specials presenting him as a menace. They dredged up footage of every firefight he'd been in. There had been more than he remembered. Most of the short programs began with a still of him carrying Quarters's bagman's head with the legend KILLER COP? under it.

"There is someone at the door," the apartment AI said.

"I've got it." Danny moved away and called for the display on wallscreen. A moment later he returned with Craig Traven in tow.

Traven noticed the nervous look on the man's face

and thought how out of place it was. A cold breath of premonition touched the back of his neck.

"I interrupt anything?" Craig Traven asked. He was dressed in party fashion with a white carnation on his lapel.

"No," Traven replied.

Craig Traven nodded and touched the carnation briefly, as if to make sure none of the petals had dropped off since he'd last checked. He didn't look at Traven when he spoke. "I'm here to pick up Danny. I've been thinking, and it's about time I started taking care of him instead of leaving him with you."

41

"I don't want to go," Danny said.

Craig Traven didn't look at the boy. "You're not being given a choice, Danny."

Traven set his drink to one side, the taste suddenly sour and hollow. "What's this all about?"

His father waved the question away. "It's not about anything, Mickey. You got enough problems around here without having to keep up with a teenage kid all the time."

"I had those same problems the last time you were here," Traven said in a measured voice. "It didn't seem to be an issue then."

Craig Traven's eyes flicked up, met his momentarily, then slid away. "You haven't had problems like you're about to have, Mickey."

"Nagamuchi was behind my suspension from the force," Traven said. He watched for a reaction.

His father shrugged. "I don't know. Maybe."

"You're telling me they aren't going to be satisfied with that."

"I'm not telling you anything. I'm just here to pick up my son."

"If busting me out of the department isn't going to be enough," Traven asked, "what will?"

Craig Traven turned to face Danny. "Get your clothes. We're getting out of here."

"I'm not going," Danny said again.

"The hell you aren't." Craig Traven stepped forward and bunched his hands up into fists. His face was crimson.

Danny stood his ground and squared his shoulders. The hard gleam in his eyes revealed he wasn't about to go willingly.

"Mickey," Craig Traven said in a quiet voice, "if Danny doesn't come with me, I'm going to make all kinds of trouble for you. I'm his father. You're not. The courts would uphold my rights, especially in view of your current public situation."

Traven stood up and looked at Danny. "If you want to stay here, it's fine with me. We'll weather whatever kind of heat comes down together."

"Dammit, boy, don't be stubborn! If you don't get your things together and follow me out of this apartment, the first thing I'm going to do when I leave is pick up the phone in my car and start calling everybody I know until we get this situation resolved. You want to bring that kind of grief down on Mickey?"

Danny waited a couple of beats, switched his gaze to Traven, and said, "I'm going with him."

"You don't have to do that."

Danny shook his head, his voice tight with emotion. "I don't want to see you hurt anymore. That's all. You know yourself the kind of buttons he can push. It'll be better this way for all of us." He looked back at his father. "Give me five minutes." He left the patio.

Traven watched the boy go. "You always win, don't you?" he asked softly.

His father waved it away. "Don't take it personally, Mickey. This is just business."

Less than four minutes later, Danny returned, carrying his bags and wearing his coat. He looked at Traven. "It's like I said—unless you've found a way out of the system, the system will beat you every time."

"Not always, kid, not always." Traven stepped forward and hugged the boy, surprised at the aching burn that jumped in his chest when Danny hugged him back. "If you need me, all you have to do is give me a call."

"I know." Danny wiped at his eyes with a sleeve and picked up his bags.

"I'll meet you in the hallway," Craig Traven said. "Just want to tell Mickey goodbye."

Danny walked off without another word or a look back over his shoulder.

"Good kid, isn't he?" Craig Traven asked. "He could have a future for himself if he plays his cards right."

"There's just one problem," Traven said. "Danny's not for sale."

His father grinned knowingly and shook his head. "Everybody's for sale, Mickey. That's something you should have learned a long time ago. If you had, maybe you wouldn't have all these problems now." He left, crossing the living room just as the latest batch of stories concerning Mick Traven appeared on wallscreen.

After his father was gone, Traven called for the lights as he walked into the kitchen and placed a pan on the stove. He pulled the ingredients for an omelet from the refrigerator, thinking a lot of the foodstuffs stored in there would go to waste now that Danny was gone.

The eggs sizzled in the pan. He added the meat, peppers, onions, and cheese, scooped the omelet out when it was done. He ate mechanically, without enjoyment. In the darkness of the living room, with the soft glow of the wallscreen playing over the furniture, he imagined Cheryl sitting there waiting for him. He banished the phantom and poured a glass of milk to wash the omelet down.

Long, silent minutes later, the phone rang and he answered it. "Traven." He recognized Escobar's voice at once.

"Amigo, I see you have been sidelined."

Traven pushed himself up to sit on the kitchen counter, put the milk glass in the sink, and filled it with water. "Yeah."

"It took some influential people to do that," Escobar said.

"Maybe you should be the detective."

Escobar laughed in sympathy. "I see that you're not happy with your present situation."

"To put it mildly."

"I thought you would feel that way. That's why I called, to make sure you still wanted to hear about our mutual interest."

Some of the uncertainty clouding Traven's mind went away. "You have something?"

"It's too early to tell. Perhaps in a couple of days." Escobar chuckled. "You're still the closest thing I have to legal aid, and I don't think you're completely cut off from your resources. True?"

"True," Traven replied, and hoped it was.

"Then I will be calling you." Escobar hung up.

A heartbeat later the *chuck-chug* noise of a scrambler echoed into the receiver before the dial tone took over.

Traven hung up and scooted off the countertop. He retreated to his bedroom long enough to change into a pair of sweats. When he returned, he glanced at the picture of the cadet on his wall and wondered where all the innocence and trust had gone. Then he walked out the door and headed for the gym. Since Cheryl was gone and the vodka wasn't working, all he had left was the gym. He didn't allow himself to think for a moment it wouldn't help.

After a brief workout with the free weights, Traven spent time with one of the heavy bags. He forced the aggression out of his system with every roundhouse kick and hammerblow he threw. He kept the pace rapid, till he was covered with sweat and his muscles felt like jelly. He ignored the attention he received from the other people in the gym, concentrated on the correctness of his movements. He could hear old Jotaro whispering in his mind, badgering him as if this were the old days, till he got the movements memorized with his body instead of his brain.

The blows and kicks landed in a drumbeat of violent rain. Instead of dissipating, the rage locked tightly inside him seemed to grow and swell till he could scarcely contain it. Even then, with the anger hammering at him more fiercely than the power he put into every kick or punch, the search for perfection was there. Jotaro had given him that. Jotaro had given him the focus he needed in his life when it seemed life would overcome him. Somewhere in between he had forged a set of rules for himself, based on the belief that right was always stronger than wrong. Right movement was stronger than wrong movement. Right answers triumphed over wrong ones.

None of that seemed to apply now.

Every fiber of the cop in him told him he was right about the connections to Nagamuchi. But being right wasn't enough. He had been the loser when the dust cleared.

There had been two systems that went with the shield—the system they taught in the books, and the system a cop learned in the streets. One had been based on the rules of society, a group-imposed morality that governed the populace. The other had been based on the rules of the individual, on who a cop could trust to repay a favor. With seven years in on the force, with three years spent in vice, with a record as impressive as the one he had rolled up, he'd found out in the end none of it really mattered. There were people in this world who could not only bend the rules and slide away from the sting of legal retribution, but also use those same rules when they chose to.

Perspiration coursed down his body. His sweats clung to him like damp rags. His hands and feet felt numb. His arms and legs were leaden. Salt stung his eyes. The only thing that kept him moving was the search for correctness within himself.

Finally reaching physical exhaustion though barely dulling the nervous emotional energy that racked him, he stepped back from the heavy bag. Skin had torn from his knuckles. He hadn't noticed. Now the pain was bittersweet. He turned toward the bench where he'd left his tote bag. The other people in the exercise area busied themselves with rowing, running, skipping rope, and bicycling.

Otsu Hayata handed him his towel, her face unreadable.

He accepted it, mopping his face and saying, "Thanks."

She wore a turquoise blouse and black leather skin-tight pants. The blouse hung open, exposing cleavage and a strand of black pearls. Her earrings were black pearl also. "You move very well," she said.

Traven nodded. "I had a good teacher."

"I did not know you were versed in martial arts. Your file didn't disclose that."

"My file doesn't tell everything."

"Neither does mine, Detective Traven."

He wondered at her words but didn't ask her about it, because something inside him said it was too early. "You know something about martial arts, Miss Hayata?"

"I've studied. Never anything as elaborate as what you were demonstrating. But I've watched some of the teachers work through their personal katas when they were alone. Not alone in the dojo, but alone in their heads. Many of them had the same look on their faces as you had on yours. Relaxed, peaceful. The incongruity of it always amazed me."

"They're meant to help you go inside yourself, to unlock the secrets you've hidden from yourself so you can put all the pieces together."

"And does it do that?"

He gave her a thin smile. "Not tonight."

"So what do you do?"

"I don't know."

She appeared to consider that. "My father taught the martial arts to my older brothers. I was only a child when he died, but he worked with me a little. The thing that most fascinated me was that he said the techniques were a way of achieving balance within a person. Do you think that is true?"

"Yes."

"Did you find it tonight?"

"No."

"But you have felt this balance before?"

"Yes."

"What is it like?"

"It's hard to explain until you've been there. It's like

having sex explained to you before you've experienced it. In order to learn it, you have to live it.''

She folded her arms across her breasts and softened the cleavage.

Traven was suddenly conscious of the sour odor of alcohol and perspiration that gathered around him. He toweled his face and forearms off again.

She looked at him. ''Do you have some place we can talk in private?''

He suggested his apartment, and she agreed.

42

"Men like you scare me," Hayata said.

Showered, refreshed, and dressed in fresh sweat pants, Traven opened two beers in the kitchen and brought them into the living room. He handed her one and she took it. "What kind of men is that?"

She lounged on the couch, legs drawn up under her. "Men who think they have all the answers." She sipped the beer and grimaced slightly.

Traven let her have the couch and took the easy chair. The lighting in the room was dim and softened her features. "Is the beer okay?"

"Yes. I'm just not used to drinking."

"I can make coffee."

"No. Thank you. I want this. The first one is always hardest."

He drained off a third of his beer as he studied her. Here, where she wasn't in the public eye, he could see the undercurrent of emotion that moved through her. It shocked him to realize the major emotion was fear.

"You think I have all the answers?" he said.

She smiled at him.

He was surprised to find that he liked it.

"I didn't say that I thought you had all the answers," she said. "What I said is that *you* thought you had all the answers."

"I like it when you do that."

"What?"

"Smile."

She colored briefly.

"I didn't know you could."

"There's a lot you don't know about me, Detective Traven. That's why it's a bad thing to think you have all the answers. You took me at surface value. You thought I was just another little tweener trying to make the grade through the squeeze of cultures. I am not, never have been, and never will be a whore for Nagamuchi. Notice that I call it what it is. I don't pretty it up by saying 'geisha.' " She waved toward the balcony. "I was born in California. Except for the last four years, I had been nowhere else. Now I have Dallas. And a few trips to the Orient when Yorimasa-san needed me to accompany him. All in all, you might say I enjoy an ideal life. I have no complaints, no unattainable goals except for a few fantasies which are none of your business, and I make a good living. For the last four years I haven't really wanted for anything. I've lived cloistered away in one of the Nagamuchi-owned apartment buildings and have passed the time very quietly. I've had only one bad experience since I've lived here, and I've been able to put that behind me and go on." She sipped the beer again and made another face. "That is, I'd been able to put it behind me until you came along."

Traven waited. One thing he had learned about patience was that it was often valuable in getting other people to talk about themselves.

"Those women died horribly," Hayata said. She gazed at him, her dark eyes depthless. "No one deserves to die that way. They were killed like animals."

"Yes." He said it softly, so his words wouldn't startle her, only emphasize that in her mind.

She shivered. "You have to understand something about me. That job at Nagamuchi is everything I've ever worked for. My parents were poor. Still, my mother managed to find enough work to put me through school. Two of my brothers are dead. One died in a Ku Klux Klan demonstration in San Francisco. The other died in a car wreck when he was just a teenager. My youngest brother is a construction worker. He dropped out of school when his girlfriend became pregnant. I was the last child in my family to have a chance of making something of myself.''

"And Nagamuchi allowed you to do that."

"Yes. You understand that, don't you?"

He nodded.

"Part of my correctness, my balance, stems from having a job with respect. Because of my mother. She is very sick and still lives in Patterson, where I am from, and thoughts of me being this very successful person make her happy. I didn't want to do anything that endangered her happiness.'' She looked away. "I don't want to now, but I don't feel I have a choice.''

Traven waited, his breath tight and still in his lungs.

Tears slipped from her eyes, and she bowed her head to catch her face in her free hand. "They shouldn't have burned that girl's head. They had no right to do that.'' She looked at him through tear-blurred eyes. "Ever since Monday I have thought of what it would be like if that had happened to me and it had been my mother attending my funeral. I haven't been able to get that headless corpse out of my head.''

Traven breathed out slowly despite the rapid beating of his heart. Part of him was suspicious, part of him didn't trust his instinct that told him she was telling the truth, and part of him kept asking what there was left to lose.

She wiped her tears away with a palm, looking like a little girl in the shadows. "You believe the man who killed those women works for Nagamuchi.''

"Yes.''

"So do I.''

"Do you know who it is?''

She shook her head. "No. Maybe. I'm not sure.''

Traven waited, fingers wrapped tightly around the beer bottle in his hand.

"I told you I worked my way up in Nagamuchi.''

"Yes.''

"I spent three years at the San Diego branch. The personnel there are primarily American-Japanese. At least they were when I was there. I've heard there have been some changes since I left. I was a public relations

person and I was good at my job. There were no geishas there. Those are found in Dallas, but not in San
Diego. At least not then. Taira Yorimasa saw me
shortly after my arrival and had me transferred to his
department. Within a week he had asked me to dinner
and arranged to take work to my apartment.'' Her wet
eyes grew bitter. ''When we arrived there, he told me
exactly what a geisha was and what he expected from
me. I tried to resist. I fought. It only seemed to excite
him more. He raped me that night.'' Her voice broke.
''I went to the hospital later, but those files were quietly lost, just as Nami Chikara's supposedly were.''

''You think Yorimasa killed those women?''

''When he raped me that night, I honestly thought
he was going to kill me. He hit me, screamed at me,
and abused me every way he could think of.''

Traven forced his emotions into neutral, forced the
cop persona to the forefront. ''Why did you stay?''

''Because of the goddam job. And because people
over Yorimasa promised me it would never happen
again.''

''Matahachi?''

''I don't want to say. There's no sense in involving
people who were only trying to do the right thing.''

Traven didn't bother telling her he thought the right
thing would have been to get rid of Yorimasa. It would
have meant imposing his priorities on hers. ''Did it
ever happen again?''

''No.''

''But there were other women?''

''Yes. Some quit. Others stayed on. For some of
them, that's what they'd hired on to do.''

''So what do you want me to do?''

She looked at him and wiped at her face. ''If Yorimasa is killing those women, I want you to stop him.''

He leaned back in his chair. ''You'll have to go to
the police to do that. If you haven't caught the wallscreen lately, I'm not exactly working for the department at present. I've been given orders to stay away
from the whole situation.''

"You've been ignoring those same orders all along," she said.

"Yeah. Only now they can lock me up for it."

"So you're afraid?"

Traven felt anger ignite inside him. "Hell, yes, I'm afraid. I'm trapped outside the system that I was sure would keep me safe."

Her voice was small. "So am I. So are all those women if Yorimasa is killing them from knowledge he has of them through the company." She shook her head. "I came to you because you were separated from the police now. You can do things on your own, without someone looking over your shoulder. What I tell you, you can keep to yourself. Do you know how much I fought with myself over whether or not even to see you?"

Traven could guess. The thought made him feel uncomfortable and cheap.

She stood up, face filled with fury. "I thought you were a stronger man than you evidently are, Detective Traven. When I met you, I was afraid of you, because you reminded me of my father. You appeared to be very single-minded in your purpose. He was like that, and I can never remember anything stopping him. That's how I thought it would be with you. I was wrong. I guess we both lost something. Yorimasa took my virginity. Nagamuchi ripped your manhood away." She walked for the door.

"Wait." Traven pushed himself out of the easy chair.

She stopped but didn't turn around to look at him.

"I'm going to need more than this to work on."

"What?"

"Personnel files. The real thing. Not the oatmeal you and your secretaries cobbled together for Higham and me."

She remained there, poised for flight.

He softened his voice. "Otsu, I've got to have those files to have a shot at this guy."

"If I'm found out, at the very least they will only fire me."

"I know. I'll try to work around your involvement in this. But to work, I've got to have information. You're the only person I know inside."

She didn't reply.

"If I can prove who did it," Traven said, "I'll nail the bastard to the wall. You've got my word on that."

"Your file suggested you were an honorable man. Honorable men don't give their word lightly."

"I'm not giving mine lightly. I want this guy as badly as you do. From the psychiatric reports I've seen and heard, the killing is only going to get worse."

She faced him. "Once I give you that, there'll be no turning back, will there?"

He shook his head.

"Hold me," she said as she walked toward him.

He met her halfway and wrapped his arms around her. She crumbled in his embrace. He held her tightly, feeling so alone, knowing the same feeling resonated in her. He looked down, expecting to see the top of her head. Instead, he found her lips coming up to meet his. He took them eagerly, wanting to get lost in the emotion.

43

Her name was Kocha Ryohei. Earl Brandstetter had never known that before tonight. He had been content with knowing her as the Queen Dragon Mother who guarded Yorimasa's private offices. Tonight he viewed her differently. Tonight Kocha Ryohei was a prize to be fought for and won.

He came up in the elevator. His dark coat overlay dark garments. The mask was folded carefully inside a coat pocket. The knife he intended to use was in the pocket on the other side. Tonight he'd brought his own weapon, a sharp little combat knife he'd picked up in a pawnshop only a few blocks away.

His heartbeat was steady. He felt loose and prepared. The anticipation that thrummed through him had started when he bought the knife.

He stepped out of the elevator into the elegant hallway and moved at once toward her apartment. Oriental rugs, real ones, not the imports manufactured in Dallas for businessmen wanting to win points with the Japanese corporations, covered the floor. He knew the difference from working at Nagamuchi.

A middle-aged Japanese couple stepped out of their apartment at the end of the hallway. They stood frozen for a moment, no doubt surprised by his presence inside a Japanese-only building.

He smiled at them and made no effort to conceal his features. He had killed four people and the police had never come close to him. Except for Traven. And even Traven wasn't a threat any longer. The news had broken on wallscreen late Tuesday. This was Thursday night. There had been no changes. He quickly amended that. The only change had been the ravenous hunger that fired him and drove him back into the street.

The Japanese couple passed him in the hallway, never looking at him again. He kept walking. His feet made no sound at all. He felt the solid lines of the knife through the coat pocket, then stroked it. Anticipation flared to new heights inside him.

She had given him the Queen Dragon Mother's name and address, proved once again how much more she knew him than he knew himself. The Cahill twins hadn't lasted as long as he would have liked, but the experience had been unique and pleasant.

Not at all what she had in mind for Kocha Ryohei, he knew. The thought made him smile again. The reflection of his smile in the burnished metal of the apartment door made him think how infrequently he had seen that expression on his face.

He didn't even have to touch the door panel to open the door, just jacked into the AI system, scanned the living room to make sure she wasn't up, and passed through.

A strong spice fragrance filled his nose as the door closed behind him. The living room was sunk fifteen centimeters. Expensive bamboo furniture gleamed in light and dark hues. Brightly colored woven blankets and plush pillows covered the framework. The carpet was Oriental. Brass incense burners streaming gray smoke hung on two walls.

He walked farther into the room and saw a side of the Queen Dragon Mother he had never suspected existed. The paintings were filled with brilliant colors that depicted imaginary scenes of samurai warriors battling mythological beasts. Flowers and plants, real and artificial, were in abundance. A long aquarium filled with red and gold fish occupied most of the far wall. The room seemed more fantasy land and garden than the austere living space he'd imagined on the walk over. The anticipation locked inside him gained a sharper edge.

The kitchen was clean and neat. Exactly what he'd expected.

He seated his senses more firmly into the apartment AI's and searched for the woman. The cyberspace lurking behind the AI sucked him into it, shared its existence with him, and, for a moment, tried to devour him. He took flight within it, then mastered the addiction to attain a newer, broader existence.

Before he had a chance to flip through the rooms, a sudden squawk drew his attention back to the physical world. He hand wrapped around the combat knife and ripped it free of his pocket.

When the squawk sounded again, he found the source.

A nightingale hung suspended from a swing inside a gilded cage to the right of the arch over the living-room space.

He steadied his heart as he moved toward the bird. He pulled the mask from his pocket, slipped it on, took control of the apartment AI's monitoring system, and switched the recording function on.

The nightingale continued squawking as he lifted the cage door and reached inside. He groped for it, finally managed to wrap gloved fingers around the bird's frail body. It crunched when he applied pressure. The bird's head jerked for a few seconds, then lolled lifelessly to one side. Blood trickled from the open beak.

The wallscreen recorded it all.

Inside the mask, Brandstetter smiled again, and pulled out his hand. Feathers and blood and bird feces caked the rough palm.

An explosion sounded behind him, and he ducked instinctively. Glass fragments shattered from a picture hanging on the wall beside his head. He spun with the combat knife in his fist.

Dressed in an emerald-green robe that hung to the floor, the Queen Dragon Mother eared the hammer back on the small revolver gripped in both hands.

There was a brief wink of chrome, then the sudden flare of muzzle flash from the pistol.

Something impacted against Brandstetter's chest. It stung. Then he was in motion, his legs driving him forward.

She fired again, and the stinging sensation in his chest repeated itself. If she was frightened by his black suit, she didn't show it.

He hit her and sent her flying with a hoarse scream of pain and terror. The gun was flung to one side.

Kocha Ryohei's composure evaporated as she scrabbled frantically toward her bedroom. She kept yelling, "No, no, no," up until the time Brandstetter grabbed her ankle and pulled her toward him.

She flailed in his grip like the tail of a kite.

He leaned over her, rested on his knees, and shook with the thought of what the bullets could have done to him if he hadn't bought the Kevlar vest. He straightened and lifted her eighty-pound frame easily in one hand. He showed her the knife.

She tried to work her head back and forth in his grip, still saying, "No, no, no, no."

He threw her into the wall nearest him. Something broke. He repeated the maneuver, used both hands now to hurl her up against the wall. He fell, repulsed by the impact. Blood dribbled down her chin. She reached for him with fingers that suddenly reminded him of the nightingale's talons. He picked her up, used another wall, hammered her against it over and over. Blood stained the wall now. Her movements grew weaker in his grasp. He heard roaring in his ears. Sweat lined his hands inside the gloves. His heart was light, happy.

He continued to smash her against the walls and the furniture. When her eyes rolled up in her head and her arms and legs hung limp, he carried her broken body to the center of the room and dropped it. Shattered furniture, cracked picture frames, and blood marked his passage.

He breathed heavily as he searched for the knife he'd dropped. He found it on a cushion. Returning to the body, he dropped to his knees again. He gripped the combat knife tightly, then bared her throat. By the time he'd finished sawing, his heart rate and breathing had returned to normal.

Pushing himself up from the floor, he carried her head to the aquarium and dropped it in. He watched, bending forward from the waist. The head sank slowly, bubbles spinning after its descent as the empty places filled. The water turned pink and stained the whites of the eyes a lighter shade. The fish seemed to lose their color, become less eye-catching. The head became the centerpiece for the aquarium. Fish circled it. After a little while they grew brave enough to swim close enough to nudge it. Later they would begin eating.

Brandstetter smiled, happy with himself. He had learned to enjoy it, just as she'd said he would. He tapped the glass to scare the fish. He smiled again when they darted madly through the pink water.

He pulled the focus of the apartment AI's cameras tighter on the aquarium, glancing up at the wallscreen to judge. When the aquarium filled the wallscreen, the slack-mouthed head canted slightly askew, he froze the picture. Every wallscreen in the apartment would keep it on till a technician broke into the system and erased it.

He got up and rubbed the sore spots on his chest. Then he reversed the coat and left the apartment. He was whistling, something he never did, by the time he reached the elevator.

"See me, Earl?"

He looked at her. The were in the drawing room, the fireplace roaring brightly. Kocha Ryohei's body fit perfectly. "Yes. You're beautiful."

She laid a forefinger on his lips and smiled. "You shouldn't lie to an old lady."

He sat on the couch and enjoyed the game she played. "I'm not. You're very beautiful."

"And wickedly old." She stroked her bare arms before her. "As small as I am inside here, I feel like a child next to you."

"But you're not."

She smiled. "No. I'm old enough to be your mother."

"I know."

She sat in his lap and started unbuttoning his shirt. "Like this you're old enough to be a man and I'm still old enough to be your mother."

He luxuriated in the feel of her hands against his chest.

"This is the last one from your immediate work area," she said in a quiet voice.

For a moment he was afraid, thinking she meant to stop everything altogether.

Then she went on. "The next woman we take will have to come from another source. Nagamuchi has plenty of subsidiaries. You have access to all those files." She smiled and slipped his shirt off. "There's a world waiting out there to entertain us, honey, and there's no sense in taking more chances than we need to."

He ran his hands down the slight arch of her back, and she trembled at his touch. He bit at her neck, inhaled the Queen Dragon Mother's fragrance.

"If we change our program," she said in a shuddering voice, "they'll never find out about our secret. We'll continue living our lives the way we want to. But there is a problem."

He looked at her.

"The personnel files have been copied. I discovered that when I checked on prospects earlier."

A knot of apprehension formed in his stomach. "Do you know who?"

She nodded. "Otsu Hayata. The transmission came from her board. Most people wouldn't have caught her. But I did. That means someone may be on to us." She held his head in her hands. "I don't think she's doing this by herself. You'll have to find out who she's working with. Then kill them."

He remained silent as the lust drained out of him.

"Do you hear me?"

"Yes." He had trouble remembering who Otsu

Hayata was, then her face clicked into his mind. He looked at the woman. "It's nothing I can't handle. No one can catch us."

She smiled, then buried his face in her small breasts. "I know, baby, I know. I just wanted to tell you so you could take care of it. Of us."

"I will." He reached for her, heard her breath quicken in his ear.

"Be careful," she whispered. "After all, I am an old woman." Her laughter faded into whimpering desire.

44

"This is the best black-market techware I could get my hands on," Zenzo said, "but there's still going to be times you have some bleed-over."

Traven sat with his eyes squeezed shut as Zenzo worked. It was one thing to know there was a biochip computer in his head, and quite another to see it. The last time had been three years ago when he'd been booted to sergeant in charge of his vice team. The new encoding had given him override capability and special tach frequencies.

They sat in Zenzo's van in an alley off Holland Street. Kowalski was there too, and it had been members of the vice team that had secured the area and marked off the two plainclothes units that had been assigned to Traven's apartment. Kowalski cracked his knuckles, a sure sign that the big man was bored.

"The problem I'm faced with," Zenzo went on, "is that your access channel has been deactivated. Given enough time, I could dummy up a name and create a new channel for you. But that would take days we don't have, as well as risk greater detection. So what I've done is build a copycat com-chip that is twinned to one of the department's rookies."

Kowalski grunted. "That should make the guy real happy. It's a bitch getting used to a com-chip the first time anyway without having interference from another chip."

Traven felt Zenzo's fingers digging behind his left ear. He tried to keep his mind from forming images, but it was no use. One of the recurring nightmares he'd had as a rookie was of the com-chip. In the dream the chip had become infected and he'd pulled it out, grabbed fistful after fistful of pus-covered wires and yanked them out of his head until he woke up bathed in a cold sweat.

"Our rookie won't know anything's wrong with his com-chip for a while. A week, maybe a little longer, and the headaches are going to drive him nuts and he'll have it checked. Once they run it through a scan, this copycat implant I'm giving you will self-destruct."

Traven had a mental image of the wiring in his head turning to dripping plastic. He shuddered involuntarily.

Zenzo laughed. "Take it easy. It's not as bad as it sounds. Nothing physical will happen to the chip. But it will go inert again. Let's just hope it doesn't take longer than we have." He pressed against Traven's head. "There. Let's switch it on and see what we have."

Traven mentally keyed the com-chip to life. From Tuesday night until Friday night, for three days of hell he could not have imagined, his world had been filled with silence. He hadn't even been able to access DataMain to find out the time. The com-chip flickered, then caught fire. He accessed DataMain, slipping through the fuzzy connections of police and emergency bands. The time was 10:12 P.M.

Zenzo rippled into his head. "Well?"

Traven opened his eyes and looked at his two friends. "Feels good to be back." The silence had gone away, beaten into submissive slumber by the familiar staccato bursts of uniformed patrol transmissions. The reception wasn't as sharp, but it was there. "Thanks, Zenzo."

Zenzo rolled his wheelchair back. "We aim to please. If things get fuzzy, just give yourself a good whack on the head." He laughed at his own humor even though Traven and Kowalski didn't crack a smile. He wiped tears from his eyes. "You guys should see the looks on your faces. Seriously, though, Mick, you're going to experience some disorientation. Since that is a satellite off the main com-chip, it's going to want to interact with any computer system around it. That chip will have an affinity for absorbing programming.''

"I'll keep that in mind," Traven said dryly.

His words sent Zenzo into renewed gales of laughter. "You'll keep it in mind? That's a biochip linked to your neural circuitry, my friend. Do you think you have a choice?" He stripped off the surgical gloves he'd used to keep the hardware sterile and dropped them into a pocket to dispose of later.

Traven shook his head and concentrated on Kowalski. "How tied up is Tompkins keeping you and the team?"

Kowalski flashed a big grin. "I forget you've been out of the picture for a few days." He shifted in the seat he dwarfed in the back of the van. "Seems this morning old Cale caught a hot flash about a coke lab over on Tremont. Naturally, he loads the team up and we go to do our Johnny-on-the-spot routine with him leading the charge. Turns out his flash is a flush. A suck play from beginning to end. We turned up a couple users, a little crack, but old Cale ended up with a .22 bullet in each butt cheek. Vinton said he caught a whiff of a Columbian sniper on top of one of the buildings. By the time we got someone up there—this was supposed to be a cakewalk, remember—the sniper was gone and Cale Tompkins was screaming like the old bull who'd been about an inch low in clearing the barbed-wire fence.''

"So you've got a free hand?"

"Until Kiley either takes the field himself or appoints somebody else.''

"How's Tompkins?''

"Facedown on a hospital bed drawing workman's comp the last I seen him.'' Kowalski laughed. "Don't want to say who, but somebody let a newsguy in who snapped a few pictures before hospital security chased him. I told Cale the guy got his best side.''

"Seems kind of odd that a Columbian sniper would

deliberately shoot a cop when they had nothing at stake.''

Kowalski gave a horse laugh that thundered above anything Zenzo had done. ''And pretty amazing to think he put both shots in old Cale's ass. I mean, everybody knows what an ass he is, but give me a break.''

Traven laughed too as he pictured the scene in his mind. Then he remembered his conversations with Evaristo Escobar and ruled out chance taking a hand in the shooting. ''Put the team on alert,'' he said. ''I think we picked up a blocker for this next play, and I want us ready to take advantage of it when the time comes.''

Kowalski grinned. ''They've already been put. I figured the shooter was one of Escobar's boys myself. Can't say that I like the guy any more now than I did, but I definitely gained some respect for his sense of humor.'' He held up two fingers. ''I mean, can you picture it? Getting shot in the ass? Twice?''

The big man was still laughing when Traven said his goodbyes and got out of the van. He faded into the darkness to skirt the plainclothes people assigned to watch him. With the constant buzz of conversations in the back of his head, it didn't seem lonely at all.

Traven heard about the fourth Mr. Nobody kill scene as he watched Otsu Hayata track Taira Yorimasa's recent movements on her computer in his bedroom. He left her clacking away on the deck while he picked up the phone and retreated to the bathroom doorway, where he'd have some privacy.

He'd been uncomfortable around her ever since Tuesday night, when they'd ended up in his bed. There had been a couple conversations through public phones since then concerning the personnel records, but no face-to-face confrontations till tonight. She had been cool toward him, cloaked herself in professionalism. Having the deck in his bedroom made it hard not to remember the sweat-soaked sheets and the desperate passion that had gripped them both that night. After it

had passed, there had been too little to talk about, and
he recognized the wall she'd erected to keep him out
of her mind, because it was the same thing he'd immediately groped for.

He stood in the doorway of the bathroom and waited
for the connection to be made as she brought up screen
after screen of information. Her back was slim and
curved, flared down to tight hips that had been so demanding three days ago. He swallowed as he remembered, and felt desire rise in him. Then the ache set
in. It was still something he couldn't understand. At
first he thought he'd been missing Beth again, remembering how she had been taken away by his father. The
confrontation with Craig Traven and Danny's loss
could have been enough to trigger those feelings all
over again. Only the pain wasn't there when he remembered Beth. It had been there months ago. It had
taken memory of Cheryl to raise the ghost of those
gnawing teeth working on his stomach. He couldn't
understand it. Maybe he'd refused to understand it.
After all, they were only friends.

"Hello." Higham's voice sounded tired and as
empty as a crushed beer can.

"It's me," Traven said in a low voice. "I just heard
about the fourth murder on wallscreen."

Quiet silence issued from the receiver. Then,
"You're not exactly somebody I should be talking
about this with."

"It's your choice." Traven felt his throat tighten.
Even wired with the twinned com-chip, Higham could
cut him out of the murder investigation. And somehow, that had become a commitment as well.

"Dammit, Mick." Higham sighed. "Is this line
clear?"

"Yeah. I had a friend sweep it a few minutes ago.
The PD had a feedoff block primed, but he scrambled
the circuitry and routed it back into itself so I can call
out undetected whenever I want to. Just don't call
me."

"This psycho is slipping over the edge," Higham
said. "The media didn't get all the details yet, but they

will. Mr. Nobody's gonna gain a lot of notoriety over this latest hit.''

"Is he still working employees of Nagamuchi?''

"Yeah. This one was Kocha Ryohei.''

The name clicked in Traven's mind and brought memory of her file in the personnel chips Hayata had given him to review. "Taira Yorimasa's personal secretary.''

"That's the one.''

Traven's hand tightened on the phone. "Where was Taira Yorimasa?''

"Don't know,'' Higham replied. "And I'm not asking. He's not the guy we're after.''

"How do you know?''

"The guy we're looking for is a lot bigger than Yorimasa. I'm talking a big guy here. He picked the woman up and threw her around like a rag doll. From what the ME tells me, her insides were pulped long before he cut her the first time. He slammed her into the walls a dozen times or more. Way I figure it, this guy has to be well over six feet tall.''

"That rules out a lot of people," Traven said. He focused on Earl Brandstetter. Yorimasa and Brandstetter were the two men assigned to computer security who would know the most about it. Either man was in position to steal techware from the company. He dropped the line of thinking. It didn't feel right. Maybe if one of them had sold the information and was discovered by Yorimasa's geisha, he could have bought the murder as an attempted cover-up. But the others had made it personal. He couldn't figure how all the pieces fit together, but he was sure they did.

"This guy's really getting into his work,'' Higham said. "We found a couple flattened slugs at the scene that came from a .22 registered in Ryohei's name.''

"Kevlar vest?''

"That's what we're thinking. It means this guy's learning more about killing. And he's starting to make more of a production out of it. He cut the woman's head off, made an effort this time to record it for its best view, and dropped it into the aquarium. When the apartment manager found the body earlier this evening, the wallscreens were all paused on a close-up of the head in the aquarium. If he's starting to think these things out and prepare for them, it won't be long before he realizes he can't kill so close to home. This city's got an animal out there with a cave to run to.''

"So you believe in the Nagamuchi tie-in too." Traven didn't feel any satisfaction. Instead, he was cold and hollow inside.

"Hell, yes, I believe it. I've been doing this kind of investigation since you were a punk kid. I just can't find a way over the wall."

"Why don't you drop by a little later and compare notes?"

Higham's voice sounded interested at once. "You think you're on to something?"

"Yeah. Hayata's here now and we're going over personnel files."

"Son of a bitch. How'd you arrange that?"

"I didn't. She did."

"Gutsy lady."

"That's what I thought." Traven waited, wondering how Higham would respond to the invitation.

The pause seemed longer than necessary. "I'll be there. Fuck it. I'd rather take a chance on working for the jackals than to see this motherfucker run free to keep on killing. Because that's exactly what he's going to do if we don't drop him. I've seen shit like this before, and I know what I'm talking about."

"Thanks," Traven said.

"Don't thank me, buddy. This isn't for you. It's for me." Higham broke the connection.

Traven hung up the handset and walked back into the bedroom.

Hayata turned to face him. She wore sexless light-blue warmups and tennis shoes. Her hair was put back in a severe bun. "Taira Yorimasa couldn't be the person behind the killings," she said. "On two of the dates, the first and third killings, he was in Tokyo on a layover to Lashio."

Traven sat on the bed, still holding the phone.

Thoughts whirled inside his head. The pieces were all spread there before him, but he couldn't make any sense of the arrangement. "Are you sure he was there?"

"Yes. Some of the corporate records I copied required his retina print on the documents as well as those of the people he met with. There is no way that could have been falsified. He was there."

Traven nodded. "There was another killing yesterday."

Hayata consulted the deck, churned through screens of information. "Yorimasa was out of country then. In fact . . ." She pressed more buttons. "He's not due back until this morning. He's flying in from Lashio by corporate shuttle."

"Lashio?" Something tugged at Traven's memory. "Where is that?"

After checking the screen, Hayata said, "In Burma. Nagamuchi has some new processing plants there."

Excitement flared through Traven as he put the phone down and stood up. "Burma. You're sure?"

"Yes."

He leaned over her shoulder to check the information contained on the screen. "What kind of processing plants does Nagamuchi have there?"

"Chemical plants of some type." She shook her head. "I could find out more. Is it important?"

"No." He smiled as some of the pieces fell into place. "Burma's part of the Golden Triangle. And I'm still after Yorimasa, though not for the murders. I've been chasing two men, not one."

"What are you talking about?"

"I'll explain later." He reached for his duster and his pistols. "I need you to do an in-depth research report on Earl Brandstetter. He's the guy in charge of corporate computer security. He's also the guy who's been murdering the women."

"How do you know?"

"At this last scene, there was evidence indicating the suspect was a tall man." He didn't want to go into everything else, because he knew he would be leaving her by herself. "Brandstetter's six feet four inches tall."

She turned back to the deck. "What kind of information do you want?"

"Everything you can get. Background history especially." He pulled the duster on. "Can you give me Brandstetter's address before Nagamuchi moved him to his new apartment building?"

Her fingers clacked across the deck. "Eight-thirteen Furgusson Apartments." Understanding dawned on her features. She trailed a finger down the handwritten notes beside the keyboard. "That's the building where the Estevan woman was found."

Traven nodded. "He's our man. She was the only one who didn't fit the pattern. She didn't work for Nagamuchi, she couldn't be researched in the corporate files Brandstetter had access to as security chief, but he didn't need them. He already knew about her."

"What am I looking for?"

"I don't know," he replied honestly. "Something had to set Brandstetter off. Before we can draw any conclusions, I have to know more about him." He buttoned the duster. "Higham will be by later. I told him we had a lead on this thing. Don't let anyone else in."

She nodded.

"When and where is Yorimasa's shuttle due?"

"It'll arrive at Love Field at one-seventeen A.M."

Traven accessed DataMain through the fuzzy reception again. "That gives me a little over an hour and a half. If something turns up, tell Higham I'll call."

She laid a hand on his arm as he turned to go. "Mick." Her voice was soft. Her eyes looked like melted chocolate, smooth and creamy. "Be careful."

The discomfort he felt at her presence and the memory of Tuesday night increased. He covered her hand with his. "Otsu, about the other night . . ." Words failed him.

Her cheeks colored, but she didn't turn away from him. "When this is over and the killer is caught, we both need to put this behind us. Since it's what brought us together, for even one night, there's no way anything could happen between us if we remained with each other.''

Traven leaned down and kissed her on the forehead. ''Another time maybe,'' he said softly.

''Perhaps, but we're both strong people who don't feel we need anyone else in our lives.'' She smiled. ''It takes a lot to tear down the walls we've put up.''

He nodded. The phone rang. He turned away from her reluctantly, feeling he was being too callous, then knew she understood. ''Traven.''

''Ah, amigo, I've caught you at home,'' Escobar said.

''Yes.''

''Do not be worried. I've had this transmission scrambled from our friends in the police department.'' Escobar sounded elated. ''I called to let you know I've discovered when Quarters's next shipment is coming in.''

Traven grinned without humor. ''At one-seventeen A.M. at Love Field on a Nagamuchi shuttle from Burma.''

There was a pause at the other end. ''This comes as no surprise to you, then?''

''No. I'm on my way there now. I'll meet you. A vice team is en route, so tell your group to relax as they arrive.''

''Of course.''

Traven broke the connection, turned back to face Hayata, and saw her busily working the deck, chipped-in now instead of using it manually. She didn't seem to notice him when he left. By the time he hit the street after signaling Kowalski, images of Love Field overlay each other in his mind. When he pulled onto the street, he felt like a cop again. He didn't try to kid himself. Instead of losing just his shield, this time he was taking a chance on losing his freedom as well.

45

The Nagamuchi shuttle arrived at Love Field at 1:13 A.M., four minutes ahead of schedule.

Traven watched the shuttle's final approach and touchdown through the polarized rear window of Evaristo Escobar's armored limousine. When the Nagamuchi trucks trundled to the cargo bay of the shuttle, he switched to the screens of the remote cameras inset against the front seat of the car.

Escobar strapped on a headset and called directions to the camera crews stationed around the airport. The Columbian drug lord had laid out bricks of money to infiltrate the airport security. But it had been money well spent. The views were perfect.

Traven leaned forward and rested his elbows on his knees as one of the cameras zoomed in for a close-up of Yorimasa floating down the escalator.

"The man doesn't seem to be too concerned about his operation, does he?" Escobar asked as he covered the mouthpiece to the headset with a hand.

"Why should he?" Traven asked. "He's got diplomatic immunity riding in his pocket for this one. Even now we're having to guess what's in those crates."

"It's no guess, my friend," Escobar said in a cold, distant voice. "I have pictures of the man he made his purchases from if you wish."

"Later," Traven said as he glanced at the two rows the eight television screens made.

The unloading went efficiently. Three dozen crates were loaded onto four transport trucks with the Nagamuchi logo printed on either side. The cargo handlers, dressed in black, wore exosuits to facilitate the handling, and they didn't speak to anyone. Yorimasa stood to one side of the corporate limousine parked at the head of the line of trucks. The combined lights of the vehicles threw pools of light across the damp runway and dock area. The rumble of jets and shuttles taking off and landing with skilled precision lended an air of unreality to the stakeout.

Traven accessed the com-chip as Escobar ordered a close-up of Yorimasa. "Zenzo."

"Here."

Yorimasa looked tired in the screen. He smoked slowly, and the sleet-filled wind whipped the smoke from his lungs as he exhaled.

"Have you got anything on the cargo declarations?"

Zenzo read off a list of chemicals.

The only thing Traven really understood was the analgesics section.

Onscreen, Yorimasa turned and ducked into the waiting limousine. On the other screens, the black-suited dock crew clambered into the ten-wheeled trucks.

"The list looks straight," Zenzo said when he'd finished.

Traven struggled through the bleed-over issuing from the computer-operated flight tower. "Kowalski."

"Go."

"Still on our other player?"

The trucks pulled into motion and followed the limousine through the gates. Escobar reached for the intercom and ordered his driver to trail the caravan at a respectable distance, then relaxed against the plush seats.

"We're on him," Kowalski responded in reference to Donny Quarters's crew. "So far he's not trying to pull any cute moves."

"Any ideas about a destination?"

"No."

Traven rippled out of the connection.

"Relax, Detective Traven," Escobar said. "Tonight

is our night, huh?'' His smile was easy. ''Relax and you can feel the truth of my words.''

Traven didn't reply. His stomach was knotted up with apprehension. Even if they made the bust, even if they took away the cargo of drugs, many people were going to die tonight. Some of them would be friends of his. If there had been another way, he would have opted for it. He already felt the weight of command though responsibility for part of the attack rested squarely on Escobar's shoulders. His thoughts wandered to Earl Brandstetter and the Mr. Nobody killings, and he reeled them back.

The trucks pulled onto Denton Drive and went southeast to Mockingbird Lane, then turned north. They moved together, didn't panic on the four-lane highway when other traffic sandwiched between them.

Traven tried to relax, but found himself watching the procession of vehicles before them. The television screens were blank now. Escobar continued to talk in a low voice as he directed his team through the side roads to keep a net over the Nagamuchi trucks.

Escobar covered the mouthpiece with a hand as he looked at Traven. ''Surely they wouldn't be fools enough to attempt taking the shipment to the corporation.''

Traven shook his head. ''No, but it makes sense they'd keep it somewhere near to increase Nagamuchi security in the area.''

Escobar studied him in the light-striped darkness of the limousine. ''You believe the corporation is behind the drug cartel.''

''Yes. It's the only thing that sounds logical. I crossed into Yorimasa's territory in another investigation. The corporation covered for him, but they wouldn't say where he was. At first I thought they were just protecting him. Tonight, when I discovered where he'd been going, I realized they were protecting their operation. If the information hadn't come to me as it had, maybe I'd never have tumbled to what was actually going on.''

"And what of the techware Quarters was able to get his hands on to pay the Yakuza?"

"Another ploy. A fail-safe." Traven looked at the man and smiled. "It didn't work. They couldn't expect me to strip the lies away as I did."

Escobar nodded. "What of the Yakuza?"

"Like we always thought," Traven replied in a tight voice. "Nagamuchi subsidizes them."

"These people couldn't have counted on our working out an alliance," Escobar said.

Traven smiled without mirth. "Would you have thought about it?"

"I had. But I thought you would reject the offer. You are not a man to be made offers to by someone you consider to be your enemy. Perhaps had I approached you first, we would not be here now."

Traven nodded. "Perhaps." But he knew it was true, and he knew Escobar knew. "It's a scary thought that I might be predictable."

Escobar showed him an empty palm. "When it comes to matters of honor, you are very predictable. If I hadn't known that, we wouldn't be sitting here either."

Traven looked through the two panels of glass at the line of trucks. Sleet continued to smash against the windshield. "Some people would say that making an alliance with you was not honorable."

"True, but it satisfies your own code of honor, and that is what makes us truly alike. You are uncomfortable with having to go outside the constraints of the laws and the order you choose to work under. There is no need to tell me this. I saw that in you the night you came to my home. But as a man of honor, you knew what had to be done. True?"

"Yes." Traven took a deep breath and felt the tightness in his chest. It hadn't been easy, then or now, but it had been the only way.

"You and I," Escobar said, "we both serve a higher honor. You fight for the survival of this city." He waved at the night lights. "I fight for the survival of my country. We both use whatever means are at our disposal. For you, that means making the law work in spite of the judicial system. For me, that means using the only profitable product my country has for exportation. The sale of drugs feeds my people just as surely as it kills yours here. And that is a type of war. We are soldiers who put aside our differences long enough to deal with a superior enemy. There is no loss of honor in that.''

The caravan turned north on Inwood Road. Escobar called out new directions to his teams.

Traven accessed the com-chip. ''Kowalski.''

''Go.''

''What's your twenty?''

''Turning south on Inwood Road off Northwest Highway.''

''Okay, look alive. The meet is set to go soon.'' Traven rippled out. He reached down beneath the seat and brought out the SPAS 15 Escobar had provided him. The ammo pouch was an over-the-shoulder rig that wouldn't impede his movements. The clips of 12-gauge double-ought gleamed like long gray bars in the intermittent light from the streetlamps.

Escobar held a full-size Uzi. The deadly little piece looked metallic and unforgiving. He smiled at Traven. ''After this is over with, I think I'll miss you. This is the world of currency and business. There aren't many men of honor left.''

Traven nodded, not knowing what to say. It was confusing to think that after the dust settled on this night's foray, the roles of fox and hound would change back to the way they had been.

''I still hope I never have to kill you,'' Escobar said.

''I wouldn't want to kill you,'' Traven said, ''but if it came down to it, you know I would.''

''I know.'' Escobar glanced at the row of television screens as they flickered to life. ''These are from helicopters I had standing by. I didn't want to tell you everything I had planned. A man should reserve a few surprises.'' He smiled. ''They are using infrared cameras, of course, but I thought it would be best to define our battleground before we blindly marched into it.''

Traven watched the screens as he accessed the com-chip. "Zenzo."

"Here."

"How're the satellites coming?"

"I'm already locked in," Zenzo said. "I've had footage rolling since the turn on Mockingbird Lane. The interference will screw up several weather reports for the next few days till the techs get my program-ming virus worked out of the system, but you'll have all the information I can get from geocentrical orbit. I've already logged the license plates and photo-graphed as many men as I can through the windows."

Traven signaled an affirmative and rippled out. Es-cobar was right. A man shouldn't give all his secrets away, and having a weather satellite system circling overhead acting as electronic backup certainly counted as one.

The trucks, led by Yorimasa's limousine, turned into Surrey Circle, a converted warehousing district owned by a subsidiary of Nagamuchi Corporation. Zenzo supplied the information a heartbeat later. Most com-puter investigators wouldn't have penetrated the title confusion the corporation had gone to in an effort not to be tied to the site. But the program Zenzo had put together on Nagamuchi Corporation holdings was any-thing but ordinary.

The helicopters passed by once and peeled off so they wouldn't attract attention. Even if Yorimasa had grown complacent about his position in the drug ring, the Yaks hadn't.

Escobar held out a hand.

Traven took it.

"God go with you, amigo."

"You, too," Traven said. He opened the limo's door and stepped out into the night. The SPAS 15 was a hard bar in his right hand. The twin SIG/Sauers were solid weights in the pockets of his duster. His Kevlar vest was lined with extra magazines for the pistols. He let the night take him and felt at home. He ran, his tennis shoes not making any noise.

"Mick." Kowalski's voice boomed inside his head.

"Go."

"Quarters has made his appearance. I'm afoot now and closing."

"Where are they?" Traven hung the automatic shotgun over his shoulder and climbed the three-meter fence separating him from the loading docks of the warehouses with a 10mm in one hand.

"Fitzmartin's Storage. Third building from the east."

"Don't engage them until the team is in position." Traven dropped to the pavement, sought the shadows at once. He pocketed the SIG/Sauer and took up the SPAS 15 again.

"Roger." Kowalski cleared, his presence still tainting the frequency.

Traven ran behind a parked eighteen-wheeler. He saw the red taillights of the trucks now, heard the whuffling cough of the diesel engines idling. They parked in front of a loading dock where a newly painted sign, FITZMARTIN'S STORAGE, hung overhead. "Zenzo."

"Here."

"Have you got a fix on this place?"

"Working color and infrared. I can't help much in calling the shots when this goes down, but you'll get instant replays on anything you want."

"Good enough. I don't want you active in this. You're an observer. Stay out until you're called for. I want you ready to receive data."

"Okay, but watch your ass down there." Zenzo rippled out.

Traven felt the headache from the twinned com-chip slamming into his temples now. He knew the rookie at the other end of the connection couldn't overhear the conversations taking place on the special frequency they'd established for the operation, but the guy definitely shared the pain. He gripped the stock of the shotgun tighter and ignored the cold wind ripping into him. He slid through the list of names of vice members accompanying him. They were all men to be trusted. Men he had trusted on other occasions like this. Men he liked. He wondered how many of them would live through the engagement. It was a given that the Yaks wouldn't go down without a fight.

Switched over to infrared, he saw Donny Quarters step out of the armored Cadillac sandwiched between two others. He knew Zenzo could have patched the auditories through if he'd wanted, but excess noise would have been confusing, as well as more demanding on the com-chip. And anyway, judging from Quarters's actions, he could figure out what was being said. At least enough for the rest not to matter. Sleet ran down the inside of the duster and made him shiver.

"I want Yorimasa alive," Traven transmitted as he went into motion, "and I want his limousine in one piece. It has the deck we need to make this case stick. Now, hit it!"

The sound of tires skidding filled the night. The harsh crackling of autofire followed. Black-uniformed Yaks fell after being spotlighted with laser sights.

Traven ran and shouldered the shotgun as a Yak whirled on him. Two rounds of double-ought buckshot lifted the man from his feet and flung him away. At least one caught him in the face. Traven knew the guy was dead before he hit the ground.

A line of 9mm parabellums from an Uzi in another Yak's hands chopped across the pavement toward Traven, splashed through a pool of ice-covered water staining the parking area.

Traven threw himself under one of the ten-wheelers as the Uzi man dropped with a double tap of sniper's bullets through his skull. He had learned to recognize Weinburger's style even in the dark a long time ago. He continued rolling under the ten-wheeler as the driver put it into motion. The thick belch of diesel fumes was almost suffocating. He blasted away a pair of feet supporting a Yak who'd started running for him, then caught the second axle of the truck as it passed. He hung on long enough to gain more of the distance toward Yorimasa and the limousine.

Autofire made hearing almost impossible, left only the rumble of the trucks, horns, and wreckage to seep through. Brass glinted and bounced crazily across the pavement.

Traven released the axle and rolled away from the oversize tires as they spun toward him. He was on his feet at once, the forward stock of the shotgun in his other hand. The SPAS kicked against his shoulder in a steady roll as he emptied the clip across the half-dozen Yaks taking cover behind a stalled ten-wheeler. They went down like mown grass. Scars flared into life against the metal sides of the truck and ripped paint from the Nagamuchi logo.

Flicking the magazine release, Traven dropped the spent clip and slammed a fresh one home as he lunged into position against the truck. One of the bodies moved beside him. A hand came up with a pistol in it. He kicked the hand away, fired point-blank. The hand dropped as crimson pulp stained the pavement. "Kowalski."

"Get outta my head. I'm busy."

Traven pushed himself off the truck and raced for the limousine. He couldn't see Yorimasa.

Metal screamed behind him. He darted a look. Escobar's men, clad in gray Kevlar, blocked the two ends of Surrey Circle and stranded the ten-wheelers in the dock area. One of the Columbians settled into position across the hood of the minivan they'd driven across the entrance. A ten-wheeler roared down at it, froze the man in the glare of headlights. There was a flare from the rear of the tube the Columbian held, then an explosion rocked the cab of the ten-wheeler. It skidded, a propelled scrap of shrapnel nothing could live in, smashed into the minivan, and formed an even more effective blockade. Fire shot up between the vehicles and a second explosion fused them together.

Bullets smashed into the Kevlar vest. Traven dropped the SPAS 15 into target acquisition and ripped the Yak from the fender of the limousine.

There were more explosions. The pavement quaked beneath Traven's feet. Standing and running took more concentration. The helicopters had returned and swept spotlights across the carnage. Traven got a glimpse of snipers hanging on to the landing gear. A heartbeat later one of them fell limply from the lead helicopter. Traven didn't wait to see the impact.

Charging through the lung-searing smoke filling the area, leaping over the dead bodies, Traven made his way to Yorimasa's limo. The rear door facing the dock area was open.

He ducked, came to a crouching position beside the open door, then whirled and extended the wicked snout of the SPAS inside first. The backseat was empty. Glass imploded from the rear window and showered over him. The drone of helicopter rotors swept the gunfire away. He threw himself inside the limo and worked his way through to the other side as bullets pursued him. Some flattened against the Kevlar body armor with bruising force. One bit into his left biceps, and sticky blood trickled down his arm. He hit the door release, tumbled through, and came up with the shotgun at once. The shooters were behind one of Quarter's vehicles. He noticed the car horn for the first time as his mind logged the presence of the dead man draped across the steering wheel of the car.

He directed the double-ought buck at the car's windows and smashed them out as burst after burst slammed home. Two men went down under the onslaught. The third tried to run. A ruby dot appeared on his face, then the cheek imploded and the headless body skidded to a stop on the pavement.

Traven glanced back inside the limo. Yorimasa's personal deck was gone too. The helicopters swung back for another pass. He accessed DataMain. The battle was two minutes old. The gray Kevlar and street clothes of the vice unit began to overwhelm the Yaks. Quarters hadn't brought many men. The ten-wheelers were stationary wrecks, most of them on fire. Different contingents of vice and Columbians broke open the seals and clambered inside to secure the crates. A gray-Kevlared man threw up his arms and went down. Traven wasn't sure if the guy screamed. If he had, it had been lost in the barrage of noise around them. The stink of death and burned cordite hung heavy in the air, saturated with diesel fumes. "Zenzo!"

"Here."

"I lost Yorimasa."

"Inside the warehouse. Quarters was with him, along with a half-dozen hardcases."

Traven pushed himself into action. Gunfire chased him. He leaped onto the concrete runway, didn't try to keep his feet under him but went with the motion, and used his hands and knees to propel him through the raised iron doors. It was dark inside. Using his infrared vision, he saw stacks of crates. The silence inside the warehouse was deafening. The smells were unrecognizable. He gripped the shotgun in solid fists. He refused to think that Yorimasa had already scrapped the deck's programming. Skylights let in a partial gleam of moon shadowed by the passing helicopters.

"Mick!" It was Kowalski.

"Go."

"I copied Zenzo's transmission. It's me coming through the door behind you."

"Come ahead." Traven swung into the semi-protection of a stack of crates.

Kowalski came into the open warehouse with a CAR-15 canted across his body. Blood leaked from a cut over the big man's right eye. He limped but didn't let whatever damage had been done slow him down.

"We've got to have that deck," Traven transmitted. "If we miss it, we've lost everything we've worked for tonight."

"We won't."

They went forward into the heart of the darkness. Traven took the lead. He moved the pace up to an almost shuffling run. His breathing was ragged and hoarse. The headache was insufferable. The bruises under the Kevlar hurt like hell. The open area between the stacked crates narrowed. He turned sideways to make it, stumbled out into the open before he knew it was there. He sensed something whistling toward his head. Ducking, he tucked himself into a roll, heard the rapid fire of Kowalski's CAR-15 open up behind him, and saw the Yak's body go rattling across the concrete as the bright-edged katana slithered away.

Another man stepped forward, the shadows stripped away by the infrared vision. He held a pistol point-blank at Traven's chest and pulled the trigger.

The first bullet hit Traven in the sternum. The second hit him over the left pectoral and brought new agony to the area. The third was never fired, because the shotgun twisted the shooter away.

Traven charged through the maze of crates, depending on his own senses and the com-chip link with Kowalski to keep him alive. He found Quarters and Yorimasa in the next clearing.

Quarters stood behind the Nagamuchi man, the barrel of his pistol screwed tightly into Yorimasa's neck. His ponytail jerked wildly as he caught sight of Traven. He tried in vain to make himself a smaller target than Yorimasa.

"Knew it would be you to take this operation down, Traven," Quarters said. "Most of these fuckers underestimated you. I tried to tell them that, but they told me the fix was in. That's why I tried to have you whacked when you started shoving your nose into Nagamuchi business. The Yaks told me to leave you alone, that fucking with you would tip their hand." He grinned. " 'Course, it seems like they fucked with us all, whaddaya think? You know who this guy is?"

Traven didn't reply. Kowalski pulled up short behind him. The computer deck was on the floor beside Yorimasa. He accessed the com-chip to reach Kowalski. "Zenzo said there was a half-dozen guys in here with Quarters. We put two of them down."

"I know. I've got another one spotted."

"When this goes down, you're on that guy. I've got Quarters."

"You don't sound hopeful about the situation."

Traven let the comment pass.

Quarters shook Yorimasa. "Don't be fucking around with me, Traven. I know you assholes got ways of talking to each other that I can't overhear. Whaddaya think? That I'm some kind of fool?"

Traven let the muzzle of the SPAS drop. "What have you got in mind?"

"I walk out of here," Quarters replied. "Me and my techware source here. And nobody stops us."

Yorimasa struggled.

Quarters hit him with the barrel of the pistol.

A line of blood, black from the moonlight issuing through the skylight overhead, slid down Yorimasa's temple.

Quarters grinned wolfishly. "You knew about the techware, didn't you?"

"Yes."

"You knew I was getting it from Nagamuchi to trade with the Yaks."

Traven nodded.

"Bet you even knew old Yorimasa here was working with the Yaks."

"I didn't know it till tonight."

Quarters shook his head. "Still knew it before I did, guy. To me, this whole setup was a piece of cake. A dream. You just don't luck into something like that. Whaddaya think?"

"No," Traven said in a calm voice. "You don't just luck into a situation like that."

Quarters yanked Yorimasa's hair and made the man yell in pain. "I didn't know a damn thing was screwy till I saw this son of a bitch trying to make the warehouse with his deck." He yanked Yorimasa's hair again. "Then I figured this asshole would mean something to you. He's the link, right? He's the guy that can make your case for you?"

Traven nodded.

Quarters grinned. "And you want that, don't you, Traven? They smeared you, man, stripped your job away from you and kicked you out on the street. The way I figure it, you want him more than me, whaddaya think?"

The shadow of a passing helicopter spilled across the square of light on the concrete floor between them.

Traven said, "I want him more than you, but I want you too. If I let you walk away tonight, you still have

all your contacts in place. You've set up a big operation. If I give you a chance to keep it together, dis-
mantling it could be even harder after this.''

Shaking Yorimasa, Quarters roared, ''You're taking
a fucking chance by being greedy, Traven. If I pull
this trigger, you got no case against Nagamuchi. And
something tells me you want that more than anything
right now.''

Explosions from outside buffeted the interior of the
warehouse.

''Mick,'' Kowalski transmitted.

''Go.''

''I got a fix on two more shooters. They're both
Quarters's boys.''

''Can you take them?''

''Maybe, but you'd better damn well be ducking
when the shit comes down.''

Quarters said, ''You can't have it all, Traven. You
can't have me and Nagamuchi Corporation too. I'll give
you this asshole free and clear and take my chances.
They screwed me too. If things went sour, they planned
on selling my ass down the river, whaddaya think?''

''That's the way I see it too.'' Traven released the
SPAS, holding it by the barrel with his left hand.

''Then make your fucking choice,'' Quarters said,
''because I'm not going to wait till the rest of the Dallas Police Department gets here.''

An eruption of orange flame overhead lit up the
warehouse interior. Then the burning wreckage of a
helicopter slammed into the skylight and scattered
glass fragments.

Traven felt the sting of cuts across his face as he
reached into his duster pocket for one of the 10mms.
He brought it out, flicked the safety off, and lined it
up as Quarters leaned over Yorimasa's shoulder and
started firing. He threw himself to one side, going with
the collision of Quarters's bullet driving into the Kevlar vest. He rolled, his gun arm straight out before him
as he dropped the shotgun.

Kowalski's CAR-15 loosed a stuttering roar. A body
dropped, followed by another.

Traven squeezed the trigger, focused on Quarters's face. The first three rounds pushed the big man's body back from Yorimasa. He kept squeezing the trigger and willed the bullets through Quarters's body. He'd put ten shots in the big man before the body hit the ground and remained still.

Yorimasa crawled desperately toward the computer deck.

Traven put five more bullets into the remaining Yak, then shot Yorimasa in the shoulder. The 10mm round flipped the man over into a groaning heap. He gripped his other SIG/Sauer and pulled it out as he got to his feet. "You okay?"

Kowalski drew a shuddering breath. "Yeah."

"You hit?"

"Yeah."

"How bad?"

The big man chuckled in pain. "Let's just say my verbal abuse of Cale Tompkins won't quite be the same as it would have been before tonight."

Traven glanced back over his shoulder and saw the blood staining Kowalski's left hip. The big man was up. The empty magazine of the CAR-15 hit the concrete even as a new one clicked into place. Traven took a step, surprised at the clumsiness of his left leg. When he looked down he saw he'd taken a round through the fleshy part of his thigh. He ignored the pain and walked toward Yorimasa. The wedged helicopter continued to rain down flaming bits and pieces. He knelt, attached the decklink Zenzo had given him earlier to Yorimasa's deck, and accessed the com-chip. "Zenzo."

"Are you still in one piece?"

"Most of me. The decklink's in place. Suck it dry."

Lights coursed across the face of the deckline, progressing from red to orange to yellow to green.

"Got it," Zenzo said.

"How does it look?"

"Complete. This is good stuff, buddy."

Traven took his handcuffs, held the muzzle of the 10mm against Yorimasa's neck, and cuffed the man.

"You can't do this," Yorimasa said in a strained voice. "I have diplomatic immunity."

Traven yanked the man to his feet. "You can walk out of here, or I'll drag your body out after me. Your choice."

Escobar came into the warehouse flanked by four other Columbians. His face was hard, chiseled.

Traven didn't miss the fraction of movement Kowalski's assault rifle made toward the Columbian drug lord. He accessed the com-chip. "No."

"I still don't trust this guy."

"Then trust me."

"Did you get everything you were after?" Escobar asked as he shouldered his Uzi.

Traven nodded.

Escobar reached inside his Kevlar jacket and pulled out a green cigar. One of the men stepped forward to light it. Escobar exhaled in contentment. "Everything outside is secured and in the hands of your men. Before this truce of ours is over," he said, "I would like to treat you to dinner."

"I'd like that."

"I believe I'm going to take my leave on that note," Escobar said. "I've been told SWAT teams and patrol cars are en route."

"So long, and thanks."

Escobar grinned. "If you should ever tire of cops and robbers, amigo, think of me. I can be a very generous employer, and I can always use someone as talented as yourself." He left and took his entourage with him.

"Still don't understand how you could be friends with him one day and plan on being enemies again the next," Kowalski said.

Traven limped toward the entrance. "It's not something you understand," he said. "It's just something you know. The same way I knew I could take my shots at Quarters and you'd cover my back."

"Yeah, but me and you, we're a lot alike."

"A lot of people are cut from the same cloth," Traven said. "The winds of personal cause just blow them in different directions.'' He grinned at the look of confusion on Kowalski's broad face. ''If the world could be reduced to black and white, it would have been done before now. I would have done it. The problem is, I found out we're not living in a black-and-white world.''

Kowalski limped after him. ''I guess that's why you're not planning on giving up the evidence you recovered tonight to link Nagamuchi Corporation to the drug cartel we just shut down.''

''That's right.''

''Wish I could talk you out of that. It'd make a hell of a bust.''

Traven paused on the concrete runway, one hand on Yorimasa's handcuffs, as he surveyed the carnage scattered over the warehouse area. ''You can't,'' he said softly.

''What if they won't deal?''

Traven gave him a thin smile. ''They will. They don't have a choice.'' He opened his hand and revealed the computer chips lying there. ''This time I'm holding all the chips.''

46

"I could have you killed and put an end to your interference," Shoda Matahachi said. Even at 3:12 A.M., the man had taken time to groom himself. The silver hair was neatly in place. His black suit was carefully pressed.

"That wouldn't stop the truth," Traven responded. "And, for a change, that's what I'm dealing with where Nagamuchi Corporation is concerned." He made his voice hard, unbending, tried to ignore the fact that he was unarmed and there were four black-garbed security officers with automatic weapons at his back.

They had met in a suite at Nagamuchi Towers this time instead of the formal office. Three large couches filled the sunken center of the floor, circling a glass-topped table with miniature rearing brass dragons as the legs. The drapes were expensive, burgundy in color, and brushed the top of the white Oriental carpet. They covered the entire opposite wall of bullet-proof glass. A wet bar filled a far corner of the room. Paintings of mythical Japan covered the walls and lent a taste of mysticism to the overall effect. A statue of a fully dressed shogun warrior holding authentic swords occupied the corner across from the wet bar.

Kema Debuchi had a sick look on his round face. Evidently early-morning meetings didn't agree with him as well as his father-in-law. He couldn't keep his eyes from Taira Yorimasa's bleeding body sprawled across the floor in front of Matahachi in obvious supplication. Baiken Matahachi was sartorially perfect, his cold face chiseled from ice. His eyes were on Traven and ignored Yorimasa.

"You speak highly of truths," Matahachi said, "yet you offer no proof of them, nor offer any indication of what the subject matter may be." His voice was thin and impersonal, as formal as his stance.

Traven resisted movement. Standing or moving made no difference. He still hurt. His leg was covered with a temporary bandage, and the bruises covering his chest and back were already swollen. Only time would take the pain away. "You know what I came here to say. Otherwise you would never have let me come this far."

"You overstate your own worth, Detective," Matahatchi said. "I am not a man to be trifled with."

"Neither am I," Traven responded.

Yorimasa's blood continued to seep from the shoulder wound and stain the white carpet. No one seemed to notice.

The doorbell rang. Two of the security officers split away from their posts and went to secure the entrance. At Matahachi's nod, they opened the door.

Craig Traven stepped inside, looking frantic, then looked even more so when he saw Traven standing between the other two guards. "Mickey. What the hell are you doing here?"

"That," Matahachi said, "is what we are trying to determine. He insisted we call you and get you here."

Craig Traven stared at Yorimasa on the floor. "What's going on here?"

Traven indicated the couches. "Have a seat and we'll cut to the chase." He gave the man a brief smile. "Now that the gang's all here." As Craig Traven passed, he caught a whiff of perfume and recognized it as Beth's. He walled away the personal feelings. There were only businessmen in the room now, and he intended to be the most professional.

Craig Traven occupied another couch by himself.

"We're here to form a dissolution," Traven said. "And that dissolution centers around the franchise of drugs Nagamuchi Corporation has instituted through the Yakuza in Dallas and the Burmese Golden Triangle.'' He locked eyes with Matahachi.

''What is it you think you can prove?'' Matahachi asked.

''Everything,'' Traven stated simply. ''I can prove that Nagamuchi has chemical processing plants in Lashio that manufacture cocaine, red satin, and other drugs illegal here in the United States. I can prove that Nagamuchi has been using its diplomatic immunity to ship those drugs into this country. The direct ties to the Yakuza faction are somewhat hazy, but I have in my possession names, dates, and places. It wouldn't be hard to turn up proof if I chose to pursue it. Even if you tried to shut the information down, you'd set off a bloodbath that would alienate the Yakuza and probably make the information even easier to get.''

''What the hell are you talking about?'' Craig Traven demanded, rising from the couch. He turned on Matahachi. ''What's he talking about?''

''Sit down,'' Matahachi ordered irritably.

Craig Traven turned away.

''I'm talking about business,'' Traven told the man. ''Business with a high profit potential. Even here in America, Nagamuchi is feeling the pressure of other Japanese competition as well as the international market. They aren't well liked here, and maybe the consumer market is slipping just a little. Drugs seemed like an easy out, especially when you had the diplomatic immunity angle to work.''

''Mickey.'' Craig Traven sounded quietly desperate. ''I didn't have anything to do with that.''

''Try proving it after the media get hold of it,'' Traven said.

''You can't do that.''

''Sure I could.'' Traven shook his head and looked back at Matahachi. ''You were sly about the setup, too, old man. You had Yorimasa in place as your sacrificial goat. If police teams had penetrated your cover, chances are they would only have gotten as far as the stolen techware Yorimasa was selling to Donny Quarters, who in turn was selling it to Yakuza in your control. Yorimasa would have been expelled from the country, and Nagamuchi involvement could be quietly swept under the table with no one the wiser.''

"You can't prove any of that," Kema Debuchi said.

"Not without Yorimasa's testimony," Traven agreed. "But then, the corporations you leased the techware from wouldn't have to have a courtroom and a jury to convince them, would they?''

Silence filled the room.

"That was another option I had," Traven went on. "I could have told the other corporations, but that would have touched off an intercorporate war that would have flowed out into the streets.'' He walked to the wet bar, aware that Matahachi waved the security guards to stationary positions. He took a glass and filled it with water from the tap. He drank slowly, then set the glass aside. He felt weak from his wounds. It was an effort to keep the room from revolving.

"How do I know you have this information?" Matahachi said.

Traven slipped an envelope from his pocket. He walked over to Matahachi. All four guards had pistols pointed at him. They'd taken his Kevlar jacket when they relieved him of his weapons. He forced his hand not to shake. "Computer chips. Check them for yourself. They're copies of the information I retrieved from the deck Yorimasa used to conduct business."

Matahachi signaled one of the guards. The man split off from the group and left the room.

"It was a good setup," Traven said, "but you got too greedy. And you didn't count on harboring a serial murderer inside your offices."

Matahachi gazed at him. "You know who this man is as well?''

"Yes.'' Traven grinned. "In fact, if you had let me search for the man instead of having me kicked off the force, I might have fallen for Yorimasa as your sacrificial goat and never looked any farther. You gave me no choice at all.''

Baiken Matahachi spoke in a hard voice. "If you

were to die here, tonight, Detective, what would happen?''

''The truth is larger than I am,'' Traven said with a slight twist of his lips. ''I've arranged that it be released to the media, to the corporations whose techware was stolen through your offices, and to government agencies. It's going to take every one of us to cover this up.''

Craig Traven looked relieved.

''I didn't figure you for a man who would indulge in blackmail,'' Matahachi said.

''It's only blackmail in the traditional sense,'' Traven said. ''The truth of the matter is that it's the only kind of justice I could salvage from the situation.''

The security guard returned carrying a laptop deck. He placed it on the glass table and switched it on. Matahachi fed the computer chips to it one by one, carefully going over the recorded material.

''You'll agree that if this information passed into the right hands, Nagamuchi Corporation would cease to exist on American soil,'' Traven said.

''Possibly.'' Matahachi closed the laptop.

''It's your choice,'' Traven said. ''We can play it my way, or you can take your chances.''

''Let me see that,'' Craig Traven said as he got up from the couch.

Matahachi glared the man back into a sitting position. ''No.'' He looked at Traven. ''Name your price.''

''I want you to understand my position first,'' Traven said. ''I want you to know why I'm doing business with you this way instead of turning everything over to the legal system.'' He paused to organize his thoughts. ''For a long time now I've operated within the law. I've been a peace officer, a good cop. I've bent the rules now and again, but I've never made deals with criminals. Not like this morning.''

Matahachi folded his arms across his thin chest.

''My problem became a moral one, a question of honor. Was it right to drive your corporation out of business when so many lives depend on the work it provides?'' Traven shook his head. ''I didn't think so.

The economic recovery of such a void would be a long time in coming. Many people would not survive it. That left me with only the avenue of pursuing justice through you.''

"Leave us," Matahachi said to the security officers. They filed out of the room.

Traven felt better, then wondered if the move was designed by Matahachi to make him overconfident.

"What are your terms?" Matahachi asked.

Traven counted them off. "I want your chemical plants out of Burma. I want the connections between this corporation and the Yakuza severed once and for all. I want anonymous financial recompense made for the companies whose techware was stolen from your corporation. You can use the monies you've made from the drug action to pay them. And I want you to be generous. I have ways of checking on the amounts."

"And if I don't agree to this, you will release the information regarding these matters?"

"You can bet the farm on it," Traven said quietly. "We'll watch Nagamuchi Corporation go down the toilet together."

Craig Traven stood up. "Mickey, you can't just come in here and expect to push these people around."

"Yes, I can," Traven said. He turned on the man. "And speaking of pushing people around, you've got a son out there who's miserable because of the way you've ignored him and made him feel about himself. He has no control over his life. Even less since his mother died. I made excuses for you as I grew up, but Danny's not as naive as I was. He stands alone, you son of a bitch, and you're not going to let him throw his life away because he doesn't think there's any decency out in the world."

"You're not going to talk to me that way," Craig Traven said. "I'm your father."

"Not anymore. I want you to stay the hell away from me and away from Danny. Remember one thing— if I bring Nagamuchi Corporation down, Traven Advertising goes down as well."

"Silence," Matahachi said as he glared at Craig Traven.

The man purpled but was silent.

"You're going to pay too," Traven said. "I expect your agency to be one of the leading factors in clearing my name of all the charges you've leveraged against me. Also, I want you to tell Danny his mother left an insurance policy with his name on it that will provide money for him while he gets an education. I don't want to take the chance he'll turn it down because it's from you."

"I'll be damned if I'll agree to something like that."

Matahachi's voice was unforgiving. "You'll be dead if you don't. Do not be so cheap as to overlook his generosity."

"This isn't generosity. This is blackmail."

Traven shook his head. "This is just business, Dad. Nothing personal." The coldness in his voice surprised him. "And I want Danny living with me if he wants to. You're going to stay away from him."

The silence in the room was tense. Finally Craig Traven sat down and looked away.

"What about demands for yourself?" Matahachi asked.

Traven looked at the man. "I want my job back, and I don't want your people fucking with me again."

"How do I know I can trust you if I decide to go along with these demands?" Matahachi asked.

"Because you know me," Traven said. "You took special care to know me. I trust that we're both honorable men."

"You can't agree to this idiocy," Kema Debuchi said as he rose from the couch. "He is only one man. Kill him and be done with it."

"Baiken," Matahachi said.

Baiken Matahachi drew a small, flat pistol from under his jacket and shot Debuchi in the stomach. Debuchi collapsed into a groaning heap on the floor.

Matahatchi walked over to stand above the man. "Never presume to tell me how to conduct my affairs again," he said in a quiet, deadly voice, "or my beloved daughter will be a widow."

"Yes, Matahachi-san." Debuchi continued to hold his bleeding stomach.

Traven stood unmoving.

The look on Craig Traven's face was one of disbelief.

"You would do well to remember this morning, Craig Traven," Matahachi said, "if thoughts ever come to you to renege on the deal you've made with this man. When I give my word, I give it for all of us."

"Yes, sir."

Matahachi came to a stop in front of Traven. "Is there anything else?"

Traven reached out and took the small knife from the dish of cut lemons on the bar. "There's the question of my honor. You've pushed me, tried to kill me, slandered and libeled my professional and personal skills, and you've forced me to perjure the sense of honor I cling to in my life. By making this deal with you, even though it's the best I can do for everyone concerned, I have still lost a sense of self. I can no longer look at myself in the same fashion. I am no longer whole in my eyes. Do you understand?"

"Yes." Matahachi never blinked.

Traven gave the man the lemon knife.

Matahachi accepted the knife, placed the little finger of his left hand on the bartop, and cut off the tip of the finger at the first joint. Blood rushed out. Instead of tending to it, he picked up the piece of finger, wrapped it in a cocktail napkin that immediately turned scarlet, and presented it to Traven with a bow. "Now we all have our losses to bear."

Traven bowed. "Yes." He left the room with the finger joint clasped in his hand.

47

Earl Brandstetter jacked into the apartment building's central AI system on the ground floor, pulled data concerning Mick Traven from it, and started up to the designated floor in the service elevator, using credentials he finessed through the computer.

Locked into the AI, he sensed the hum of the elevator through electronic ears, felt the grind of gears through the system's automated pulleys and traction feeds. He felt his weight through the frame of his body. He felt his weight against the floor of the elevator. Both felt comfortable.

The combat knife was a hard length in his coat pocket. His hands were gloved. His heart rate sped up as he watched the floor indicator rise.

Traven wasn't home. His link with the building AI had told him that already. But Otsu Hayata was in the apartment alone. He closed his eyes, formed an image of her at the deck in Traven's bedroom. Lust stirred within him, a leviathan now, no longer the timid beast he'd shared all his life with. He existed outside himself, traced his intellect through the skin of the building where it hovered like a bird of prey. Traven would be home soon. Then Brandstetter could end the menace of being discovered.

His thinking was rapid, cyber-fast. Only one floor had ticked by. It seemed as if he'd been in the elevator for at least an hour.

Curious, he extended his avenue of investigation into Traven's apartment. The deck drew him like steel to a magnet. He pulsed through it, took in the information byte by byte. It was about him. His name, his date of birth, his job history, address, age, criminal record— blank, of course—his financial situation, family . . .

"No." His mother's voice came to him sharp and strong, and broke the connection. "Stay away from that, honey."

It hurt that she had yelled. He tried to hide his feelings.

"It's okay, baby," his mother said. "What's on that deck doesn't matter to us. The only thing that matters is that Traven and Hayata can force us apart. You don't want that, do you?"

"No."

"Okay. Make me proud of you. Get in quietly, kill the woman, and wait for Traven. He'll be back soon."

"I know." Still, the curiosity pulled at him. An image of his mother formed inside his head. She screamed, tried to cover herself and him, her mouth wide and afraid. Then the image popped like a tired soap bubble, left only the residue. He shivered. Goosebumps suddenly covered him, and he felt nauseous.

She shoved the image of Otsu Hayata into his head, stripped the woman as if on the other side of a curtained window. She stoked the hunger governing his actions, promised him dozens of delights without uttering a sound inside his mind.

He rasped the ball of his thumb across the sharp blade.

The elevator door slid back.

He stepped into the hall and stared at the closed door of Traven's apartment. He started to lay his hand on the access panel and augment the door.

"Hey, get the hell away from that door!"

Brandstetter raised his hand automatically as he turned. The man held a gun. He remembered the detective's name with difficulty. Higham. He'd been with Traven during the interview session.

"I know about the vest, buddy," Higham said, "so

you'll take care to notice where I'm pointing this gun.'' The barrel winked darkly, aimed at his face.

Brandstetter stood unmoving as Higham came closer.

''We're going to do this nice and easy,'' Higham said, using both hands to steady the pistol. ''We're going back down the hall and we're going to stop at the public phone. Then I'm going to call in some backup and we're all going downtown for a little chat.''

Between physical and electronic senses, Brandstetter had an extremely complete picture of Higham and the situation. He controlled his body functions, waited till the proper moment arrived.

''Give me a hand,'' Higham ordered.

Brandstetter lowered his right hand.

Higham brought out a pair of handcuffs. The double-C of steel clicked tightly around Brandstetter's wrist.

Without pausing, Brandstetter yanked on his captured wrist and ducked. His right hand found the hilt of the combat knife in the pocket of his coat. Higham's pistol fired and gouged plasterboard from the wall behind him. Using the building's AI system, Brandstetter triggered a burst of static from every wallscreen in the building to disguise the report of the pistol. He dropped his shoulder into Higham's chest and ran the man across the hallway into the wall. Higham's breath exploded from his lungs. Then the combat knife bit through the fabric of the coat and penetrated the detective's ribs.

Warm blood gushed over Brandstetter. He reveled in the feel of it. The security cameras gave him three different views of the first puncture as he stepped into cybertime and gave himself over to the flow of it.

He leveraged his left arm under Higham's gun hand and slammed it into the wall. There was a sharp crack. He grinned at the pain wracking the detective's face. The combat knife slid free of his pocket, slid just as easily into Higham's left ear and into his brain. The shuddering body dropped into Brandstetter's waiting arms.

He shut out the smell of death that clung to the man.

The taste of warm blood smeared his lips. He ran his tongue across it and relished the saltiness. He lifted the body easily, knew at once what he was going to do with it. She told him it wouldn't do to have it found in the hallway. People passing in and out would notice and perhaps call other police. He wanted this to be between him and Traven, because she told him it had to be that way.

Pausing at the service elevator, he used the building AI to bypass security. He stepped inside, removed the roof panel, and settled the corpse on top of the elevator cage. He reseated the roof panel, took time to get it straight.

Satisfied, he tucked his combat knife back in his pocket and walked to Traven's apartment. The door hissed shut behind him. He ran his fingers down the blood covering him, enjoyed the slippery feel of it.

"There's more to come," she whispered into his mind. "Lots more."

The apartment door slid away at his touch, and he stepped inside.

48

Traven answered the yellow blink of the mobile phone in the Cherokee as he pulled off Musashi Boulevard onto Oak Lawn Avenue. He hurt in what seemed like a thousand places. His head throbbed constantly. "Traven."

"Earl Brandstetter *is* the man we're looking for," Otsu Hayata said in an excited voice. "I've been trying to reach you for the last hour. Listen to this. At age thirteen, Earl Brandstetter was admitted to Gaston Hospital for multiple gunshot wounds. I came across the information in a sealed file in Juvenile Hall records. I don't know why Nagamuchi application researchers didn't find it."

Traven pulled her back on track. "Who shot him?"

"His stepfather." Computer keys clacked in the background. "A man named Wayne Hollister."

"Why was he shot?"

"According to the police reports on Hollister I cross-referenced, Hollister came home and found his wife in bed with her thirteen-year-old son, Earl Brandstetter. Hollister was drunk. He took a pistol from a closet and shot them both. The mother, Catherine Hollister, was dead when police arrived."

"Brandstetter had an incestuous relationship with his mother?" Traven had to force himself to think. Everything sounded right, but so much had happened it was hard to put himself back into the serial-killings investigation.

"Yes. I uncovered a psychologist's report in the file.

From the evidence suggested there, Brandstetter's relationship with his mother lasted for at least five years.''

"A sexual relationship? At eight years old?''

"It started out as heavy petting, sleeping with her naked, that sort of thing. I don't know. I thought maybe you'd be more familiar with this than I am.''

"I've never worked sex crimes,'' Traven said, "but it sounds right.''

"The psychologist went on to note that Brandstetter had trouble adjusting to other people after the murder of his mother. He remained alone while he was at the institution. He was never adopted.''

"He was raised as a state child?''

"Yes.''

"Where's the stepfather now?''

"The report didn't say.''

Traven logged the name in his memory.

"Why is Hollister important?''

"I don't know that he is, but something had to set Brandstetter off. I'm trying to figure out what it might have been. Where's Higham?''

"He hasn't arrived yet.''

Traven accessed DataMain. It was 3:58 A.M. Higham should have been there. He heard the sound of the apartment door whisper open.

"Maybe that's him now,'' Hayata said.

Gripping the phone tightly, Traven said, "Otsu, get the hell out of the apartment. Higham doesn't have a pass to get through my security system.''

A hollow click sounded as the other phone was placed on a hard surface.

"Otsu!'' Traven put his foot down on the accelerator. He hit the siren and pulled into the middle of the two lanes of traffic. "Otsu!'' A cold, hard knot filled his stomach, washed away thoughts of the pain that clung to his body.

A muffled scream sounded, then the harsh rasp of a man's breathing filled the connection. "Traven?''

He forced his voice to remain calm. "What do you want, Brandstetter?''

"You, Traven. I want you. If you want to see Hayata alive again, you'll come here alone. It's going to be me and you, Traven. If you win, you get to walk out of here with the woman. If you don't, you won't walk anywhere. If I see any other cops, I'll kill her and leave. You won't be able to catch me. I'll just disappear the way I always do. I'm Mr. Nobody, remember?" Ragged laughter filled the telephone till the connection broke.

Traven hung up the receiver and put both hands on the steering wheel. He cut through traffic and earned several horn blasts from the early-morning crowd on their way to work. He tried to match the insane voice to the man he had interviewed at Nagamuchi and couldn't. If he'd had to guess, he would never have put that voice and that man together. Earl Brandstetter had seemed too much in control of himself ever to sound that way. The memory of the bitter laughter sent chills down his spine.

He thought of calling the police, then put it out of his mind. Even if he hadn't been persona non grata at the PD, Brandstetter was too good at getting in and out of places. He had the man's name filed on the long-term memory of the com-chip. If he was killed, Zenzo or one of the techs would be able to dig the information up. Brandstetter would be known whatever the outcome. The thing that mattered now was to get Hayata out of the apartment in one piece if at all possible.

Turning southeast off Oak Lawn Avenue, he roared down Holland Street and parked the 4×4 halfway on the curb. He had one of the 10mms in his hand when he touched down on the street and raced for the main entrance. He walked through the door and toward the bank of elevators. With the SIG/Sauer tucked safely away in the folds of his duster, he thumbed the elevator button.

None of the elevators responded. He was about to take the stairs when the doors of the service elevator opened. Without a building pass or his shield, he wouldn't have been able to enter under normal conditions. He didn't doubt for a moment that Brandstetter had arranged the same transportation.

"Come in, Traven," the elevator's mechanical voice whispered. "We're waiting for you."

The security camera mounted in a corner of the elevator cage whirred and locked onto him as he stepped inside. He reached up, grabbed the lens, and yanked. It came off in his hand, and he threw it to the floor. He noticed the pool of blood staining the tiled floor as the elevator skyrocketed up. He was thrown back against the wall of the cage. For a moment he considered the possibility that Brandstetter might use the elevator to kill him. Then he realized he had accepted the fact the man had somehow become part of the whole building without reservation. He wondered how the hell he could stop someone like that.

He looked up as the elevator came to a stop on his floor, tried to judge where the blood came from. A circular patch, like the stain left by rainwater collecting on a leaky roof, covered one corner of the access panel. Still holding onto the SIG/Sauer tightly, he reached up and batted the access panel away. He groped in the darkness, touched cloth, made a fist of it, and pulled.

The elevator jarred suddenly as the weight came crashing down on top of him. He went to his knees under it before he realized the weight belonged to Higham's body.

Brandstetter's maniacal laughter filled the cage. "He couldn't stop me, Traven. Do you still think you're good enough?"

Traven made no reply. He checked for a pulse on Higham's neck and found none. Higham's blood streaked his duster, and the smell of it was overpowering in the small elevator. The doors whispered open.

"Get out, Traven," the elevator's voice commanded. "Get out now, or die!"

Traven jumped into the hall as the elevator dropped away beneath him. He lay flat on his stomach. The security cameras tracked him as the *whump* of the elevator filled the shaft.

"I can see you," Brandstetter's voice whispered through the emergency intercom system in the hallway. "You're afraid, Traven. I can see it all over you. But you can't stop me. None of you can. She told me I was too good for any of you to catch."

"She?" Traven asked as he walked toward his open apartment door with the 10mm fisted in both hands.

"Yes," Brandstetter replied. "She's here with me now. No one's ever going to take her away again."

Traven listened for sounds coming from the apartment. There weren't any. The only thing he heard was the rapid *whumpf-whumpf-whumpf* of his heart. "Your mother? Is that who's there with you?" None of it made sense, but he wanted to keep the man talking, maybe keep him off balance.

"Yes. She told me you would know about her. She said you were the dangerous one. She said you were the one who would know."

Traven paused at the doorway and swept his darkened living room with the SIG/Sauer. The wallscreen was on and reflected his larger-than-life image. Disoriented for a moment, he watched it zoom in for a close-up. Tracks of Higham's blood showed across his face. He put the image out of his mind with difficulty. "Your mother's dead, Brandstetter. She died when you were thirteen."

"Liar!" The voice came from the apartment AI's speakers now, triggered so that each room was a fraction of a second off from the others, creating a thunderous roll of echoes.

The pain in Traven's head increased. For a moment he thought he was going to pass out. Then the vertigo left. His hands shook from the intensity of the feeling. The com-chip felt like a live thing in his head, pulsed like a worm trying to ooze through his mind. Shadowy images collected at the fringe of his reception, both sharper and duller than the bleed-over Zenzo had described that might happen.

"She told me you would say that," Brandstetter said. "She told me you would lie about her. They all tried to make me think she was dead."

"Look at the deck," Traven said. He went forward. The reflection on the wallscreen moved too. His senses continued to swim away from him. It was getting increasingly harder to know what was reality and what was fantasy. "Wayne Hollister killed your mother when you were thirteen. He almost killed you."

"Lies," Brandstetter responded. "All lies. They tried to keep me away from her. They all tried to keep me from her. But I knew she was still alive. I knew she would come for me one day if I would just wait."

Traven stepped into the hallway leading back to the bedroom. Nausea gripped him, stemming from the com-chip. His knees felt weak from the pain and the disorientation. For a moment he wondered if he was really in his apartment or if Brandstetter had somehow managed to warp his perception of reality. He considered the possibility that he was being led over the edge of the building following a scenario painted by Brandstetter. "Where did you find her?"

"In the computer at Nagamuchi. In my construct. She had been waiting for me. I almost failed her. I almost didn't get the job. I almost turned it down. I didn't know. I didn't know she would be waiting there for me. She couldn't tell me. I almost didn't find her." Brandstetter sounded frantic. "Now that I have, no one is going to take her away."

Traven tried to visualize a construct. He'd never been in one, never been in cyberspace, but Zenzo had described constructs to him. Zenzo had called them paradises on earth, told him whatever a deckjockey wanted could be found there. But none of it was real. Even a madman's dreams could find life there, he realized. A ragged chill skipped down his spine as the remembered images of the murdered women flowed through his mind like beads of quicksilver, ended with Higham falling out of the elevator. He took another step and wondered if Hayata was still alive. "Why did you kill the women?"

"I killed Nami Chikara because Yorimasa was threatening my job. Then I realized how much she needed them."

"The women?"

"Yes."

"Why?" Traven stepped around the corner and looked down at Hayata.

"To make herself beautiful for me. She always told me she wanted to be beautiful for me. She told me not to be afraid. She told me she wanted me to touch her."

In the lambent glow of the deck screen Traven saw the pulse pounding slowly in the hollow of Hayata's neck. The woman was only unconscious. He looked for Brandstetter. The room was dark. The wallscreen was vacant. "That's why Hollister killed her, isn't it?"

"She's not dead!" The response roared from the AI speakers.

It was as if Brandstetter had vanished. Traven crossed the room to Hayata's side and reached down for the woman.

Brandstetter stepped away from the wallscreen, suddenly visible against the black background. "She's alive, damn you!" he yelled in his own voice.

Traven triggered two shots. Both holed the wallscreen and neither touched Brandstetter.

Brandstetter's foot lashed out and caught him on his chin.

Lights exploded in Traven's head as the ache ripping at his temples scaled to new heights. He felt his body go over backward from the impact, felt the SIG/Sauer slip away from him. The big man loomed over him suddenly, eyes glowing in the dark.

Brandstetter's free hand held Traven by his lower face. His other hand gripped a bloodstained combat knife only centimeters from Traven's unprotected throat. Brandstetter's hair was in disarray. His breath smelled like death. The look in his eyes was wild and crazed.

Traven tried to struggle, found his motor action impaired by the sudden attack. His arms were too heavy to lift.

"She's alive," Brandstetter said. "I'll show you."

The com-chip twisted sickeningly in Traven's head,

seemed to turn white-hot for a heartbeat under heavy cybernetic interference, then swallowed him whole.

Traven was on his feet. There was no pain. He ran his hands down his body, surprised at the sensation. His duster was clean. His guns were gone. He looked up, studying the room they were in. Brandstetter stood by the fireplace. Walls of books surrounded them. A bearskin rug covered the floor.

"She's here," Brandstetter said. The man was naked and moved with the frantic liquidity of an enraged lion.

"Where are we?" Traven asked.

"In the construct," Brandstetter replied absently. He walked out the door.

Traven followed, telling himself nothing he saw was real, that he was still lying on the floor of his apartment with the blade of a psychopath's knife at his throat. They walked past labs, past bedrooms decorated with mirrors and colors, past rooms with closed doors, followed the twists and turns of hallways that seemed endless. He clutched at objects that could be used as weapons: brass candlesticks, ornate glass ashtrays, picture frames. Nothing came loose in his hand. It was as if he were a ghost, unable to apply physical force in this surreal world. He was as helpless here as he was back at his apartment. For a moment he wondered if Brandstetter had already killed him and if he would be doomed to wander throughout the construct until someone ended the program.

"Mother!" Brandstetter's voice thundered through the house. Echoes of it came back, crackled thunder of their own.

Traven focused on a lighter in the shape of a DNA helix sitting on a table in a room that resembled a saloon in a western movie. While Brandstetter was occupied with searching the room, he tried to lift it from the table. Even if it wasn't solid enough to use as a weapon, he could burn the construct down. Maybe. He strained against its weight, unable to move it.

"Everything here is mine," Brandstetter said.

Traven released the lighter and looked up at the man. "Everything here is under my control."

"Where is she?" Traven asked as he pursued the only chink he'd found in the man's armor. "She isn't here."

Brandstetter turned away with a confused look on his face.

"She's dead," Traven said again. He wanted to break the man down, but fear of the unknown filled him. If Brandstetter lost his control on reality, it could mean he was trapped here as well. Zenzo had told him time could stand still in the real world when you were in cyberspace.

Brandstetter whirled without warning. A massive hand slammed into Traven's face, knocked him backward with more than mere physical force.

Traven splintered a table he landed on and spilled the chair around it in all directions. There was no pain. Only the sensation of the incredible force. He stood up. There wasn't even any debris clinging to his duster.

"She is here," Brandstetter said as he stared at the ceiling. Reflections of the kerosene lamps played across the polished wood. "She's afraid of you. Why?"

"I don't know," Traven replied.

"She said you would be the one to find out about us," Brandstetter said. "But I want to show her that I can take care of you. I want her to see for herself that you hold no more threats for us. You're going to die."

Traven racked his memory for the things Zenzo had mentioned about constructs and cyberspace. Something was lodged there, but he couldn't grasp it.

"She must be there," Brandstetter said suddenly. "It's her place. She would go there if she was afraid. It's her place. She made it for herself." He went back into the twisting hallways.

Traven followed the man, no longer sure the decision was completely his to make. Brandstetter's words clashed with something in his head, something he almost remembered. Something Zenzo had said.

Brandstetter led the way, walked up staircases that

seemed to lead down, walked down staircases that seemed to lead up. Nothing existed but the staircases. Blackness hung greedily on either side of the narrow passages. The door appeared suddenly. Brandstetter unlocked it, and they passed inside. "This is her place," he said in a reverent voice.

Traven stood as his mind struggled with the impossibilities strung before him. The room was small, yet gave off a feeling of immensity. Clothing racks and shoeboxes covered the walls and sat in stacks all over the floor. A lighted vanity with a horseshoe-shaped mirror filled the other end of the room. Dozens of pornographic pictures covered the walls. A dark, gloomy haze stained the room. Above it all, the smell of death clung to the room.

The woman stepped from the shadows behind the vanity. She was younger than Traven would have guessed. She couldn't be much older than he was. Then he remembered she'd died young. Glossy black hair framed her face. She was naked, her skin pallid in the gloom. The expression she wore was one of disgust and anger.

"You shouldn't have brought him here, Earl," she said. "You should have kept him away from me. I told you to keep him away from me."

Brandstetter approached her. "He told me you were dead. I wanted him to see for himself that he was wrong." He took her hand.

Traven watched in disbelief as the years and bulk of Brandstetter dropped away and left a thirteen-year-old boy in their wake.

"Kill him, Earl," the woman said. "Kill him and be done with it before he destroys us." Her face, cold and pallid, was a mask of rage.

This time Traven saw it. When the woman spoke, Brandstetter's lips mouthed the words as well, as if he was lip-synching along with her.

The woman regarded him with dead eyes. Her voice was a frozen whisper. The smell of death swelled in the room. "He knows. He knows the truth about us."

Traven forced himself to remain calm, unable to look

away as Brandstetter faced him and spoke the same words as the woman. Then the memory he'd been searching for surfaced in his mind. Zenzo had explained constructs so long ago.

"I only wanted to make you happy," Brandstetter said. He sank to his knees before her, still holding her hand. "I wanted you to see how I could protect you."

"She's not your mother," Traven said.

Brandstetter looked up at him, tears in the thirteen-year-old eyes. "She is." He looked at the woman. "Tell him. Tell him you're my mother."

She reached down to smooth his hair. "I'm your mother, you know that. It doesn't matter what anyone else thinks. As long as I'm here, you never have to be alone again." Their lips moved in unison.

Traven stepped closer, captivated by the scene. "She's not your mother. Think about the possibilities presented by the construct. It operates off your conscious and subconscious minds. Two minds, with only a thin connection between them."

The boy looked up at him, fear etched on his young face. "No, no, no, no, no," he sobbed in a choked voice. He held on to the woman's legs tightly.

"Don't listen to him, baby," the woman said.

The boy's lips moved as well. His body shivered.

"Two minds," Traven said as understanding filled him and sickened him at the same time. He grabbed the woman's face, felt the skin stretch under his fingers. He pulled. The features came away in his hand.

Suddenly grown again, Earl Brandstetter looked up at himself as the head and shoulders of his dark twin shoved through the thin fabric that had been his mother.

"Your subconscious," Traven said. "Your subconscious created your mother while you were here. You fooled yourself."

Pushing himself to his feet, Brandstetter stared wildly at the pictures on the walls. They didn't show the woman anymore. Only him. He was the seducer and the seduced. It was Earl Brandstetter clothed in the Marilyn Monroe dress on the closet door now.

"Kill him!" the other Earl Brandstetter shouted, frantically trying to pull the torn fabric back into place. The voice was feminine.

Brandstetter's lips still moved with the other's. He threw himself at Traven. "You murdered her!" His screams ripped the world apart.

Traven felt the bite of the combat knife go deep into his chest through the Kevlar, and realized he was back in his own head, back in his own apartment. Brandstetter's body was heavy across him. There was no air in his lungs. Pinwheels of bright, smoking pain flared to new life inside him. The com-chip felt dead.

"You bastard!" Brandstetter screamed almost incoherently. "You murdered her! You murdered her!"

Using leverage, Traven rolled the man from him, gasping for breath. The knife cut him again, a long line this time, just above the neck of the Kevlar jacket. He felt the blood course down his chest. He ducked under the whistling knife as Brandstetter swung at him. He couldn't find the pistol he'd lost in the darkness, but the backup was still in its ankle holster. If he could get to it.

Brandstetter still screamed. The words weren't understandable.

Blood roared in Traven's ears. He felt weak, hurt, and alone. Even without the knife he was giving away several centimeters in height and almost twenty kilos in weight. He blocked Brandstetter's next swing and felt a bone break in his forearm from the impact. The pain was only an added inconvenience. He went with the force, rocked back on his bad leg to deliver a roundhouse kick to the big man's head. Something broke in his foot.

Roaring in pain and rage, Brandstetter rushed at him again.

Traven caught the knife hand on his bad arm, stepped inside the amateur swing, and rocked the man's head with a palm blow. He felt Brandstetter's nose break and slick blood cover his palm. His breath was ragged, whistled in and out of him.

Brandstetter stepped back and roared like a wounded beast. Dark blood trickled down his face. The wallscreen went wild as image after image flickered across it in total confusion.

The com-chip sucked at Traven's mind with bleedover. He forced it away, focused on the physical world. He reached for the ankle holster.

Brandstetter body-slammed him, spread him across the wallscreen and shattered the high-impact-resistant glass.

Traven couldn't get his breath, couldn't make his hands or legs obey him. He tried to push Brandstetter off.

Brandstetter bit him, strong teeth tearing into his neck.

Traven leveraged the man's face from him with a forearm. He hammered an elbow into Brandstetter's cheek, felt the elbow and the cheek go at the same time. He grabbed weakly at man's shirt, felt his fingers slide over the edge of the Kevlar vest, and pulled. The closure opened with harsh rasping sounds.

Brandstetter grabbed him and threw him to the floor.

Traven hit hard, almost giving in to the unconsciousness that swam just outside his vision. The kaleidoscopic images triggered by the defective com-chip interacting with Brandstetter's programming kept trying to print on his retinas.

Growling like an animal now, Brandstetter tried to bite him again. The knife in his fist rose and fell like a precision clock.

Pain burned through Traven, and he felt his own blood covering him like a second skin. He struggled under Brandstetter's bulk. His fingers groped at the butt of the 10mm in its ankle holster until he finally got a grip on it. He brought it up, refusing to give in to the blood loss, shock, or pain until he made sure the man was down. The knife bit into his back, hung in the bones between his shoulders. He screamed with the pain as Brandstetter yanked it loose.

He used the sudden shift in momentum to push the 10mm into Brandstetter's chest in the gap of the open

Kevlar jacket. The first bullet shook Brandstetter's body, but the man refused to release him, buried the knife deep time after time.

The last thing Traven remembered was the sound of the 10mm firing dry. Then he fell into the darkness waiting for him.

49

Traven woke up in a hospital. He blinked at the white walls and fluorescent lights. It felt like daytime, but he wasn't sure. There were no windows. His breathing was stifled, and his throat hurt. When he swallowed he realized there was a tube running down his throat from one of his nostrils. An IV bag hung over his head, and a bank of monitors bleeped quietly to his left. He turned his head, closing his eyes with the sudden onslaught of pain.

A man wearing a doctor's uniform and a sterile face mask stepped into view. He held a microrecorder in one hand as he read off the figures on the monitors. He turned to Traven, brown eyes muddy above the mask. "How're you feeling?"

"Worse than I ever thought I could and still be alive," Traven replied honestly. He had trouble talking around the tube.

"You came close to not being here," the doctor said. "Flat-lined on me on the operating table a couple of times. But I do damn good work." Wrinkles formed around his eyes to let Traven know there was a smile under the mask. "Of course, it helped that we were both stubborn."

"Where am I?"

"At Parkland Memorial. I'm Dr. Todd."

Traven tried a smile and found it worked. "I'd shake your hand, but I'm afraid something might fall off."

Wrinkles formed around the eyes again. "Nah, we got all the important stuff sewed back on."

Traven nodded and regretted it. The tube through his nostril and throat twisted. "So how am I?" He felt the fear crowd in on him as soon as he asked the question.

The doctor poked a penflash at his eyes. "Healing, Mick. Healing. You won't have any permanent damage that will keep you from leading a normal life, but you're going to have to spend some recovery time with us. I won't say that you'll be at a hundred percent when we cut you loose, but you're going to be pretty close. As I said, I do damn fine work. You do your part and I'll do mine. Deal?"

"Deal. Can I have some water?"

"How about some ice? Only enough to wet your mouth and no more." Todd held up a spoon and a cup of shaved ice.

Traven wet the inside of his mouth and pushed the spoon away with his tongue. "How long was I out?"

"Four days. This is Wednesday." Todd put the cup away. "There's somebody wants to see you. She's waiting outside. I told her to keep it brief, because you need your rest."

Traven closed his eyes as the doctor went away then blinked them back open when he felt a hand touch his face.

Cheryl Bishop looked tired, but her hesitant smile was cheerful. "Hi, cowboy. How are you feeling?"

He smiled. "How do I look?"

She shook her head. "You can't feel that bad."

He laughed, and it hurt. She laughed with him, but there were tears in her eyes. "What about Brandstetter?" he asked. Memory of the knife caused his heart to thump in his chest. He had to fight to control the nausea.

"He's dead. He was dead when the police arrived."

Traven nodded.

"They know he was the killer. Hayata filled in the pieces that weren't covered in the files." She paused. "The media are calling you a hero. It's been everything the police department could do to keep the news people from your door. Even Nagamuchi Corporation has been concerned over how you were doing.''

The thought brought another smile to Traven's lips when he realized the corporation's concern was based on a totally separate and totally selfish bias. "How is Hayata?"

"She had a concussion, a couple of minor lacerations, but nothing serious. The hospital kept her one day for observation, then released her. Nagamuchi Corporation gave her some time off to visit her family. She said she'd see you when you got out of the hospital."

"I'm glad. She really put her neck on the block for me."

"Danny's out in the hall. He's asleep, but he's been here since you were brought in. He wouldn't go home."

"Let him sleep. We'll talk later." Traven felt lassitude creep into him to douse the fiery images of Brandstetter and the knife and the madness that had dwelt in the computer construct. They would live with him for a long time. Then he looked up at her. "I've missed you."

Tears ran down her face. "I came as soon as I heard," she said. "I was afraid you were going to die before I got here."

He reached for her hand, felt it glide into his. His throat felt tight, and he didn't trust himself to speak.

"I met Captain Kiley out in the hall a couple days ago," Cheryl said. "He told me to give you this when I saw you. He said he wanted to give it to you himself, but they're only allowing the family in right now, and you'd want it before then."

He took the shield and felt it, hard and sure, in his palm. He put it on his chest, then took her fingers in his hand again. He gave her a smile, forced his words through his dry throat, past the pain of the tube. "I really have missed you," he whispered. "A lot of things have happened to me in the last few days." His voice broke and he couldn't go on.

"I know," she said. She ran her fingers through his hair.

He made himself speak. "There's a lot I have to tell you, about me, about the things I've done."

"It doesn't matter. I talked to Hayata. She came to me in the hallway when she found out who I was. She told me what you did about the serial killings." She tightened her grip on his hand. "She told me about the two of you."

"I'm sorry," he said.

She smiled through her tears. "All that matters is that you're going to be okay, don't you see that?"

Traven looked at her, saw the hurt in her eyes, and wished he could take it away. "I was afraid of you for so long. When you left, I couldn't ask you to stay."

"I know."

"I didn't want you to go. I wanted you to stay. I just couldn't ask you."

"I know."

He looked at her. "I'm asking you now, Cheryl. I want you to stay with me. I love you."

She squeezed his hand. "And I love you, Mick Traven." She leaned over him and kissed him on the side of the mouth.

With his hand in hers, with the taste of her tears lingering on his lips, Traven let sleep claim him, denying the nightmares and thinking only of the future.

About the Author

Mel Odom lives in Moore, Oklahoma, with his wife and four children. He's the author of twenty-five novels under various pseudonyms. *Lethal Interface* is his first solo SF work, and the first novel under his own name. His comic-book series, *Harte of Darkness*, is currently being released. And he's hard at work finishing up his second novel for ROC.

SENSATIONAL SCIENCE FICTION

If you and/or a friend would like to receive the *ROC Advance*, a bimonthly newsletter featuring all the newest and hottest ROC books and authors, on a complimentary basis, please fill out this form and return it to:

ROC Books/Penguin USA
375 Hudson Street
New York, NY 10014

Your Address

Name _____

Street _____ Apt. # _____

City _____ State _____ Zip _____

Friend's Address

Name _____

Street _____ Apt. # _____

City _____ State _____ Zip _____